FROM THE CASELOAD OF

AMBROSE O'DONOVAN,

BARRISTER, SLEUTH

About the author

Pat O'Donnell was born and raised in Coalisland, County Tyrone. He divides his time between Ireland and his home in Ontario, Canada, where he lives with his wife, Lenore, and their daughter, Melissa.

FROM THE CASELOAD OF AMBROSE O'DONOVAN, BARRISTER, SLEUTH

PATRICK O'DONNELL

First published in 2005 by

TownHouse, Dublin
THCH Ltd
Trinity House
Charleston Road
Ranelagh
Dublin 6
Ireland

www.townhouse.ie

1 2 3 4 5 6 7 8 9 10

A CIP catalogue record for this book is available from the British Library.

ISBN: 1-86059-226-0

Cover design by Sin É Design

Text design and typeset by Typeform

Printed and Bound in Great Britain by
Cox & Wyman Ltd, Reading, Berkshire

Contents

For Melissa, I do it all for you

BY WAY OF INTRODUCTION

First of all, I suppose I should have the good manners to introduce myself. My name is Noble Alexander but you likely will not have heard of me for, unlike my famous employer, I have always been a man to stay in the background, to remain in the gloaming of things. I am content that it is so and the only reason that I have dragged out all my old notes and am writing down these things in a fuller form is that I have so much time on my hands, for my master has less need of me now, as he has largely abandoned the practice of law for his work with the Catholic Association, the repeal and reform movements and rural land redistribution, and there seems not much for me to do nowadays.

I must tell you that I was born, not in Ireland at all, but in Ayrshire in Scotland, although both my parents were born Ulster Scots and very proud of it. I returned to Ulster with my father, who was a Presbyterian parson, when my dear mother and two little brothers died of the diphtheria. My father wanted better for me than to have me living on a parson's stipend that was as much begrudged as freely given by his congregation. And so he endeavoured, by begging or borrowing – I forbear to add stealing – to get me the best lay education that he could. All about reckoned, no doubt, that I would take holy orders and some were duly scandalised when I instead took up the law as a barrister's clerk. But I was well suited to my calling for I had always a good, fast, clear hand and my mind is an orderly one. I modestly say that I have always been able to connect things seemingly unconnected by time or appearance, and that talent has proved to be a boon to myself and my employers. I also found the workings of the law most absorbing. But please do not attribute what I say of my talents to base pride, I beg of you, for pride is a deadly sin and one that I have always done my utmost to avoid.

Even while taking up gainful employment in the law I was most interested in and concerned with the struggle of the small-sect Protestants and their Roman Catholic brethren to obtain full rights under the law of the land. I was smitten by the cause and was duly inducted into the United Irishmen in Belfast at the age of eighteen, and I met all its northern leaders, including that brave and noble man Theobald Wolfe Tone. My own mentor was none other than Henry Joy McCracken and I declare that he and his sister were two of the finest, gentlest people I have ever known. When the rising came in '98 I was with him, as one of his *aides-de-camp*, for I will admit that I did not much relish the actual fighting. Not, I hope, from any fear of death and injury to my own person, but rather from a fear of inflicting death and injury on others.

The rising in the North was a shambles and was soon quashed. Henry Joy and many others were hanged, the army ran roughshod over the population and the people suffered greatly. The aftermath was terrible and should have caused another rising if the populace had any energies left to it. Miraculously I was able to escape arrest for, just as miraculously, my identity seems to have been unknown to the authorities and their numerous spies, or perhaps they thought me only a sprat and not worth the bother. In any event I hid myself away in my father's home until it was safe to go out and about again. The rising in the South had initially been more successful but also came to nothing in the end and was crushed, if you can credit it, even more brutally than in the North. The army killed thousands of innocent people and non-combatants, and I have been told that every tree in the land seemed to have at least one corpse hanging from it.

The rising may have failed, but it did alarm those sly, vicious men in the seats of power in Dublin and London, who used it as a base excuse to do away with the old Irish parliament and to enforce rule on us from Westminster. Another change made to our society by the frightened English was the granting of near enough full rights to the small-sect Protestants, mainly in the North, but the same rights were denied to the Catholics. To our shame, my people largely accepted this injustice and actually began to treat the Catholics as shamefully as they themselves had been treated until lately by the members of the Established Church. The government further drove a wedge between the natural allies among the lowest orders of the people by scaring the small-sect Protestants witless with the spread among them of the idea that full rights for Catholics would only result in Ireland being ruled over by Rome. I have never accepted those changes as just and I have been happy to devote my time and energies in working for Catholic emancipation and repeal of the Union, although to be honest with you, I do greatly fear the power of Rome.

In the meantime, rebellion or no, I had to work and for many years I served the same master in Belfast, until he quit the bar on marrying a newly widowed woman of extraordinary wealth and girth. Then I was clerked to a young barrister from Belfast who, for want of a better place being available, went to train further and to assist an old barrister in the south-west of the country. We ended up in the town of Kilrush in County Clare.

My new young master was inexperienced in the wiles of courtroom practice, and so was put under old Bumbo Green for finishing. Alas the poor young fellow died of the typhus within a year of us going down to Kilrush, and I would have been without any position at all if Bumbo Green's own man hadn't taken ill of the same malady and died a week later.

I was, I know, the completely wrong personality to be dealing with old Mr Green, for I have never tasted strong drink even once in my life, and Bumbo was a great toper, though a man with winning ways and well liked. He was without a doubt the largest man that I have ever seen. He was well above six foot and a half in height, but his girth was so vast that he actually appeared to be a squatter man and less than even the average in height. I attended with him often in court and it was something to see him attempt to sit down on the narrow benches reserved for the attorneys. He had no distinguishable 'small of the back' but he did have a huge, wide and deep rear end on him, enough for three men in fact. He was fat and beyond obese, yet if you could have seen him on a dance floor, you would think he weighed but ten stone, he was so light on his feet, and until the gout had him near crippled he dearly loved to dance with all the young lasses, the wives and daughters of judges and king's counsels, whirling them around many's a law ball.

Now, I was mortified on a daily basis by the man's actions and the disarray of his life but, do you know, I came to tolerate and then to ignore his faults, for he had many more redeeming qualities and a perpetual sunshine of good temper gleamed lightly over them all. After I became his clerk I tried constantly to convert him back to Christ, but alas I failed miserably in that regard, for even on his deathbed he remained a reprobate.

I would have found myself once again out of a position when he died, if Bumbo hadn't taken on another junior just a few years before he passed on. That young man was Ambrose O'Donovan, and I bless the day that I met him. That is a strange thing for me to utter, for I am what he would call a dour Presbyterian and he is and always has been a devout idolater of the church of Rome – and something of a *bon vivant*, though nothing on the scale of Mr Green. How often he has participated in that abomination that is their Mass I cannot imagine, but I fear his soul is forever lost.

So you can see the grand irony of it all, no doubt. I have spent most of my life in the service first of a libertine and a reprobate and latterly a Papist adherent of the anti-Christ, but let me just say that they are two of the finest men that I have ever met in my long life and so I have been rewarded for what many of my co-religionists would have deemed my 'burden' by having had the privilege of knowing those men so well.

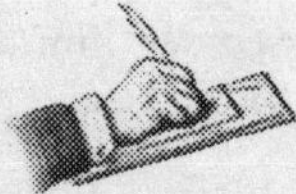

Ambrose O'Donovan is the youngest son of the O'Donovan clan of Kilrush, one of the old families that ran the country before they lost most of their power and possessions to James the First. The O'Donovans may have lost nearly all their traditional lands but they were always able to make money from their trading with Spain and France, and so by one means or another they had been able to recoup some of their ancestral territory over the intervening generations. The father of young Ambrose, old Hugo, put his youngest boy and his only girl off to schools on the continent as they could not be educated in Ireland in what he thought of as a proper fashion under the Penal Laws, and so they both were well educated, in fact much better educated than the vast majority of their Protestant fellows who remained for schooling at home, even though their schooling was of necessity tainted greatly by Papism and its purveyors.

When the bar was thrown open to Catholics in 1792, old Hugo O'Donovan made plans for his young son to eventually join the law and all his education was turned toward that very purpose. 'We'll give the wee lad a hap'eth of law,' I believe he was fond of saying, and I am happy that he did so. Ambrose O'Donovan was called to the bar in or about 1815 and practised in the Four Courts in Dublin among the droves of the Junior Bar for a season or two before he was taken on as a junior by old Bumbo Green.

Mr Green did this for several reasons. As an act of kindness; to rub his fellow-Protestant enemies' noses the wrong way; and, much less honourably, for a tidy sum of money from old Hugo O'Donovan. Let me say in his defence that he told me, privately, he had always liked the lad, having known him for many years, as he had acted for Hugo O'Donovan in the most of his legal work and was at one time a regular visitor at their home.

Bumbo had a good practice once, not only from the Protestant gentry and tradesmen, but he had nearly all the Catholic custom as well. Catholics couldn't practise the law in his young day and Mr Green was always seen by them as a very even man, a sort of honorary Catholic, if you will. I suspect that many of them were fond of consuming vast quantities of whiskey punch with the man as well and that would certainly have cemented their relationship with him.

In his latter years, Bumbo spent far more of his energies in getting tight than in pursuing the enemies of his clients in the courts of law, and his practice had fallen off considerably by the time he took on young Ambrose. So much so that I found I spent half of my days idle and it constantly grated upon my conscience to be taking his money for less than a full day's work.

Well, all that was to change when young Ambrose joined our chambers, for we got back the Catholic clients almost immediately, and they were ever a litigious lot. Then young Mr O'Donovan had a major coup when he represented old General Humphries, who was at the time the local military governor, in a case over the leasing of hunting and fishing rights. It was but a small matter but he showed a great deal of acuity in the manner of its winning and his reputation flourished. The old general took to him personally as well and introduced him about into society where, because of the old military man's patronage, he was soon well accepted in spite of his faith. He was rich and handsome in an athletic way and many a matron had soon spied him out as a match for one her daughters.

Less than three years after taking on Ambrose, old Bumbo died from the many wounds inflicted on him and his poor innards by the demon drink and, lo and behold, he shocked the country by leaving the remaining half of his practice outright to his young Papist protégé. I have been with him ever since, and even though he has little need of me these days I would rather die in harness for, if the truth be told, I have no real interests in my life outside of our chambers, the ancient Greeks who inhabit my books and my dearly held religious beliefs.

One of the remarkable things about Ambrose O'Donovan, even as a young man, was his ability to go beyond the courtroom side of things, the planks and nails of the law, and to fully investigate the right and wrong of a matter on his own. He had a great facility for seeing through things, for linking facts seemingly unrelated and for drawing logical conclusions that would have totally escaped the mind of most other men and not only in the courtroom, for he flourished outside of those narrow confines as well. He has always been a man who tempered his vast talents with a fine sense of justice, mercy, generosity, fair play and an overriding regard for his personal honour, and those are the qualities that have always endeared him to me.

I have notes in my files of over a hundred interesting cases which we investigated together; some are what you would call court cases and others, while in many instances tied to court cases, were far beyond the crosses and dots of the law and entered the realm of the criminal, his mind and aberrant behaviour. If you have ever sat through a murder trial you will be thankful to me for the synopses of such proceedings which I give to you in these few pages. A court trial is like an iceberg, with the small interesting part above the water but with a vast body of tedium below. The hours of motions, depositions, the long-drawn-out process of entering evidence, would try the patience of a saint. To spare you ennui, let me promise that the moments of cut and thrust, the unmasking of false witnesses and the winning *coup de grâce* are near all that I will include for your edification. If you want more detail then I suggest that you take up the law and see for yourself the tedium it can involve.

MURDER IN TRINITY

My association with Ambrose O'Donovan had not been of very long duration when he first brought me to Dublin to ply our trade in the halls of the Four Courts during the spring and summer sessions. He had practised in the rotunda hall and courts of that impressive and renowned edifice for over a year after being called to the bar and his return to it was of the same note as a return to an *alma mater* for a recently graduated student. By that I mean that there was not much changed about the place itself and he knew almost all the varied personnel who usually gathered there, from his previous tenure.

It was in the year 1820 that we first went to Dublin and, whereas my employer, who was inured to the city, found the experience exhilarating in comparison to Kilrush, I found it exhausting, for I did not possess his boundless energy. The next year I learned that I was to be dragged away from Kilrush once more for several months, leaving behind the most of my little library, my privacy and seclusion, while my master in his turn would be separated from his dear spouse, Ellen, and his new little daughter.

It was late in April, the last day of the month but two in fact, and I had several leases which had to be signed by my master that day for them to be legal, as it was a Friday. The leases were for two large farms on his family estates and even though I was his law clerk and was not officially connected with the management of the estate, I felt duty bound to have them executed properly and in good time. I therefore locked up our chambers and journeyed on poor old shank's mare the nearly two miles out to the military cantonment of the Kilrush garrison. It was quite a substantial place filled with horses, military men and their various attendants. The common soldiers lived in low barrack buildings, while their officers dwelt in vastly more comfortable quarters. There were numerous stables and exercise yards laid out for the practice of equitation and for the endless drilling of the troops.

I knew that my master would be there, as it was his habit to go to the cantonment for physical exercise on nearly every Friday afternoon, and I knew where he could be found. I entered a walled exercise square reserved for the officer class and I spotted him immediately. He was among a group of young officers and at sword play with them, and, as I did not want to interrupt and my legs were wearied, I sat on a rough bench under a plane tree and watched for a while.

I could tell my master at a mile's distance, for he had a fine, tall, straight figure and he was made distinctive from the others by his short, black hair. He wore a loose white shirt, black close-fitting knee-britches and dark stockings above black shoes with small silver buckles. My master was always wont to be fastidious but more than a little puritanical in his style of dress, which I found to be an attractive trait in him.

He was obviously demonstrating, in fact showing off, the Italian art of fighting with both rapier and long dagger to the assembled youngsters, and they whooped and cheered and were suitably impressed at his skills. He had pinned his opponent with a flourish and they were all vying to clap him on the back and they brought him over to sit at a long deal table set up under a tree in the yard, where they poured him a large tumbler of chilled claret. I knew that the fencing was ended for that day and I approached the table, still unseen. The young officers were paying rapt attention to Mr O'Donovan and seemed to hang on his every word. These were the best of the general's youngsters, for some others in their ranks had too much side about them to associate with a Papist, even one such as my employer, and I can tell you the loss from that bigotry was all their own. These others worshipped him as a hero, though, for his skills with horse, sword and pistol; further, he was nearly of an age with them and did not hold his sway over them by dint of a high rank.

I neared the table and at last Mr O'Donovan became aware of my presence. He rose to greet me and introduced me to a dozen young men by name, but for the life of me I cannot recall a single one of them today. I presented him with the leases and my small travelling pen and inkwell, and he signed where I indicated. I shook some sand dust on the wet ink from my ivory flask, refolded the documents and made to leave again.

'No, stay a while, Mr Alexander,' Mr O'Donovan said. 'I have news for you. I have decided to travel to Dublin for the spring and summer sessions. I wish to renew some old friends and to make new ones, and perhaps to get an interesting case or two to try in the Four Courts. I intend to leave on Monday morning by way of one of Mr Bianconi's excellent coaches. I will need you to pack up what law books you imagine will be needed. As I recall, you were not particularly enamoured of our sojourn there last year and, bearing that in mind, I shall of course not impose another such on you this year and I will travel alone.'

'Very good, sir,' I said evenly, but I was fairly shocked that he would be leaving Kilrush so casually for several weeks, months even, and leaving me behind, for I had grown used to his company and, to tell the truth, I had grown very fond of him. I knew that I was in for an empty and tedious summer, for the old man of the chambers, old Bumbo Green, while still extant at that time, was by then bedridden, from his brandy as much as from any unsolicited infirmity.

I turned and made to withdraw from the company, but Mr O'Donovan hailed me and said, 'Oh, of course you will accompany me, for where would I be without you, Mr Alexander, what justice could I possibly achieve for the masses without your assistance?'

I was suddenly lifted from my feeling of growing misery, which I could not disguise, to one of elation at the news and in spite of myself it showed on my face. I know that I was smiling as I said, 'Very good, sir, I shall be ready to go as you wish.'

Now the practice of law in Ireland in those days and the procedures of the courts were precisely the same as in England, but the system of the professional life of the proponents of the law was in some ways quite different. There was, and is, a custom of the Irish bar of assembling daily for the transaction of business or to seek business, if they lacked it, in the hall of the Four Courts in Dublin. The building itself is magnificent and a source of pride to the people. In the centre of the interior and over-canopied by a massive and lofty dome is a spacious central hall into which the several courts of justice open. Its columned spaciousness is a busy place between ten in the forenoon and four in the evening and is a motley scene.

Every barrister who was anyone, and many who were in truth no one, thronged the place and there were an equal number of 'civilians' there as well – plaintiffs and defendants seeking out the best counsel for their cases, and the political hangers-on, come there to hear the latest gossips about their friends and enemies alike. There were, no doubt, many Castle spies among them. One could see men from all walks of life, from dukes to small freehold farmers. A man who could claim relations among the greatest houses of England might be seen next to a tenant farmer in his rough frieze clothing and much-mended boots clutching an equally seedy and tattered lease that contained some small clause that his landlord was using to effect an ejectment upon him and each, for all the difference in their stations, could have the same worried look upon their visages. One might see an affluent and angry father, suing to punish some rake for a breach of promise, or you might see the litigant and the defendant in some vicious slander suit glaring at each other across the floor, only restrained from physical attack on each other by the pudgy arms of their briefs.

The place looked to be in total chaos, but after only a few days as an inmate, one could put some sort of order to it. At one column one could see several of the Junior Bar, newly minted, men from good families, discussing arcane matters with nary a worry between them, being well insulated from care by their paters' thickened wallets. Immediately after at the next pillar might be found some of the myriad of the chronically impoverished members of the Bar, without a brief between them, but still shrilly arguing some trivial and pointless bit of law. Then there were the big men, the successful briefs simply thronged with applicants for their services, and next some up-and-coming barristers favoured by those elite and receiving their cast-off cases, thereby aspiring to build a great name for themselves.

On the steps outside the court of Chancery one might see a famous brief waiting there for his turn to refute some long-winded argument going on within the chamber and to which he disdains to even listen as a nice piece of forensic finesse. A case might be getting under way and the tipstaff might call out for 'the gentlemen of the special jury' to go to the box or a clerk might be heard screaming for his brief to attend in court, as the case was started and would be lost if he tarried more.

In any given day there would be many distractions. Once, more than once in fact, a pickpocket was discovered and all about rushed to the scene where the man had been caught *in flagrante* to see him pinioned properly and receiving a good cuffing before the police were summoned to remove him. Or now and again a bevy of country beauties might parade through in their finery, awash in large bonnets and colourful parasols, as was the custom during a city visit, to see the sights of the court building, and to show themselves to the members of the Junior Bar. Public horse-whippings took place too, from time to time, in the rotunda, to the general entertainment of those about the place, but the fuss died down as quick as it started, as often as not, and all went about their noisy business.

Incongruously with its regular hubbub and bedlam, there came in many cases of an interesting nature and these my master sought above all others. Each morning when the courts were sitting he would commingle with some other noted barristers in the hall, where he would be approached by various clients needing good representation in their cases.

It would be my duty to take any client with an interesting case aside and, with my writing board, metal pen and ink bottle, to make a précis of their case on a page or two. My employer would then go into court with no other reference at his disposal and, do you know, in most cases he was able to get a satisfactory verdict for his new clients with no more preparation than that. It was a style of law practice that he had learned from his mentor, Daniel O'Connell, himself, the Great Liberator, who, shall we say, 'held court' each day in the rotunda of the place, but you will hear more of him anon.

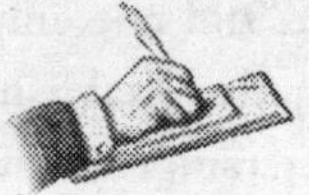

This visit to Dublin I want to tell you about took place in 1821 and it was absolutely the most ill-chosen time for a sojourn in Dublin because it was the year of the historic royal visit, the coming of King George the Fourth across the ditch to the other island of his kingdom. The visit did not interrupt the flow of legal work in any way nor deter the populace from the commission of their various crimes against the penal codes or their native willingness to become litigious over any real or imagined civil transgression from a neighbour or the like, but rather it increased that industry. Alas it also made suitable lodgings in the city very tight to obtain that year. Most of the 'Who's Who' of Ireland wished to be in the old capital for the fullness of the visit, to attend the various functions to be held during the king's lengthy stay or to be available to be invited along to meet the fat, bigoted, pompous rake should the opportunity arise. And so, the great and the good, the elite and the chosen and, in greater numbers, herds of unwanted kindred swarmed Dublin that year. They took up every available room in the whole city, in the best areas of course, for they stayed away from dreadful places like Drumcondra and the Liberties, which were crammed full of humanity, or a semblance of it, every day of every year in any case.

We arrived, like neophytes, with no more planning than we had made the previous year, with no lodgings booked for the season and we were forced to take up residence in a room at an inn called the Brazen Head, somewhat down the quays on the southern bank of the Liffey and even then we were not to have any privacy. My master and I had shared close lodgings before in hotels in countless little market towns in Clare and Limerick as we attended the various assizes and we were not put out by that at all, for we were both respectful of each other. But on this occasion the one large room available to us contained not two but four large beds and these were filled with drunken sleepers each night, and not only because of the royal visit. The Brazen Head was a popular establishment among a certain class of men. Not tinkers or guttersnipes, mind you, but not drawn from the cream of society either. They were the poorer members of the bar, for it was handy to the Four Courts, and also the likes of travelling representatives were drawn to stay there. Many of these men had homes in Dublin, comfortable places, no doubt, in Rathmines and suchlike, but they liked to imbibe the devil's buttermilk every night, and then, unable to go to their homes either through the condition of their legs and the distance to be travelled or from fear of their wives, they would 'take rooms' in the hostelry. This meant being carried upstairs by one of the inn's burly attendants and then being thrown unceremoniously into a space in the first available bed.

That was the condition of living which we found ourselves enduring that spring. This intolerable situation went on for a few days and we had so far not found nor even entertained the glimmer of a hope that we would find a decent set of rooms when good fortune smiled upon us. It was in the rotunda of the Four Courts on only the second morning of our attendance there that we met with Mr Darcy Latimer, barrister-at-law and a good friend of my master. He hailed Mr O'Donovan immediately upon entering and after I had been introduced to him they fell to that activity of the reunited known as 'catching up on old times', although to my mind it should be called 'catching up on new times', for all they talk about is what has happened to them and where they have been since they last met. The maudlin recapture of old times comes later, unfortunately usually over too much drink.

I don't doubt we served up a wretched aspect to his eyes that morning. We were both of us far from being well rested for, even though we had retired at a fairly early hour the night before, myself totally sober and my master with only a mild nightcap of whiskey punch in him, we were kept awake from the singing and roaring from the carouse in the public bar below us. I'm sure there was a verbose and physical altercation in the courtyard under our window in the wee hours, some students likely. Then when that had petered out we were further tormented by the snoring and other much worse noises emanating from the new guests brought up to us to stew in their own juices until morning. We were tired of face and lacked our usual vim and vigour and our clothes were crushed and wrinkled, something unheard of in my master, and Mr Latimer knew my master well enough to make comment upon it.

'My God, Ambrose, but ye look as if ye've been sleepin' rough, don't ye just, in a doorway or the like,' he said in a mock whisper that they could have heard back in Clare.

Mr O'Donovan explained our situation and our inability to obtain any lodging and he had no sooner done so than Mr Latimer put before us a solution to our housing problem. We must come and lodge with him, he said. The Provost of Trinity College was an uncle of his mother's, and as many of the students had gone home or to the continent for the long vacation, he was able to get part of a suite of rooms for himself with no bother. He explained for my benefit that each set of rooms in the college was set up with at least four bedrooms and sometimes as many as six, around a large common living or sitting room and, as an added attraction, each such set of rooms was attended by a man, one of the porters, or 'skips' as they are peculiarly called in that establishment. These men saw to the tidying of the rooms and the making of tea and chocolate and other minor duties. He insisted that we move into two of the other bedrooms in his own suite. The fact that he had automatically included myself in the invitation endeared the gentleman to me, and I soon found that, rich and privileged though he was, there was no side to the fellow at all. He was from an old Leinster family, a branch of which had sensibly turned Protestant after William's victory and so had kept their lands, but he wore his religion lightly and had been among the first to befriend my master when he attended Trinity and studied at the King's Inns and he even shared rooms with him when they studied further at the Inns of Court in London.

Mr O'Donovan agreed, after a quick glance at me to see that my dour old face was not filled with disapproval. We forgot all about the practice of law that day and went at once to collect our things from the Brazen Head, which was a blessed relief. Our new rooms, while not of the best quality and not well appointed or decorated, were nonetheless immeasurably better than our previous situation amid the topers, and we spent the day unpacking our things and placing them in the best and most convenient order in our own chambers. I gave the porter the fresh linen sheets and pillow covers that we had brought with us from Kilrush on the instructions of my master's wife, and he made up our beds with them. The furniture in the rooms, while once fine and heavily made of blackened oak, was exceedingly worn and no doubt misused by the untold numbers of students who had lived there.

It was the first time that I had been in the college and I was most impressed by the large square one entered after passing through the porter's gate and the arched entryway. The square was spacious and adorned with statuary and enclosed by many fine buildings from several centuries. To one side lay a chapel, near the size of a cathedral and as beautifully designed and wrought, and on another side of the square was a row of modern-looking residential houses but which were, I do believe, Elizabethan in origin. Alas, the large library was closed that day. We enquired why of one of the jockey-capped porters and he advised us that the librarian had taken advantage of the fine day that was in it and had taken his spouse and twelve offspring away to the seaside at Dalkey. I was disappointed, for I longed to lay eyes at last on the legendary, endless shelves of its millions of books.

We had to content ourselves with a visit to the college's museum instead, which proved to be a dismal place and a dreary experience. We walked behind an unkempt young porter, who had the look of a 'fly-boy' about him, up a narrow, dusty stairwell. The walls of the hallway about us were festooned with 'artefacts', spears, canoes and war clubs. One of the more esoteric of the exhibits was a large pair of jackboots, nearly two feet long in the foot that had apparently belonged to O'Brien, the Irish giant. Although I looked at them carefully, I could discern no wear at all of the sole and heel and so I concluded that they were manufactured by some enterprising cobbler to fool an anti-quarian or two and, I don't doubt, make himself some money at the same time. The room of the museum proper was as dirty and untidy as its annexe, and the porter proceeded to tell us a series of astounding fabrications about the dusty, decaying contents of the glass cases, all of which we had to view by whatever light managed to get through the tall but extremely dusty windows. The scope of the fellow's mendacity was remarkable indeed. There was the harp of Brian Boru, here was the sword of Strongbow, the doublet of Silken Thomas and the quills used by old Dean Swift. He also pointed out to us a huge pair of leathern drawers which, he said, once preserved the modesty of none other than Finn McCool. There was a large stuffed giraffe, very mouldy in the legs, and several species of sea mammals, equally stuffed, hung in festoons from the ceiling, and I could imagine all sorts of vermin falling from their decrepit furs onto our helpless heads. I should mention that we actually saw the death mask of the Dean there that day, lying in a fly-blown glass cabinet. The poor man's plaster visage was a pitiful thing, sunken and drawn with age and his fine forehead, which must have fronted an astounding quantity of brain matter, was fallen in like an old eggshell.

I was glad to get out of that depressing hovel and away from the prating cant of the porter who, in turn, was most gratified with the coin that Mr O'Donovan slipped into his hand.

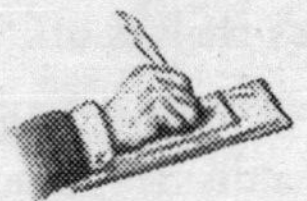

At the end of the day we went, all three of us, at Mr O'Donovan's treat, to Trocadero's fine new restaurant in Dawson Street. There we enjoyed a grand meal of oysters and Dublin Bay prawns, followed by braised lamb chops and all that went with them. I suffered from the unaccustomed richness of that meal for several days thereafter, I can tell you. That meal was also made memorable for me by Mr Latimer, who was gracious and ebullient throughout. Though, to my distaste, he cheerily punished the claret bottle, he seemed to delight in doing anything at all to make us happy and put us at our ease. He was well connected, as I have said, with Trinity and he did all that he could to see that we were more than merely accommodated. He and my master went to the various parties and functions among the dons and to soirées each night in the most genteel of Dublin salons. I know that I would have been welcomed at these as well, but I have always been limited in my wardrobe and further I do not drink – in fact I will admit that I abhor frivolity in all its forms. I cannot help it – and so I was content to sit at home and to work on the next day's briefs, to sip my China tea and nibble at cheese and hard biscuits while deeply involved with the various activities of the ancient Greeks as described in my most treasured books. I found that I was grown content in how things were, but my peace of mind was soon to be shattered. On one morning after a party, when my master was already gone out again, Mr Latimer, in all innocence, told me something which disturbed me very much.

He said that he and my master had been the night before to a party in the home of Lady Frances Fox that was attended, in his words, by the elite of the city. He had been attracted to a fetching plump girl of less than twenty and had been imagining himself 'coming to grips with her' – I was used to Mr Latimer's sometimes unfortunate turn of phrase by then. He noticed that his companion, my master, was standing beside him looking dumbstruck, like a pig which has just received a good clout of the knacker's mallet. He was staring at a woman who had been introduced to them both in the same company as the plump lass. Mr Latimer said that the woman was a rare, cool beauty, dark-haired and blue-eyed, dressed in a dazzling ivory gown and with her long pale neck encircled by a blue cameo on a black velvet band. Mr Latimer said that she was perhaps a bit too thin for his own taste, but my master was enthralled by her. He could only mumble out his charm at being introduced to her before they passed on, she pulling the plump object of Mr Latimer's new interest along with her.

Well, he said he had the devil of a time getting more than a word or two from my master all the evening after that, and an even harder time in getting the plump young lass on her own. He did manage it at last and took her out into the garden to attempt to give her a 'squeeze or two', when he noticed that there were some people standing on the balcony above them. He recognised my master's voice mixed with the voice of a woman, although he could not tell what they said to each other. He obtained a vantage point where he could look up and see them and it was the woman in the white gown who was there on the parapet with Mr O'Donovan. He said they were standing very close to each other, closer than two people in polite society would be if they had just met. They were not touching but were speaking earnestly to each other. He watched them so long that the girl he had with him grew bored with his lack of attention and successfully gave him the slip. Afterwards he left with a party that was going off to Cicchio's restaurant for a late supper, but he noticed that my master and the lady were not among their company, nor did they put in an appearance at all.

'What was the lady's name, do you recall?' I asked, as casually as I could manage it, but I was sitting there full of apprehension, my throat as dry as ashes.

He thought for a moment and seemed perplexed by my question but then brightened and said, 'I've got it, Noble, it was a Mrs Talbot, I'm near sure of it. I recall asking my little one about her and she said that she was the wife of a wealthy man, a landowner, a Captain Talbot, from the West, like yourself and Ambrose, a man who loathed society and had fled at the first opportunity away to Scotland for the fishing or the grouse-shooting with his cronies. The girl said that he spends fully half his year there and in other climes seeking sport.'

I said nothing, but inside I felt a great weight had been placed across my shoulders. I knew who the woman was – none other than Celia Talbot, née Scanlan, a woman who had exercised a great grip on my master at one time. She had married Captain Talbot soon after she had broken off with Ambrose, had moved to his estate and then up to their townhouse in Dublin, which was in the very fashionable Merrion Square. I had heard all of that from the town tattlers of Kilrush. After the rift between them, my master had avoided her company and the society that she moved in, and in the interim he had wed Ellen Walsh, and I always thought her a much better match for him than that bissum Celia Scanlan would ever have been.

But now they had met again, and from what Mr Latimer had told me, she had not shunned him but they had had a private meeting together. It bothered me inordinately that they had met again, and it bothered me more that she had seemed so civil to him, and most of all

I was troubled when he failed to mention his meeting her to me, although I knew every detail of their previous relationship and had nursed him through his heartache and mental anguish as best I could. I worried a great deal about this serious new development, for her husband was away out of the country and for the next few nights my master was away from our rooms, without Mr Latimer. I could only guess at where he had been and what I imagined vexed me sorely.

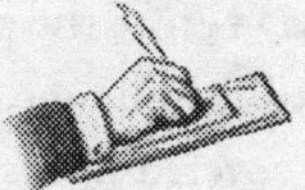

I slept badly for many a night after my chat with Mr Latimer and was no easier in my mind until I heard Mr O'Donovan come in and enter his own chamber. After a week or more I was on the very point of challenging him on it, something that might well have ended our relationship forever, when the college and our little world within it was shivered by a night of singular horror.

In that one night an old porter, the Provost of Trinity himself and the Dean of Students were all violently murdered. The porter was found with his throat cut behind the refectory in the main square, the Provost was got dead in his chambers, beaten on the head with some heavy object, and the Dean was found at a desk in his study with a blade still in his throat.

We knew the porter in question tolerably well. He was Cornelius Flynn, our own skip, though we shared his services with the next set of rooms, as it was summer and there were only about thirty or forty students in that whole wing of the college. The next set of rooms had only five students there at the time, all well advanced in their studies.

Cornelius Flynn had seemed a decent old sort. He had been very solicitous of our well-being, thanks to the odd guinea from Mr Latimer and my master, and we had been treated exceedingly well. My master and Mr Latimer both called him Mr Flynn, by dint of his age; for he was quite old for a college servant, well into his late fifties, making his jockey's cap seem ludicrous on the grizzled head perched upon his round body. He was obviously raked with pains in his joints, for he moved carefully and slowly about. I pitied him, stuck in a post he was no longer fit for, carting coal and wood up to the fireplaces and ashes down again, emptying the chamber-pots, fetching water and boiling it up for us all to use for our ablutions or to brew into tea.

Things could not have been easy for him, looking after two sets of rooms, and now he was dead, his throat cut from ear to ear. Unfortunately, I saw his body before the police took him away and his white, blood-drained face still haunts me, with its eyes stretched wide with horror and his hands, covered in his own gore, still clutching at the rent in his throat, as if he was trying to put it back together again. He had been found lying on one of the pathways near one corner of the square.

I came down to the square pretty sharply when the hullabaloo was first raised. Soon my master was beside me, and as we viewed the remains he said, 'The poor old lad, sliced open like a marrow. From behind, by a fairly tall person by the looks of it. See how the slice there is undercut. As if the blade were drawn upwards as well as across.'

Mr Latimer, his eyes still full of sleep, stood beside him in a long brocaded dressing gown and slippers, whereas my master was already fully dressed but, strangely, had not yet shaved that day. Of course, Flynn had not come up with our water for washing and that might have explained his lack of shaving, but my master would never have been fully dressed and with his neck stock tied before he did his ablutions. I realised with a shock, as he bent down to touch the dead man's skin on his neck and under his tunic, that he had not even been to our rooms as yet and he was just returning from his outing of the night before. He had chanced upon this scene on his return, attracted by the crowd of police, dons and students gathered there.

'Cold as a skate,' he said. 'Been dead since last night. Probably the wee hours. I'm no doctor, but the night was warmish and this fellow has no heat left in him at all.'

The police were there in force. One of their chief men in an ordinary plain suit of dark clothes was obviously in charge. He stood there with his hands on his hips and ordered us back and was having his men load the poor devil onto a litter when there was a sudden 'view-halloo' from across the courtyard. A woman, a college servant by the looks of her, some sort of cleaning maid, I supposed, was waddling towards us waving her hands about her head and screaming 'Moreder, moreder,' at the top of her lungs.

'Yes, we know it's murder, you stupid bloody woman,' the officious policeman shouted at her. 'The man didn't cut his own throat.' Then he turned and yelled to one of his uniformed men, 'Get that damned woman out of here and away from me.'

When the man intercepted her she did not go quietly but struck the fellow about the head, with a small whisk-brush, dislodging his cap, calling him names and babbling about a murder in the Provost's office. That was picked up by the chief peeler and he told his man to let her go, which he gladly did.

'What is this about a murder, woman?' he asked, shouting down into her face.

'The Provost hisself is lyin' dead in his study, sur, kilt stone dead, wit' the head bate off him, so he is,' was her convoluted reply.

'Good God, are you sure?' the policeman asked her.

'Sure as I am that your father was an *amadán*,' she answered most testily. 'Do ye think I lived through the '98 in the Wesht and don't know the look of a dead man, sur?'

'Show us where he is then, and if he's only sleeping or died from a stroke I'll have you cleaning the Bridewell with the smallest nailbrush I can find for the rest of your miserable days.'

'He died of a stroke all right, sur, the stroke of a stout iron poker or the like,' the woman replied very angrily.

The policeman followed the serving woman back the way she had come and he must have been very preoccupied with the status of this new victim, for he hadn't yet noticed the woman's unmannerly tone to him nor the fact that myself, my master and the dressing-gowned Mr Latimer were hard on his heels. We ascended some broad steps and entered the house of the Provost through the large, open double portal and followed the puffing skivvy up the stairs and along a corridor to the man's study. Then she stopped, put her hand on her hip and the other against the wall and wheezed a while.

'I was just come up wit' a bucket of turf and some shticks to set a fire for him,' she said to us over her shoulder, 'he likes that of a mornin' even in the summer for he's kilt with poor circulation, when I saw him in der, fell across his desk wit' blood all over the place. I'll niver forgit it till the day I die.'

We all filed into the room through the open doors and I must say that the dead Provost offered our eyes no prettier a sight than had poor Corny Flynn. He was in a gown of dark blue silk over his nightshirt and his feet were clad in black leather slippers. He was sprawled across a large oak desk and was obviously dead, as the servant had said, from a clout or two to his head with a very hard object. There was a great deal of blackened blood pooled about his smashed head on the table's leather surface, and once again his face was turned to us but, unlike Flynn's, his was only the face of a sudden, stunning death and not throat-cut terror. His mouth, near toothless, was agape and his eyes were open, but otherwise he had a fairly reposed visage.

'This one didn't suffer a bit,' my master whispered in my ear. 'He died without knowing he was about it. He must have known the killer to have been taken so easily. From behind once again, but this time the killer did not have to lie in wait for him. I see no sign here or at the doors below of a forced entry.'

Mr O'Donovan stepped forward and felt the dead man's neck under his chin and then ran his hand under his nightshirt. He frowned as he stepped back to my side.

'Who in blue blazes are you?' the senior policeman asked in sudden surprise and anger. 'What do ye mean by interfering in police business, and who the devil are these other two jackanapes come up here to gawk?'

Mr Latimer spoke up stoutly: 'That dead man is my beloved uncle, sir, and I am grieved to see him so, and I would ask you to keep a civil tongue in your head when addressing myself and my companions. I am Darcy Latimer, and these gentlemen are my friends, Mr Ambrose O'Donovan and Mr Noble Alexander. They are, like myself, both gentlemen of the law. And now you know us, who the blazes are you?'

The policeman was taken aback. 'Ahem, beg your pardon, Mr Latimer, your uncle, eh? Well, please accept my condolences and the condolences of the Dublin police force. I am Inspector Bermingham, and I will be in charge of this dreadful affair, ... er ... both of these dreadful affairs.'

He then took Latimer aside to speak to him, and my master whispered to me that from his guess the old man was near about as long dead as the porter, from the feel of him.

Then the inspector turned back to us and said, 'You gentlemen may remain here, but I command you to touch nothing at all until I return with my men.'

Saying so, he left us, chivvying the old skivvy out before him, as she asked him if we'd not be wanting the fire lit after all.

As soon as he was gone, Mr O'Donovan sprang into action. Over mild protests from Mr Latimer, he examined the corpse more closely, turning it this way and that and searching the pockets of his gown. He then turned his attention to the unbloodied surface of the desk and the table tops and shelves of books, before getting down on his hands and knees and examining the floor. He seemed to find something of interest near the desk, but he quickly put whatever it was in his pocket without saying anything at all to us. He had only straightened up from this unlawful search when the inspector huffed and puffed his way back into the room. We left then and went down to the courtyard together, my master and myself both offering our condolences to our friend.

'He was a sort of uncle all right,' Mr Latimer replied, 'my mother's half-brother's uncle in fact, but to tell you the truth I hardly knew the man. He only acceded to my request for lodgings on the strength of family ties and not from any real affection for me. He seemed glad to get rid of me out of his sight, if you want to know the truth.'

Mr O'Donovan spotted the old skivvy seated on the grass near the white marble statue of some college luminary, smoking the little black pipe known as a dudeen. He brought us over to her and introduced us all to her as if she was the Duchess of Argyle herself. She was pleased at the compliment and at my master's manner. Having won her over, he proceeded to ask her some questions about the Provost and his habits. From her we learned that the Provost liked his bed warmed with a pan of coals at ten o'clock each night and was always risen and dressed when she arrived in the early morning to set his fire. He was in the habit of warming his own shaving water over a spirit lamp in his dressing room. She had never seen the man in his night-clothes until that very morning.

We went back to our rooms and my master was full of talk about the two killings and in fact was more animated than I'd seen him in months. He actually rubbed his hands together as he expounded on his early theories as to the deaths. The surprised horror on the poor old porter's face and the repose on that of the Provost, he said, were telling things. The second man must have admitted his killer in the early hours, woken up after several hours of sleep. It must have been an unusual occurrence, but not a startling one, for he was struck down, defenceless, from behind. He also stated that the assailant must have brought the murder weapon with him, or else he used something at hand and carried it off with him. He subscribed to the first theory, which meant that the murder was premeditated and not done in a fit of passion. He said that the fireplace implements were all intact. The old porter was killed by someone who had waited patiently for him to travel a well-worn path, a path of nightly habit, and had struck with the certainty of killing, taking the weapon away with him. He wanted to find out if the porter was robbed of the few coins he would have had about him. He would ask the inspector, he said, but was confident that the man was not killed for his purse, and even if it was missing, it would have been taken as a subterfuge.

There was quiet then in our sitting room. Mr Latimer said that he was composing a letter to his mother, advising her of the death of her relative, and my master sat lost in his own deep thought, fingers steepled before him. I wondered if he was thinking of the two dead men or a living woman. I had grown weary of thinking of the mayhem I had just seen and remembered that I wanted to ask my master where he had been all night, even though I feared an honest answer. If he had been with Celia Talbot, then I knew that my good opinion of him would be lost forever. Even though fearful of a straight answer from him, I was about to broach the subject in an oblique manner when we heard another commotion in the courtyard below us.

'What the devil can that be?' my master said, rising to hurry to our stairway.

He was gone in a flash and we both followed him down and into the morning light again. The first person we met was a uniformed policeman with the face of the most uneducated peasant on him under a pulled-down kepi and with a pair of lugs the like of which one would find on a buck goat stuck on the sides of his head.

'What's happening, man?' my master asked authoritatively.

The fellow must have seen us before when we had followed his own master up to the Provost's chambers, for he was obviously in error as to our status and answered us as if we were the police ourselves.

'They're only after finding anudder body, so they are, the Dean of somethin' an' somethin', dead as a doornail he is. In his office. I'm off to catch the inspector, for he's walkin' back to the cashle, so he is. I'm thinkin' this place has more dead men in it than the churchyard at Skibbereen.'

He beetled off to the main portal of the college and we all headed in the opposite direction, for both my companions were graduates of the college and so they knew that the policeman was talking about the Dean of Students and Admissions and they knew exactly where his office and living quarters were situated. My master explained to me on the way that the Dean was the personage who was responsible for registering and quartering the students who could be accommodated in the college precincts, and he was charged with levying fines upon them for their various offences against the college rules. He was the penultimate disciplinarian of the institution, the final say, of course, being left to the Provost.

We reached the Dean's office on the second floor of a building at the far end of the square, near to some other student residences. We found the door ajar and no policemen about, only an old man who had the aspect of a clerk with *pince nez*, a myopic look, narrow hunched-over shoulders and ink-stained fingers. It turned out that he was indeed the Dean's own clerk, and the one who had found his dead master when he had opened the office that morning. We entered the room to find the Dean seated facing us in a straight-backed chair at a narrow table, his hands on the top of it and his head thrown back against the top of his seat. He looked unscathed until one noticed a small blemish of blood on his neck and a little rod of beaten bronze protruding from his throat. On closer inspection, it was the handle of some small weapon and the blow that drove it home must have been delivered by someone standing near to him.

'It looks as if a single stab killed him instantly,' Mr O'Donovan said as he bent over the corpse. 'It must have pierced some important nerve or other. I confess I don't know the right name for it but there is one there, in the throat. It can cause instantaneous death. This man would hardly have known what hit him. There is little blood about the wound and that is significant in itself, for there is little or no bleeding after the heart stops pumping. Notice that his hands seem not to have moved at all after he was struck.'

He touched the man's neck again and his chest under his shirt, and then went about the room examining the table and then the large desk at the other end of the room. Then he went under the desk and examined the dead man's feet before going through to the Dean's living quarters and searching about in there. I saw him through the door, rooting in drawers and armoires. I waited in the outer office for him.

Unfortunately, Bermingham returned and was in a foul mood. He seemed to have forgotten any trepidation he harboured regarding our standing and demanded that we leave the site at once or face prosecution for hindering a police officer in the pursuit of his duties. Just then my master came back in from the Dean's bedchamber, at the worst possible time.

'What the devil do you think you're playing at, sir, prowling about through a man's private quarters and in the middle of a murder investigation?' yelled the inspector. 'I should have you locked up for that alone. Now be off with all of you or I will have you in the Castle, just you see if I don't.'

The poor old clerk was still outside on the landing, quaking with fear at what he had seen and had just heard. My master asked him to accompany us to our rooms for a cup of tea, at which the man seemed most unimpressed, but when a bracer of good brandy was added to the prospective comestibles he brightened immediately and fell in beside us. He was a thin man, pale and spare as myself, but the purple veins on his narrow nose spoke loudly of a liking for strong drink.

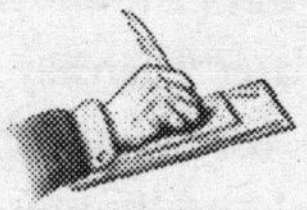

When our man was seated in our room with his second glass in his hands – the first I swear did not even touch his mouth or the sides of his throat when he quaffed it down – my master began to make him pay for his hospitality. 'Tell me, Mr – ' he began.

'Sloane, sir, Andrew Sloane, at your service.'

The man spoke well, almost too well for a man born to aspire only to clerking at a university.

'Tell me, Mr Sloane, your poor master, was he usually in his office before you?'

'Why, no, sir, he was what is known as a night owl, he burnt more candles than a dozen Papist churches. He always said that he worked best at night. He was the man who knew all about the college's finances, you see, he took that work very seriously and guarded his information closely. That is why he worked so much at night. That is how he put it to me at any rate.' The clerk gave us a sly look at that before continuing. 'As a consequence, he was a bit of a lie-a-bed of a morning. Why, some days he would not appear until after eight o'clock.'

'I see. Now, why do you think he was dressed and at his table this morning? Did he rise early or do you think did he stay up all night?'

'I doubt if he rose early,' said Sloan, 'for he was dressed exactly as he was yesterday and the Dean was a clean man and most fastidious about his dress. He never wore the same things two days on the trot.'

The man talked on and on about his master and Mr O'Donovan no doubt obtained a lot of information about him from it but I must admit that it was nearly all lost on me. Eventually, the clerk rose and left us, when there was no movement made to fill his glass a third time, and when he left my master took an opportunity to ruminate aloud as to what we had learned. 'The Dean was still vaguely warm. Cold about his forehead to be sure but warmish under his clothes. He died much later than the others, hours later. I can say that with certainty.'

'Still, some maniac is loose about the place,' Mr Latimer said morosely, as he took a third brandy himself. 'Three murders in one night! Tonight I shall sit up with a loaded pistol in my lap and every candle lit that I can find. Perhaps whoever it is knows that I am a relative of the Provost and wants to finish the job. You two are all right,' he added, 'he doesn't know you from Adam, in all probability.'

I had a dreadful vision of a tipsy and startled Mr Latimer shooting one of us by accident when we came in late.

'I doubt if you are in the slightest danger, Darcy, old friend,' said Mr O'Donovan. 'I will show you the reason for my belief in due course, but in the meantime you mustn't fret. The Dean died much later than the others did, that is one of the most important things that we have learned. He was still up from the day before when he died, the Provost was abed and roused for the slaughter and the old porter was ending his duties for the day and was doubtless going to his own quarters when he died. He died first, incidentally, then the Provost some time after him.'

'How in blazes do you know that?' Mr Latimer asked in as much surprise as doubt.

'For now suffice it to say that I know it; all will be explained in due course. Now I suggest we rest a while and perhaps that fool Bermingham will stumble upon some truths in his plodding wanderings.'

He turned and went into his own bedchamber, where he slept away most of that day. In the evening he rose, freshened himself and before leaving to eat supper he asked me to go with him to seek out Bermingham. Mr Latimer, not wanting to be left alone, accompanied us. We found the man, even at that late hour, by the knot of uniformed police loafing about in front of the Dean's building, and he was far from glad to see us. The three bodies had been taken away by then and were in the city morgue awaiting examination by the police surgeon to gather evidence for the coroner's jury. There was a magistrate, Cumyn was his name, standing with Bermingham, and he was a little more receptive to us. He expressed pleasure at meeting us and asked what we were doing in the college. Our presence as lodgers was explained to him and he laughed affably.

'I know,' he said. 'The city is bedlam. My own house is full of people who claim to be my wife's nearest and most cherished relatives but I'm sure half of them are mere chancers, willing to endure anything to see the king. Well, let me tell you frankly, I've seen him times aplenty and I can say that they'll not be missing much.'

I must say that I was impressed with the magistrate, for he seemed a sharp fellow. My master later agreed and we were proven right, for the man went on to become one of the best judges that ever sat on the woolsack of the London High Court, an intelligent and humane man all his days, who only hanged those that truly needed it.

'My friend Mr Latimer is distraught at the loss of his dear uncle, Mr Cumyn,' said my master, as innocently as an acolyte, 'and so we are hoping that Mr Bermingham will let us know what progress he has made in the murder investigation. And the other two of course.'

The policeman was obviously irritated at my master, but with the magistrate present he was at least civil. He cleared his throat and said, 'We have made up a list of all those in the college at present. Servants, porters, lecturers and other staff and students who are staying here over the summer. There are over three hundred names on it and we intend to question all of them. With your forbearance, I believe we will start with the three of you, for you were all in at the "view-halloo", as it were. Now, please stay here and I will call you in one by one to take your statements.'

We were stuck of course. I could see that Cumyn thought Bermingham to be an idiot of the first water but he could not be seen to be interfering with a police investigation, and so allowed the man to badger us individually for an hour, which made us late for our supper and upset my stomach terribly as a consequence. I was quizzed the first and told the man that I was asleep in my bed all the while until old Corny Flynn was found. Then my master was questioned and the policeman seemed content at the story he was told by him, but he kept Mr Latimer longer than any of us.

I learned that Mr Latimer had no real alibi for the night. He had been in many places listlessly looking for sport and, finding none, had finally come home to bed. My own alibi was every bit as bad, but for some reason Mr Latimer's story was looked at more askance. The inspector let him know that he was a suspect in the three deaths because he was a relative of the Provost and also because he knew the old porter. He intimated to him that if he found some connection with the Dean he would arrest poor Mr Latimer at once and charge him.

'The man's a dolt, that is sure,' my master said on hearing this at dinner from a worried Latimer, 'but at least he is trying to find a link to the three men in the one suspect. At least he has that in his favour. But good luck to him, for he is on the wrong road totally.'

'What do you mean?' I asked. 'Why should the horrors have not been carried out by one villain, a chance robber who stole into the college? And what alibi did you give him that shut him up?'

'He will no doubt check my story, but that is neither here nor there, and it is a very private matter,' he replied enigmatically, which aroused my suspicions about himself and Mrs Talbot once more.

I was about to ask him point blank about that when our plates of mutton arrived steaming hot and accompanied by all that a reasonable man could wish for.

I know that I slept little that night, I was upset at the lateness of our heavy meal and my mind was playing on both the murders and my master's liaison with Celia Talbot. I rose as early as there was light in the apartment to find my master at the table in the sitting room with paper and pen and ink before him. The gutted-out candles were heaps of wax on the candlesticks at his elbow. We had no brief to try that day and so I knew that he was working on the trinity of murders that had been committed almost in our laps. I sat opposite him and he ignored me, as was his habit when he was deep in thought. At last he looked up and shoved the paper in front of him over to me for my perusal. It was merely a list of names.

'I have managed to whittle down Bermingham's list of over three hundred to a dozen or so. See if you can follow my reasoning, Noble.'

I looked at the list. The first three names were our own group, us and Mr Latimer; the next two were the names of the students who shared our particular set of rooms, Messrs Clarke and Adams. Then he had listed all the students in the set of rooms next to ours in the corridor. There were five of them as I have already stated, tabled as follows:

Thomas Quinty, student of medicine
Peter Easterman, student of medicine
Albert Havers, student of medicine
Peter Quinlan, reading classical arts
Ronald Thompson, student of divinity

Then he had listed five other names with no heading over them:

Jack Wallace, student of medicine
Oscar Dunne, reading mathematics
Horatio Gunn, reading ancient history
George Osterman, student of medicine
Piers Morgan, reading classical arts

I read the list several times before giving up on trying to divine what its real meaning to me should be.

'It is simple, Noble, our chambers and the next set were seen to by Mr Flynn and so that connects all the names to him. There is little point in trying to establish a list of all those in daily contact, or even possible contact with the Dean and the Provost. They were available to everyone. Flynn is our man to start with, for his sphere is far narrower. If he had been the only one murdered I would have put it down to chance, death dealt out by a footpad, but it is without a doubt only the part of a larger scheme. The people who saw him on a daily basis must be the prime suspects in my mind, but some connection to the other murdered men will be our only hope of uncovering the culprit. The last five names on the list are those of the students in the chambers two removed from our rooms. They exit by the next staircase, which is why we have not seen them much. They are normally seen to by another porter, but the man has married this summer and so has taken several weeks away from his duties and, as there were so few students about the place, poor old Corny Flynn was pressed into service to see to a third set of rooms as well. He got some extra for it and had been doing the additional work for three weeks or more. That is why he was so late in going to his own room, as it took him so long in a day to perform his duties. He was a bachelor, you see, and had his own small place under the stairs of the lecturers' residence across the square. Now, that being said, I have not yet eliminated the other porters from possible involvement in his death, for whatever motive, but I doubt that any of them would be involved with all three murders. I think, and I may be shown up later to be a goat, that one of the students listed may be involved, to some extent anyway. I have too little to go on as yet and so I must rely on your help to get more information. Are ye with me, Noble?'

I averred that I certainly was, forgetting all about Mrs Talbot for the moment, and very late that evening I found myself dressed in dark clothes and with my employer at the door of the dead porter's cubbyhole under the main staircase in a building across the square from our own. We had waited for the small hubbub of the day's activities to die away and for those about the place to go to their rooms for the night. We carried no light, only the unlit stub of a candle in a pierced toll lantern. As a consequence we could see little in the dark hallway and my master had to feel the lock on the door.

He harrumphed quietly at his discovery that it was to be no great obstacle. I heard him fumble about in his tail pocket and then heard the faint scrape of metal against metal before the door creaked open and he pulled me into the room after him. I wondered where he had learned to break a lock in such a fashion, for it was a skill he was exhibiting to me for the first time that night. He closed the door and, finding the dead man's cot, he took a blanket from it and threw it onto the floor along the crack of the door. Next he applied himself with the flint and steel from his tinder-box and soon was able to light the candle from it. The lamp gave off just enough of a glimmer to let us see most of the small room. The place was well enough ordered but smelled stale and heavy, as if the normal occupant was not very fastidious about his personal hygiene. The chamber was not over ten foot long by five and a half feet wide. The headroom at the door was ample, but it sloped to the back at the same angle as the stairs above it and a man of any height at all would have constantly been knocking his head until he grew used to it.

There was not much to see in the place. A cot, a chest of drawers, very chipped and with its top covered in mug rings, and a floor chest with an old oil lamp on it comprised the only furniture. The man's longer garments were hung about the walls on nails. As well as the scent of an unbathed body and cheap tobacco there was also a smell about the place which I recognised as being the devil's buttermilk. The fact that I could still detect it at least twenty-four hours since the late owner's last presence there speaks as to the liberality of his nightly imbibing.

The place was, as I say, quite neat except for the blanket on the floor and my employer whispered that obviously the police had not searched it at all, for in his experience they were wont to leave things behind them in a chaos, especially when they imagined there was none left to complain after them.

With me holding the dim lantern to the best advantage, he began to systematically search the place, examining even the floor and the base boardings. Then he searched through the floor chest and the chest of drawers, even taking out the drawers and looking under them as well as pulling out the chest and looking at the bare wall behind it. It was there that he saw something of interest. A difference in the baseboards, which soon revealed itself to be a miniature door, about six inches in width, with a shallow cavity scooped into the wall behind it. It was empty, but the piece of wood was obviously well used to being removed and replaced from the amount of grime about its edges.

'Well,' he muttered, almost to himself, 'it looks as if someone was here, someone who shouldn't have been, and the old dead fellow has been robbed after all.'

'How do you know that?' I asked. 'Perhaps the poor old lad had nothing to begin with.'

'Hardly likely, he was an old man, as you say, and had been employed here for a small lifetime. With his remuneration and the customary gratuities from all the students in his charge he must have had some left over, even after his whiskey and tobacco were paid for. I spoke to the other porters about him and was told he was quite parsimonious and feared living out his last days in penury.'

'Perhaps, but it is still a speculation that he was robbed.'

'Not altogether. Early on the evening of his death, Mr Latimer gave him a guinea for his continued kind service and I did the same. The coins were not found on him, although some few of a smaller denomination, coppers mostly, were still in his pocket, nor are they here. I don't believe he could have drunk them so soon. Two guineas worth of bad whiskey would kill off a dozen Corny Flynns.'

I said nothing, but I felt that the theory just espoused by my master was exceedingly weak. The old fellow could have given those last coins away or used them to repay a moneylender or such.

'Well, if someone was in here they didn't want it to be obvious to anyone, but they left a trace or two for us nevertheless,' Mr O'Donovan said, holding up a small dark object, shaped like a wedge.

'What is it?' I asked, for even on close examination I had no idea.

'It is a piece of hard-packed soil, loam from a flowerbed, dark and rich, and it was carried in here jammed into the corner between the sole and heel of a boot or shoe.'

'The old man could have tracked that in himself,' I said.

'I think not. This is fairly fresh stuff. I looked at the soles of the old fellow's boots where he lay on the pathway and saw no soil there. This soil seems the same as that of the flowerbed near where he was found murdered, though. I suspect that his assailant, knowing the man's habit and duties, waited for him in the shadow of the refectory wall and so had to step across that freshly dressed bed to get at him with his knife. I couldn't tell for sure of, course, for whoever found him and the various police had stamped about the place no end before I got there.'

'That is still a stretch of imagination, Mr O'Donovan. Anyone could have tracked it in, we cannot very well age the specimen.'

'Ah, but we can, for it is not muddy but it is still held together by what moisture remains in it. It was very damp to begin with. See it does not crumble like caked mud but more falls apart in friable pieces. More than two days in here would have it different, it would likely be just a pile of black dirt by then.'

I was still sceptical and thought he was fitting everything to match his own theories. I did not know him so well in those days.

He arched his eyebrow at me in the dim light and said, 'My, but you are recalcitrant tonight, Noble, you are forcing me to defend my honour with my last card. The reason that I know the murderer brought in this piece with him, and on the night, and likely straightaway after the slaying, is that I found a similar but smaller fragment of the same stuff in the room occupied by the dead Provost, under his desk in fact. Now, does that convince you? That soil is what makes me certain that the porter died first of all and then the Provost, for their body temperatures were not so markedly different and the old man had lain out in the chill of the night and one would expect him to be colder in any case. Incidentally, I also found similar soil in the chambers of the Dean of Students, but that is a matter we will discuss later.'

I was still not satisfied. The dim light and the fact that he could not really glare at me in his minatory way made me bolder.

'Why do you say that so conclusively? The killer could have gone to the Dean's office after killing the old porter and before killing the Provost.'

'No, when I felt the body of the Dean it was still a good deal warmer than either of the other two. I'll grant again that the porter lay out in the night air but the Provost was well sheltered. The Dean died last of all.'

I accepted defeat and owned that he was likely correct. It seemed he had a response for everything at his fingertips. He looked at me quickly, at my use of the word 'likely'. He was quite vain where his skills of observation and logic were concerned, more so in his youth, and he only learned to be more easy-going about such things later in life.

We slipped out of the porter's room, my master re-locking the door with his unseen metal device, and we stole back to the light of our own sitting room. Mr Latimer was there much earlier than he usually would have been and, being stuck for company – he couldn't seem to exist without it – he had invited in several of the other occupants of the floor for a 'libation' as he called it. He had a cupboard in the place full of bottles of drink well before we had taken up our temporary abode there.

He beamed as he greeted us. 'Ah, O'Donovan, let me introduce you properly to our esteemed and learned new friends and neighbours. Come in, have a drink, for God's sake. I even have a bottle of most refreshing barley water for our dreary old friend as well as a good Armagnac for yourself.'

We were soon introduced to all gathered there and seated with drinks in our hands. I thought mine far too sweet and I sorely missed the China tea and cheese and hard biscuits I might have had if I was alone. I feared that I would not sleep a wink without them.

As the bright talk of intelligent people waved back and forth in the circle of the room I kept my silence and watched and evaluated. I was instructed to do so, in a hurried whisper, by my employer before we even sat down. I only learned after that he had actually asked the innocent Mr Latimer to arrange this little soirée so that he could see some of his 'suspects' in an informal setting, free from the fear of authority. Mr Latimer must have been insistent, for all the students from the next two sets of chambers were there but one. Albert Havers, a young man from near Dover who was reading arts, was absent on some dinner engagement with his aunt who lived somewhere about Dublin.

I sat and strained my mind with my attempts to remember all the names and where they were from and what was my impression of them and how they acted and reacted to mention of the murders, for that was naturally the main topic of conversation and speculation. I wrote it down hastily later that night and have expanded it since.

Firstly there were Quinty and Easterman, both medical men and both from Guernsey. They seemed studious and quiet to me.

Next was Peter Quinlan of London, who was reading arts. He was small, wiry and weaselly looking, another quiet fellow, sitting there with his bright little eyes darting back and forth. His glass was always ready to be replenished.

Next were Thompson, Clarke and Adams, the last two from our own rooms, divinity students, all from Ulster and bound for ministries in the Established Church. And welcome it is to them for they were far more boisterous than one would expect from future guardians of the flock and both got quite tight on the free port, if I recall correctly.

The next were Messrs Morgan, Dunne and Gunn, the first two from Wales and the last from the city of Dundalk and all reading arts. They seemed uncaring of anything and enjoyed the brief carouse as much as anyone else, save the divinity students. They were all three big and burly men and Gunn exhibited a flash of temper when Morgan advised him that he was becoming drunk. He offered no real violence, though, and was soon mollified.

The last two of our guests sat together, for they were apparently lifelong friends and neighbours and were both studying medicine. Of the two, Jack Wallace was the bigger, bluffer man, one who looked as if he was more suited to the athletic field than the medical amphitheatre. His small friend George Osterman was a different sort, slight, quiet and almost effete. He drank sparingly and said little to anyone but his friend Wallace. He had a good-looking face, almost pretty in fact, fair hair and fine skin and delicate hands, perhaps well suited to a good surgeon, whereas Wallace had a pair on him that would have better suited a rough butcher. The smaller man appeared to me to be the more intelligent of the pair by far.

The talk, having carefully avoided it for the first half hour, finally turned to the three killings and was all theories and clues and motives; the scenarios that sallied forth from their mouths were too myriad, fantastic and frankly sometimes too asinine to write down here. Strangely the only one who had a decent grasp on the thing was big Jack Wallace, who claimed it was a case of multiple robbery by some dangerous thug, plain and simple. I thought it an eminently sensible explanation and took great pleasure in endorsing it in front of Mr O'Donovan. I looked at him briefly for his reaction to my abandonment of his own theories and only got a smirk for my trouble, a smirk that told me he knew what I was about.

The evening broke up well after the eleventh hour, but not before my master, who seemed to have imbibed a lot and was consequently full of bonhomie, advised everyone that he was thrilled to meet them and intended to throw a splendid party and dinner for all in one of the private dining rooms of the college just as soon as he could arrange it. They must all attend, he said. All had to agree for he pressed each one on it, tipsy as a lord and taking each one warmly by the hand in turn.

Immediately after they left and Mr Latimer had donned his own cloak and made his way off to the city to seek better sport, my master was once again as sober as a judge and assisted me with the transposing of my mental notes concerning our guests. He explained to me that likely the killer was among them. I hardly credited it, for of all only Quinlan looked shifty and Gunn bad-tempered enough, and it was very difficult to imagine any of them capable of hurting one man, never mind brutally dispatching three, all in one night.

'I can tell by that statement, Noble, that you lag far behind me in this matter, even farther than usual, if you can imagine that,' he said casually.

I was shocked and a good deal hurt by his statement. He saw the effect on me but he did not bother to try to soothe my feelings and went on.

'Just because there were three murders on the one night does not mean that there was only one assassin involved. Free your thinking, Noble, or you will never make a good solver of enigmas. Do not discount those things that are obvious but also do not marry yourself to them.'

He said no more then and just as well, for the next morning Inspector Bermingham solved all the crimes and took the killer by the collar. It was soon bruited about the confines of our little society and caused a right hullabaloo. The inspector had finally woken up and had searched the dead porter's room, thankfully when we were all imbibing, and had found nothing. To his credit that had made him suspicious and his suspicions had already fallen on one of the junior porters, the custodian of the tatty museum, who had attempted to divert us with his lies about the various exhibits. His name was Seamus Tollin and he was known as a great liar by all in the place. He also liked the drink and, being a young, single man, had the repute among the other porters of using the services of the streetwalkers who strolled about the outer walls of the college at night.

He could not give a good account of his whereabouts on the night of the murders and so Bermingham had raided the man's small cubbyhole and had found there, hidden in the untidy midden the young man lived in, gold coins and several other valuable-looking objects taken from the Provost's quarters. A gold locket of the dead Provost's mother and various other valuable items of jewellery were also recovered. The personal items were later identified by the Provost's maid, roused from her bed for the purpose, and Tollin was by first light being browbeaten by Bermingham down in the police barracks. Most tellingly of all, a ceremonial knife with a vicious-looking curved blade and an Iroquois war club, both bloodied, were found in his room as well. The man protested his innocence and bewilderment at the objects found in his room, but because of his reputation for mendacity, among other things, none believed him. The case was being treated as closed but for the man's trial and execution, and that was that.

When Mr Latimer brought us a breathless verbal account of this my master treated it with all seriousness. I thought he must be feeling foolish over his prognostications to my poor wounded self about the crimes and, rather than feeling smug, as I should have done, I felt sorry for him. I needn't have bothered, for later, when we were first alone together he laughed and said, 'That fool Bermingham has grabbed the first thing that will give him the credit for a solution to the case, has he not?'

'Well, it seems plausible enough to me, sir. I didn't like that scruffy young porter from the start. Then there are all the things, weapons and the rest, supposedly seized in his room.'

'Don't let your visual prejudices cloud your judgement or your ability to judge, Noble,' he began.

I was in no mood to be patronised by him – there had been altogether too much of that recently – and I pshawed him and went off to attend to my toilet.

We went to court that day and I said hardly a word to him nor him to me outside of our business. I regretted my sullenness after an hour and I could sense that he did as well, but we were both too thickly stubborn, cut from the same cloth in that regard, to make the first approach.

I was about to do so as evening and our usual mealtime approached, for I did not fancy enduring a frosty dinner, as it would play havoc with my poor digestion. Therefore I was on the cusp of opening my mouth when he said, 'Noble, old friend, I apologise from the bottom of my heart. I have treated you abominably. What must you be thinking of me, still wet behind the ears and talking down to the likes of you as if you were the schoolboy and not me? Please forgive me. I value your good opinion far too much to let it fall away from me over a trifle.'

We had a pleasant enough dinner after that – though to tell you the truth his apology was so elaborate and overwrought that it took all the good out of it, and ended by making me feel not better at all but guilty – and he explained to me some part of his notions of what had happened on that notorious night, and I admit that I felt like a blinded dolt for not seeing much of what he related for myself, but my own mind doesn't work in the same fashion as his. Incidentally, since I have accepted that fact as engraved in stone, I have been a far happier man.

The evening of the soirée he had promised to provide came sooner than I had imagined it would. Mr O'Donovan, partnered by Mr Latimer, who dearly loved such a gathering and wanted to share in the glory of hosting one, quickly arranged all with the folk of the college and soon invitations were written out and delivered by me to those at the recent get-together in our rooms and to a few others, mainly members of the academic staff. These men were encouraged to bring their spouses along as well.

The night of the big do we had toileted and dressed carefully and my two companions were just enjoying a preparatory drink when there was a knock on the chamber door. I went over and opened it to find a coachman in full livery standing there.

'Are these the chambers of Mr Ambrose O'Donovan?' he asked in a flat Clare accent.

'Why, yes,' I answered, 'among others. Mr O'Donovan is here, but what ...?'

I received no further words from the man, who simply stepped aside and allowed me to see who our visitor was to be. I almost fell over when I realised that it was none other than Celia Scanlan, as was, dressed as fine as any woman could be and looking as if she had just stepped from a picture by Raphael – only more fine of feature and far less stout that his normal subjects.

'Good evening, Mr Alexander, it is so lovely to see you again,' she said, giving me her silk-gloved hand and wafting past me into the room. My master and Mr Latimer had sprung to their feet at the sound of her voice and they both bowed elaborately and kissed her hand in greeting.

'Mr Latimer, Mr O'Donovan,' she said, 'how very pleasant of you both to invite me to your soirée! It'll be a first for me. My first dinner in these halls of academia. I hope that I am dressed well enough for it all and not too dim of wit to participate in the conversation.' False modesty, that was, on a par only with my master at his fullest.

I wondered who had penned her invitation for it certainly wasn't myself.

'Far too well dressed and versed, O loveliest of ladies,' Mr Latimer exclaimed with unfeigned delight. 'You'll have all the students agog as well as their lecturers, and the lecturers' wives, frumps the lot of them, will be mad with jealousy. They won't know where to put themselves.'

She looked worried at this but he continued, ''Twill be a perfect night, perfect, I tell you, made so by your presence.' He seemed to shiver with further delight at the prospect.

'You are lovely as ever, Mrs Talbot,' my master intoned and, from my vantage point, I could tell that, unlike the rote and ingrained flattery of Mr Latimer – although her appearance deserved that and more – he meant it in all seriousness and couldn't seem to take his eyes from her own two pools of deepest azure.

She returned his look as steadily and candidly, and I hemmed to break the silence and the invisible thread between them and found myself for the first time in my life asking another human being if they would like to take a drink. She declined even barley water, saying that she was saving her appetite, and her colour for the party.

She was soon seated among us, for we had an half hour to dispose of before crossing to the dining hall, and that was passed in polite converse, in which I was included. I was in a dither, I will admit to it, and I was forward enough – I didn't care – to bring my master's wife and child up as often as I could. Miss Scanlan, I always thought of her as such, didn't seem perturbed by this and asked Mr O'Donovan all she could think to ask about his daughter. She had no children of her own as yet and was not likely to, I imagined, as her husband evidently spent so much of his time away and all his energies on hunting and fishing.

For the life of me I could not comprehend what her presence signified at all. She hardly knew Mr Latimer and so the invitation must have come from Mr O'Donovan. I went across to dinner that night a very unsettled and unhappy man. Thoughts of poor Ellen O'Donovan, out of sight out of mind, constantly in my aching head.

The dinner party was, I suppose, judged to be a great success by all the others who attended. The talk was not all frivolous for it was concentrated a great deal on the porter Seamus Tollin, his apprehension and his obvious guilt. We actually learned something new – that a triumphant Inspector Bermingham had determined that the murder weapons, the Burmese ceremonial dagger and the Red Indian club, had both been taken from the museum, and, as Tollin had full access to that dusty room, his culpability was established even more.

My master shook his head sadly at hearing this, but otherwise he seemed to be the cock-of-the-walk going about with Celia Scanlan glowing like some lustrous heavenly body on his mortal arm. That night he actually out-socialised Mr Latimer, who couldn't keep up with him at all. He was patently popular with all the guests, but I was very annoyed and disappointed with him. He brought her to every corner of the large ante-room where the guests were enjoying their various aperitifs and introduced her at great length to every single person there, himself hanging on her every word and gesture like a schoolboy. For the first time in our acquaintance I thought my master was a complete fool. To be risking all, his family and his good name, in this manner, over this woman. I was so angry, seething inside, I vowed to myself that I would leave his employ immediately we returned to Kilrush and I could barely look at him directly the whole evening without feeling revulsion.

The dinner fare was well prepared and delicious. Fourteen courses, of which I sampled three, the thin game soup, the plain green salad and the cheese and biscuits at the end, all washed down with Adam's ale. The others for the most part simply gorged themselves. Jack Wallace the medical student sat with his little friend George Osterman and showed himself to be not just an athlete but a mighty trencherman as well. Even though there was plenty of food, he threw manners to the wind and cleared up that left of each course by his tiny, picky companion, and so he fully ate the most of twenty-eight courses on his own, washed down by a lake of claret, port and brandy.

It was midnight before we rose to retire to where my master and Mr Latimer had arranged for coffee and what Mr Latimer referred to as *digestifs*, to be served in the ante-room. Contrary to custom, the ladies in attendance had been kept with us the whole evening and were not expected to withdraw even then. Much more conversation took place, as nearly everyone else was half tight, and for the same reason I took little direct part in it. My master was continuing as the most genial of hosts, beaming idiotically at every word from Celia Scanlan as if she was some goddess come down to earth. The rest must have all remarked upon it, but for once he didn't seem to care what others thought.

When we left the gathering, around midnight, Celia Scanlan did not go to her coach but, to my further horror, accompanied us to our rooms again. She had left her blue velvet over-wrap there, as the night was warm, and she came to retrieve it. I volunteered to run ahead and fetch it, but my master told me to bide myself: 'By the time you hobble there, Noble, sure we'll likely be right on your heels. No, Mrs Talbot will come up and grace us with her company for a few minutes more, will you not, dear lady?' He said this so blatantly that it was almost as if he wanted to annoy me further, for he was too keen an observer of men not to have noticed the condition of my temper and feelings towards him.

She in turn beamed and said that she would like nothing more and I sat there like a guardian dog from the Greek myths making sure that they were not left alone until we all went down in search of her coach. My master lingered overlong over her gloved hand as he kissed it in parting and when he raised his lips from it I noticed in alarm that all the time she had held his own hand in a grip between her thumb and fingers, as if she was loath to release it. I hemmed and mentioned the lateness of the hour and the coach was soon gone, my rewards being her leaving us and a stern look from my master.

The next day in court we were, to any casual observer, nearly back to normal, although I was still determined to leave his employ at the earliest possible moment. We worked well together, as always, and dined plainly before returning to our rooms. Mr Latimer, who had yet to try a case that year, was of course out on the town again. It was a Wednesday night as I recall, and we were alone. I was in a quandary as to whether to suffer on in silence or to speak out of my station about Miss Scanlan. My master sat reading a brief by the light of the candelabrum. It was dark, for it was past ten o'clock. There was a knock on the door and my heart jumped, for it seemed to my ears the same knock as the night before. It was indeed the same liveried coachman and he stood aside once more, to allow Celia Scanlan to enter our sitting room. This time she was much more plainly dressed, in dark green velvet, which even I found breathtakingly fetching on her pale skin. My master greeted her, more informally this time, more as a valued old friend, without the elaborate flattery or show of gallant courtesy, but he was still inordinately pleased to see her.

She was soon seated opposite to his armchair and after a moment or two she looked at me and then my master said, 'Noble, I have something to discuss with Mrs Talbot. Would you mind leaving us alone for a little while, a half hour at the most, say. A walk, a turn or two around the quadrangle will do you the world of good.'

He rose as he said this and took me by the arm, almost lifting me up and ushering me toward the door without waiting for my assent. Before I could protest the impropriety involved in my leaving the two of them there, the door was shut and I saved myself from the indignity of shouting through it at him. I went for my huffy walk and even the cool night air could not settle my rising choler. I was in a rage and a great deal hurt for my good and gracious friend Ellen O'Donovan as well as myself. I almost wept with the frustration of it all.

I walked and occupied my time by counting my estimate of each minute until I had amassed thirty and then returned. I made an elaborate and sarcastic ritual of knocking. The door was opened and I entered without a trace of warmth on my face. I looked quickly at each of them but could detect no dishevelment in their dress nor flush of any passion about their faces. Not that I can claim to be an expert in such things, but I supposed that it was sensible in the circumstances to look for those signs.

Celia Talbot rose before I could say a single word and said that she must be off; she then startled me by taking my arm and asking me to accompany her safely to her coach. Much as I didn't want to do any such thing, I could not very well refuse, and I reckoned further that if I went with her then my master would not, and so they would be that much less together. She took my arm again as we exited the main building and I could see that her coach was nowhere about and so must be waiting for her outside the college grounds, on Dame Street. That meant more than a short walk in each other's company and I resolved to be polite and yet say not a word to her, but as it turned out I did not have to.

It was she who broke the silence between us: 'Those days in Kilrush when we first knew each other seem far off now, do they not, Mr Alexander?'

I replied, evenly, that they were only a short three years past us and while that might seem a long period of time for a youthful person such as herself it was like a fortnight to a Methuselah like me.

She forced a small laugh. 'Come now, sir, you're not that far advanced in age. My father is your senior by half a decade. But I wanted to say that those days, near or far, have been and still are much in my mind. So full of promise they began and yet ended up in so much horror and pain. I wish that those times of our great hope had never ended so badly. I dream ill dreams of those days yet, but recently I have found that I am moving past all that happened.'

'The circumstances were indeed unfortunate, Ma'am.'

'Yes, Mr Alexander. Afterwards, my parents sold me, *de facto*, to Captain Talbot ... James, and Ambrose had married another, a fine and good woman, and he too is a fine and good and honourable man.'

'Yes,' I agreed warmly, 'and he is too honourable to consider casting aside his family, even if he could ...'

My tone was high and she noticed it.

'Hush, Mr Alexander, I know that well, better than anyone else. However, I still have the deepest regard for Ambrose and I know that he has the same for me ...'

I grew alarmed beside her. I started to extract my arm from her own. She knew that I was about to make strenuous protests as to the impropriety of her last revelation. I wanted her to go no farther.

'... but we are both honourable people, Noble, nothing can or will ever happen between us, you must believe that, I beg you. He and I are both wed to others, his wife is the mother of his child and a good spouse. My own husband is away from me and that is not his fault. It stands to his own strength of character, if you must know the truth of it. In his own way he is an honourable man, he stays away so that there will be no strain between us.'

'Mrs Talbot, you are telling me more of your private affairs than I need or desire to know. I have to say that I am very uncomfortable with it.'

'I apologise, that is unseemly, but I can see that you are angered and miserable to see Ambrose, I mean Mr O'Donovan, and myself so much together and I want to ease your fears. You have my word that as long as either of us is married there will not and cannot be anything more between us than the deep affection and respect that we now hold for each other. I swear that to you before God. Now, here is my man.'

I was trying to find some words to say in reply when she left me abruptly, without looking back. I walked to our rooms feeling gradually lighter in my mind at her assurances and guilty at my own suspicion of them. I half expected to hear a similar speech from Mr O'Donovan, but here I was relieved and at the same time disappointed, for he had already retired and quenched his lamp by that time, and the next day he uttered not one word on the subject of Celia Scanlan, nor did I say a word myself.

After we were done with court that Friday evening, we supped lightly in a small eatery that did a good poached fish and Mr O'Donovan advised me that I would be returning to Trinity alone for he had business elsewhere. I feared the worst and my peace of mind, so recently restored, was severely rattled. He hesitated before going on. I think he divined my thoughts and wanted to let me stew in them for a moment or two.

'Aren't you interested in where I'm off to, Noble? That's not like you, for you are usually the divil himself where my business is concerned.'

That was not accurate or fair, as I only ever questioned his comings and goings as they applied to his profession.

'Why, no, sir, what you do in your own time is your own business entirely, you are your own conscience in such matters,' I replied, with some ill temper showing in my tone.

He laughed: 'Well, 'tis no deep secret to tell you, nothing nefarious or dishonourable. I'm only off to question that young porter Tollin, Bermingham's convenient killer, in his cell. That young magistrate, Cumyn – you recall him? – told Bermingham to co-operate with me if at all possible. Bermingham hates me for it, no doubt; he's a devil with a very thin skin on him.'

'But the man's an inveterate liar,' I protested. 'A rascal. Do you not recall the museum? He'll be sure to tell you that he didn't do it, any of it.' I thought it a fool's errand he was about.

'Liar he may be, and an entertaining one in the right circumstances, but in this instance he would be speaking the truth.'

His reply shocked me. 'But the evidence against him, apart from his low character, is overwhelming – the money, not to mention the weapons, the weapons which he had full access to. Don't waste your time on the likes of him.'

'And let the real killer be in peace, is that it? That mountain of evidence against him is my exact point, Noble. A liar is not, thank God, necessarily a murderer, but a good liar must be sharp of mind not to trip himself up, and this fellow was a good liar. Now, I ask you, why would such a sharp lad turn out to be such an untidy murderer? Why would he leave such a litter of incriminating evidence against himself, literally where he would step on it, shoving murder weapons under his cot? I grant that he did have access to that war club and the knife, but then I had to ask myself, who else did? You'll recall that big black and venerable iron key which Tollin used to open the museum for us. Besides his professions of innocence, with which he will no doubt flood us, I want to find out who else had such a key and where is it now.'

He was off as soon as he said that and I didn't see him again until the morning. I heard him come in, it must have been in the early hours, and I thought that he could not possibly have been with Tollin in his cell for all of the intervening time. He was humming a happy little air to himself as he prepared for bed. A popular ballad that I recalled had been stuck in his head at the time when he had first become smitten by Celia Scanlan.

The next day was a Saturday and so we were not required in the Four Courts, but my master did not take advantage of this spare time to sit and read as I did, but was up and bustling about, ready to go abroad.

'I'm off to see that fool Bermingham at the Castle, but I still have the instinctive fear of the native Irish about me when I walk through those bloody gates. Will you not come with me, Noble? As a Protestant gentleman you could perhaps afford me some protection.' He laughed.

I realised that it was an attempt at humour or to get my goat and I did not rise to it. 'I'll be glad to go with you, but only for my interest in hearing what you have to say to Bermingham after your many long hours with Tollin yesterday – and so late last night,' I replied, setting down my book and rising.

If he sensed my sarcasm he said nothing but picked up his hat, cane and gloves and went to the door.

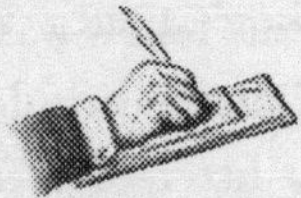

Dublin Castle is a very dark and ominous place, with its closed-in square and grey stone buildings. It had sealed the fate of many an Irishman in its time, and still does, I suppose. We eventually tracked Bermingham to his lair, a cramped, white-limed, slope-roofed little room with brown files tied with ribbons stacked on every surface save for the man's own chair.

He was not well pleased to see us. He made a point of telling us how busy he was and he treated my master with no more regard than he would have afforded any other Catholic Irishman. He was rude in fact and sat on while we stood.

'See here, O'Donovan, I'll be frank with you. I've no time to spare and if you had sent me a note asking for a meeting I would have declined, in spite of Cumyn. I cannot imagine what you want at all.'

My master showed no reaction to the man's insulting manner. 'I've come here only as a courtesy to you, sir. I value your time as well you see and I don't like to see you wasting it.'

'Wasting it, what's that you say? You're a nervy beggar ... '

'Wasting it by chasing down that poor gossoon Tollin for crimes which he patently did not commit.'

'How do ye know he didn't commit them?' Bermingham asked.

'Because he told me so,' my master replied beatifically.

'The man's a known and proven liar. Why would you credit a word he says? A jury certainly won't. I've checked up on you, sir. You have the repute of being a very clever man, but I must say I find that reputation surprising in light of what you have just said.'

Once again my master went on, seeming quite unperturbed: 'It takes an intelligent man to be an entertaining liar, Inspector, and speaking to the man last night I could tell that he was not only intelligent, if acutely wanting in morals, but cute in the ways of the world as well. He is no fool when it comes to life. But if he killed those men for gain and then was foolish enough to hide the loot and his gory weapons in that hatbox he lives in, then he would have to be the stupidest murderer I have met so far.'

'That is a very nebulous theory when all is said and done, sir. No law of God or man says that a criminal has to be clever, that he can't be a foolish dolt. If that was the case, then we'd never find a one of them for the courts to try. Now good day to you, sir. That is all the time I have for you.'

We left the rude fellow, myself bridling so that I thought my neck stock was about to choke me, but my master merely chuckled as we walked to our rooms.

'That man is as thick as a rick of hay and as unmannerly as a dunging pig, so he is.' He reflected for a moment before adding, 'Don't you think that as a consequence he'll likely go very far in the Dublin police?'

We walked out of the Castle grounds and he said, 'Well, Noble, we'll just have to uncover the real killer or at the least prove that young Tollin did not do the deeds he stands accused of.'

As it turned out he did both.

We went back to our rooms at a great pace which even my long legs were not up to. I huffed along beside him and finally asked what his rush was for.

'Why, to see that all is in order for this evening,' he replied without elaboration.

I looked puzzled no doubt, and he finally explained: 'I am giving a small soirée, a light dinner party for the three of us and a very special guest.'

As it turned out, he had arranged for a meal to be brought in to our rooms by the owner of the Pearl Diver, an eatery in Lower Baggot Street. It was a cold collation, a brace of pheasant, two brace of woodcock, a small boiled Limerick ham and a poached salmon. To accompany this we also had a marvellous and huge platter of salmagundi of an extraordinary variety and freshness, and I would have been well content to have made my supper from that alone.

Our guest arrived when all was in place, and an extraordinary figure he was. He had on a military-style cloak with good enough evening clothes under it, but he had topped his large head with a gaudy tartan hat, the type known as a tam o'shanter, of the most ludicrous aspect and ill suited to his natural gravitas, and on his feet I noticed that he wore common brown boots of the heavy rimmed variety favoured by cattle dealers.

My master introduced the stout little man to us as Professor James McPherson, lecturer in medieval history at Trinity College for over thirty years. We sat to dine and even though the Pearl Diver had supplied a man to carve and serve us, my employer was up again and again and cutting and passing and filling the wine goblets of the others. McPherson's cup seemed to have been made with a hole in it, for it was never long full, and he had the face of a long time toper on him. His nose was a round and flaming lantern held before his pink face, which itself was dotted and streaked and beribboned by the colours of burst veins. The man was, however, very tidy in his dress, unusual in such an overweight toper, in my own experience, and although undoubtedly Scottish by birth he spoke English with no accent other than that employed in the best English universities.

He supped up his umpteenth glass of white wine, wiped his mouth, turned to me and said, 'I believe, Mr Alexander, that you are like myself a good and devout disciple of John Knox, a good Presbyterian. To your health, sir.'

This coming from a man whose face had the aspect of the foyer of hell, who was already more than half drunk! He was even then eyeing the brandy and port bottles that stood like soldiers in nervous readiness on the dresser behind me and his eyes were swimming, looking as though they were watered by the devil himself every day.

'Is that so, well, well, imagine that,' I said politely, turning away on some pretext, but quick enough to see my master hurriedly wipe a smirk from his face.

He had obviously told McPherson of my religious leaning as a source of some future sport, and he had been rewarded by the look of horror on my face caused by my co-religionist.

Before the man had arrived amongst us, I had quizzed Mr O'Donovan as to who our guest might be and what was the ulterior motive he must have had for throwing the little party. He told me that he wanted only information about the personages involved in the killings and after asking about, he had learned that James MacPherson had the longest tenure of any of them. He actually recalled much about him – who could forget him once having met him – from his own time at the college, as did Mr Latimer, although he had not lectured them. They very likely thought him dead of the drink by then.

McPherson had been there thirty years or more, stuck in what he referred to often as his prison, and had seen many Provosts and Deans and porters come and go in that time. He would prove useful, for he had the memory of an historian and, even better than that, a repute for being as inquisitive and curious as any scandal-mongering old slattern from the Liberties. He was a lonely old stick at the back of it all, I suppose, and had been glad of an invitation out for some good food, pleasant conversation and not least a veritable bucket of drink. He had been, in his youth, a lecturer in history at Oxford, but had got into trouble over his drinking and the madcap pranks it led to, and thus it was that he had found himself in exile in Dublin. Because of his reputation from his Oxford days and the wild antics he had got up to in his youth, he was still barred from mixed functions at Trinity, for even in Ireland the proprieties had to be observed. He was as eccentric as a man could be and soon became a great favourite with the students. My master remembers a good many 'Old Mac' stories from his own days at Trinity, and said that someone should write a book about the old codger, that same old codger who sat now with one of his raw hands clutching a good bumper of brandy, while my master judged him sufficiently lubricated to prod him for the extraction of candid information. He turned out to be very candid indeed.

'Here's to eternal rest for Professor Oliver Petrie, Mr Latimer here's dear old uncle. May he rest in peace,' my master said by way of a toast, but really to get the ball rolling. 'Mr Latimer unfortunately didn't really know his uncle over-well, Professor, even you must have known him a good deal better. How long had he been the Provost here, can you tell me? He was after my own time anyway.'

'Not long in the scheme of Provosts, though,' the Scotsman sniffed. 'Five years or less. Not a patch on old Joshua Hargate, as was before him. Beggin' your pardon for saying so, Mr Latimer, your uncle was a good and decent man, but not of a nature to be running a university, even one like this. A university is a business, you see, to any sensible mind anyway, and can only continue as a business. It should be run by a man of commerce and not an academic. Your uncle was an academic, a damned good scholar, I don't mind telling you, but altogether too wrapped up in his ancient Greeks to be the least bit of use otherwise.'

Here thinking of my own passion for the old Greeks I shrank a little in my clothes.

McPherson took a swallow of spirits that would likely have killed off Bacchus and continued, and once started off he rolled along on his own with only a tweak and a nudge needed to point him in one direction or another. 'The late Provost took no heed of anything to do with or that smacked in the least of commerce. To him the world of pounds, shillings and pence did not exist. It was his nature and it is the nature of the things he studied.'

'How so?' I asked, receiving a stern look from Mr O'Donovan for interrupting.

'Well, where in the history of the ancients, I ask you, does it speak of money and gold and how much a man was worth and how much he made either by honest toil or by plunder? Nowhere, that's where, and I've read it all and the whole thing is most impractical. My own sphere, the middle ages, early, middle and late, is crammed full of records of their commerce and guilds, ransoms and prices of all things from armour and silk clothing to corn. The costs of the cathedrals, the cost of a milch cow or a hide of land or dried peas or a common trollop. We, in the sphere which I teach, are the more practical men, not living in the airy-fairy world of the likes of that old pederast Socrates and his ilk.'

I was about to leap to the defence of one of my greatest heroes when my master nudged the old fellow.

'So, Professor Petrie was not much at running the place, but do ye know, it doesn't show, for the whole thing seems to hum along, even though it is the quiet season.'

'That is through no fault of our late Provost, I can tell you. I wouldn't have put the old fellow in charge of a privy door, beg pardon again, Mr Latimer. No, he left all that "commerce" to the Dean of Students and Admissions, James Lockhart. Now, I try never to speak ill of the dead, *de mortuis nil nisi bonum* and all that, the recently dead at any rate – for I have never cared much for Richard the Third – but

Lockhart had the stony heart of a moneylender. Where old Petrie cared not a whit for a pound, with Lockhart every shilling was a prisoner – with a life sentence. The man had the inner heart of the meanest miser, he knew where every nut and bolt was in this place, what everything was worth and what all cost down to a nicety. He knew what the sum of the annual fees was to a penny, the rentals of rooms, the profit from the university's fee lands in the North. The man was as hard as iron nails and used his power over the students – and over the rest of us where he could – most mercilessly. He delighted in fining students for any infraction of the college rules and he had made himself a true expert on those. They have not been changed much since the time of Queen Elizabeth, you see, more added on to than anything else, and so a good many of them are arcane in the extreme. A transgression against them is therefore an easy thing for a novice. The poor students, the newer ones, would be stripped by him in a few weeks and soon took to looking about for him before they so much as crossed the quadrangle or ventured into the supper hall. James Lockhart will not be missed by anyone, for he hadn't a friend in the whole place. But do ye know, for the university's sake, I hope that they appoint a similar in his place, though perhaps not one quite as grasping. In any event, the old Provost would have been lost without Jimmy Lockhart, 'tis lucky they both perished on the same night, what!'

My master and even Mr Latimer laughed at that, I hope more from a willingness to keep on the good side of their guest than from anything else.

'So this Lockhart was the factor of the university. Was there not a bursar or a treasurer to look after money matters?' Mr O'Donovan asked.

'There was indeed, sir, always, but when the last of them retired four years ago Mr Lockhart offered his services to replace the bursar, without cost to the college. The Provost and the board of governors were only too delighted to accept, crowd of penny-pinching skinflints that they are, I mean the board, not your old uncle, Mr Latimer, I assure you, sir. The strange thing is that, even given Lockhart's mean disposition and almost satanic love of money, the old Provost had complete confidence in him and would hear no ill about him at all. I suppose it suited him to do so.'

'Not so surprising,' my master observed, 'for the Provost's love lay elsewhere. As I understand it, he only stayed in his post as a means of allowing himself the luxury of constant study of his chosen field.'

'Damned right, but he stood too close to his work, don't ye know, and that is always a bad thing for a man to do, it blinds him, don't ye see. He stayed in his rooms as much as he could, and that was almost all the time. He would have a porter bring him the books he needed from the library. Funny, but 'twas old Corny Flynn that he used the most. He would lean out of his door and shout for Mrs Harrigan to "fetch Corny, for I have an errand for him". I think that he liked Corny for some strange reason known only to himself. Personally, I think that old Petrie may well have seen Corny as what he might have become but for the grace of God – and his father's wallet.'

The brandy was by now taking its toll on the old fellow and my master moved ahead with his schedule. He wanted any information he could get from him on the students in the next two sets of rooms.

McPherson knew only some of those by reputation and some who were reading arts and were also attending his lectures. That was only four men in total. He said that Peter Quinlan was a twerp and a know-it-all, that Wallace was only good for playing sports and foolish pranks. (That was rich, coming from him, I thought.) He estimated Ronald Thompson as a studious humbug and Gunn as a ne'er-do-well who had a dark character to him. He was in his fourth year at the college, but was only in the second year of his course to a degree. He was constantly short of money and was likely up for any means of getting it. McPherson said that he fully intended to fail him again.

That concluded our evening, for the old fellow shortly after fell asleep, empty glass in hand and all of his chins resting on his chest between snores. Mr Latimer and my master looked at each other and sighed. They woke the old man gently and took him, one on each arm, back to his own chambers.

When we had all reassembled, there was a lively discussion as to what we had learned, if anything.

'We have learned that Professor Petrie was a trusting, decent old stick,' my master began, 'and that Corny Flynn was a favourite of his and so possibly his confidant. We have also learned that the Dean was a grasping, hard-hearted man who was also possibly a scoundrel. We must bear in mind that he had apparently unbridled control of all the moneys flowing into and out of the college.'

'That is all by the way, though,' I interjected, 'for he was a victim as well and so cannot be our man.'

Mr Latimer nodded at that, saying that the Dean's character didn't signify as he was a dead'un too.

'I can tell that you both have yet to grasp any of the real tails of this thing,' Mr O'Donovan remarked. 'I will say no more, but would ask you to think, just to think. Between you, you know as much as I do about the matter.'

I sat chastened but angry at his high-handed manner, but Mr Latimer only laughed and poured another brandy for himself. 'Damn, but you're right on my score, Ambrose. I've no head for these things at all, that's likely why I'm such a complete lout as a barrister.'

I was about to rise and retire when I learned that our evening was not yet over, even though it was well past eleven o'clock by then. My master stood and arranged his cuffs, a habit of his when he was about to do something important.

'I've some necessary work yet to do this night,' he said. 'I'd appreciate the company of a good friend for it. Are ye up for a little stroll, Noble? Nothing dangerous, I assure you.'

His words heartened me again and I readily went with him, but once more I soon wished that I had not, for our destination was not a far one, just outside the walls of the university in fact.

We soon found ourselves in the heart of the area where the local ladies of the evening paraded for the benefit of students and others in the darkness. When I realised that fact, I wanted to leave immediately, but my master restrained me with a tug on my sleeve.

'Steady, Noble, I need you as a fly on the line from my rod. These doxies might not approach me, for I am too old for a student and too well turned out to be short of female companionship, and so I might be a member of the law come to harass them. You, on the other hand, are too old to be a policeman and you have the mien of a minister from the country or a circuit judge or something, both species that would be favoured customers for these girls. The great thing is that you are not a judge nor a country parson and so none of them will recognise you.'

I considered the implication in this. That I might have been recognised I knew was another jibe at my expense, although Mr O'Donovan had a straight and serious expression on his face. But his eyes were sparkling in the light from a single dim lamp overhead and gave the devilment in him away. I was about to speak up with the intention of excusing myself from the night's venture when we were approached by two tawdry bissums of indeterminate age, linked in their arms and exuding a strong odour of gin mixed with a great quantity of stale scent.

'Evenin', surs, lovely for the toime of year, is it not?' the taller of the strumpets said by way of greeting.

I said not a word, for it was the first time in my life that I had met with a streetwalker and I was not enjoying the experience a bit.

'Lovely, almost as lovely as a pair of doves such as yourselves,' my master replied, to my horror.

The shorter one smiled at that and the wreckage of the dentition she revealed would have put a pig off his dinner. She was the older, for the other one was less lined under the thick plaster on her face and her teeth were as yet largely intact.

'Would yous kind gintlemin be wanting the company of two of Dublin's foinest this night?' the older brasser said.

My master almost howled with laughter and I knew the cause of his mirth, for Robert Peel had started the slogan that his police force was composed of 'Dublin's finest'.

'We'll walk a piece with you, ladies,' he said, and fell in beside them as they ambulated off down the street.

We talked a little with them and when we got to a small park – it was no more than a bit of green and some shrubs at the corner of two streets – we separated into couples. The shorter one fell to my lot and my master was soon gone off into the darkness with the other before I could say a single word of protest. Immediately the little gorgon on my arm tried to lead me off into some of the scant shrubbery, I can only imagine for what purpose.

'Come on now, me old love, 'twill only cost you a shillin', or two if you want anything that might offend me. Oi'll be as gentle as a kitten wit' ye, I promise. Now, don't be afraid nor a bit shy.'

'Leave your dreadful hands off me, you trollop,' I replied exasperated. 'I want nothing to do with you, and will give you not one copper penny.'

Well, when that sank in, that she was to have no custom and what I thought of her, she began to rant and rave, to wail and screech, and I was afraid that the scene she was causing would get a complaint from the neighbours and perhaps even bring one of the police watches along to officiate at our sparring match, although it was not much of a match when all is said and done.

I tried to quiet her. My master's trollop was not causing a disturbance and I did not want him to be disappointed with me or blame me for ruining his plans, whatever they were. He was seeking information, that was all, and we could ill afford to put the possible source of that information off talking to us so soon.

'Tell you what, I'll give you a shilling,' I said, pinching the relevant coin from my waistcoat pocket, 'on the strict understanding that we will stand quietly until my friend is er ... finished – and that you will not touch me or speak to me further. Now, is that agreeable to you?'

'That is very offensive to me, sur, and loike Oi said before dat is going to cost ye a florin.'

I tossed the shilling to her and turned so that I did not have to look at her. I did not even say that she would get no more than a shilling under any circumstances and she must have accepted it, for she was silent. She was fishing about, rustling in her clothes, though, and I feared that she was about to disrobe or do something equally immodest. It turned out that she was only seeking her bottle of poteen which she took out, unstoppered and sipped at, demurely as a tea matron, only spoiling the effect by belching softly when she was done. She nudged me for my attention and I turned to her involuntarily. She smiled at me horribly and offered me the foul bottle, wiping the opening of it with her shawl.

I declined abruptly. I have been offered drink a thousand times in Ireland, but never in quite so disagreeable and loathsome a fashion.

'Aw, go on, sur, ye might as well get somethin' for yer money, some wee pleasure. Who knows the sup might even put some fire back into your old – .' Here she used a word I will not repeat, for modesty, and out of deference to barnyard fowl.

I had reached the limit at that and was fully determined to leave when my master reappeared with his doxy, neither of them with their clothes in any way disarranged, I was glad to see.

He bade them both a hearty good night and we left them sharing the shorter one's bottle and cackling among themselves.

'I trust that you are happy, sir,' I sad stiffly. 'Your doxy was at least fairly clean of stink and sober and, more important, quieter. What on earth you dragged me down here for I cannot imagine, except perhaps to mortify me and to make fun of my …'

'On the contrary, Noble,' he interrupted. 'You were greatly needed, for I had to get the young doxy alone to question her. It cost me a guinea to hear what she had to say – and to have her leave me alone. Remarkable how expensive her information was when the normal business would have been a florin at most. But she was canny enough to know that a man can get a doxy for two shillings anywhere in Dublin but a man seeking knowledge of a specific sort is stuck with paying whatever the traffic will bear. It was worth it, though, every farthing.'

I asked him what he had learned, but he would not tell me until we were back in our empty rooms and seated.

'Did you not find yours pretty, Noble? She was a fine wee stout woman after all and she took an immediate liking to you, I could see that.'

I had been waiting for just such an attempt at a witty sally and I flew at him at once. 'Listen, I have given you service this night, and now I want to forget that it ever happened. If you mention it again, even in jest, I shall have no choice but to leave your employ.'

He was chastened by my reaction and apologised over and over and said that I had behaved admirably. I gave the appearance that I was mollified, but the next day I was suspicious that he had not lived up to his penitence when Mr Latimer spent the morning singing some evil little ditty about a woman of the Dublin streets who lived by selling shellfish and, by inference, from the sale of her personal charms as well. I have no doubt that he was doing his crooning to get my goat. My master must have told him of our brush with the two street whores.

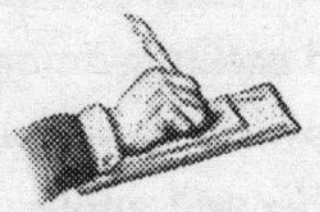

Getting back to our discussion after the meeting with the strumpets I asked my master what he had learned and he replied, 'Quite a lot, Noble. I learned that our young porter, Tollin, who seems to have Bermingham's rope tightly about his neck, is a *bon vivant* of the lowest and most unsavoury variety. He is a man of unfortunate habit and a near moral wreck for one so young. He is addicted to ardent spirits and drinks freely, but his main failing is the use of narcotics, and opium was his choice in that pursuit. He was constantly in need of money to buy his evil substances and also to avail himself of the services of various ladies of the evening about the college from time to time. It was usual for him to spend the whole of the night in their company, in their rooms and at some considerable expense. He had four or five favourites, who also indulged in his narcotic practices with him. I got the names of them from young Rosie last night and now I have the task of tracking them down.'

'Why?' I asked.

'I'll tell you. The young rogue is in a right fluster with the charges against him and rightly so, but he swears that on the night in question he was in funds and so had left his post at the university to seek out whiskey and the stupor offered by opium, together with the company of one of his women. He does not remember which one, though, for I suppose he is an inconstant swain. The fault of his straying that night is mostly mine and Mr Latimer's, I fear, for you recall we gave the rogue money for showing us that dreadful museum. He strove to put it aside and was successful for some days, but alas it burnt a hole in his pocket and at last he succumbed to temptation. That begged another question. He was given over the responsibility for the museum and had turned it into a small industry for himself. It was not a great money-earner, but remember there was one in the university who was avaricious, according to Old Mac and many others. I could not imagine that individual letting someone else make money from the college right under his nose without interference, but apparently he did. The young porter said that Jimmy Lockhart 'the grasping Dean', never said a harsh word to him about it and he had been doing it steadily for several weeks before our arrival, since the beginning of the summer vacation, in fact.'

'That is interesting. But what does it matter that Lockhart lost a shilling or two?'

'It matters when you know that the only other key to the venerable lock on the door of the museum door rested with the late Dean himself. He was the only other in the college who had access to the room's exhibits – if they can in truth be termed as such.'

'So he could have taken the knife and the Iroquois war club as readily as Tollin – but what of it? I mean to say, James Lockhart was a victim as much as was the provost and old Corny Flynn. The fact that he had access to the weapons doesn't change the other more important fact that he too was murdered.'

He looked at me with pity written plain upon his face. 'I'll grant you that he too was murdered on that dreadful night, Noble, but until you think it all out you will not see the insignificance of that particular detail.'

'I hardly think the death of a man, no matter how vile, to be an insignificant thing,' I said with all the sanctimonious asperity I could manage. I could see no real point in his theory about the museum. 'The fact that he had the only other key, he being a third victim, makes matters even worse for young Tollin. Does it not?'

'Only to those who cannot see, my friend,' he replied enigmatically and ended our discussion by challenging me to a very late game of chess. He was obviously too exhilarated to sleep. I salved my scalded pride by trouncing him solidly in three straight games.

The quest for the proper harlot, if there is indeed such a thing, took some time and, to put it as delicately as possible, involved my

master's roaming the al fresco bordellos about the college for several nights. During that time he located and eliminated all but one of the four women as the companion of Tollin that night. That night was an infamous one in all of Dublin because of the three murders and so stood out in their minds, and the women were helpful in providing further information regarding the night-time antics of Seamus Tollin, even though they were not the one that my master sought. There was only one left of the handful of names that young Rosie had given to Mr O'Donovan, and unfortunately she had vanished almost without a trace. He offered a good reward to any strumpet who could locate her for us and so the woman was found, or accounted for, after long days of having resided in the deepest recesses of the Bridewell. She had been there near a week all told, incommunicado among the other female felons, or accused felons, of the city. She had lifted a good gold watch from a client, in the same bushes where I had been mortified, and unfortunately for her, the gent had noticed his loss before she could get away. He grabbed her and yelled for the police and held her firm in spite of her screams and her nails until they arrived. She was searched, the watch was found and she was now expected to be taking a trip to Van Diemen's Land at the earliest opportunity.

My master dragged me off to interview her, and what a sight the depths of that dismal jail was to behold and what an impression that young girl, a true wreck of God's humanity, made on me! Her face was scabbed and pocked, flea- and even rat-bitten, her hands were raw, her clothes were little better than dirty rags and she wore not a trace of shoes on her bare feet. The worn flagged floor was damp, cold and covered with mouldy straw and must have caused her a great deal of discomfort, as it was also her bed and dining table. My master asked why she was not shod and she said that her shoes had been stolen from her by a large woman prisoner, Biddy Kiernan, within hours of her arrival. The other inmates were terrorised by this Medusa and so made no complaint. She said that the turnkeys knew only too well what was happening and were happy to turn a blind eye in return for the large woman's keeping the others in order for them.

The girl before us, although at twenty a hardened strumpet, was plainly terrified at her new surroundings, shaking and scared to distraction about her future and pleaded with us to help her. My master assured her that we would do all that we could, and when he had settled her he asked about young Tollin. She said that she knew him well, and that he often retained her services for a whole night. She said this to us without one trace of shame on her face or in her tone. She and Tollin it seems shared a common addiction to opium and the girl had now been denied the drug for over a week and that deprivation in part explained her sallow, drawn and nervous appearance. Tollin would bring a quantity of the vile substance to her room when he visited and they would afterwards smoke a pipe or two and pass into a drug-laden sleep to enjoy what she termed as the most marvellous dreams. She said that they smoked a pipe or two and were not in it at all until the morning.

I got the impression from the way the harlot spoke that she had some small but genuine affection for Tollin. She was well aware of the murders on the night in question but knew nothing of the arrest of her young friend. My master asked her what she recalled from that night for such news must have made some impression on her. I doubted this for the victims of opiate addiction seldom have a great deal in their memories.

The hussy surprised me, however, by mulling over the question for a few moments and then answering that she remembered part of that night at least. It had been a fine evening and she had strolled about for her own enjoyment until after dark. After that she had received the attentions of three or four men who paid her for her services. She recalled that the last of them tried to pass off a counterfeit florin to her, and when she protested, he threw her another coin. He made off quickly before she realised that it was only a shilling. She gave up following him and turned to see another customer walking towards her. He came up to her but he was walking with his head down and his rough coat pulled up around his chin, as if he was cold or had a toothache. He was not a customer, though, and only wanted to walk past. She got the impression from the way he was walking that he was on an errand. He was a workman of some sort and did not even answer her when she greeted him, but pushed her aside and went on his way.

My master seemed surprised at this information, and pleased, for he rubbed his hands together. 'There would be few workmen about the college walls at that time of night, my dear, is that not so?' he asked her gently.

'Yes, sur, come to think about it, you are right, few workmen who would not be customers at any rate.'

'Where did this workman go after he left you, do you recall?'

'I think he was headed for Dame Street, sur, I seem to remember that, but I cannot be sure.'

'To the front gate of the college, I'd wager. Now, think carefully – did you notice anything unusual about him, in his dress?' Why my master was so interested in this faceless anonymous fellow I could not then imagine but if young Josephine was perplexed at his quizzing she did not show it, but seemed to think hard on it.

'No, sir, on'y he was a tall man and he had on rough clothes and work boots.'

'Were the boots really work boots or were they high leather boots with yellow tops? Please think.'

'Yes, why yes, I can see them now as we speak, sur, they wus like you said. Not what a man'd wear for work boots but high leather yokes, just like gintlemin's riding boots only old and worn. The tops was folded over and showed the yellow lining.'

'I hoped that you would say as much. Now, later in the night, where were you?'

'I stayed about the college walls for a only a while longer for the night had grew quiet and I was about to return to my own room when

Shamey Tollin approached me. He had money on him and gin and told me that he had a pipe or two of opium as well. We went to my room and drank off the gin. After that we smoked the opium and I recall nothing until I awoke the next morning.'

'Were you alone when you woke?'

'No, Shamey was there beside me and I had the divil's bother waking him for he was due at his college post by eight o'clock that day. He told me that the night before, to be sure and waken him up. He was good and late at his station that morning, that much I'm sure of.'

We left her in near as much despair as we found her but my master gave the warder some money to see that she was looked after a little better and protected from the malicious giantess, Biddy, and then we went upstairs to the police and, using what influence he had, he obtained the name of the man who had accused the trollop of theft and he went off to visit him. He told me of it later, that he went prepared to offer the man money to withdraw the charge against Josephine Doyle. He was delighted to find the man, in his tea-shop, apron tied about his waist and him in a blue funk. The fellow was married, you see, and while seizing the harlot who was robbing him and turning her over to the law seemed the best course of action at the time for an angry man, he had since come to realise that there was every chance that his wife would learn of his involvement with the whore if he had to go to court and testify. She would, he said, skin him alive for wasting good money on that foolishness and he obviously went about in great fear of his spouse. Dublin and its courts were small places in those days and he was sure to bump into someone he knew and that someone would doubtless take a great delight in advising his wife of his night-time activities. My master only added to the man's trepidation by suggesting that it might even make it into the newspapers if it was a slow day with no murder trials taking place. My employer escorted the man to the police station and had him withdraw the complaint at no cost to himself. He went to a magistrate that he knew and had an order for the release of Josephine Doyle issued within the hour. We then brought her home in a horse cab to the evil hole that she inhabited and he saw to it that she had money for food and new clothes, garments of a more modest nature to what she normally wore.

Then we travelled back to the college, for he said that he had a meeting planned with none other than Harold Cross, who had been appointed as Provost, pro tem, some days before. He had already gone to see this man once, ostensibly to congratulate him on his apparent rise in the world of the college's hierarchy. That is what he told me, but he spent almost the whole afternoon with the fellow, which led me to think that it was more than a courtesy call.

A couple of hours later he came for me and we went back to the harlot's digs. I waited in the cab while he fetched her down. She had obviously followed his instructions, for I tell you she looked a totally different woman. She wore a modest high-buttoned dress of dark green with ivory trimmings and on her feet were dark shoes of a very sensible kind. Her fair hair, no longer stringy but remarkably clean and brushed, was drawn up behind her into a severe bun and she had a loose-knitted black shawl about her shoulders. He had explained to her the fix that young Tollin was in and the need for her to tell the police that he had been with her all of that night.

The change of clothes seemed to have somehow changed her character as well, for she was very sober and serious and actually reddened at the prospect of telling a stranger that she had spent the night with a man she was not married to – this after telling us near every foul detail of her trade and life during our first meeting!

She realised that the life of her young friend was in the balance, and she also realised that but for Mr O'Donovan's intervention she would soon have been taking a ten-year tour to Australia, and so she agreed to go with us to Dublin Castle. That part of our mission was not as easy as one might think. We almost had to barge our way into Inspector Bermingham's office again and there was a bit of a shouting match when he tried first to oust and then to ignore us. Reason, to a small extent, and the mention of Magistrate Cumyn's name to a larger extent, prevailed, and my master at last convinced the dolt that he had better listen to the witness who waited for our summons, trembling, out in the hallway.

At length Josephine Doyle was able to tell her story to the obstinate policeman, with myself as a witness, and even though she admitted to sleeping with a man not her husband and was really only a slightly mundified strumpet, Bermingham did not seem to notice but was to my surprise greatly inclined to believe her. He confided to us after she finished that, on serious reflection, the young porter had acted in a very stupid – even for an Irishman – almost suicidal manner, if he was indeed the killer. To go to the trouble of waylaying a victim and then killing two more in their rooms and then to leave the most damning evidence lying about his cupboard-sized quarters was too ridiculous to be credited. To throw the weapons away or to clean and replace them in the museum would have been the work of only minutes and they would have been available to him again if he ever needed them. The whole thing was just two cut and dried. He had come to the conclusion that the evidence had been planted in the boy's room by the real killer; which meant that the killer had planned it all out most carefully. Taking the weapons, doing the bloody work and fitting up young Tollin for it all. That much is to Bermingham's credit, but do you know, if we had not faced him with the testimony of Josephine Doyle I believe that he would actually have buried those reservations – along with Seamus Tollin.

The girl's statement was recorded, by yours truly, and signed by her in a neat hand. We left the man's office some time later – the girl and myself, that is, for my master remained there after us in conference with Bermingham and I had the task of bringing the odious woman home again on my own.

He came back to our own rooms an hour after me looking very pleased with himself. I was anxious to ask him what transpired after I left, but we were not there together two minutes when Mrs Talbot's coachman arrived for him and he left me there without so much as a by-your-leave. I went to the top of the stairs and heard the coachman saying that he had waited for my master to return for over an hour and that Mrs Talbot had been expecting him back ages ago and would no doubt be worried.

I went back inside with a heavy heart, for obviously my master was off to another private meeting with the woman. I slept not a wink before three in the morning, I am sure of it, and I did not hear him return. All her earnest words about the honour between them fell in ruins about me.

I had slept badly and the next morning was to be a busy one. We went to the Four Courts and my employer seemed his old self, cheerful and invigorated. I feared even more that Celia Scanlan was the root cause of it all, that she had her hooks into him again, taking a hold that might destroy him and all who belonged to him. We whisked through three of our small cases in the courts of Chancery that day and were supping early in an ornate public house near to the college when I brought up the subject of the murders for the first time that day.

'You seem well pleased with yourself, Mr O'Donovan. The murders are not weighing as heavily on your mind now, I take it.'

'No, well, not from any sense of mystery anyway, Noble. I have made great advancements in the matter as you well know,' my master replied, a little too smugly for my taste.

'If by great advancements you mean proving that Tollin did not commit the crimes, then I beg leave to say that it is no great advancement. I could say that Mr Latimer did not do it and so have achieved as much, could I not? And it would not put us a whit closer to getting hold of the real felon.'

I spoke in quiet triumph, for he seemed for once to have walked himself into a trap I had set up for him. I fully intended to take a little of the wind out of his sails, as they say.

'You cannot compare the two, Noble, and there is no truth at all in your statement. I have proven to Bermingham's satisfaction that Tollin did not, could not do any of the murders. Bermingham is a callous bigot to be sure, but in spite of that and my first assessment, he has a spark or two of wit behind him. On the other hand, you have proven nothing. Your statement that Mr Latimer is innocent in the matter is quite unsupported by the facts. He might well be the murderer, though an amiable one to be sure.'

'That is monstrous to suggest! Why, Mr Latimer was with us when the first murder was discovered. With me, at any rate, for you were mysteriously not about,' I said, to remind him that I knew of his night-time visits to parts unknown.

'Ah, but you are wrong, Noble, for I was about. I was watching from the main gate as you tumbled out the door and scurried across the yard. Mr Latimer came after you some minutes later. You were no doubt horrified by the sight before you and did not notice him coming up to your elbow. I noticed that he had a dressing gown on over his outdoor clothes. Under it he was dressed for the streets right down to his boots. And anyway,' he went on, with the twist of a sarcastic smile at the corner of his mouth, 'how do you know that he was in his room at the times the murders were actually committed? You have no idea where he was then. Admit it.'

I sat dumbstruck, my mind racing. I felt like an ass and was heartily sorry that I had claimed innocence for Mr Latimer just to try and prove my point and belittle my employer's achievements. I was also horrified by a new possibility.

'My God, so you think that Mr Latimer may have killed his old uncle and the others ...' I began.

'Nonsense, Noble, he had no more to do with it all than young Tollin. Put your mind to rest on that score. Whoever did the crimes had a very definite reason for carrying them out. Mr Latimer had none – none apparent to me at any rate. Perhaps he didn't like old Corny's tea or he couldn't stand the way his uncle ate his biscuits or had a pick at the Dean for some unknown reason. No, I know that our friend Darcy Latimer did not do any of the murders for the simple reason that I know who did and am in the process of proving it. That is why I have asked Bermingham to hold on to young Tollin for a while yet, two days at the most. The young rascal's continued trepidation is a small price to pay for the uncovering of the real story. It will, I hope, be a good lesson for him as well.'

'But the poor lad is innocent of all ...'

'Yes, yes, I know, but he is in better circumstances now, eating better and in a cleaner cell, incommunicado. Bermingham will see that he is all right for a day or two.'

'But why not release him as justice would indicate that you should?'

'We are holding him because the thought of his imminent execution for a crime he did not do is doubtless hanging heavy on the conscience of the real killer,' he replied, to my great shock.

'That is far-fetched,' I said with almost a snort, when I had recovered. 'I don't think that any man who can go about slashing, braining and stabbing willy-nilly can have much of a conscience.'

'You are only two-thirds of the way correct, my friend, and if you had used your intellect you would know why that is so.'

I tried to continue, to find out what it was I had missed, but he cut me off by changing the subject, abruptly, to tennis. He had been invited to play in a new court at Ringsend and was wondering if he should go.

'I played at tennis in France, *tennis royale* they call it, but 'tis not a sport for a man at all, to my evaluation of a man's game, that is. Why, you cannot get to grips with the other fellow at all!'

I said nothing. I was still smarting and lost in a fog with no hopes of being able to ask him anything that would lift the mist for me, for he wouldn't answer. I knew that from experience. I also knew that he detested tennis, for I had heard his little speech on it before. My master was a conundrum to me in many ways. He was a man who could argue the niceties of Baroque music or describe and interpret the plot and significance of some esoteric play, a man who loved the art of the Renaissance as I love the ancient Greeks, but he would leave off an intellectual pursuit to climb on a horse and gallop off to challenge the local cock-of-the-walk at an impromptu crossroads boxing match of a Sunday afternoon. He always preferred fencing and wrestling and boxing or a good game of football or a full day's hurling between rival villages to more sedate sports, if only for the opportunities they provided for rough-and-tumble, head-cracking and general mayhem. How a good mind such as his could be attracted to such rude endeavours as hunting and cock-fighting was, and is still, a mystery to me. I was not about to rise to the fly he had cast, however, and so embroil myself in an argument about the merits or lack of merits of what are known as 'blood sports'.

The next day was to see everything to do with the matter put right and I will do my best to relate it to you just as it happened.

We all rose early, for Mr Latimer was to go riding with a new belle and I was to work in the Four Courts with my master, who was already risen and gone from the rooms and only returned when I had made my frugal breakfast and our new skip had tidied up the rooms a little.

'Well, Noble,' said Mr O'Donovan, 'are ye ready to face the legal giants of the Dublin courts? We have an easy enough day ahead of us.

One or two bracing torts and a breaking-and-entering before we unmask the true murderer for all to see.'

He would say no more and was, I'm sure, more than content to leave me in a great state of ignorance and anticipation. The day's business hung heavy on my mind as I waited for the sudden flash of exposure that I expected from my master, but the day passed without incident, no matter how expectantly I looked at him. He lost one of the torts and his breaker-and-enterer was deported for ten years. The lout had only himself to blame, for he broke into a house in the Upper Rathmines Road and proceeded to get beastly drunk on the owner's best brandy and was caught there, red-handed, when he fell into a dead sleep.

Such a result from a day's labour would normally have upset Mr O'Donovan, but he seemed to have other things on his mind and took his losses with equanimity. But then he was not the one about to be deported for ten years.

That evening in our chambers he was nervous for once, prowling like a cat. He passed about and checked the clock on the mantel often, although it registered only ten minutes past six and had apparently done only that for some years.

Finally there was a knock at our door and, when I opened it, I was shocked to see two students standing there. They were from the chambers two over from our own, Messrs Wallace and Osterman, both medical men. You will recall them, the hale and hearty Jack Wallace and the frail, almost effete George Osterman.

The big fellow did the initial talking for them and he was in no sociable mood as he brushed past me into the room.

'See here, O'Donovan, just because you treated us to a soirée and a drink or two don't give ye leave to order us about as if we were your bloody servants. Osterman and myself are our own men and we are very busy with our studies besides. We do not appreciate a summons such as this, even from you.'

He fairly bellowed the last and threw a balled-up piece of paper at my master, who batted it aside. I picked up the scrap, unnoticed by anyone else and read it. I have kept it since:

> *Dear Mr Wallace,*
> *Please do me the honour of attending at my rooms at no later than seven o'clock tonight. Be sure that George Osterman accompanies you. You should both be warned that failure to appear will cause me to involve the police in your affairs. I am having you watched so do not attempt to flee,*
> *O'Donovan*

The note seemed very terse to me and not of his usual manner, with its threats of police involvement. The fact that the two were there, however, even in a foul, reluctant mood, of course indicated that it had been successful.

'Have a seat and quit your bluster, sir, we have other guests arriving shortly and I would ask you both to be quiet until then. I intend to say nothing until all are here.'

I thought that the burly Wallace was about to strike him, but Mr O'Donovan left off leaning against the mantel just then and straightened himself up to face the fellow. The man sighed and sat down on the couch, where he was joined by his little companion.

Within a minute I was at the door again and to my horror was admitting Celia Scanlan to the company. She smiled sweetly at me as if butter wouldn't melt in her mouth and was then re-introduced to the two young students by my master. She sat on a straight-backed chair facing them and she looked the cool beauty in her light summer dress and with her pale, unsunned features.

Mr O'Donovan then went to Mr Latimer's room and asked him to join us before he started the proceedings.

'Firstly let me just say that I have not yet advised the police as to any of my findings or suspicions,' he began. 'I will tell them some of what goes on here, but if you both play your hands right you may benefit from my continued secrecy. Is that understood?'

The big fellow was about to protest that it was not understood at all, when his smaller companion stayed his arm and said softly, 'Hush, Jack. We understand, Mr O'Donovan.'

But Wallace was not ready to be quieted and Osterman continued, 'Let us at least hear what Mr O'Donovan has to say.'

George Osterman had spoken more words then than I had yet heard from him altogether and he had a soft, pleasant, almost sunny voice in spite of the dire nature of our meeting.

'Good, very sensible, Mr Osterman,' my master continued. 'I am prepared to name the murderer of Corny Flynn and Professor Petrie. I am sure of my facts. I have been since the morning after the killings. I would ask you to hold off any comments until I am done, or until you are asked for your observations.'

He stood where we all could see him in front of the mantel.

'James Lockhart was the murderer of both the old servant Flynn and the Provost. He did the murders in a fully planned manner, for he even fetched the necessary tools from the museum, to which, incidentally, only he had a key besides the young porter.'

There were gasps at this. I know that I emitted one myself. He held up a hand to remind us of his previous instructions before continuing.

'I knew at once the order of the killings, for Lockhart had walked in a particularly loamy bit of flowerbed when he lunged at the porter and he had carried away some of the soil packed between the heels and insteps of his boots. I found traces of the soil deposited in the rooms of the Provost and the young porter, Tollin. When Lockhart was found dead in his own room I took the opportunity of the police not being there to search his private quarters, where I found the rough old boots he had worn for his night of crime. They were in his closet, worn riding boots that were the only flawed items in the disguise of a workman which he had affected to enter the college grounds. The rough clothes were there as well, bespattered with blood. I left them all where I found them, including some of the earth, but the police made no attempt to search the place after me and so missed it all.'

Here he looked directly at me and I remembered the tale told by the young harlot, Josephine, about the workman who had rushed past her wearing the yellow-topped boots.

'He made his way,' Mr O'Donovan went on, 'garbed as a workman, out of the college by a side gate and came around to the front on the open street. If he was spotted it would be reported that a ruffian had gained access to the college grounds and had no doubt carried out the mayhem. If not he had other plans for laying off the blame on another.'

I forgot myself at this and interrupted him: 'But why did he not dispose of the boots and the bloody work clothes?'

He looked at me frostily but answered, 'Because, Noble, he did not believe that he had to. Not then anyway and he did not have the chance to do so later.'

'But why would he do those horrible things?' Mr Latimer interjected.

I had opened the lock gates for questions and knew that I might be rebuked for it later.

My master answered, nevertheless, for the question was one he was about to answer in any case: 'For one of the oldest motives – greed for wealth ... and self-preservation.'

He let that sink in for a moment or two.

'The man was a scoundrel, low-born and impoverished as a young man. I believe his credentials to have been a total forgery, prepared to enable him to obtain the position of Dean here. It would be a simple (but to my mind unnecessary) matter to write to the institutions where he claimed to have received his education and to have worked in previous employments. He was a man driven by greed for material gain and I think by an instinctive hatred for his betters. Let me say that he respected no one. I have read some parts of his private journals. They were his only confidants, and they betray a poisoned and merciless mind.'

'But he cannot have made much by way of income from his position,' I observed. 'A living at most, surely.'

'Quite right, Noble, but his position, coupled with the fact that the old Provost had completely removed himself from the business of the college allowed him – acting with, I believe, the collusion of old Corny Flynn – to rake off a fair amount of coin each year. I have been meeting with the *pro tem* Provost, Professor Harold Cross, for the last few days and that good man has had a brief audit of the college books done by the people from Curzon's firm of accountants. Even that cursory review has shown that a pattern of fraud and deceit was present for almost the whole tenure of the late Provost.'

'And no one ever noticed?' I asked.

'Apparently not. The funds running through the college each year are substantial and so the funds taken by Lockhart did not show up as clearly as you would think. He was careful to ensure there was never a deficit but always a healthy surplus.'

'How did he manage to steal the money in the first place?' Mr Latimer asked.

'His position offered him a myriad of ways to pilfer. He fined students regularly and then simply pocketed the funds. But that was only a small sideline for him, more a vicious sport than anything else. The main of his illicit income came from the taking of monies paid over by resident students for their living quarters. He had, over the years, shown more and more of those living quarters for students as having been converted to other, non-revenue-producing uses – such as faculty rooms and even lecture halls – so making room for fewer and fewer students to find lodgings in the college proper. The numbers of resident students actually increased in that time and he put the spare rentals and other costs borne by the students right into his own pocket.'

'That is a remarkable claim,' Mr Latimer observed.

'Yes, Darcy, it is to be sure, but this college is large and the board of governors is old or frankly indolent; and the Provost was a man with his head firmly in the clouds. Lockhart was able to pull the wool over his eyes completely. He was seen as a godsend by the old man, for he took away all responsibility and duties from him, thereby turning his position into the sinecure he desired. This could have continued until the provost retired or was replaced, but, I believe, for one thing.'

'What was that?' It was my turn to make a noise.

'The arrival of George the Fourth in Dublin. He has, as we all know, put any suitable lodgings at a distinct premium in the city and its environs. The college had few students about and it was seen as a way to increase revenues in the summer months. The discrepancy between actual and recorded living quarters finally showed up. I believe that old Corny Flynn noticed it first. He must have got hold of an official roster to distribute the quarters and noticed the supposedly missing rooms. I believe that he foolishly confronted Lockhart about it. Lockhart was forced to forestall the old man's marching off to the Provost about it and took him on as an accomplice, or pretended to. The old fellow made the fatal error of taking Lockhart's fine clothes and cool manner for the qualities of a gentleman and so was, to his own surprise, put to death by the true savage that the man was. He was not foolish, though, and I guess he wrote down a note or two, which he left in his room as a kind of reserve. No doubt he told Lockhart that such a thing existed, to be shown to the Provost. Recall if you will that old Corny and the Provost were thicker than such a man and his employee would normally be. Lockhart, a master of blackmail probably in his own right ...' here he looked at the two students sitting quietly among us '... feared the grip of an extortionist and struck out. He killed Flynn and searched his room for the letter. Not finding it, I think he concluded that the Provost must have it already. Perhaps Corny did not feel that he was being given enough, or was having pangs of conscience over being a party to theft – and other things. And so the Provost was also killed. The killer must have had that in mind as a distinct possibility all the while, for he stole two weapons from the curio cabinets in the museum. He had keys to every room in the college as part of his function and so was able, first to search through the old porter's room, and later, to plant all the false evidence in young Tollin's cubbyhole. He could even have let himself into the Provost's chambers without any commotion. He may have raised the old fellow from his bed on some pretext – perhaps the old man knew of his thievery by then and expected him. The old man wouldn't have known the true type he was dealing with and trusted that no harm would come to him. He probably wished to settle the whole matter without attendant publicity or the involvement of the police. He likely even expected that Lockhart would resign his position and, as a gentleman, make some attempt at recompense to the college. But the assassin was not interested in going back to a life of unemployed penury; and besides, he had already dispatched Corny Flynn and that was sure to be investigated. The Provost might even put two and two together and not get five for once. The whole thing took only an hour or so, and Lockhart was soon back in his chambers, dressed but dressing-gowned and relaxed, confident that he had got away with it all. He could guess at the type of man that the board would appoint as Provost and felt no doubt that he could manage the new man for a while and so at least give himself time to clear out with the spoils.'

'That is a remarkable piece of conjecture, Mr O'Donovan,' big Jack Wallace observed. He sat there red-faced and fidgety, as if he wanted nothing more than to get away. Little George Osterman sat beside him, but was pallid and had a look of great concentration on his visage.

I spoke then, voicing something which had been concerning me: 'But Lockhart was as surely a victim of the murderer as any of the others, so how can ...'

'... he be guilty, because he was murdered too? I'm afraid that he cannot hide his guilt behind his own murder, Noble. Death does nothing to exonerate him in any way, for there is no law that a murderer cannot himself be murdered. Have you never heard the old saying about those who live by the sword? He killed twice and was himself killed by another; that is all.'

The big student considered this for a moment as I did myself.

'I mean, with all due respect,' Wallace went on eventually, 'that you have no real proof of what you say, of any involvement of Dean Lockhart, other than a few bits of soil, when all is said and done. It could all still have been the work of an outsider.'

'You are right in part, sir, I have not, nor cannot have any substantial proof to support my assertions and that is why I have asked you to come here this evening.'

'Me? Why me, and why George here? What the devil have we to do with it all?' Wallace said, once again reverting to blustering.

'A great deal, sir, as does your friend here. I ask you to remember that there is at this moment a young man accused of the three murders and he will surely hang for the crimes of Lockhart – and for the crime of one other.'

Here Mr O'Donovan looked at me as if to tell me to keep my mouth shut about Bermingham, about Seamus Tollin's impending release, et cetera.

He turned back to his small audience: 'He will die, I'm sure of it, and he is innocent, of these crimes at least, and his execution will be nothing short of a fourth murder. The person who killed James Lockhart, if they do not come forward, will to my mind have done a real murder and not merely have cleansed the world with the dispatch of a depraved swine.'

The big student, Wallace, was growing white in the face now and obviously had become very frightened. His companion looked stricken as well and, in the silence that followed my master's last speech, he seemed to physically crack. His lost his cool distant look and his frail-looking shoulders slumped and shook with some new emotion as he put his head forward into his hands.

'I cannot live with myself as it is,' Osterman groaned through his fingers. 'How will I ever hope to live in peace with innocent blood on my hands?'

'No, don't. I beg you, George,' his large companion screeched at him, with a look of real terror on his broad face. 'No, say no more, for we are safe, none can prove a thing against us, please, I beg you.'

To my surprise, he even took his companion's hand tenderly in his own great paws as if to assuage his fear.

'No, Jack, dear, innocent, true Jack. I am following the ambition of my life against all odds to become a healer, a doctor, and I cannot start out my career by taking life when I am to take an oath to preserve it at all costs. Now, hush. I will explain myself in good time to these people. You need fear nothing, for you have done nothing wrong, except to be a faithful companion.'

'Fear nothing! I know nothing but fear for I cannot live a day without you,' the big man blurted out to my further surprise.

I now feared there was an unnatural relationship between them, and the idea of it repelled me.

'I am glad that you are seeing sense, George, but that is not your real name, is it?' my master said, sending my own mind off onto another tangent. 'Your real name would hardly be George. Georgina, perhaps, but certainly not George.'

The young man sat up as if struck. 'How did you guess? I know that we have never had an inkling, not one, in three years here that my disguise was not perfect, or perfect enough not to arouse undue suspicion. We never put a foot wrong.'

Wallace started to speak again, but my master waved him to silence. 'You would have taken me in as well,' he said. 'Your years of impersonation have made you practised. You mostly had taken me in, in fact, for at first I saw you only as a frail and somewhat effete student, not such a very rare thing, and so I would not have suspected you of actually being a woman. I could hardly have taken the chance of challenging you on it, for if I was wrong what would the consequences have been? There was something not quite right, though, and I had my suspicions, and so I asked my dear friend, Mrs Talbot, here to attend at our recent soirée where she met you among all the other students and immediately she knew you for what you are. She is a very perceptive person, Mrs Talbot. Now, are we not correct?'

The young man looked steadily at him with tear-filled eyes.

'You are,' he, or rather she, said. 'I have lived the lie so long that I am nearly relieved that it is out. I am in reality Pauline Wilson, from Devon in England, like my dear friend and fiancé, Jack here. We have been affianced since we were children. He understands me as no one else possibly could and he has always been my champion. I have longed to become a doctor all my life that I can remember and, as you must know, I was thwarted in my ambition on account of my sex. My father is of the old school and would not hear a word of it. He barely educated me at all and so I had many of my lessons at second hand from Jack. At length I decided that the thing could be done, with dear Jack's assistance, and so I ran away to Dublin. We both did, and that is why we reside here all the year. I dare not go home, for my father would now imprison me. I know that it was hard on my parents, my absconding, but I have written to them to say that I am well, posting the letter in England, and so I hope that they have not been fearful for my physical safety at any rate. I bought some forged letters and papers as to the scope of my lower education and enrolled here at Trinity to learn my chosen trade. It was my intention to graduate, with Jack, who shares my love of medicine, and then to emigrate with him to the new lands of America where my talents would be valued and where my sex might not even count against me, if I was a good enough doctor, for the land there in the Americas is filling up with new towns and populations and my help will be needed. It is to become, I firmly believe, a land of new ideas as well.'

There was complete silence for a moment in the room.

'Those are admirable ambitions, Miss Wilson,' my employer said kindly. 'It is surely a folly that such as yourself has been denied an education when all you want to achieve is some good in the world rather than laze about all your days in idle comfort. I have already spoken to several of your lecturers, and to a man they have said that you will make a first-rate doctor, combining skilful hands and a good brain with a kind and caring nature. But tell me, when did Lockhart learn of your subterfuge?'

The young lady was startled again and answered him almost involuntarily: 'Why, only recently, just a few weeks before his death. I may as well admit now and get it over with that he died at my own hands and I have asked myself since what kind of doctor will I ever make now?'

'No, Pauline, I beg of you to say no more, for nothing can be proven against you,' her fiancé said, putting one of his big arms around the little person in men's clothing.

'Your companion is quite correct,' my master said. 'If you say nothing, then we are powerless, but can you live and escape by letting an innocent man die? Ask yourself that question.'

She did not hesitate for a fraction of an instant.

'No, I cannot. Please let me continue, Jack, for I must tell my side of things and be judged against them. I was discovered, accidentally, by our temporary skip, old Corny Flynn. He was unused to my long-standing request for strict and full privacy. One morning I was surprised by him in my room as I was binding down my bosom as an essential part of my habitual disguise.'

Here she was not being indelicate, I hope you will understand, but was rather speaking of things as clinically as any doctor would.

'I was risen late that day and, thinking me gone, Flynn came in to straighten up my room as he would for any student, and he saw me.

He turned and left the room at once, but I knew that I was found out and was at the least facing expulsion. We had some money, thanks to Jack, and I followed and approached Corny with a bribe, which he accepted and promised me his silence. I was nervous of course, for once a secret is out it is no more a secret, but as the time passed I became more assured of my faith in Corny and the power of the guinea that we gave him each week. Then I received a dreadful shock. It began with a curt note from James Lockhart demanding that I come to see him in his office on a most important matter. I still did not imagine that he knew my real secret, but when I complied with his request he faced me with it all. He had it from the perfidious Corny Flynn who, Lockhart said, was now his associate in other matters, and had told of my real identity as a gesture of "good will". He claimed that he did not wish to take the trouble to expose me, but wanted a profit from it of his own. He got it as well, over twice what we paid Corny, and we both accepted it, Jack and I, as another burden upon us. I thought that if I could continue the subterfuge until I was at least qualified with my degree, then we would disappear from the ken of Flynn and Lockhart and all would be at an end.'

'That was not to be?' my master asked.

'No, indeed. Lockhart knew as well as we that we would, one day soon, be placed beyond his power over us and so he increased the cost of his silence each week. He would have broken our small bank in a little while, so I begged him to let us pay him a little less. I wrote a long letter to him – I know now that was foolish – and I asked him to be more reasonable.'

'And of course he was not amenable to that,' my master concluded.

'No. At first I thought he would be more lenient, but he then summoned me to a meeting in his chambers, specifically without Jack, for four o'clock in the morning and I was to make sure that I was not seen coming or going. I had no choice. I pray that none of you will ever find yourselves in the grip of such a blackmailer. When all was dark and still about the place, I went to him. I was frightened but had no option but to go. Even then I hoped that I could persuade him to be reasonable. He only sneered at me, becoming more and more abusive as I wept and begged. He seemed that night to be strangely excited, his face was red and his eyes were shining and dancing in his head. Much as I have seen Jack when he has just won a great victory on the field of sport.' Here she patted her companion's beefy hand. 'I am embarrassed, even now, to say openly that he told me that he would reduce his monetary demands only on one condition, and that I had no choice in the matter and must tell no one.'

Here for the first time she seemed unsure of herself. Big Jack bristled beside her but she eventually continued.

'He … he … told me that I must submit to his will, abase myself to him for the satisfaction of his lust; and only then, and as long as he was content with me, would he safeguard my secret. He actually wanted money as well. He said that when I was qualified I could leave with my papers and he would be happy never to see me again.'

She sobbed then, 'What did he think of me, what did he expect, that I would do the vile things he wanted for any reason under the sun? The man was a scoundrel and he must have been mad with his own power. I believe that now, that night he was insane.'

'The swine, I would have choked the life from his scrawny throat, so I would,' Jack burst out, flaming with anger.

'I know you would, Jack, but you were not there, thankfully. Lockhart was as smug as I've ever seen a man. He sat at his desk and showed me the written report that he proposed to send to the Provost and to the board of governors exposing my subterfuge, along with my own letter to him, and he told me to disrobe for him in almost the same breath, so that he could get a look at me, he said, for he didn't want to be buying a pig in a poke and couldn't tell what was my true shape in my man's getup.'

'The monster,' Wallace erupted again. 'I wish I had killed him.'

She didn't seem to notice his useless outburst and went on: 'He saw my hesitation and thinking me only frightened and shy he grabbed my hand and tried to place it on himself. I can tell you that I fought at that and told him what I thought of him. I was prepared to give up my dream rather than do what he was bidding. I said I would expose myself and him and Corny Flynn the very next morning and we could all face the consequences. He was taken aback at that, he glared at me and called me names that one could not apply to the vilest strumpet. Instead of releasing me, he pulled me half over his desk to his mouth, saying that if I would not do his bidding willingly then he would take me as he pleased. I was desperate, I had no escape, even the public admission of the ruse that I was playing would not save me from degradation at his hands. It was then that I felt his letter knife on the table under my other hand. Without thinking, I found my arm shooting out to fend him off with it. To my surprise he released me at once and grabbed at the blade, which somehow I had jammed deep into his throat. I had felt so little resistance to the blow that I first imagined that he was unscathed. I truly believe now that I was guided in my desperate stroke by a merciful God, for the foul creature died instantly. I panicked at what I had done, but I kept my head enough to take away my letter and his letter to the Provost and I ran back to my quarters, where I told Jack all that had happened. We sat in a frightened state all the night fearing that our future together was over, but then the events of the night began to unfold, three murders had been done and suspicion seemed to fall everywhere else but on me, and why would it be otherwise? I said nothing but I have been plagued by conscience since the young porter was locked up and charged with all of the crimes. Even if he had done the first two, he had not killed James Lockhart. I had.'

Finishing her tale, she dropped her head into her hands and I confess that I felt a great pity for her.

'I believe every word that you have just told me, Miss Wilson,' my master said. 'You did not intend to harm Lockhart, that was not ever the point of your visit. You took no weapon with you and the stroke, though seemingly expert, was a piece of pure luck on your part, even for a near-trained surgeon. It was the result of a panic and striking out blindly only to defend yourself. I suspected Lockhart of being a man vile enough to not have been able to resist having such power over a young woman. As if the scoundrel was not laden for his voyage to hell with enough other vices.'

I instinctively felt a renewed pity for the young woman whose life now lay in ruins. She would be exposed and banned from the practice of medicine and worse she would be tried for murder and at the least transported for life. My heart was indeed heavy for her but I was shocked out of this by my master's next words, for I have already told you of the great store which he sets by his honour, justice, the strength and necessity of the law.

'Well, I don't speak for Noble here, or Mr Latimer or Mrs Talbot, but I for one can't fault you in anything you have done and I firmly believe that you would never have let Tollin swing for even one murder he did not do. I have therefore absolutely no intention of making any of this public or of assisting the police in any way, shape or form. Your secret will be safe with me and I will be greatly disappointed in my three companions if they are of any different mind.'

He stopped and let us digest this.

'I will say nothing,' he went on, after a moment, 'but my proviso is that you must leave the college with your Mr Wallace in the next few weeks and travel to America. There I hope that you will marry and practise medicine in that land of new frontiers. If you have any daughters, I hope that they will be as good as you and that the new world will see past the silliness of the old and let them become whatever they want to be. I wish only the same may come to pass for my own little girl. Now, what do you say to that?'

'But, Mr O'Donovan, you are forgetting one important fact,' Osterman, that is to say, Miss Wilson, protested. 'I cannot walk away from this matter. What of the fate of young Tollin?'

'Miss Wilson, you have just this second confirmed all the good opinions I hold of you. You have not immediately grasped at the chance of freedom and escape to a better life with Jack, but your first thought has been of your duty to an innocent man. I am more confident than ever that I am making the correct decision in this matter. Now, let me ask, what do the rest of you say?'

I for one was greatly relieved and felt the welling of a tear or two in my eyes at these sentiments. They were tears of relief for the young lady and from pride in the deep humanity of my friend. Mr Latimer was more than willing to let the matter be, and Mrs Talbot smiled and nodded as well.

My master resumed: 'There you have it. You have been brought to justice and tried in the minds of us all and have been found innocent, a verdict any sensible court would render. But one must not ever put too heavy a reliance on the common sense of any Irish court and I think it best that this be your only trial in the matter. Seamus Tollin is quite safe from any legal harm, I can assure you. You are free to go with my blessing, as your judge, and, dare I say, with the blessings of Mr Latimer, Mrs Talbot and Mr Alexander, who have acted as your jurors.'

He smiled broadly at the two huddled together on the couch. When the full gist of it had sunk in Miss Wilson and Jack Wallace were very relieved. She wept softly and he was manly and effusive in his thanks to us all. I personally thought that the passing of the murderous Lockhart was no bad thing and that the young woman deserved praise rather than castigation and I said as much.

'Let us not spoil the moment we are enjoying by speaking ill of the dead, Noble,' my master said primly, letting his Catholic superstition shine through his veneer of civilisation for a moment. He was being such a prig about it that I was set to remonstrate with him, when I noticed the others in the room looked as if they shared his view. I was suitably chastened and said as much.

The rest of the story is simply told. Tollin was released and, at a meeting in his office, my master admitted to Bermingham, who was obviously most pleased to hear it, that he had got no further with the matter since the very first day. He told the policeman of the strumpet's meeting the working man in rough clothes and Bermingham fell at once into a new theory that the killings were random acts of mayhem and robbery carried out by a person or persons unknown. It is amazing how a mind weak in logic will adapt any facts to fit a theory or vice versa. My master, having softened up the policeman, then let him know what he had learned on the first day after the murders.

He showed the man the college's financial report, demonstrating Lockhart to be a thief, and told him of the evidence, backed by myself, of the soil found in the rooms and gave his proofs of the order of the killings. He soon convinced him that Lockhart had killed Flynn and the Provost to cover his own criminal tracks.

'But then who the devil put that knife into Lockhart's throat?' Bermingham asked, as if musing to himself.

My master waited a moment or two before admitting that in that regard he was as stumped as the policeman. Then he added casually that it was Lockhart's own letter knife and there was little sign of violence at the scene.

Bermingham mulled this over a few minutes before sitting up with a shout: 'I have it. No one killed Lockhart, the dastard. I believe that he did himself in!'

My master said the word 'himself' at the same time as Bermingham and the man looked more pleased than ever to receive his backing for his new theory.

'Yes, that's it, it must be,' he continued, on the hunt now. 'The man was obviously labouring under a great terror of being discovered. And rightly so for if he had lived I'd soon have had him by the heels. Or perhaps as well his conscience was eating at him. He had just done two dreadful murders after all, killed two men he knew well, and only for vile profit. I think that his mind suddenly snapped as he sat contemplating all this at his table and he drove the knife into his own throat. Well, what do you both think of that?'

'Admirable, Inspector, admirable, you have it. I can think of nothing that you have not hit upon and I must own that you have the whole thing solved.'

Bermingham was not long in obtaining the police surgeon's sworn statement that the blow which killed Lockhart could only have been self-inflicted and he closed the case by convincing his superiors that he had been able to lay the other two murders directly at Lockhart's own door. Everyone was delighted at his success and he was slated for further promotion.

A new Provost and Dean were appointed for the college by the creaky old board of governors and the place was soon back to some form of normality. My master scoffed when he heard the name of the new chief of the college, for it was not the worthy Harold Cross but another fellow he recalled from his student days there as being 'as useless as an udder on a bull'. He said that it was a sad thing that by far the best Provost of Trinity College, that bastion of established Protestantism, had been a Catholic (the only one ever), named Dr Michael Moore, who was made up to the post by King James in 1689. He did much to save the valuables of the college and its singular library from pillage and destruction by the king's army and made himself responsible for the safety of the numerous Protestant prisoners kept within its walls. A secular priest, he also successfully opposed the handing over of the college to the Jesuits. His noble and humanitarian efforts are acknowledged in Trinity by numerous plaques. My master went on about the great Dr Moore so long that he brought me from an initial interest in the subject to near falling asleep.

As for the two at the very kernel of my story: Jack Wallace and George Osterman left Dublin by the end of the summer for parts unknown, and I hope that they found happiness there. The fat

German-English king came to our shores and soaked up as much drink, food and gelt from Dublin as he could for four months before he went back to London. We too returned to Kilrush and our other business there by the middle of September.

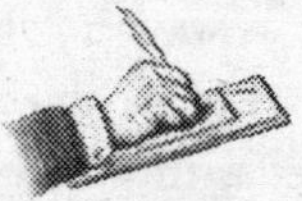

You may recall that I had determined to quit Mr O'Donovan's employ over his blatant relationship with Celia Talbot and you will wonder that I did not do so. In my own defence let me say it was fully my intention to carry out that decision and I wanted to broach it with him before we even left Dublin. He carried on in the meantime spending several late nights a week in her company, brought to her in her own coach, and this only made me more set in my determination to quit him.

I was actually on the verge of telling him one evening as he was preparing to go out. He turned as he was putting on his gloves and asked me: 'Tell me, Noble, do you still place as great a stock in the rights of man, of all men, to freedom from the interference and injustice of bigotry?'

The question, out of the blue, took me by surprise, but I said that I certainly did. I was a true follower of Tomas Paine, even though that great thinker for the American cause was an Englishman.

'Then, if you will be prepared to be sworn to secrecy, I believe that you should accompany me tonight. Will you?'

I agreed, for I knew that he was likely headed for the Talbots' city mansion, but I could get no more out of him until we arrived there in her coach. Once greeted by her man and led into the drawing room, I saw with a shock that we were to be far from alone. There were upwards of twenty people in the room. The first figure that I spied was that of Daniel O'Connell, who stood by the mantel, speaking to a much smaller man whom I knew as Richard Lawlor Shiel. They were both lawyers of course, and denizens of the rotunda of the Four Courts. I recognised several other barristers there in the room, some Protestant as well as Catholic. I was then greeted by Celia Scanlan with a handshake, as she did with my master, as bold as a cattle dealer.

I was still in a quandary as we were all ushered into what was her dining room but was now bare of all objects used for dining. The long mahogany table was now set with a covering of green baize and had notebooks and ledgers spread out upon it. All but myself took what were obviously accustomed seats. Mr O'Connell was installed at one end of the table and my master at the other. He pulled me down into a chair beside him and I sat there quietly until Mr O'Connell rose and called the meeting to order. I learned then that I was attending a meeting of the newly reformed and invigorated Catholic Board, the successor to the Catholic Committee, an organisation whose principal aim was the emancipation of the vast Roman Catholic majority in the country and the abolition of the last of the Penal Laws. As a first order of business that night my master rose, bade me rise also, and introduced me to the rest of the governing committee. He had me sworn in as a new member and I found myself immediately assigned to assist the committee's secretary, none other than Celia Scanlan, in writing down the various minutes, a task near to my own old clerical heart.

That is enough said about the matter for now, though I remained a member of the board and all its later incarnations and rendered all the service I could, at my master's side.

As we returned to our rooms in Trinity in the wee hours of the next day my master advised me that on the first night when he had become re-acquainted with Celia Scanlan she had told him of her involvement with the movement and that Mr O'Connell wanted men like him to make up the committee with which he planned to shake the board out of its lethargy. She had cajoled him into coming along to a meeting, where he had been indoctrinated. Mr O'Connell had already known my master well but could never have been so persuasive, and he was a mightily persuasive individual, as Celia Scanlan in getting him to join with them. The new interest had grown in him over the summer, for they had their secret meetings three or four times a week and so I realised that he had never really been alone with her. It was all an innocent thing, noble in fact. Ellen O'Donovan, sitting in Kilrush, was not betrayed, but the poor people of Ireland had gained a true champion in Mr O'Donovan, and a good clerk in myself through the auspices of Mrs Talbot. I spoke often with her about her aspirations for the people and soon realised that she was no bored dilettante, nor a woman out to cross her people for spite, but a passionate believer in the desperate need for social change in Ireland. How she had matured so in three short years I cannot even yet begin to imagine, but any ill feelings I harboured for her were to an extent replaced in a short time by admiration.

I slept like a baby that night, for when I had imagined that my master was doing wrong it was as if I was doing wrong myself and I had been conscience-racked. In my relief I rested well and was quite happy for the remainder of that year's sojourn in Dublin.

I recall the day that we left the city with a good deal less pleasure, though. We were all packed and awaiting a coach to bring us to the Bianconi depot for the western stages when Celia Scanlan arrived to take her leave of us. We shook hands warmly and she wished me well as my master quite naturally walked her back to her coach. I stayed in our rooms to make final preparations for our departure. Mr Latimer had saddened us by leaving over a week before, without darkening a courtroom door once that whole summer, and the rooms had seemed empty without him. I stood by the window using its light to put papers into a leather satchel when, from the corner of my eye, I noticed my master and Mrs Talbot at the entrance to the vaulted arch over the front gate of the college. I had almost turned away to put the fastened satchel on top of our other bags when I saw the thing happen and my heart dropped again.

As they stood together in the shadow of the building Celia Talbot reached up quickly and put her arms around my master's neck, pulling his head down to hers and then she kissed him. Not the brief kiss of a dear friend taking leave of another but a far longer kiss than was seemly. Long enough for him to put his arms in turn around her waist and practically lift her off the ground. Just as suddenly as she had begun the embrace she broke off from him and hurried away through the portal to where her coach would be waiting for her in Dawson Street. She did not look back, but my master from his vantage point on the ground could see her go and he watched where she went until she must have been long departed.

THE BURNING OF THE SHEAS

In the year 1823 we were once again in Dublin, where my employer was plying his trade in the vestibules of the Four Courts during the spring sessions, for he had taken to going to Dublin for some months each year to look for interesting briefs, to relieve the tedium of life in Kilrush.

The city of Dublin was still a fine-looking place, although it had lost its parliament to London almost a generation before, and the beautiful building that had housed it was sold off, for a bank of all tawdry enterprises. There was likely a good deal less bustle about the place since the transfer of the seat of government and anyone coming from London would no doubt have considered it to be only a provincial backwater, but what the ancient city had lost in prestige it had striven to regain in social comforts. It boasted a reformed and largely effective, if oppressive, police force in the Castle, a good transportation system, a clean water-supply system, good wide streets and there was even much talk that those streets would soon be lighted by gas. The city still had some of the aspect of the dazzle put on it by the citizenry for the royal visit two years earlier. There were numerous new and convenient bridges across the Liffey and a grand

and efficient post office with its headquarters on the broad avenue that was Sackville Street. There had been a plethora of fine buildings erected since the Union to house churches, hospitals, asylums for every class of the deprived, from the insane and the poor to the deaf, dumb and blind. As a symbol of its modernity there was a frequent, but to my mind not quite safe, steam packet service across to Britain from Kingstown harbour.

I have been to London – I accompanied my master to England sometimes when he went over to try cases in the courts there and to dine with his fellows in the King's Inns – and so I can say that in my opinion Dublin need not have stood to the back even when compared against the English capital, except in the matter of size. If anything Dublin was the better run of the two, besides which it had many fine eating houses and theatres and suchlike, which my master frequented, though I must declare that when he was away from home and his dear, indisposed spouse, Ellen, he never behaved at all in any dishonourable way.

In the particular year I speak of we had been very busy with several serious capital cases, and Mr O'Donovan had been successful in every one of them. It was all down to his manner in the court, his ability to destroy a witness before the jury as well as his ability to see through to the true crux of any matter at once. He was a fine looking man, for he was descended from an ancient line of the Gaelic nobility, and his face had a distinct air of openness about it. He could turn flinty hard in a split second, though, and his fine blue eyes would fairly blaze and glare at an adversary who had irked him.

He had always a wonderful versatility as a speaker. In the courts of law, he was occasionally very jocular with the jury, dragging them into his view of the case, by jest, subtle argument, strong declamation and an irresistibly natural manner. They often as not became his allies against all else in the room. Later at political meetings, where he spoke to the masses, he could, alternately, bring them to smile or cause them to become enraged as he jested or moved their feelings on the subject of some great wrong; and when investigating a matter outside the courts of law he had the ability to put people at their ease and so draw information from them while they did not even realise that they were rendering any service at all. I have often witnessed this.

I was at my usual position one morning, quill and stiff pallet in hand, by the third pillar in the vestibule of the Four Courts, while Mr O'Donovan was inside arguing against a charge of malicious wounding brought against a man from Drumcondra, a disreputable area of north Dublin, when I was approached by a stiff-looking man in a most ornate form of military uniform. He said not a word to me but merely handed me a sealed letter addressed to Mr Ambrose O'Donovan and to be seen by his eyes only.

Immediately the man left, of course, I opened the missive, as my employer, I knew, would wish me to do, and I read it through. I realised that it was most important and I spent an impatient hour or so waiting for a recess in his case. When he emerged from the arena, flushed but certain of an acquittal, I pressed the note into his hand and said that he must read it immediately. He fell to the perusal of the epistle. I still have that letter in my possession even after all the intervening years and I reproduce it here:

> *My Dear Mr O'Donovan,*
>
> *Please excuse the brevity and informality of this note but I must see you on a most urgent matter. I hope that you will oblige me by coming to my private chambers at ten o'clock tomorrow morning for a very important meeting. If you cannot attend at that time then please send your man to me with details of when you will be available. I sincerely trust that you can assist me and I thank you in advance for your patience and gentility in this matter. Please tell absolutely no one else of my request as this whole matter must remain entre-nous.*
>
> *I am, sir, your obedient servant,*
>
> *James Griffin*

Let me explain that James Griffin was also known as Lord Harland and was Lord Chancellor of Ireland at the time as well. His powers were enormous and he was not a man to be ignored. Mr O'Donovan didn't, I believe, care a fig who he was but was more intrigued by the last warning than anything else, for it bespoke a mystery, which was always so attractive to him. He had a case, a minor matter of breaking-and-entering without bodily harm, set for the next day and he handed it off to a young barrister of his acquaintance to plead it for him.

That night saw a frenzy of activity in our lodging house as the landlady prepared Mr O'Donovan's clothes for the next day. She didn't know why, of course, but he instructed her that he wanted to be absolutely pristine in his appearance in the morning. His best suit of clothes and waistcoat were brushed, sponged and pressed with flat irons, he put out new white silk stockings with his black britches and his shoes were polished and buffed to a mirror finish. He was ever a man of refined but simple taste, especially in his clothing, for he wore mainly black or dark green with a boiled snowy white shirt and a plain neckerchief; I've often thought he would have made a good puritan if he hadn't been thoroughly tainted by the false dogmata of Rome. He set off to the offices of the Lord Chancellor in a rented carriage that morning while I went off for the Four Courts to attend to his business. I wasn't at his meeting with Jimmy Griffin, that little Welsh scoundrel, but it is safe to tell you now that even though he was technically sworn to secrecy he told me every detail of it that night over a late supper of cold pheasant and woodcock. He forgave himself his fracture of discretion, on the conceit that I was his 'right hand' and so should be an 'ex-corporeal' party to the whole thing. It was the purest sophistry to be sure.

He had been met at the Chancellor's offices in the Castle by an equerry who whisked him up through a private entranceway to the great man's inner offices. The Chancellor had greeted him warmly and when they were truly alone he told him directly that he needed his services, not just for his own good but for the good of justice and the whole population of the island. Mr O'Donovan later said that he told the man bluntly that he could promise nothing, as he owed nothing to a state that did not represent him because of his religion. The Chancellor had countered that the current laws were indeed ridiculous, but that this was a matter to do with the common people not of the state and that he should wait and hear what was asked of him before turning him down.

The Chancellor then reacquainted him with the details of one of the most gruesome occurrences in the recent history of Ireland, the awful burning of the Sheas. It had taken place on the night of the twentieth of November in the year 1821 in a farming area to the north of Clonmel in County Tipperary, at the very base of the mountain of Slievenamaun. The house of one Patrick Shea had been burned to the ground, its thatched roof and its wooden parts consumed by fire, the stout oak door burnt down to its iron hinges. The walls had given way and stood gaping in rents through which, the next morning, the people who approached the still smoking site could see the awful scene within the one large room of the dwelling.

The bodies of nineteen human beings of both sexes lay together in a mass by the door. The door itself must have been closed tight when the fire broke out and the inmates had precipitated themselves against it *en masse* in an attempt to flee through the only point of egress and in all likelihood mutually counteracted their efforts to burst into the open, life-saving air. They lay piled on each other, stacked like logs of driftwood, the topmost burnt beyond recognition, right to the bone, and the undermost suffocated but not so much burnt as melted. One of the spectators was horrified to report that the rendered fat from the corpses ran from the heap in a black flood across the slope of the flagstone floor. But terrible as this sight must have been, there was another horror even more appalling in that hell-hole. A young victim, one Catherine Mullally, a servant girl of the Sheas' who normally resided in the house, had been married some time before and was advanced a considerable time in pregnancy. Her unfortunate child had been delivered of her in the midst of the conflagration, brought on by her great fear no doubt. She and her child made the number lost up to twenty-one. They were found, not with the rest of the dead, but in a corner of the room. A tub of water lay on the floor beside the woman's body and she had evidently placed the new infant in the water in a futile attempt to keep it from being killed. She had succeeded in preserving only its torso and limbs, for its head had been held out of the water by her and had been burned away. She was found with the skeleton of the arm that supported the baby hanging over the tub. The constabulary was there by then, sent from Fethard, a village to the north, and they attempted to find out what it was that had occurred.

It might be supposed that this spectacle would cause a feeling of great dismay among those who saw it, but they were affected by a variety of sentiments and they had long ago learned caution and silence in the face of the authorities – which, incidentally, I have always found to be deeply characteristic of the Irish peasantry when faced with the law and its power. And so they deemed it wisest not to comment on the Sheas or on the manner of their demise. Tipperary had a fearsome repute in those dark days for being a place with a very fractious population and it was the venue of many spectacular and huge faction fights and innumerable murders of individuals, landlords and their agents.

The deaths of the Sheas caused a sensation in Dublin at the time – we had even heard of it in Clare – and a massive public investigation was launched. The crime was thought to be a Rockite act of revenge over the dispossession of some land, but no one wished to believe that so many innocent people had been killed over a few paltry acres of poor soil; and so, gradually, with the silence of the people, a surmise was conveniently adopted by the authorities that the fire was purely a dreadful accident. Griffin, however, was convinced that the investigation had failed to achieve any effect simply because no one would come forward with information despite a large reward posted by the government. It was a thousand pounds as I remember, a veritable king's ransom.

The Chancellor had reminded Mr O'Donovan of this much about the case and then he had shown him a letter recently received under cover of a letter from the Papist priest in Fethard. The attached missive was anonymous and my master had it on him when he returned from the Chancellery and I reproduce it here in all its misspelled glory:

> *Yous are not the smart men yous thinks yer eir. The shays wus burnt over a yeer ago an stil noboby is hung for lightin the fire what kilt thim all. If yous was smart yous would do somethin, it is a disgrace afore our true God Almighty that the murderars is stil alive. May God above have mercy on yer soles if ye do nottin about it.*
>
> *A frend of the people.*

The Chancellor had received it from the priest, who asked in his own letter that something be done, for the whole country knew that there was more to it than an accident and they held the Crown's forces in contempt over their powerlessness. He wanted someone brought to justice, but as I say a reward and a full investigation by the men from the Castle had produced absolutely nothing. Griffin, the sly little beggar, asked Mr O'Donovan to undertake the matter as my employer had come to the man's notice by his having been very successful in several other criminal investigations, even though in most instances he was never mentioned in the official police reports of the matters. Little Jemmy knew the worth of a man, though, even without laying his little eyes on him in person. There was also the fact that all the previous investigators had been policemen and Protestants, marked out plainly in what they were about and could not ever hope to establish any sort of rapport or trust with the populace. In fact the very presence of these men engendered an even greater silence. Mr O'Donovan, on the other hand, was both respected and a Catholic, and could move among the people with less notice and they might open up to him more; they would never dream that he was a government agent. Mr O'Donovan said that his first impulse had been to turn down the Chancellor's request, but the old man had seen his reluctance and had forestalled his refusal. He was a canny wee man.

Griffin said that he was not asking Mr O'Donovan to play the spy on his people for the Castle – which meant Dublin Castle, the home of England's spies and the symbol of English authority in Ireland – but to gather evidence in a crime which had killed twenty-one of those people in a most savage and senseless manner, worse than even Oliver Cromwell had done. That did not have the total effect on my master that he expected and so he continued. He said that it was only a matter of time before men like Mr O'Donovan and Mr O'Connell had achieved full emancipation for the Catholics of Ireland and then they would no doubt come to run the country. How would they ever expect the Irish to be taken seriously as a race if they allowed such calumnies to go unpunished, he asked.

Mr O'Donovan had finally agreed to go to Tipperary for a week and to see what he could learn, but he said he would do the work *gratis* and he further declared that if the whole thing appeared to have been a political act, no matter how misguided, he would pass on no information to the Crown. That was agreed to by the Welshman, and now I sat with my employer making plans to take a sightseeing tour around the natural beauties of Slievenamaun.

I worried, as did Mr O'Donovan, that so much time had elapsed since the deaths that it would be difficult to unravel any crime connected with it as the trail would have grown very cold by now. Mr O'Donovan replied to my concern by saying that, certainly, our only hope of success lay in getting information and testimony from those who had some definite knowledge of the crime, for there would not be an abundance of other evidence available to us. He knew that the populace would be reticent about talking to any new investigators and therefore the secrecy of our true mission was to be our only real weapon.

We journeyed to Tipperary across the country by way of a good rented gig and a sound horse. We did not hurry but stayed at an inn halfway to our destination on the first night. The Chancellor had given Mr O'Donovan a letter of introduction to the priest who had received and forwarded the ill-written note complaining about the crime, and also another letter of introduction to the commander of the local constabulary in Fethard, ordering the man to give us every assistance possible under threat of being cashiered. I should say here that I had almost baulked at making the trip myself. My master had advised me that he would travel about Tipperary under his own name but that I would have to travel as his manservant, one Seamus O'Toole, a Mass-going member of the church of Rome, for I would attract too much unwelcome attention as a Presbyterian law clerk in the village of Fethard, where he planned to make his initial headquarters. Also, he said that my assumed identity might be of some use to us in that I could so mingle better with the people.

After many blandishments he convinced me to accompany him, for in all honesty I truly did not wish to be left behind, as I might miss something. The next day saw us packed and installed in the well-sprung shiny new trap, to be driven by myself, as got up as a peasant in frieze clothing and rough boots as I could stand to be. We drove slowly but steadily and arrived about the foot of Slievenamaun by the afternoon of the second day. The rising mountain was an imposing sight in the clear spring air, well grassed and green about its lower parts and purple-heathered above that, ending in a whitened, rocky crown. Not a steep and sheer mountain, but more tapering than anything else. The local idolaters believed it to be the closest part of Ireland to heaven and that all the souls of the local dead left for their final journey from it, as from one of the Bianconi stations. We could see white-walled cottages up on the side of the mount at what seemed to me impossibly steep heights and above those, even without a spyglass, we could make out the small white dots that were grazing, hardy, mountainy sheep. The landscape brought to my mind the yarn of the careless mountainy farmer who fell out of his hayfield and broke his arm. The road was not overly populated by dwellings or inns and we drove on to Fethard in search of our lodging. We found a small hotel there which was well enough appointed, as it had been long in the service of catering to travelling representatives, cattle-buyers, horse-traders, tithe-proctors and the like. It was clean enough and the bill of fare was honest if plain. My employer took a small suite of rooms for himself and I looked forward to a few days of reasonable comfort myself. My ideas soon took a knock, however, as I was handed over to the landlord's wife and shown where I was to spend my sleeping time, on a shakedown in the loft over the long horse stable. I must say that I have never been partial to the smell of horses and after that trip I found them to be even more nauseating and gaseous creatures than ever before.

I was, however, allowed to dine with my master. He ordered his evening meal in his room and I was summoned, supposedly to serve him at table but in reality we ate a hearty meal together, though I tend to pick at my food more than anything else.

He had noised it about that he was on his way home to Kilrush, but that he had no pressing business there and so had decided to explore the countryside about as a sightseer of sorts. Our landlord seemed to accept him at his word and later spent some considerable time speaking with him and relating the history of the area and telling of the various points of interest to be seen. He was apparently well used to tourists by then, for the French and Germans had been coming to the area for some years to take the air, *en route* to the rugged coasts of the West. The roads were excellent for light travel and Mr Bianconi and his coach services had opened up the hinterlands to visitors in the island as never before.

Mr O'Donovan listened politely and attentively to our new host, although he was a bore – he could have put a wooden eye to sleep – and his sense of history was very erroneous and much distorted by the peasant's mind of which he was in possession. My master asked many questions about the countryside and the happenings in it but was most careful to avoid asking anything about the burning of the Sheas, and the landlord himself said nothing of it, in spite of its being, without a doubt, a most significant event in the recent history of the locality.

My employer asked the man for directions to the priest's house, which was, as it turned out, at a significant distance from the local Mass-house. We had passed that edifice on our way into the town and a most unprepossessing pile it was. It was a squat, almost windowless block with no spire and no cross about it at all. It was thatched in its roof and the thatch looked to be threatening to fall in at one end. This might have seemed strange to a visitor, for nearly everyone in the local population was a devout Papist and the area was quite wealthy compared to the more western counties, for it was favoured with much better farm land and weather. One would have expected an edifice as good at least as the fine stone, slate-roofed and spired Church of Ireland building in the middle of the town, with its attendant large parsonage and outbuildings. The answer to the conundrum was a simple one at the time we speak of. The Protestant church had been built and maintained and its priests paid through a tithe levied on all the people, the few Anglicans and Presbyterians and the teeming millions of Catholics as well. Also, under the last vestiges of the Penal Laws, the Catholics were not supposed to have a Mass-house at all, even such a one as the shed on the outskirts of Fethard. Their public worship was now tolerated, to be sure, but no Catholic community would dare to erect a spire with a cross on it beside a Mass-house for that would be seen by the established church as very provocative indeed.

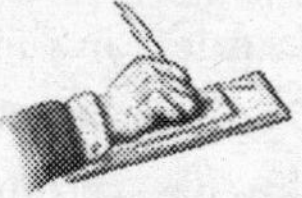

Mr O'Donovan told the landlord that the local priest, Fr Foyle, was a distant cousin of his dear mother's and that he would have to visit the man or his mother would never forgive him for the omission and we got directions to his house. We found the man, black skirts hiked up in his broad leather belt and shod in a pair of most disreputable yellow-topped boots, digging the soil in a part of his garden for a late spring planting of seeds. He was a man in his forties with carrot-red hair, cropped short to reveal a pair of ears protruding like those of a buck goat. His beefy red agricultural face was scraped clean of all hair and his big top front teeth, well browned, pushed slightly through his lips.

The man seemed delighted to be called away from his task, for the soil he dug looked heavy, muddy and anything but friable. I would have drained it properly first if I was depending on it for any decent crop of vegetables at all. We hailed him and he came to us through the gate in the stone wall that surrounded his plot, and when he heard from my master who we actually were and what was our mission, he brightened further and grasped my master's hand in his mud-splattered fist, which was as large and raw as a Limerick ham.

'I'm most pleased to make your acquaintance, Mr O'Donovan,' he said with obvious sincerity. 'I was hoping that Dublin would get up off their dainty arses and do something about the poor Sheas.'

It was apparent that he didn't really know my master from Adam, but then he was not so famous in those days and his more public glory was all in front of him.

He ushered us both into the kitchen at the back of his manse, though 'cottage' would be a more apt description of it, and sat us on two straw-seated chairs, my master in the one with arms to it and myself off in the corner one with no back to it at all that was little better than a high stool. He accepted me as the servant-man of course and then ignored me, but I was able to hear all that passed between them and my memory was faultless in those days.

'Well, Fr Foyle,' Mr O'Donovan began, 'your transmission of that anonymous letter to Dublin has certainly stirred things up again regarding the Sheas. I have been given this introduction to you by none other than the Lord Chancellor himself, so you can see how high it reaches. You may keep it if you want to. I am here to try and unravel what occurred on the night in question and as I have nothing else to guide me then I must start with you, our only source.'

'Of course, I will help you all I can, sir,' said the priest. 'This was a terrible thing and must not be allowed to go unpunished, but, other than the letter which I forwarded on, I know nothing – there is nothing more I can tell you. I found the thing on my seat in the confession box one morning. I have no idea who put it there.'

'Forgive me for saying it, Father, but I believe that you do know more,' Mr O'Donovan said, and it rang out as a blatant challenge and made me sit up and take notice in my corner.

'What! Are you accusing me of lying to you, man?' the clergyman exclaimed angrily.

'Not at all, not in the least, I assure you, Father, but you must know something more than the authorities in Dublin and the police about here do, for until your letter they had come to put the thing down as a mishap, all for their own purposes, don't you know, to save face, and you clearly stated that it was a crime just now. Contrary to the official line, so in your mind at least you must know more.'

'But I tell you that I don't know anything. I can tell you nothing.'

'Perhaps, but from the manner of your last two statements I think that you may know things … but that you cannot tell me or any other man, by your priestly vows. You say that you can tell me nothing. The secret of the confessional. I would hazard a guess that someone involved in the atrocity or deeply troubled in conscience has confessed to you and you cannot say anything about it.'

'I don't like to speak of matters of the confessional ... even in abstract terms, Mr O'Donovan, I can tell you nothing of what transpires in the box.'

'But, Father, I don't intend to ask you to reveal any such secrets or the name of a murderer who has come to you to be shriven, but there is one question that I can ask you and that I believe you can answer without in the least sinning yourself.'

'I fear that will be impossible. The vow is, as you may know, specific,' the priest replied uncertainly.

My employer looked down at his hands. 'No, you can answer this question, Father. Has someone come to you and stated that their conscience is plaguing them with the knowledge that a great crime has been committed and they have done nothing about it?'

I was watching carefully from the side as I had been instructed and the priest did not change his expression.

'Or more to the point –' my employer went on, 'someone who knew what was going to happen on that dreadful night and yet did nothing to prevent it.'

Mr O'Donovan was still looking away as he spoke, and the priest sat up, involuntarily, a shocked look on his face, as if someone had just looked into his mind. My master looked around in time to catch it as well.

'I see that I have struck a chord with you, Father,' he observed. 'Now I don't need any other response from you. I'm sure that you will never tell me the name of that person just as I am sure that in your capacity as confessor you have done everything you can to make that person come forward, though obviously to no avail, so far.'

The priest seemed very relieved that the interrogation was so mild and at an end, that my employer thought he had done all he could, and that he would not be required to break any of his idolatrous and ludicrous vows – the very idea of one man forgiving the sins of another.

'We'll bid you a very good day for now, Father. We may call upon you again, though,' Mr O'Donovan said, adding to me, 'Come along now, Shamey, give yourself a shake, man, no spilling your soup in the corner.'

As instructed I had been watching every twitch and expression on that priest's big face as he was questioned. In the cart my master was quick to ask me what I thought of that session.

'Well, Mr O'Donovan,' I began, 'I think that you have hit the spike on the head, cleanly. The man hasn't heard from the murderer or murderers, I think, but from someone who knows of the crime, in fact, as you said just now, from someone who knew that the crime was going to take place and yet stood by and let it happen.'

'You're right, my friend, that's exactly what I believe. Do you know, there's hope for you yet, Noble. That big priest would, likely as not, strangle any murderer who came to him for shriving without turning himself in to the temporal authorities. It must be someone more innocent in the matter, and think what a burden that person must be carrying in their heart of hearts. They can't be knowing a peaceful moment in their days and nights, for I know that I wouldn't if I was in the same situation.'

I agreed with him over my shoulder. 'And so, logically, if we can but identify that mysterious person, then we have the thing mostly solved,' I opined.

'Perhaps, but I fear it will not be as simple as that, Noble. If the priest cannot get someone well known to him and who is under his sway and no doubt respects him and the cloth, to come forward, then we will have no more profit than he has had. We might just frighten that person into fleeing the land altogether.'

He was silent then and so I took a chance and spoke up: 'In any event, how can we identify the person? We know practically no one in the area and if we ask too many questions then the locals will take a dim view of it all.'

'Correct, Noble, but let us not get too far ahead of ourselves, for we have some other avenues to explore. I want to meet the sergeant of the local constabulary. He may have some information for us – some suspicion but no real proof – but I dare not go directly to his barracks in Fethard, for news of that would flow about the countryside like free whiskey. I will pen a note to the man and I will rely on you to deliver it for me, without being seen.'

I looked over my shoulder again, expressing some doubt with my expression.

'No, I know that you can do it. I will ask the man to meet us out in the country somewhere and to bring what documents and evidence he has about the case. And by the way, I now fully believe that Fr Foyle himself penned that mal-written note to draw official attention to the crime once again and so make an attempt to salve his own conscience in the matter without breaking his vows. His secret penitent had nothing to do with it. It was almost too ill-spelled not to have been done by an educated man in imitation of a near illiterate, don't you think? And surely you noticed that the part about 'God Almighty' was properly capitalised and not misspelled at all, where much simpler words were mangled. The good father couldn't bring himself to do that when it came to the divinity, I suppose. But his note did serve a good purpose, for it enabled us to find him, and every investigation needs a starting point. He will be of further use to us, I have no doubt of that at all.'

'Why did he not just forward the note to Dublin without a covering letter from himself?' I asked, looking for a hole in his reasoning. 'He could have remained anonymous and so avoided the attentions of such as ourselves.'

'Well, Noble, there is possibly more than one reason for his stepping out into the light. Firstly his covering letter showed the Dublin authorities that he knew of the note and so they could not very well just file it away as an inconvenience or simply lose it in their bureaucratic maze. It would be easier for them to ignore it, after all, if the writer was in no position to complain of it later. In my experience, civil servants never seek extra toil or responsibility, as long as there is a handy carpet edge to lift and to hide their sweepings under. Secondly his position in the community, even as a priest of Rome, would lend weight to the thing: he could always tattle on Dublin to his bishop if they ignored him. But thirdly – and this is as likely as the rest, though it might have been a motive hardly even admitted by the man to himself – I think that he actually wanted whoever investigated the matter to approach him, even though, when put to it, he could not bring himself to break his priestly vows. He is a man in great turmoil, as any good shepherd would be with a known malignancy in his flock. You can see that in him, and I hope that we can put his mind at rest before we finish.'

When we returned to the hotel in Fethard, my employer wrote out a short note to a Sergeant Grimes, who, he had been told by Griffin, led the small detachment of police in the townland. He enclosed his letter of introduction from the Lord Chancellor with it and I was dispatched to deliver it without being seen. That was a far taller order than my master would admit to but I think that he knew the difficulties involved nevertheless. The village of Fethard was a market centre and even though it was not a market day there were still plenty about going to one of its two shops or eleven grog-houses. The proportion of taverns to population in Irish towns is a continuing source of puzzlement to me, though I did once hear a landlord say, 'Sure all any one pub needs is six good drinkers,' which is an example of the senseless intemperance among the native Irish.

At any rate, the squat barracks of the constabulary was right in the middle of the place, in the centre of the west side of the square, and was surrounded by loungers who, while seeming inattentive, no doubt missed not a single minute thing that happened in the place. I walked past it several times, ignoring the odd pair of constables that entered and left it. I knew that there were seven police in the detachment including the sergeant, but I didn't know the look of him at all. I daren't approach any of the other constables as to my mission, for I was admonished to show the letter to none but this Grimes man. My master said that no other could be trusted, for some of the constabulary had been, no doubt, recruited from the local peasantry or knew the locals well, or drank among them, and their loyalties as well as their ability to keep a secret might be suspect. We could not afford for anyone to know the real purpose for our sojourn in the area for then all mouths would be shut tight to us and we might find ourselves in corporal danger to boot. The burners of a new-born and his mammy would not baulk at the killing of a couple of strangers.

I did not see anyone come out of the barracks with a sergeant's stripes on his arms and so I determined that the man was either away from the town or was still in the building. I wracked my imagination to divine a method of gaining an anonymous entry, but could come up with nothing, and so I decided to try something drastic. I went to a shebeen at the edge of town and there for the first time in my life, and the last, I purchased a black bottle of liquor. It was only an expenditure of a few coppers, for the stuff was of the sort made in the mountains nearby under the most insalubrious of conditions and when I uncorked it to spill its contents into the mud and cow dung of an alley it smelled very vile indeed, as if something had crawled into that flask and died and rotted in it. I put some of the vile stuff in the cup of my hand and rubbed it about my mouth and onto the collar of my disreputable frieze coat. I waited a while and after I had been away from the square for half an hour or more I staggered back to it, playing the part of a very drunk man. I was no doubt effective at it, for if one lives out one's daily existence in the setting of an Irish market town then one will see countless examples of the shambling, reeling, falling, drunken scut. I worked my way unsteadily to near the front of the barracks before making a show of draining an already empty bottle and throwing it with a crash against the low wall in front of the barracks door. I then pulled up my coat sleeves in a most pugnacious fashion, reeled about and started shouting, 'God save Ireland! Away with the Sassenach! Death to the English!' and the like.

I would have sung a rebel tune too, if I had known one, and if I had not been tone-deaf all my life. I could tell that the loungers were delighted for this unexpected diversion and some of them gathered very near me, murmuring, 'Good man yerself!', 'Stout fellow!' and the like.

Within a few moments of the start of my show, two constables came out, took one look at me and rushed forward to seize hold of me. I struggled with the two brawny men and was warned that I would get a good box or two in the ear if I didn't settle down. I replied by collapsing in their arms, as if I had passed out and so offered no resistance as I was carried into the station house, one of my long white legs sticking out of my pantaloons and pointing towards the sky.

I was hurled into a cell at the back of the largest room. It was a cage more than a cell and I had a good view of all in the room through the slits of my supposedly unconscious eyes. There was little of furniture in the room but a few benches around the white-limed walls and a dark wood desk near to the cage where I lay. There was a stand of arms near it and on the wall behind a board containing many keys on rings. The room was very clean, floor scrubbed to its deal finish and the walls white-limed and with a tidy and ordered appearance overall. I marvelled at how the authorities could be so much above the population that they ruled in matters of neatness and hygiene and so below them in humanity, for their penchant for orderliness does not by any means excuse the fact that they have ever been brutal oppressors. Perhaps a penchant for extreme order should be viewed with suspicion in a race.

I determined that the sole desk in the place must be for the use of the sergeant and I was disappointed to see that he was not seated there at that very moment, and it was three long hours or more before a man with a neater, more carefully cut uniform bearing a sergeant's stripes arrived back from some destination or other, took off his forage cap, hung it on a brass hook behind him and sat at his desk.

There were other police in and out for a while before Sergeant Grimes spoke and confirmed his Englishness: 'Take yourself off for your potatoes and buttermilk, Donnelly, and see you come back in good time and in good order, for if I smell any drink on you I'll have you flogged,' he said in a cold, authoritarian voice, without even looking up at the other man who was sitting on a bench by the door.

'Yes, Sergeant,' the man said and raised himself up, saluted and made to leave.

I lay there on the floor of my cell and watched the sergeant for a good while before making a sound, and then I said 'phist' to gain his attention. He ignored that low sound from me, and I did it again, only far louder this time. He looked over in my direction and I could see the total disdain for me plain on his face.

'Beggin' yer honner's pardon, sur, but I need a word wit' ye,' I said in my best approximation of a peasant accent.

It must have sounded correct to his English ear for he rose and came over to my cage, but not too close, as if he was convinced, no doubt, that I had to have an extremely bad smell about me and attendant vermin in my clothing.

'What the devil do you mean by addressing me, you dirty, drunken, bastard,' were the first charming words which he spoke to me, angry words to be sure but spoken in his oddly cold, clipped tones.

'Nothin' yer honner, sur, but I hiv a litter here fer ye dat you must look at,' I said, keeping in my part, and reaching the folded paper to him through the bars.

He took the letter from me with his fingertips and brought it to read it under the good light from the window. When he had finished with my master's note and had examined closely the Lord Chancellor's orders, he rose and came over to me again in my suite.

'Are you this O'Donovan fellow, or what?' he asked.

I told him that I wasn't, reverting to my normal speech and do you know he showed no surprise at all at that sudden change. I told him that I was Mr O'Donovan's clerk and that I had only feigned drunkenness so as to see him privately. He hesitated, looking at me, then nodded as if that made perfect sense to him, and went to get the key to release me. Much as I did not want to, I advised him that I should remain in the cell for a while longer before being released, so as to make the watchers outside and the other constables think that I had been kept until I was sobered up, just like any other drunken scallywag. He nodded again and said for me to tell my master that he would meet him at the place specified in his letter the next morning at ten o'clock. Then he returned to his seat and ignored me completely.

That night, on being released, I returned to the hotel to find my employer dining in the public rooms, and I was mortified that the tales of my drunkenness, my rebel bravado and subsequent incarceration had reached those quarters and had been bandied about all evening. There was a loud, mocking cheer as I entered, beaten felt hat in hand, feigning the face of a man in the tortures of a poteen hangover, and everyone thought it great sport that I had been urged to truly rebellious utterances by drink. Mr O'Donovan for his part castigated me for my conduct and told everyone how hard it had become to get good help and that this was only the latest in a lengthy list of drunken escapades that could be laid right at my feet, and me with a loving wife and sixteen young children at home, and me the right-hand man of the parish priest in Kilrush, in charge of the collections at all the Masses, grave-digging and all the rest.

I suffered this comedy in bitter silence and I even had to feign interest in the supposed cure, a large glass of whiskey, pushed in front of me by our solicitous landlord: 'A wee hair of the dog, Shamey – on the house, like.' Mr O'Donovan pretended to take the man to task for encouraging my great weakness of character, my chronic intemperance.

Afterwards I was sent to the back to the scullery for my own meagre supper, but I was able to visit my master in the privacy of his rooms afterwards and I told him what I had done and I think that he was honestly appreciative of all my efforts and the personal shame that went with them. He avowed that there was not a man in Ireland who would have had the style or wit to do better and I found that, in spite of my nature, I was inordinately pleased at that and I forgave him all the wicked jibes he had passed my way in the public dining room.

The next morning we were away after an early breakfast of good ham and eggs for my employer and stirabout and more raillery for me – it came from every quarter in the kitchen where I supped my gruel and I could see how readily a man could acquire a false reputation for himself, a bad one at any rate.

Sergeant Grimes was already there at the crossroads. Having already met the man, I introduced Grimes to my master and he looked at me as if I truly was a verminous peasant and not a respected law clerk; but, fair man that he was, he gave Mr O'Donovan not much more respect than he accorded me, for Sergeant Edmund Grimes had either been born with or had in life developed a total lack of regard for anyone at all.

'You are to investigate the burning of the Sheas, Mr O'Donovan – good luck to you with that. My predecessor, Captain Briggs, was in command here then and he was able to get nowhere with these bloody people at all. I have his papers here, and I have read them more than once, for this is a boring station. I believe it to have been murder all right, for the fire started on the roof, far from the only chimney, although it *could* have been set off by a wind-blown spark from their damnable turf fire, I suppose. But even if it was a murder, unless someone comes forward with useful information, then I am positive that we will never lay a single charge in the matter.'

'That is certain, Sergeant, and that is why no one must know the true reason for my presence hereabouts as we tour around the mountainside. Not even your most trusted man.'

'Frankly, O'Donovan, I wouldn't trust the smallest of them as far as I could throw him,' Grimes replied, with no hint of irony in his voice.

'Quite,' my master said, seeming not to notice that Grimes had so soon dropped the title of 'Mr' when addressing him. 'If I am to have any hope of getting to the bottom of these grisly murders then I will need your co-operation, and also to have sight of any papers that your predecessor, this Captain Briggs, left for you. I shall also need your men, I hope, to make some arrests at the end of it all, but in the meantime, perhaps you will tell me if you have formed any theories of your own as to the motive behind the crime or of the identity of possible suspects.'

'Motives? Not really. The most usual motive among these people for any killing is revenge, for any slight, real or imagined, or to get back at someone for cheating them or taking over a stony patch of leasehold from them or bettering them in a horse trade or some such trivial thing. But those killings are always, in my experience, individual slayings, one man murdered from ambush. This country is still alive with guns, you know! But even when killing a landlord who has greatly displeased them, the peasants are fairly careful. Last year, quite near here, a landlord was waylaid and slain in broad daylight, but the miscreants dragged him from his carriage to shoot him, and his wife who rode with him was left unharmed, in her body at least. The usual thing is a beating or the lighting of a hayshed or a bloody wounding, but never a mass murder. It is unheard of even for these wretched people. I mean, Shea did have some success as a small farmer and had increased his leaseholds, at the expense of others no doubt, but I cannot believe that such would ever create the atmosphere where something as drastic as this could happen. If someone had a grudge against Shea senior, he would have waited to ambush him with a blunderbuss or would have taken the head off him with a bill-hook some dark night.'

'I agree that it is a strange case, Sergeant. I have never known a death toll to a single clan like it – outside of the army's reprisals for the '98 rebellion, that is. First, before all else, I should like to see the scene of the crime. Would you oblige us by going there in our company, Sergeant? There will be few about to see us, I hope, and I will need your direction to get there. Perhaps I can peruse these papers as we go.'

Grimes agreed with only a nod and climbed in beside my master. I tied his horse to the back of the gig and we set off.

'There's damn little to be seen in the Sheas' hovel now. It's been open to the elements for over a year, for briars and weeds to choke the place and you know how it can rain here for weeks on bloody end. Still, if you must see it for yourself, then you must,' Grimes said with an increasing bad nature.

Mr O'Donovan, already deeply engrossed in the papers on the case, in that deep study normal to him, did not even reply to this, and Grimes began the journey staring off to the road on his side with no real expression on his face, only occasionally barking directions at my back. We travelled by several byroads, twists and turns until we reached the rough track that led up to the cottage of death.

It was a long, low building, abandoned forever now, for who would live on that site even in a new-built mansion? It was a rough one-roomed cabin but was actually long enough for two or more rooms. How these people are content to live in great numbers in such conditions is hard for a stranger to credit. But in fairness I must say that it is not entirely their fault that they live in such dire homes, nor are they content to have to do so. You see they are all tenants only and if they do improve their houses or outhouses – at their own expense – then the landlord's agent will simply raise their rent at the time of renewal, based on a higher property value. If they cannot pay the new rent they are evicted and the improvements made by them accrue to the landowner. A new system of tenancy would change things greatly for the better, for conditions could not be worse. I still have great hope for the future of land reform in this sad little island.

We dismounted in the yard of the Shea farmstead and Mr O'Donovan inspected the outside of the place, looking up to where the vanished roof should have been and then peering through fire-made splits in the stone walls. He went through the doorless portal – the hinges from the burnt door had long been pilfered – and stepped into the room beyond and its tangle of badly burnt roofing timbers. He stepped about carefully and it took him some time to complete his inspection of the place. I walked about the outside of the building and I could see at once that the few windows of the place were pitifully small and would hardly have permitted the Sheas' house cat to have escaped the inferno of that night. He returned to near the door and asked Grimes and myself to enter. When we did, he showed us some marks on a flagstone embedded in the floor, just by the entrance. He bent down and indicated that we should also take a closer look. The fragment of flat stone was blackened about the edges, but its grey granite was vaguely showing at its centre, where the elements had patiently scoured it over the many months since the fire.

'What is this, do you think?' he asked Grimes, scraping some more of the black from the stone with a small knife as he spoke.

'That, according to Captain Briggs, is cooked and rendered human fat. It is as black as night and apparently it covered this floor to a fair depth after the conflagration. It smelled dreadful hereabouts by all accounts. My men were detailed to clear out all the reeking corpses and not a one of them is over it yet. I hear them speak among themselves of recurring nightmares. There was little else left to see in here and this stone would have been as black as the others were then.'

'But now it is well rain-scrubbed at the crown, is it not? You can plainly see that someone has scratched something into it with an iron nail or a knife tip. The stone is much fractured from the heat in its other parts, but we can still make out some of the letters on it. It seems to read '...ORM...'. Tell me, Sergeant, does that mean anything to you?'

'Is it the end or the middle or the start of the writing, O'Donovan?' Grimes asked. 'Offhand, I would say that it means little to me. ORM, ORM... Well there is a Lord Ormond hereabouts, a branch of the great family itself, but more only a twig if you take my meaning. He is still a big landlord around here, though, and a powerful man. He spends nearly all of his time in London – it ... er ... apparently holds many attractions for him and his ilk. His son – I've met him, Harold, he is called – supposedly looks after his business interests, but in reality they have a devil of an agent who takes care of everything on the estate. They even own this very land we are on and so they were the actual landlords of the Sheas.'

For the first time since I had first laid eyes on him, the sergeant seemed near to being excited. It was almost as if a very pleasant thought had occurred to him.

'I suppose he could have something to do with the business,' Grimes added thoughtfully.

I wondered at a member of the constabulary being so ready to suspect a member of the nobility, for the opposite was usually the case, in my own experience of the application of the law of the land to the lords of the land.

'Provided that the writing was actually done by someone during the fire in a desperate attempt to apportion blame to his murderer or murderers,' Mr O'Donovan remarked.

'My thoughts exactly,' said Grimes.

'Perhaps it is part of some other longer word, or perhaps it was scratched there well before the fire – the work of an idle child's hand, a lad left to his own devices one day, maybe.'

'I suppose,' said Grimes, but even given the man's innate flatness, I could detect no real enthusiasm for that last theory, and I supposed that he very much preferred his own first thought.

'Would someone in a conflagration have the presence of mind to scratch a name into the floor for someone to find?' I asked from behind them, thinking myself the voice of reason.

My employer spun around.

'Quite a good question, Noble, and perhaps they wouldn't have done it. But there have been many instances in the history of forensics where a dying victim has written out the killer's name in their very own blood. And we do not know how long an interval there was between the starting of the roof blaze and the last gasp of the last victim, do we? I mean it could have taken some considerable time.'

We spent an hour there before Mr O'Donovan was satisfied and suggested that we travel back to town, separately, and he also asked that he be allowed to keep the case papers with him until I could copy them out for him. It took me several hours to do that while my master was in the taproom playing the tourist and getting any information from the topers there that he could.

When he came up and before I left for my perch in the stable, we spoke for some time about the case and what we had learned so far. He always tries his ideas out on me in such times and I pride myself that he evidently values my opinion. He was quick, at any rate, to credit me with acuity when I spotted or thought of something that he had so far missed, although that was not a frequent occurrence. To my chagrin he would castigate me equally for anything that had escaped my own ken.

What we knew of the current case was very little, to be sure, but he was gratified that we had learned from the priest that someone was feeling guilt over the crime and that someone likely could, and most definitely should, have prevented it. He surmised that such a person would not be a close kin to the actual murderer or murderers, for familial ties would have swamped any deep guilt – I have seen it happen a hundred times – but yet he felt that person had been privy to the planning of the thing far enough in advance to have been able to do something about it if they so wished. Someone in a position of trust. If we could only determine the identity of that person, then we had a chance of bringing him or her forward as a witness. The …ORM… marked on the stone, he thought, would be of some future significance, but on its own it meant little and might well signify nothing at all.

We perused the papers I had copied, taking one set each so that we could compare ideas as we progressed. The scene of death was described in clinical but still unnerving detail on the first page and the untangling and removal of the bodies on the next. Then came a list of the dead which I will reproduce as follows:

Patrick Shea, aged fifty, tenant
Henrietta Shea, aged forty-seven, wife of Patrick Shea
John Shea, aged forty, brother of Patrick Shea
Harry Shea, aged thirty-seven, brother of Patrick Shea
Clementine Shea, aged twenty, brother of Patrick Shea
Ellen Shea, aged twenty, sister of Patrick Shea
Martha Doherty, aged twenty-seven, married sister of Patrick Shea
John Doherty, aged thirty-three, husband of Martha Doherty
Enda Doherty, aged nine, son of John Doherty
Paul Doherty, aged six, son of John Doherty
Sally Doherty, aged three, daughter of John Doherty
Tomas Shea, aged twenty-seven, son of Patrick Shea, tenant
Bridget Shea, aged twenty, wife of Tomas Shea
Andrew Shea, aged twenty-five, son of Patrick Shea, tenant

Peter Shea, aged fifteen, son of Patrick Shea, tenant
Oonah Mooney, aged twenty, widowed daughter of Patrick Shea, tenant
Olive Mooney, aged four, daughter of Oonah Mooney
John Mooney, aged two, son of Oonah Mooney
George Mullally, aged thirty-one, employee of Patrick Shea, tenant
Catherine Mullally, aged twenty-three, house servant and the wife of George Mullally
Unnamed infant of Catherine Mullally, born and died in the fire.

Truly it was a dreadful litany when read out in a whispered tone in that dim room.

Mr O'Donovan studied the list until he could have almost recited the names, ages and levels of consanguinity from memory. There was little else of note in the file, if one could even call it that, except several brief lists of those interviewed by Captain Briggs in the matter and there was no written record of what was said by those people, except an enigmatic line at the end which stated that no one admitted to seeing the start of the conflagration or to knowing any least thing about it.

'It is a fairly stark record, Noble, is it not?' my employer remarked sadly. 'What an epitaph for that little child, "Born and died in the fire." That alone would make me give up all that I possess to bring the culprits to justice. When I think of my own dear wife, my mother and sister and my two girls at home, it fills me with a great rage and great dread that so much could be lost, in an instant, to a blazing torch being thrown onto a thatched roof, not a shot fired or a knife unsheathed, but twenty-one beings dead, killed in the most horrible manner imaginable. I will admit that I would like to be in Kilrush with my own family at this very moment, Noble.'

I could make no such wish myself, as I have no family, outside of that of my master, but I thought of how pleasant it would be in his parlour and to be dandling his elder daughter on my knee at that very moment. I was deeply moved as well, but I do not take well to being moved; it causes me to tend to speak out of turn, inadvertently, at the most inopportune times.

'Yes, it's about time that these scurrilous landlords are made to put back doors in these hovels,' I said, 'for they are fire-traps one and all.'

My employer looked at me in surprise at my remarks, which I had meant sincerely, but which perhaps sounded pragmatic and callous to his ears, and in truth I was immediately ashamed that I had not spoken more warmly, from human feeling; it is a fault in me, I know.

'We must rest now, Noble, we'll start "sightseeing" again in the morning. I believe,' he said in dismissal of me, 'that we will start with the local Catholic burial grounds.'

The next day dawned fair again, if a little breezy. I recall that as I harnessed the horse I looked to the south of us and the sun was illuminating and causing the shadows of any small, wind-chased clouds in the sky to seem like furtive rodents as they scurried across the green and purple side of the big mountain.

We drove in the gig to the Catholic burial grounds which were located about two Irish miles out on the road to Slievenamaun. It was, even with the landlord's directions, a hard place to find. It had no wall around it but was instead enclosed by a high hawthorn hedge and its small gateway was not facing onto the main road at all but opened onto a muddy and grass-centred boreen. We got down from the gig and entered the field. There were two sturdy-looking gate pillars, but no gate hung between them. The place looked to have been in use a long time and appeared quite full to me. Every square inch was covered in headstones and markers, casting shadows on the graves of countless poor idolaters. The graves themselves were mostly grassed over and thick with thistles, except where families had marked off and bounded the measurements of a plot with stones and had covered the enclosed surface with small pebbles to keep the weeds and the voluntary grasses down. We spent a good quarter of an hour individually scouting about the dreary place before I found the final resting place of the Sheas. I called my employer over and he and I inspected the headstone at the centre of the long grave, the original outlines of which could still be seen under the new grass.

Mr O'Donovan took out his list of the dead and he seemed to check off each name with a pencil as he sounded off the engravings on the granite slab.

'Well, Noble, they are all accounted for in the line of the Sheas. All the brothers, sisters, sons and daughters and their children. Even the sons-in-law and sisters-in-law have been interred here. But there are two, three actually, missing from this plot. Let us look about here a little more and try to see if Catherine Mullally, her husband and their unfortunate child are buried in this place.

This time it was my employer who discovered what we were looking for. The grave was in a far corner, in the least-used part of the cemetery, and it was the grandest monument that I had seen in that place. It was a true headstone in almost the Protestant sense, replete with engraved fond wishes and surmounted by a finely worked finial. The only gesture to Papism was the angel carved in relief above the names. That stone was inscribed as follows:

In Loving Memory
of
Catherine Mullally,
Her Dear Husband George,
and their child, Shaun.
Died on November, 20th, 1821.
May they know Eternal Bliss
with our Saviour in His Heaven.
R.I.P.

Even I could tell that the thing was well wrought and the grave itself was neat, squared-off and nearly free of weeds.

'Someone with more means than most peasants has erected this stone and is carefully tending the grave, Noble. I wonder if we can find out who that person is. Someone thoughtful enough to give the dead child a name, though it was never near a formal baptismal font. I believe that it must be one of Catherine's relatives and not her husband's who has stumped up the coin for it all.'

I asked him why he thought that.

'If his family had erected it they would have put his name to the fore. It is the usual thing to put the husband's name first, is it not? The priest must be a humane man, Noble, for he has interred the unbaptised infant with its mother in consecrated ground, allowing himself to presume that the loving mother baptised the child in that bucket … as any good Catholic can, so making it a faultless angel.'

I sighed as I again contemplated the absurd man-made tenets of my master's faith.

Later that morning we found out who had paid for and planted the stone by the simple expediency of going back to town and asking the priest. This information was not covered by his vaunted secrecy of the confessional, but he still seemed quite reticent about giving it to us. Mr O'Donovan forced the issue by almost shaming the man into it and he finally told us that the cost of the funeral, the headstone and all the work on the grave was paid for in cash by someone named Mary Kelly of Slievenamaun. She was a relative of the dead woman.

We left the clergyman and went back to our hotel for luncheon. At least my master did so, and while he ate of fine boiled mutton I ate bread and hard cheese in the scullery while being teased by three or four slatternly maids who were in and out of the place.

Fortunately we went out on the road again directly after the meal for we had arranged to have a daily rendezvous with Sergeant Grimes at the same crossroads. He was already there and if he was impatient in waiting for us or indeed if he was under the sway of any emotion at all, we could not have told it from his face.

'Good morning, Sergeant Grimes,' my master called out to him as we drove up. Grimes did not answer in words but merely nodded his head to us, or should I say he nodded to Mr O'Donovan, for the man usually ignored my presence entirely.

Mr O'Donovan went right to business when Grimes joined him in the gig. 'I'm interested in a person named Mary Kelly, who lives hereabouts. I think she must be fairly affluent. Tell me, do you know of her, Sergeant?'

Grimes thought for a moment, and then said, 'Yes I do, I know of her, if it be the same woman, for there are many Kellys about and they seem to call half the women by the same Christian name – where are these people's imaginations? I often wonder. If it's the hussy that I'm thinking of, she is well known to the constabulary, for she runs a not entirely respectable establishment at the foot of Slievenamaun. Not too far distant from where we were recently, not a gunshot from the Sheas' cottage, in fact. Tell you what, I have inherited files on nearly all the locals of ill note from my predecessor, for like myself he trusted none of them, and I have added to many of them during my own tenure. If you return here this afternoon I will bring you what information I have on her. But in the meantime, O'Donovan, I believe that I have uncovered some much more important information regarding the deaths of those people. I have enquired through my men about the local Ormonds and I've come up with some telling things.'

Mr O'Donovan was immediately interested and he listened attentively, as Grimes said, 'I have come to believe firmly that one or both of the Ormonds, pater and son, were behind the murders, either done by their own hands or by others hired for the purpose.'

'What possible motivation could they have had for killing their own tenants?' my master asked.

'There are several possibilities. The most basic one is that the Ormond family is trying to clear large parts of their holdings of small farms, some of which are only three acres, and Patrick Shea had a long-term lease on his bit of land. With a clan the size of his, he would always be able to pay his rents somehow and so was near immune from eviction.'

'But I was given to understand that Patrick Shea was not long in possession of the lease. Why would the Ormond family have given it to him if they planned to turn that whole area into a sheep pasture or whatever?' my employer asked.

'True, he only had the part of his lease for a little while, but this idea of a clearance was only very recently sent from the old lord in London to his agent, Charles Flint, and to his son Harold. I understand that those men in London to whom the Ormonds are deeply in debt – they are mortgaged to the hilt – have threatened to call in their loans if this action is not taken to make the estate more profitable from the raising of wool, mutton and beef. The so-called lords are becoming desperate, and are in fear of losing the estate. Perhaps their agent, Flint, put a light to the Sheas' hovel to get rid of them from the land.'

'Do you really believe that the agent would kill twenty-one innocent people to follow his master's command?' O'Donovan asked. 'If you would even believe that such a thing was possible from him then this Flint must be a bad'un and have a heart as hard as his own name.'

'No, I do not believe that he is so callous, but I am inclined to believe that perhaps it was that he meant only to burn them out of the cabin, not to dispatch them all. He could hardly have known that the inmates would stampede into the doorway like a herd of frightened cattle and so cause their own entrapment and immolation.

I believe that it might just have been an eviction tactic gone horribly awry.'

'Nevertheless, and in spite of my experiences of landlords' agents, I find it hard to credit that. The man would be putting his freedom if not his neck at grave risk even by starting a fire which injured no one,' Mr O'Donovan said, evenly enough, though I could tell that he was repelled by Grimes and his single-minded thinking.

The man was undeterred. 'Also, there are other possible motives for the Ormonds to have taken drastic action against the Sheas, more personal reasons,' he said slyly, waiting for the effect of this to hit us before continuing. Satisfied that we now knew he had intelligence unknown to us, he continued: 'Young Ormond, the only son of the house, this Harold, was apparently, according to my constables, totally besotted with Ellen Shea, the youngest sister of the tenant, Patrick. He had met her while she worked as a maid in his father's manor house and had, for whatever reason, fallen under her spell. She had her hooks set well into young Ormond, and old Shea, her brother, was delighted by it all … at first. Then something happened which made the young Ormond most unwelcome in the Shea home, and Ellen began to spurn him as well. I hear that he was distraught. Frantic. Out of his mind over the whole thing. He drank sometimes in the taproom of your very hotel and swore more than once in drink that he would be revenged on Patrick Shea for keeping him from his love. For the addled young fool still believed that she wanted him, you see, and it was only her brother who was keeping them apart. I think that he might have fired the Shea home out of some want for revenge, some misguided retribution thought up by a deeply troubled mind.'

'And so he burned the object of his desires, only to get back at her brother? No, that won't wash, I think,' Mr O'Donovan said, shortly now, for he could no longer disguise the fact that he found the man Grimes both petty and tiresome.

'Or, then consider this, O'Donovan: young Harold Ormond's

father knew of his son's infatuation with the girl, a mere peasant and a Papist after all, and decided to get rid of her and so cure his son of his madness. He might have believed that the lad would grieve a while and then take up with some other, such as the horse-faced daughter of the master of the local hunt. Apparently the old fellow had told his son that if he did not give the girl up and stop any foolish notion he had of marrying her then he would formally disown him and thereby entail away the estate to the son of his late younger brother.'

'Was that not enough to end the young man's infatuation, Sergeant?' my master asked, already knowing how the man would answer.

'Apparently it was not, for he was constantly getting drunk and moping about the environs of their foul cottage at night, hoping to catch sight of the woman as she went out to the privy, no doubt.'

My master looked at the man with open disgust now. 'That is a possible motive and I'm sure that the lord in London could, with the collusion of his agent here, have had the deed carried out. It wouldn't have taken much, an oil-soaked clod of turf in the dead of night, hundreds of years worth of burning thatch coming down, perhaps even a spike or two driven at an angle into door and doorpost to lock it tight against the victims getting out. Two men could have done it – even one if he was determined enough. But it was a terribly cold-blooded thing if that were true. I almost hate to think that men walk the earth who could do such a thing. Thank the Lord that I have yet to meet such, though I fear that it will soon be my lot to do so.'

'There are far worse things done in the world every day, O'Donovan, don't be so bloody naive, man,' Grimes responded, almost with triumph in his voice.

That was practically the last word that passed between them before we parted from the policeman at that time.

'What do you make of our friend Grimes, Noble?' my employer asked me as we trotted back to Fethard once more, going slowly to let the policeman get well ahead of us.

'My word, but he's a cold fish, sir. I've never met colder,' I replied, though I myself am thought as cold as a man can be without actually dying.

'I believe that he has some particular pick against those counted among the nobility of the country. He seems ready to believe anything of them. But he has raised some valid points, at least valid to his own mind, against the Ormonds and I fear that he has a good pair of blinkers on by now and will see no other explanation but that they were behind it in some way. No doubt he will continue his investigation in that direction, but you and I will not be so waylaid and we will move today to lodgings somewhat closer to the place of the Sheas' demise. At any rate, I believe this crime was not likely to have been politically motivated, and so I will be able to report all of my findings to the Lord Chancellor with a clear conscience.'

He asked our landlord to make up our bill promptly upon our return to the hotel, explaining that we wanted to move along to the foot of Slievenamaun, and the inn-keeper was civil enough to recommend two or three boarding-houses in that vicinity to us. My master then asked about a place owned by a Mary Kelly, saying it had been suggested to him by someone in Dublin who had lodged there, and the man's face froze at the sound of her name.

'I'd not send yous there, sur, not in a million years, that is a bad place and run by a bad woman, so it is. Don't yous go near it, take my word on that, sur!' He spoke with a great deal of bluster, meant, to his mind, to keep us from any peril. Then he added, 'God, forgive me for spakin' it, but she is a trollop and runs little more dan a brottle.'

This seemed to amuse my master, but I was not amused. However, I did as I was bid and I packed up our belongings and put them in the gig while my master paid the account and enjoyed a final glass with the landlord. While not ever a waster by any means, my master drank far too much of wine and ardent spirits in those days and was often party to what could only be termed a carouse with his closest friends, especially in Dublin, but I could not very well attend at such gatherings due to my sensitivity over religious matters.

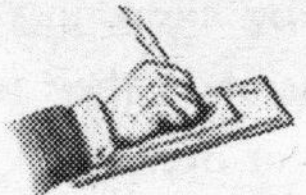

We were to meet Sergeant Grimes again on our way to Slievenamaun, and this time we had to wait some time for him to arrive. When he rode up to our standing gig he seemed almost flushed. He dismounted and joined my master in the conveyance.

'Well, sir, I've not been idle since this early morning, I can tell you. I've bearded the lion in his den, so to speak, for I have paid a visit to young Harry Ormond and his agent Flint. I met them separately and I asked them directly about the fire and the Sheas. Their reactions were a study in opposites. The young man, who seems pale and worn beyond his years, actually started to weep at the mention of the Sheas and I fear that from the look of him his mind cannot be far from being lost. I could hardly get a rational word from him, he was blubbering and crying so much and so I think that I can discount him as a suspect – unless his madness has been caused not only by grief but also by a guilt-racked conscience at having destroyed the object of his lust. Flint, on the other hand, was a portrait in evasiveness as I asked him my questions. He would hardly speak about the Sheas except to own that it was a great tragedy and that he knew nothing further about it. When asked, he would neither confirm nor deny that his lord was anxious to clear his land of tenants and I could not move him on it. I do not intend to let the matter drop, though. I have warned both Flint and Ormond of as much and that I will be back to see them again and again and that if I am able to gather any evidence against them they will be up in front of the magistrate in a trice.'

'Did you find out anything material about the Sheas' leaseholds from this Flint fellow?'

'Why, yes, but not from the devil direct. I examined the land book in his office. He didn't like it overly – the face on him was as black as ink. And I looked at his dockets on the Sheas as well. As it turns out you were partially wrong, you know, in your opinion that the Sheas had not been long in possession of their lease. I found to the contrary that they had been tenants for over ten years and were always in good standing with the estate.'

Grimes stopped to see what effect that would have on my master.

'I'm sorry, but I was given to understand that they had come only lately into a new lease,' he said.

'They did,' Grimes continued. 'They were given two new leases by the estate, recently relinquished by tenants by the names of Lynch and Gorman, and under very favourable terms. They got these leases just a few months before their deaths.'

'Why would a man like Lord Ormond give out two new leases to the Sheas when he was determined to clear his land? Surely he would have been delighted to have two such leases fall vacant, so why would he fill them with a long-term tenant? Did you not ask the agent to explain this?' O'Donovan asked.

'Of course I did, man, do you take me for a fool? And I have the answer to your question. Flint stated that the leases were given to Shea on the express orders of the old lord in London, and this is the reason – I cajoled it out of him. It seems that the old lord had made a secret pact with Shea, through his agent, to turn over the vacant leases to him in return for Patrick Shea's shunning of his son and his suit, and guaranteeing that his young sister would have no further truck with the younger Ormond. It makes sense when you think about it: Shea did, in fact, turn the young man away from where he had been an honoured and most welcome suitor at one time. So, his slattern of a sister seems to have sold her "love" for the sake of her brother's betterment.'

'Then, Sergeant, your theory as to a motive for the old lord having engineered the crime is gone, for he had, evidently, solved the problem of his son's ill-advised infatuation,' my master observed.

'Yes, but it was hardly a successful outcome for the old lord, was it? He had given up two leases which he needed vacant, and he would have been under an obligation of sorts to Patrick Shea for many years to come. As a gentleman, he would have no doubt found that irksome in the extreme. He was stuck with the Sheas for the foreseeable future, and his failure to effect the prompt clearance of his lands would have aroused his creditors; and even at that, he could not trust that the woman in question would not, later, when all was settled, throw caution to the wind and take up with the young lord again for, even if the pact was broken by them, he would never get the Sheas off his land. Further, the old man might die at any time, sodden with port and brandy, and by some accounts, boys; and there was always the danger that the young fool, once free of parental ire, might have actually married the Shea woman and attempted to make her a lady. Ormond might still have wished Flint to make it a permanent thing after all.'

'You have a valid point there, Sergeant,' said Mr O'Donovan, 'many valid points to be sure. You have been most assiduous in your investigations, and you are to be commended.'

We drove off a few minutes later heading for the 'inn' run by Mary Kelly and her husband Francis. As we moved along, my master expressed the opinion that Grimes was like a dog with a juicy bone as far as the Ormonds were concerned. He would follow that false track till he dropped.

'How can you be so sure that they were not involved? I asked. 'There is much scope in Grimes's argument for such a conclusion to be drawn.'

'But, think, my friend, think, just think, for a moment,' he said to my back. 'Do not emulate that man. Poor Grimes does not know what we know. Something which puts the Ormonds out of the picture completely as far as I am concerned.'

'What? We know little more than him, he has all the files and ...'

'Hush, Noble, and listen. We are certain from the priest's own non-admission that someone knows the details of the crime who was not a direct party to it. That someone is evidently a Catholic and so likely is a peasant or near enough to it. That person, by reason of fear or misguided loyalty, will not come forward to name the guilty. Now, if the Ormonds were behind it or even their agent Flint, a hard-hearted and much-hated Protestant by all accounts, then the person known to the priest would come forward without a second thought. Therefore, neither the Ormonds nor Flint can have been involved. Also, I now believe, as a consequence, that the person we seek actually witnessed the murders.'

I kept quiet at that. I pride myself on an orderly mind and I must have reddened at my own lack of perception, but Mr O'Donovan said nothing more and slept with his head in the corner of the gig seat until we arrived in the vicinity of the mountain.

He missed seeing much lovely scenery by his slumbering. The land we travelled through was broken by low hills, lushly grassed, and the countryside still looked well wooded … for Ireland. Which I believe was once a mass of oaks cut down later to build the new navies of England. Our road crossed several lovely streams and rivers and the bird-life along these seemed profuse. The fields were well tilled and the pastures looked to be teeming with healthy-looking beasts. It was like a biblical land of milk and honey. But it was milk and honey that defied Isaac Newton's ideas of gravity, for the milk and honey for the most part flowed uphill and away from the toilers of the soil and into the mouths and coffers of the elite of the land.

We arrived at a rough crossroads, which I recalled from our recent visit to the Sheas' ruined cabin, and my master had me ask at the first inhabited cot we came to for the residence of Mary Kelly. The house, when we finally came to it, was long and low, positively sprawling for a mountainy establishment. I later found out there were six rooms in all and some small outbuildings and a mean-looking stable and carriage house, which all formed a large loose square. I breathed a silent prayer that I would not have to sleep there in the stables while playing the part of Shamey O'Toole, the serving man. The house was spruce enough to look at and had evidently been recently limed and its wooden trim was painted a bright green throughout. The thatch was new enough to still be a honey-yellow colour and the edifice boasted three chimney stacks. At both gable ends there were huge stacks of black dried turf bricks and there was a fine-looking cock perched on top of the farthest heap, where he could keep a lookout over his clucking, pecking harem below.

The clatter of the horse on the cobbles brought a woman from the central door of the abode, drying her hands on a very grey-looking cloth as she came. She was fifty if she was a day and stout about the middle, but she was nearly comely, in a matronly sort of way. Her face had once, I dare say, been deemed handsome, but now it was touched by time and she had a most tired look about her, a sadness even, especially in and about her eyes. To me she looked a deal less lively and jolly than a woman of her girth and stature would normally be. She looked forlorn, in fact. That was our first look at Mary Kelly.

She approached our stationary gig, having forced a slight smile onto her face. Ignoring my presence, she looked at Mr O'Donovan and said, 'Good day to yer honner, sur. Welcome to my humble home. Is there anything that I can do for you at all today?'

In view of what Grimes had told us about the woman, that was a question tinged with great irony.

'Well, I certainly hope so, ma'am,' my master said. 'You see, I'm travelling about sightseeing in the area and I'm hoping to find decent lodgings in the vicinity. I believe that you provide for travellers in your establishment. We will be in the area a week or so, Mrs … er… '

'Kelly, Mrs Mary Kelly, at your service, sur. Indeed we do for travellers here and I would be delighted to do for yourself, sur. A week is it? 'Tis fortunate that our best room is available at the moment. Perhaps you would like to see it?'

Mr O'Donovan alighted and followed the woman in through the low doorway and I was left to my own devices, until he emerged five minutes later and motioned for me to bring our bags in. I did so, but with an ill will for I was grown sick and tired of playing the fetch-and-carry lackey. Once through the doorway I discovered that the house was split in two across its girth by a hallway. To the right side was what appeared to be a public taproom-cum-dining area and beyond that the kitchen. I later discovered that the family's living quarters were off beyond the kitchen. To the left was 'the accommodation' available for paying guests. I followed my master along the hallway with two doors opening onto it on my left. The second door was open, and he entered it with Mary Kelly at his heels. I struggled along, almost bouncing down the narrow passageway, for the master's bags were encumbering me greatly in the dim, narrow space.

His head re-emerged from his new room and he called to me, 'Come along, Shamey, shake a leg, man and don't take all day. Lay out my things now, while I accompany this good lady for some much-needed refreshment.'

I heard her cackle at this, and then saw her simper horribly when he made a shallow bow in her direction. I had no sooner gained the room, with my burdens, but the pair of them left me alone. The chamber was low-ceilinged but a good deal larger than I imagined it would be. There was a fire-hearth on the inside wall and a small window on each of the far side and back walls. There was also a large, lumpy-looking, bed, a pine chest of drawers, an armoire, a table and one straight-backed chair in the room. Two full peat buckets stood on each side of the hearth and a small washing area had been created in the corner with a dark-painted wooden stand on which was a large bowl and ewer and a much fly-specked mirror was affixed to the wall behind it. I set about opening my employer's bags and putting his things into the drawers and the armoire, having first checked them for evidence of vermin. Then I laid his items of toiletry by the wash-stand and placed his writing materials and a few books on the table which could serve as his desk.

When my 'duties' were done, I went in search of my master and found him in the taproom, seated at a table with Mary Kelly and a man. The man was huge, with a truly leonine head on his shoulders, complete with a flaming, flowing mane of red hair. He was unshaven that day and his face had a most rough-used look to it. I noticed that the hand that held his horn beaker of what, no doubt, were ardent spirits, was like a pork butt it was so red and huge.

As I approached the table I heard my master say, 'Well, Mr Kelly, that is most interesting, the holy well of Saint Finbarr, and so close. My word, I can see that I shall have plenty of curious sights to see this week and the scenery on the mountainside is simply breathtaking. I am sure that I will have a most interesting time about here.'

I have rarely heard him be so verbose and full off light banter. His manner would have given the impression of his being rather vacant, to anyone who did not know him that is, and I realised that was part of his disguise.

'Yes, yer honner, this is a grand place for a bit of a holiday, so it is. There's nothin' as grand or unbespoilt in Europe at all.'

'Capital, Mr Kelly, but just two more things: I will need decent accommodation for my man here. Poor old Shamey has a tender disposition for a servant man, and he couldn't stand anywhere too damp or dusty. Secondly, I have to ask you, is the nearest Catholic chapel all the way back in Fethard, for Shamey and myself go to Mass each and every Sunday without fail, isn't that a fact, Shamey?'

The Kellys both looked toward me at that and I was forced by circumstances to own that it was so, to my eternal mortification. Mr O'Donovan was, I realised, showing them that he was a good Catholic gentleman, and therefore very unlikely to be an agent of any branch of government.

'We'll fix Shamey up wit' a good warm den in one of the out-offices, so we will, he'll be as snug as a bug in a rug, and we'll see to it he gets all the stirrabout that he can ate three times a day,' said the woman, barely glancing at me.

Grand, I thought. I would apparently be spending a week in a vile shed eating nothing but oaten porridge three times a day.

'And as your honner has requested, he can serve you at table while you are eating here, as befits a foine gintleman like your honner's self.'

Wonderful! I was not only to survive on gruel and the odd boiled potato but I was to stand and watch my master eating whatever succulent things the Kellys might put before him as well. I realised that I was getting myself into a serious huff over this, which was slightly ludicrous, for in my own life in Kilrush I ate and still eat porridge nearly as frequently and take a great pleasure in it, as it settles my stomach as nothing else seems to.

'Now, to answer your question of a more ecclesiastical nature,' Kelly went on, 'the nearest chapel is not in Fethard at all but just down the west road from here about two miles, right handy for you ... and me missus goes there every Sunday and a half dozen other times besides in a week, for, do you know what I'm goin' to tell ye, she has got very pious in the last year or two has Mary,' Mr Kelly volunteered. 'The parish priest der is Fr Rourke, a youngster, but a good'un all de same,' he said almost as an afterthought.

'Grand, well I think that we'll be off and do a bit of touring now, we'll be back for the evening meal at say ... six o'clock,' my master said airily, as if he could not wait to see their dreary mountain at close quarters.

'That'll be grand, yer honner, six it is; and we're to have a big rib roast of beef this night with plenty to go with it and we can even offer some good red wine to accompany it as well,' Kelly said, proudly, draining off his bovine tumbler and politely half-rising as my master prepared to leave.

I followed him out after the goodbyes were completed, and we drove off in the direction of the Catholic chapel. It was as disreputable looking a Mass-house as I've ever seen, even worse than that of Fethard, and with no churchyard around it at all but merely a limed thatched cabin leaning lazily against one end of it, with little more shape to it than a turf pile, which I imagined was the priest's residence. Mr O'Donovan had me stop, and he alighted and approached the cottage door. It would seem the most natural thing in the world to any passerby or nosey neighbour that a travelling Catholic gentleman would call on the local abbé while staying in the area. As he knocked on the half door to the hovel, he turned and motioned for me to follow him. I secured the horse to a nearby post and did so just as the door opened and a small dark woman in black came out to see who was there.

My master asked for the priest by name and we were soon admitted to the 'drawing room'. The old maid bade my employer take a seat and hurried off to what must have been an adjoining bedchamber to fetch the priest.

I stood dutifully behind the straight, hard-seated chair that held my master, and soon the priest emerged. He had evidently been lying down, for his dark soutane was wrinkled and he had the red crease marks of rumpled bed-coverings on his pale cheeks. He was a tall, spare figure with dark hair and the saddest eyes that I have ever seen on a man.

'I'm sorry to have been lying down when you arrived, Mr O'Donovan, is it? I have been unwell of late and find that there are times during the day when all my energy leaves me and I must rest, for I do not sleep well at night when I'm supposed to.'

'Yes, Ambrose O'Donovan, at your service, Father. I am most sorry to hear that you are indisposed. I trust that we are not disturbing you with our unheralded visit. Shamey here and myself are staying a week in the area. I want to do a bit of sightseeing, don't you know, before heading back to Kilrush. We've been in Dublin a good long while, you see. We'll be here on Sunday for Mass, if God spares us, and I thought as we were passing that I should pay you the courtesy of a visit.'

'Quite right you are to do so, sir, and I'm glad that you have. Now, I'm a native of the area myself, even though I was schooled and ordained in France, and so I know a fair bit about the various places of interest hereabouts. There are several holy places. I could tell you all about them if you wish.'

Mr O'Donovan acted as if he was delighted and as if he hadn't already had chapter and verse from that red giant Kelly not an hour before, so I was forced once again to listen to a litany of Romish idolatry and superstition from the mouth of an educated and travelled man, for the priest was well spoken and obviously of an intelligent and sensitive nature. When he had finished his druidish cant and had offered us tea, which my master graciously declined, he was thanked profusely for his information, and we took our leave of him. As I was going, I bowed my head to him as a sign of respect – I was playing a Papist peasant, you will bear in mind – and the man, he was as tall as myself, put his left hand to the back of my head like a skullcap and gave me his blessing with his Latin mumblings, signs of the cross and 'my son' and all the other rot he had learned in France. I was horrified, let me tell you, and I know that my grey cheeks were burning crimson as we drove off. My mood was not helped when I distinctly heard my master unsuccessfully suppressing his chuckling as he sat in the gig behind me.

He had me stop up the road so that we could talk face to face.

When I turned to look at him, he saw the remnants of my discommoded demeanour and involuntarily he laughed again.

'I beg your pardon, Noble, I really do, but if you could have seen your face when young Fr Rourke put hands on you! Glory be, but I will never forget it if I live to be a thousand, you had a look about you like the last goose in the butcher's pen on Christmas Eve,' he said, wiping his eyes on a kerchief and laughing again. 'But tell me, all the rest aside, what do you make of our clerical friend – and his condition?'

'Well, I would say that he is not a well man,' I began. 'He is young, so he is likely not so ill in his body as in his mind. He is, I don't doubt for an instant, an honest, decent man, holy and devout by his own lights, but he has the aspect of one who carries a great burden on his shoulders. The care of the world, in fact, and it seems to be robbing him of sleep and of his peace of mind.'

'My thoughts exactly, Noble. I suspect that the same penitent that went to the priest in Fethard has also visited Fr Rourke and has placed a heavy burden on his priestly shoulders as well. He has been made privy in the confessional box to dire and dreadful things and I pity him. We will visit him again when we know more.'

'Who do you think is the penitent in question, Mr O'Donovan?' I asked.

'I suspect, as no doubt you yourself do, that it is none other than Mary Kelly, who is the cousin of Catherine Mullally. Mullally and her husband were the two victims not directly part of the Shea clan. I know now that they were not even distant cousins of the Sheas. The only other non-Shea by blood was the husband of Martha, one John Doherty, who was a man from the depths of County Donegal, according to the police notes, and so has no relative in the area who would fill the role of a penitent struggling with his or her conscience.'

'And the baby,' I interjected.

'Yes, quite right, Noble, yes, the poor baby, born into an inferno, it was not related to the Sheas either. I suspect that Mary Kelly feels no remorse or pity for the Sheas themselves, but is deeply troubled by the death of her poor relative and the child. Unless her husband is the killer, which I doubt, she is not coming forward from fear of the murderer, even though she desperately wants to. These are suspicions only, of course, and we will have to try and find out if we are correct in that assumption before we can take any action. Didn't we hear from her own husband that she is haunting the chapel this last year and more?'

'That is all well and good, sir, but do you not think it is a dangerous thing to make speculations before you have gathered all the information that you can?' I asked him.

He looked at me in some surprise, for it was not often that we crossed words or that I had the temerity to contradict him.

'Why no, Noble, I do not, if you must know, unlike yourself. I think you must own a very inflexible mind indeed to fear that early speculation might send us permanently down the wrong road.'

We drove back that evening for my master's fine repast of beef and my bowl of porridge with salt and buttermilk. A not unpleasing meal in itself – if one is in one's nineties and has lost all sensation of taste for food, together with the will for continued existence. I had to stand at my master's elbow while he was served a large cut of juicy roasted beef. I could tell by the smell of it that it was perfect in a gravy worthy of Olympus and it was accompanied by a variety of tasty things. Instead of ordinary potatoes boiled in their skins, which was the usual fare at places such as the Kellys, the landlady gave him a platter full of golden potato cakes, fried crisply in butter and lard and sprinkled with caraway seeds, along with mashed turnips with a knob of melting butter on top the size of a cock's head.

I stood by doing nothing and with my mouth watering, for I was not there really to serve my employer, you see, but was set there to watch Mary Kelly as she went about her business in the room. He had further instructed me to try and make her acquaintance and also that of the other servants of the place. I smiled graciously at her at every turn and at last she noticed and seemed to warm to me. I watched her in unguarded moments and at those times there was a great wearisomeness about her eyes and brow. When the meal was ended and my master had retired to his room, she took me into the kitchen and I was given a good slice of beef with all the trimmings except for the potato cakes, which had all been devoured. I sat and munched that very late repast at the long deal work-table, my backside to the open fire. Fortunately I was not offered wine or other strong drink, for I would have had to refuse and that would have marked me out as an oddity among the Irish peasantry and it was an important requirement that I should fit in.

As she served me, Mrs Kelly chatted on and on about what a fine gentleman my master was, so handsome and well made, and with such immaculate manners to boot. She said that I was lucky to have such a master, and in spite of my circumstances at that moment in time, and for many other more substantial reasons, I had to agree with her.

After I had eaten my fill and far more than I would normally consume, I was by then feeling much more affection for our landlady. I excused myself, saying that I should go and see to my master's needs before retiring to my own 'suite', and she smiled sweetly at me as I left, saying that I was a most attentive servant indeed.

In his room, my employer instructed me to keep a close watch on Mary Kelly and to let him know where she travelled to and to whom she spoke. It was another tall order indeed. Then he went back to the taproom for a nightcap, as he called it, and I went with him, not to imbibe but to watch. The landlord and one other man were the sole occupants that night, which I gather was an unusual thing. He called my master over immediately we entered and introduced him to the other fellow, who was called Peter Maher. He was a swarthy-looking, sharp-faced little man, not bad-looking, but with a harder look in his eye than that of most of the peasantry. He spoke fairly well and seemed very pleased to be making my master's acquaintance. He was a self-avowed expert on the lands about us and he had many more places of interest that we must visit before our week there was up. He had been passed along the subterfuge that we were only tourists by our host. It is a strange thing, knowing what I know now of the smaller man's suspicious and vicious nature, that Maher should so readily believe from Kelly that we were only harmless visitors, where he would have doubted it or at least have been suspicious of the same tale direct from our own lips. It is ever thus with human nature.

He proved to be good enough company for my master, who seemed to be delighted with his information and took down notes on sites of interest on a scrap of paper. In conjunction with Kelly, he passed several hours of relative bonhomie with Maher. As I sat there, doing not much, Mary Kelly motioned for me to follow her to the kitchen. I did so and was rewarded with a large tin mug of hot milk, which she had beaten up with sugar, raw egg and a pinch of ground ginger, for a nightcap of my own. When I was done, having drunk down the posset most greedily, I wiped the froth from my upper lip and rose to leave again. I was shocked when my landlady came up to me, embraced me and pushed me up against the inner door. I was flabbergasted and taken aback and hardly knew what she was about when she seized my head, pulled it down to her and kissed me hard on the lips. The bissum, Lord forgive me, even forced her tongue into my mouth. I recovered myself and pushed her away, but not roughly.

'What's the matter?' she said with some asperity. 'Don't you like me? I've seen you staring at me all the while. What was that all about if you didn't want me?'

'Sure, you're the loveliest woman I've seen this many a day,' I replied in the voice of a peasant. ''Tis only right that I should look at ye, but I can do no more, for I have a faithful wife and a house full of childer at home, and so no more can come of it than lookin'.'

'But sure, I'm a married woman as well, and you're not at home nor anywhere near it, so who's to know the difference?' she said, attempting to grapple with me again.

Again I repulsed her onslaught: 'But I'm a good Catholic, 'twould be a mortal sin to do what you want. I couldn't do it, so I couldn't. Now for mercy's sake let me go and tempt me no more.'

I reflected that since I had donned the mantle of a Papist peasant, the lies had dripped constantly from my mouth. I shuddered at the thought as I made my way to my own quarters. For the sake of my soul I was nearly tempted to throw the whole thing in and go to the taproom and tell my master that I was resigning from our mission, but that would have placed him in danger. I will admit also that I was pleased, much against my will as I thought on it, that so fine a woman as Mary Kelly had found an old fellow like me in the least attractive, even dressed as I was in the homespun clothes of a peasant. May God forgive me for the sin of vanity.

I sat in the loft of the small shed that was supposed to be my abode for the next week, by the open window, and thought of all that had happened for a long while before I retired. I slept immediately on turning in, thanks in part to the effects of the warm milk, but I woke in the wee hours of the morning and I could not get back to sleep, for I had consumed far too much for dinner. Please do not think me indelicate, but I could detect the first symptoms of a certain looseness of the bowels. As I sat there, innards in some animation, I was trying to use my master's methods of seeing the truth in things, and I thought of what we had learned of Mary Kelly from Sergeant Grimes.

Apparently when young, Mary Girvin, as she was then, had led a most dissolute life. She had later married a servant, James Kelly, who left his employment and together they established their inn, which was at the start little more than a shebeen. They sold spirits with no licence and provided board and lodging to any travellers who thought it expedient to stop there. Further, it was said that if a young man and woman had any wish to be alone in their accommodation at a late hour of the night, then they could do so without interference from their hosts.

According to Grimes's report, Mary Kelly appears to have superintended and conducted this establishment, her husband merely giving it the sanction of wedlock and joining in with the licentious conviviality which took place under his semi-lucid auspices, for he was a hopeless toper. By wedding her, he had merely allowed her to be transformed from harlot to procurer and assured himself a constant access to whiskey. For all the bad that I had heard of her, she seemed to be quite kind-hearted, though, and I thought that her husband could nearly be discounted as a suspect in the deaths of the Sheas by reason of his almost constant drunkenness.

As I sat once more by the high window of my hovel, musing over these thoughts, I was shocked into full wakefulness when I saw the very woman in question leaving the front door of the inn. She looked about her and then stole away from the yard and onto a rough track through a small wooded area. The figure that I saw was wrapped well in a dark cloak but I knew in an instant it was Mary Kelly from her shape and gait.

I pulled back on my shirt and trousers and shoes, went down into the yard and followed in the direction that she had taken. I never did overtake her, for she had hurried along, and I was unfortunately forced to stop to answer an urgent call of nature. However, I followed the path along, and I soon recognised the destination as the burnt-down home of the Sheas, for it was a clear night and the half moon had risen. The path led through a growth of scrubby bushes and only opened out at the yard of the former home of the unfortunates. I stopped just before this and allowed my eyes to adjust to the gloom before going further. Even with the moon in the sky I could not see Mary Kelly, but I could hear her and I will never forget the sound. There could have been nothing more unnerving in that site of tragedy with its tumbled building than the low moaning that came from within the life-forsaken abode. I ventured further and dared to look through a small frameless window from where I could just make her out, sitting there in the back corner of the chamber, among the burnt and tumbled debris. I realised that it was the part of the room where Catherine Mullally had breathed her last hot breath as she held her doomed infant's head out of the water tub.

Mary Kelly was rocking herself back and forth and wailing loudly, working herself up until she seemed to break and then collapse onto the floor, speaking some phrases over and over again in what I knew to be Irish, but did not understand other than a word of endearment or two. Then she stopped, but still weeping, she said in English, 'Ah, my Katie, my Katie, I failed you. I am a sinner as bad as ever was, ah, my Katie, forgive me, forgive me, a foolish, weak, evil old woman, for I fear I can be forgiven by neither God nor myself, hell fire only awaits me.'

Her voice was as spectral as her form and it fairly raised the hair on the back of my neck. Though I have never placed any credence in the existence of ghosts, I can tell you I felt an immediate impulse to flee the place. My recent corporeal relief, I found, had been only temporary, so I didn't run but continued to watch her vague form, my innards a-writhing, until she made to rise from her vigil and come back out of the house. I scurried off then and hid myself in the bushes near by and watched again as she came out and knelt there in the moonlight before the door and commenced to say her rosary beads in a clear voice, in Irish.

After that string of half-idolatry was ended, she rose slowly, solemnly crossed herself and went quickly off down the path by which she had come. I waited a safe time and then followed her and I will admit that I was most impatient to get back and tell my employer what I had seen and heard. I was further unnerved when I heard a rustling in the scrubby growth at the other side of the pathway and thought, no I was certain, that I glimpsed a dark figure moving along stealthily behind the woman. I stopped and gave them both a good head start before I went back to the stable.

Of course I had to wait until full morning before I could go to my employer's room to 'see to him', as the other servants called it. He was awake, shaved and near dressed when I arrived, and he was greatly excited by my relation of the happenings of the night before. I omitted Mary Kelly's failed seduction of me, as I was still shamed by it, and I did not want to risk that he would tease me over it or, worse, spread it about as a droll yarn in Dublin or Kilrush.

'Just as we suspected, Noble, well done!' he said excitedly. 'We know for sure who the sorry penitent is now. Our next obstacle, and it may prove much more difficult than finding her, will be to work out how to get her to come forward. There must be something we can do. I am sure that the good Fr Rourke has been at her to come forward and from what I've seen and from what you have reported, I think the poor woman is so racked and haunted by guilt as to be near a mental collapse. But first things first: today we must meet Sergeant Grimes again, for he has a little more information to impart to me. But, bless us, you are near dead from lack of sleep, old friend. I'll tell you what, when we are out of sight of the Kellys, we'll switch roles for a morning. I will drive and you shall laze and slumber peacefully in the gig for a change.

And so we progressed, but if you imagine that I slept or even rested on that journey you have never seen my master drive a fleet horse and a light gig. He always drives the beast as if the devil himself were after him, standing up like a charioteer, and we dashed along the narrow road bouncing over every pot-hole and rock on its surface, brushing the briars and thorn bushes of the hedges as we careered to either side. I clung for dear life to the upholstery of the seats, so tightly my knuckles looked as though they were about to burst through the skin of my hands, and I prayed that I would not be thrown from the vehicle or that we would not tip over into the ditch. I was a happy and relieved man, I can tell you, when my 'rest' was over and we reached the crossroads where we were to meet Grimes.

The man was not yet there, but my master was exhilarated by the morning so far. He walked up and down by the gig, rubbing his hands together, his head cocked to one side, as I had often seen him do when he was well pleased or expecting to be pleased.

'Damn, excuse my language, Noble, but I love to drive a horse. I don't know why I let you do it at all, 'tis such a pleasure to me. What say from now on I drive and you laze?'

Fortunately, we were just then interrupted by the clatter of Grimes arriving on his horse. He had great and ghastly tidings with him as well as the mysterious further information that my master had asked him for. The man looked almost excited, for all that his visage had the aspect of a recent cadaver.

'Well, Mr O'Donovan, I have come to tell you that I believe your task is at an end, for I have solved the thing for you while you dallied about this bloody mountain,' he said, pushing up his sharp chin at us as he finished.

'You don't say! Why, that is most remarkable, Sergeant, you must tell us all about it,' was all my master replied, as genially as possible.

'The younger Ormond has broken under my hounding and has done away with himself this very morning,' the man exclaimed, almost with a whoop. 'He shot himself with a pistol in his own chamber, racked with guilt and shame and knowing that I was onto him, no doubt.'

'The poor, tortured young man. And how do you know this?' Mr O'Donovan asked.

''Tis simple. He left a note that tells all. I have it here.'

The man seemed to be actually enjoying himself at my master's expense, and all over the newly dead body of a young man. I thought him even more reprehensible than ever.

'I went back to the Ormond family seat again last evening to get the information which you had requested from that scoundrel Flint, and I took an opportunity to put it hard to young Ormond that we were onto him for the killing of his worthless paramour and her kin. I told him how his father had bought off the slattern and her family with two paltry leases and that the depth of her affection for him could be measured out in a few boggy acres. I said that I believed he had torched her and her foul kin in revenge for her perfidy. He fairly howled when he heard it all, I can tell you, and he collapsed straightaway, but I heaped on my imprecations as to the foulness of his deed. When I felt that it would do no more good, there I left him. He was a shaking heap by then anyway, incapable of speech. Some time this morning, to escape the hemp, he shot himself. Here is his note.'

I read the note over my master's shoulder and it said:

To this evil world,

I am ending my own misery this fine morning. I am twenty-three years old and I have seen enough of God's earth and the vileness that he has put here to stalk it. I believe that His hell will be no worse than this life that I have endured since my beloved Ellen was taken from me. When I embarked on the journey of our true love I never dreamt that it would end so. It could not be, my hateful father told me so, over and over. He even bribed her grasping, vile brother to take her away from me, but I know in my heart that her love was true in spite of what that odious fellow Grimes has said. I can tell by his cut that he is no gentleman and more suited to being a shopkeeper's assistant than a policeman of any rank.

I believe that my father has done the dastardly deed, not by his own well-scrubbed hands but by his minions, for he has great power here and I have none. He will roast for it in the next life even if he does not swing for it in this world.

I welcome my death and I pray that it will reunite me with my Ellen, no matter how unlikely that dream may be.

Ormond.

'You can see some splashes of his blood on the other side of the paper,' Grimes observed clinically.

My master did not turn the paper over but simply handed it back to the man.

'He comes very close to insulting your good self, Sergeant Grimes, doesn't he?' he said. 'His words seem to be very telling against the old lord all right.'

Grimes looked at my master strangely for a moment, mulling over the first part of his comment before going on.

'I'm hoping it will be a damned sight more than telling, O'Donovan. I'm determined that it shall serve to put a rope around the old lord's neck before too long. I'm sending this off with my full report to London and I will ask – no, demand – that the authorities there arrest the man immediately.'

Mr O'Donovan only nodded at him and then said, 'But anyway I will still require the information that you were asked for. You have it with you, I hope?'

Grimes immediately showed anger; he was on the point of saying something nasty but thought the better of it, remembering the Lord Chancellor, no doubt.

'Well, for all the damned good it will do, but here it is. Now, will there be anything more, Mr O'Donovan?' he asked grudgingly, putting as much sarcasm into the *Mister* as he could muster.

Grimes then handed my employer another sheet of paper. Mr

O'Donovan looked at it briefly, seemed satisfied with what he saw, and put it into his waistcoat pocket.

He stopped Grimes from remounting his horse. 'One more thing, Sergeant, if I can beg your forbearance before you go after your prey: do you know anything of a man in the district of the Sheas' cottage named Peter Maher? Do you know him at all?'

Grimes started as if he had been struck. 'Yes, I bloody well know Maher, Wee Black Peter he's called. He's a vicious thug with a band of his like gathered about him.'

'Is he a rebel do you think?' my master asked.

'No, that he's not. He's not noble enough to have even any misguided patriotism in him. He lives for gold and mayhem alone and I could not tell you for certain which one he most prefers. If I could get any information against him I would see him roped up quick enough, but it is unlikely for not a one in the countryside would want to get on the bad side of the same man. He lives by his crimes and is willing to do anything under the sun or moon for money. He dwells alone in a hovel with no land to it at all. He raises nothing, he trades nothing and he does no work, but still he lives very well. I have seen the rogue often in Fethard – he dresses in the best of cloth and is fond of good drink and food, and is always treating his cronies to something or other. If you can supply him to me, or give me a means of condemning him, I would be most grateful.'

'If ever I can do so then I will, you have my word on it, Sergeant, now we will hold you back no more from your work,' my master said as affable as ever he was.

The man seemed mollified by his tone and almost smiled as he said, 'Well, O'Donovan, I hope there will be no bad feeling between us. I imagine that I got there first, not only from my long experience as a policeman, but from knowing more of the district and the locals than you – as well as taking the direct approach. A full frontal assault is always best, it works every time. Now, good day to ye, sir.' And Grimes jumped on his horse and rode off hell for leather.

I asked Mr O'Donovan if the man was really onto something definite.

He laughed ruefully and said, 'Why yes, Noble, he is onto something, very definite, and he deserves it if ever a man did, for I believe he's onto the road that leads straight to perdition.'

'You don't think that he has solved the case then?' I asked.

My master looked at me quickly as if I was an imbecile. 'No, far from it. He has merely driven an innocent, unfortunate young man to kill himself. Our friend Grimes will pay for that in due course, but if he bruits it about the country, then it might well make our informant come forward or our real killers more careless, or both.'

He indicated then that we should be off to do a little sightseeing and so put a good look on our tour. We drove around the foot of the mountain for a long while and then returned to our 'inn' for luncheon. Again, my master ate well on grilled mountain trout, but I got porridge, salt and boiled kale in the kitchen, and this time my landlady was content to let me eat that alone, without adding tidbit or tasty treat. In fact she ignored me pointedly. Was love ever so fleeting, I ask you.

Do you know that the speed of communication of information amongst the Irish peasantry, especially that concerning horrors, calumnies, scandals and just ordinary malicious gossip, has always astounded me. It defies the speed of the signal fire or even the new semaphore signals used by the military. If the battle of Marathon had been fought in Ireland, a score of miles from Dublin, then the news of it would, I believe, have reached the city an hour before the fastest Hoplite runner. By mid-afternoon the news of the suicide and apparent confession of young Ormond reached into the very depths of the Kellys' busy kitchen. I was there myself when a slattern named

Bridget brought it in and told her garbled but still pertinent version of all to Mary Kelly and her maids. The great news was that the old Lord Ormond was the killer or the procurer of the killers of the Shea clan and was to be arrested in London. A dispatch rider had been sent post haste to Dublin with the documents to set the wheels in motion. Grimes had browbeaten the local magistrate into swearing out the arrest warrants and the man's clerk had let the word of it out in the tavern a half hour later. The maids clapped their hands to their mouths in apparent shock and horror, but I was quietly supping and watching Mary out of the corner of my eye and I noticed that she almost collapsed and would have keeled over if she hadn't had the work-table to support her until she had recovered herself a little. Then she ran from the room, her apron piled up about her face, saying, 'No, no, no, no, 'tis not right, not right at all, 'tis another crime in the making. Merciful God, deliver me.'

I immediately sought out my well-replenished master in the taproom and whispered to him what had happened. He signalled me to follow him to his room and he seemed very pleased with himself as he shut the door

'I cannot believe that Grimes's news has reached out to here so soon. I thought it would take a full day at least, but this is capital for our purpose and we must strike while the iron is hot. Grimes may well have done us a great service, but I wish that the foolish young Ormond were alive yet. He threw his life away for nothing. Mary Kelly has, as we know, from her appearance and her night-time ramblings, been suffering from a long bout of bad conscience, and this may finally force her to come forward. Don't you see, Noble, she now knows that another man has died by her silence and yet another man is to be falsely accused of the crime. No doubt, to her mind, the Sheas and Kate Mullally and her little family are dead and cannot be brought back and she feels great guilt over that already, but this is something that she can yet stop from happening. I believe that with the proper handling she will not be able to restrain herself from talking now. But first let us revisit young Fr Rourke, for I believe that he can help us with some "local gossip".'

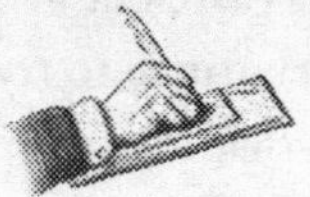

We reached the priest's low house a half hour later, and we were soon in the young cleric's parlour again. This time Mr O'Donovan did not play the idle sightseer but went right to the point. He told the priest that we were here in the area specifically to investigate the murder of the Sheas and that he now knew who had done it and who knew about it; but without concrete proof or, more to the point, witness testimony, the loathsome, savage swine who had burned those people and the newborn baby would ever walk free on the earth. He said he fully realised that the priest knew the same information as we did, and that we needed his help.

The priest was taken aback by all this and his careworn expression changed to one of great alarm. 'I can tell you nothing, Mr O'Donovan. I am bound by the secrecy of the confessional in this matter. Please believe me when I tell you that I would dearly love to help but I cannot.'

'I'm not asking you to break any sacred vows, Father, but merely to tell me if you are actively asking a certain person to come forward. I don't expect you to name that person.'

The priest hesitated, then seemed to make an internal decision. 'Yes,' he said. 'I have been doing nothing else this near a year and a half. What I know about the thing is putting me in an early grave. I will perish from it if it is not ended very soon. But the person I speak of is deathly afraid to come forward, still more frightened of temporal retribution than eternal damnation.'

'Speak to that person again, Father, and assure them that they will have the full protection of the law and the personal protection of

Ambrose O'Donovan and Mr Noble Alexander, my good Presbyterian Ulsterman, here.'

That last made the priest gasp, but he said nothing.

'I … I will try, sir. I will continue to try, that is, but I have made no headway so far and I doubt that my trying will do any real good.'

'Make another attempt at it anyway, Father, now there is some information that you may know, being the shepherd of the flock and a local man to boot. This Mullally man, who died with his little family in the flames, does he have any kin about here still? I saw nothing of it in the official records.'

The priest thought and then said, 'Yes, he has an old mother and a younger step-brother. Their name is Butler. They live two miles to the east of here. She is Alicia Butler and the half-brother is named John. He's about eighteen years old. Her second husband has passed away now as well, poor old woman, and she was in paroxysms of grief over the death of her fine son and his family. The doctor despaired of her, for she took to her bed and seemed to have turned her face to the wall. I visit her as often as I can and slowly she has recovered some of her strength. Mullally and his wife were only working for the Sheas to raise money for the rent on her own smallholding. I fear that the Butlers are not far from the roadside by now and so the woman has another helping of grief to be soon heaped on her dish.'

Mr O'Donovan took the man aside and they spoke more on other matters and did so privately, huddled together, as if the very walls could hear, and it was some time before we were out on the road again. East this time, in search of the Butlers and their abode.

We found it handily enough and we only had to ask one suspicious peasant the way. The place was almost derelict although one could tell that someone, probably working alone, was making a valiant effort to make a go of the place. Someone had put a new roof of sorts on a shed recently and had limed the front of the house. That was all, as they had run out of either whitewash or their initiative at that juncture. We both went to the door and halloed to the occupants.

A woman, old and bent though she wasn't in truth above sixty, all dressed in dusty, ashy black, came to the half door. She saw my master's fine clothes and beaver hat and started as if she had been struck across the face.

'The grippers, the grippers is come!' she roared, much louder than one would ever have imagined that she could. 'They're here and we were to be given another month to pay up our back rent, and my wee John working night and day to get the coin to pay off that scut of an agent. False thieves ye are, away with ye to hell, coming early to throw a poor twice-widowed, old done woman out onto the road. Shame and curses to you and yours, may the devil make a ladder out of yer back bones, may he sweep the two legs from yer bodies, may every beast ye own be choked be its halter.'

She went on in this vein for a few more moments and her turn of phrase and her invective against us, while vile in the extreme, was at the same time a wonder to hear for she never once repeated herself.

'Mrs Butler, ma'am, we're not the bailiffs nor anything near them, we're good Catholics like yourself, only come to try to help you,' Mr O'Donovan shouted over her own clamour, looking at me apologetically for labelling me as a Papist once more.

It took us a full ten minutes or more to calm the old woman down and when she finally understood that we were not the law come to throw her out and to tumble her cabin walls in with the battering ram she was as rapt in delight as she had been flaming in ire. She apologised for the things that she had said in anger at us, and then spent some minutes blessing us, once more without repetition, and beseeching the Lord for long and happy lives for us, his holy bounty on us and ours for countless generations to come.

At last Mr O'Donovan coaxed her out of her home to sit on a stool by the door and he asked her where her son John was that day. She replied that he was away working and she seemed to be turning to suspicion again.

'And what would yer honner be wantin' wit' him, the innocent wee lad?' she asked slyly, looking at Mr O'Donovan from the corner of her eye.

'I'm fully sure that he is innocent, Mrs Butler, but I wish that he was here. I want you to tell him something from me that may make his fortune, and yours. There is a sizeable reward out from the Dublin government for any valuable information leading to the arrest of those people who were responsible for the murder of the Sheas and your own son and his family. If John and yourself know anything at all about this crime, directly or indirectly, the reward, or a good part of it, will be yours. You can redeem your farm or move elsewhere, for the reward is a thousand pounds, as I'm sure you know already. Tell John that if he has knowledge of anything he must come forward to testify, for justice and for the memory of his brother if not for the money.'

'That has been put down to an accident long since, so it has,' the crone said craftily, looking down at her wrinkled, hardened hands joined in her lap.

'I know it was murder and so do you, ma'am, so let's not talk foolishness. It only remains for the culprits to be brought to justice.'

'I'm thinkin' that one wee lad like John couldn't do it on his own. There needs be two witnesses to prove a case, does there not, and John is on'y one and I know nothin' direct-like, and so I'd be as much use as udders on a bull,' she said, demurely. 'Not that wee John has anythin' to say or knows anythin' at all,' she added hastily.

Once again I was amazed at the depth of knowledge of the law and the rules of evidence that was possessed by the average Irish peasant. I'm quite sure that almost any legal problem could be solved over the course of an evening in any tavern in the country without the use of a professional attorney at all. She was quite correct: in Ireland the

Crown would need two independent witnesses to prove its case, unlike in England where a man could be stretched on the say-so of a single eye-witness. The authorities here had long ago divined that the temptation to put paid to a rival or someone who had caused a slight or had got the upper hand in a business deal, or who was owed money, by merely testifying against him in a court of law might prove too much for many of the Irish, and so they had wisely required corroboration from at least one other unrelated worthy before considering a case as proved.

'That is entirely correct. John cannot do it alone, but I am confident that we can obtain a second witness, or even more witnesses to the crime; and if we do he can then come forward – rest assured that he will be fully protected if he does. If he waits too long, he may lose his chance of the reward.'

'But he knows nothin', yer honner, I swear it,' she muttered.

We left the old lady then with her pledge to us that she would speak to no one of our visit but her son, although she said that it was pointless. We were confident that she would say nothing – not from her pledge, which likely meant nothing to her, but for fear of losing her second son to the killers, for they would no doubt silence anyone that they imagined could or would talk against them.

The next stop we made was back at our inn, for my master had not eaten for several hours. I was impertinent to note that to him and to remark that the current case was taking its toll on his girth. He was still a young man and fit as a butcher's dog, but he was fast approaching that point when a man's physical stature is decided for him for once and for all and he must begin to watch his intake of victuals or carry the consequences forever before him.

At his evening meal he acted as if he had just heard the gossip about young Ormond and had not been aware of the crime against the Sheas before. Oh, to be sure, he admitted that he had heard of it a good many months ago, but had not put it together with this area in his mind. He cornered Kelly in the taproom and quizzed him for every possible detail of the thing, interrupting often with comments and questions, many of which were inane or stupid. The landlord suffered his silly remarks with great patience, and when his friend Peter Maher arrived, he invited him to have a bumper and join in with the educating of the fine gentleman about the famous matter of the burning of the Sheas. I could see that Maher was anything but pleased at the topic for that night's conversation, and he said that the thing was a dreadful accident and was best forgotten and that the dead should be left to rest in peace. If he truly believed that, he was the only man or woman in the townland that did, I thought. He did sit down and listened to the landlord talk on and on about the tragedy, but he became more and more impatient and fidgety as he did so and eventually he rose and left the tavern after only one drink of whiskey.

Mary Kelly was in the room clearing and serving through their whole conversation, and Mr O'Donovan was very forthcoming with his cries of anguish as he 'heard' the details of the dead and their grisly end from her husband. He repeated the worst of these details aloud, repeating himself, followed by many's a 'God in heaven above, save us,' and the like. Once Maher's intimidating presence was removed from the room, he took his plan to the next stage. He exclaimed, purposefully, so that she could hear it, that if it was not an accident then those dastards who had perpetrated such a monstrosity would surely be damned forever and also those who assisted them – and even those who only knew of it but lay abed and did nothing that night – well, they too would roast in the fires of hell. He acted as if he was quite tipsy and said that if he had lost a dear relative in the fire, then he would not rest until he had brought the culprits to justice, regardless of the cost to himself and even at the loss of his own life. He actually had tears in his eyes and he slammed his fist down on the table in front of him to emphasise his point, spilling the two beakers of spirits that rested on it. Mary Kelly was near at hand when he said this, right behind him, clearing off another table and I saw her jump and then blench. She dropped her wooden tray with a clatter of dishes and cutlery on the floor.

Mr O'Donovan turned in surprise to face her and said, 'Sure isn't that as little as any genuine Christian could do, now isn't that so, would you not agree with me, Mrs Kelly, would you not say I was right?'

I had watched Mary Kelly throughout this last speech and saw that this direct question had a deep effect on her. I do not doubt it for a moment, for she ran crying from the room and through the kitchen door. No one else seemed to notice, much less to care, and a few minutes later I ventured in after her and found her huddled at the hearth, weeping into the apron gathered up in her hands.

'I'm sorry, ma'am,' I said, 'Oi only come in for to get a dipper of buttermilk, for I've an awful throat on me, so I have,' I explained.

She looked up at me, eyes red and streaming, and said, ''Tis over in the corner, Mr O'Toole, help yourself,'

'You're in distress, ma'am. Is there anythin' I can do fer ye?' I asked her.

'No, go away! What do you care about me? Go away now and leave me in peace.'

'Ma'am, I do hate to see a woman weepin'. Is there nothin' I can do, are ye sartain?'

She softened to me a little at that.

'I'm sorry, Shamey,' she said. 'I hold nothin' agin ye, but there is nobody can help me in this whole wide world and now I'm scared stiff of the next one, so I am,' and she commenced weeping again.

'Well, whatever's troublin' ye, what about the Lord above and the Blessed Virgin?' I asked, praying for forgiveness from my own God. 'Ye can always seek divoine help and forgiveness, can't ye?'

'Ach, you really are a good man, Shamey,' she replied without looking up at me. 'That wife and childer at home is lucky to have you, so they are. But I fear what I have in me heart is too much even for God and the Holy Family and all the angels and saints that ever was to forgive me, so that is that. I wished I was dead meself. Now please get your sup of buttermilk and leave me alone, I beg of you, there's a good man.'

I took a dip of the buttermilk, wiped the white moustache of it of on my sleeve like any peasant and left her again.

When I returned to the taproom I had to wait a few minutes until Kelly's much-abused bladder forced him to go out to the privy. I told Mr O'Donovan of the condition of Mary Kelly, and he was most impressed at the deep effect of his words on the woman. When Kelly returned, my master cleared out his glass, thanked the man for his company and said that he had some paperwork in his room to look after and bade him a very good night.

Once there, he penned a note on plain paper, writing the text of it in block print. He said it was for Mary Kelly and her alone and sent me off to see to its delivery, without myself being seen, mind you. I seemed to have been relegated to the position of invisible deliveryman since our visit to Tipperary had begun. I managed to pass Mary in the kitchen. She now seemed to be somewhat recovered. Probably she was afraid of others in the household seeing her in that condition and word of it getting out. The other maids were all working there again and in the crush, as they were telling me to get out and to leave the kitchen to the womenfolk, I managed to slip the note onto a corner of the long work-table before I left. Even as I quit the room, I heard one of the maids exclaim that there was a note there and then Mary Kelly stated that her own name was written upon the outside of it.

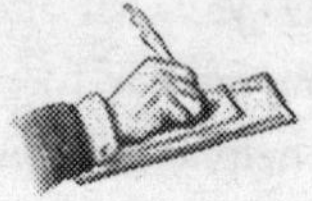

Then my employer decided that we had nothing to do until the night came upon us. We stayed in his room and played chess on the small wooden board with ivory men in red and white that he always brought with him on a journey. It was fortunate that he loved chess so much and not cards or dice, for chess I could play in good conscience, as there was no element of gambling about it at all. He lost two games to me before it was time to go. He was not at all inexpert at the game, but I had played it for a good many years longer than he had. Still, he was improving all the time, and it was becoming more difficult to best him.

At last he deemed it time to leave and I went and prepared the gig. I noticed Mary Kelly hurrying out along the west road as I walked over to the stable. I dawdled over my task as instructed by my master and when I drove along the road he bade me slow the horse, and over and over he cautioned me that we must not overtake the woman or even let her hear our horse's clip-clop behind her. Our destination was the house of the priest, Fr Rourke, which was also the destination of Mary Kelly, and we wished her to reach it and to enter well before us.

We went at a slow walk, and in the darkness we both heard a crack of noise and then the whirr of something passing between where I sat as driver and he reposed as passenger.

'A shot, Noble, I'm near sure of it. Get us moving at a good clip for a yard or two.'

I did as he asked and raced the gig for a hundred yards or more until he reached up and made me constrain our speed by grabbing and pulling me back by the shoulder.

'Mercy, sir, do you really think we were fired upon?'

'Yes, Noble. That was not a bee that buzzed between us but from the sound of the shot it came from a good way off. It was likely more in the line of a warning than anything else. We are being watched, I fear. Someone has seen us snooping about or in the company of Grimes.'

I went along the road after at a tremulous crawl, and I expected to feel the slap of a ball into my back at any minute. I looked back at my employer and he seemed to be sitting there as calm as a clocking hen.

Mary had evidently hurried along at a good pace and when we neared the Mass-house and the priest's cottage she was already inside. We left the gig some distance off and continued to the curate's door on foot. Once there, Mr O'Donovan did something totally out of his own character: he opened the door and we entered the house unbidden. In the short hallway we heard the voices of the priest and Mary Kelly, both speaking heatedly. Mr O'Donovan did not tarry to listen but opened the door and we burst into the priest's parlour.

The clergyman and the woman both started at the intrusion and looked over at us. The priest was incensed and said, 'What the devil do you mean by barging into a priest's house? You as a Catholic gentleman should know better, Mr O'Donovan. I am with a penitent and you must leave now, at once! This is a very private matter.'

The woman looked at us dumbstruck the whole time.

'No, and with all due respect, Fr Rourke, this is not a confessional in any of its forms, for how many times can this woman confess the same sin to you?' Mr O'Donovan said evenly.

'What sin?' Mary Kelly exclaimed, shaken from her stupor.

'The sin of omission at the very least, woman. You know who killed your cousin and the Sheas and you will not speak. That is a terrible enough thing in itself and if, as I suspect, you knew beforehand that it was to happen and did nothing to prevent it, then that is certainly a far greater sin, and under God's eyes you are as guilty of murder as is William Gorman and probably that fiend Black Peter Maher and his vicious minions as well. If my recollection of Catholic dogma is sound, you will not be forgiven that particular sin until you do all that you can to put the thing right.'

Those words had a remarkable effect on the woman. She collapsed onto the rushes that covered the hearth. She would have injured herself had my master and the priest not supported her in her fall. Together they put her into one of the priest's uncomfortable parlour chairs.

'Who told you anything of William Gorman?' she asked very fearfully, when she had recovered a little.

'Never mind that. I know that he was behind it all. It was carried out at his request and I have another witness in reserve to prove it. My God, woman, the whole countryside must know that Gorman was behind the thing. If I bring a case against Maher and Gorman and then tell everyone about that you knew of their plans – no, don't look at your priest, for he didn't tell me anything; I surmised it from the reaction of the priest in Fethard – if I tell that you knew beforehand, then you, Mary, will be a pariah in the land. You could no more continue keeping your inn hereabouts or even living here than if you were a rotting leper.'

'But I tell you, and I've told Fr Rourke often enough, that I cannot tell a thing, for my life would be in grave danger. I would lose everything.'

'What does it profit a man if he gain the whole world and lose his soul?' I quoted from behind them, using my normal clipped northern tones and all heads turned to me in surprise.

The priest exclaimed, 'Exactly! Well said, sir. Now, Mary, I have been after you for months to do the right thing. The burden of this is killing me and I fear that I will go mad if the thing is not resolved.'

The woman had begun to weep by now.

'And, Mary, what type of life will you have if you remain silent?' my master said to her, in more reasoned, gentler tones. 'Would it be worth living? I ask you, is your burden lessening with the passage of time or is it worsening? Tell me the truth. They say time is a great healer, but for your wounds there can be no healing; they will only continue to putrefy unless you take some action.'

Mary Kelly, sitting there, sniffling, said, 'You're right, sur. You know, I nearly feel worse over it now than I did at the start, worse than I did a month ago. Lord, what am I to do at all at all?' She began to wail anew, rocking her body back and forth on the chair.

'You must come forward, my child, you must,' the priest intoned and put his hand on her shoulder.

And eventually, after a great deal more prodding and tears and my master reminding her that young Harold Ormond had been the twenty-second victim of the fire that killed the Sheas, and that another innocent man was to be arrested for the crime, she agreed to act. She swore on her life that she would come forward and she told us the whole sorry tale of what had happened to the Sheas, and it brought us almost halfway to the dawn before she had finished and Mr O'Donovan had done with his questioning of her on it. She agreed to go the next morning with us and the priest to the home of the local magistrate, a Captain Despard, and there to make a formal statement before him.

Then we drove back to the Kellys' inn together, to pass the time until the day had reached a decent enough hour for a visit to one of His Majesty's magistrates. As we drove off with Mary in the deep darkness of the middle of the night, we did not know it but we had been observed in her company and the news of our strange threesome was on the way to where our observer owed his true allegiance.

Mary Kelly had brightened considerably after her admission and solemn promise to testify. She was greatly fatigued by now and said that she felt like sleeping for the first time in a long while, and so she went to her chamber immediately upon our halting at the door of the inn. We went to my master's chamber and spoke together for a little while.

'Your note to Mary Kelly obviously summoned her to the priest's home, on his behalf,' I ventured.

'Exactly, Noble. There is little of hard evidence to be seized on in this case, so I knew we had to use the weapons of the mind. We both realised that Mary Kelly had to be moved if the case is ever to be solved. We had to get her to come forward, without getting her killed for her pains. I needed first of all to get her well and truly upset by bringing up the case on top of the latest news from Fethard, and by my ranting about justice and punishment for the miscreants, the killers of my relatives and the duties of a true Christian. When I judged that she was at the breaking point, I still had to get her away from the inn and any support that she might feel that she had here. I could think of no better place to face her than in front of her confessor, who, as we are well aware, has been after her for months to speak up. He did have the cork in the bottle somewhat loosened up for us, I think, and so we were able to obtain this successful result from our efforts. No doubt there will be others to come forward now, for I find that the silence in these small villages is not unlike the stemmed flow of a river – once even a small hole is made in the obstruction then the water cannot be held back for long and the dam is doomed.'

I quizzed my master about this man Gorman, and he reminded me that there had been two tenants dispossessed by old Lord Ormond to enrich the Sheas as part of their pact with him over his son and the young Shea girl. Grimes had said as much. The two dispossessed tenants were William Gorman and Charlie Lynch. On discreet enquiry in the taproom that evening, Mr O'Donovan had determined that old Charlie Lynch had been a bachelor and a recluse all his life and that he had died broken down in the workhouse before the burning of the Sheas had taken place. Moreover, Mr O'Donovan had learned from the priest in their private conference during our second visit that William Gorman was known locally for his great spite and vile temper, and had, since his eviction, been living with his large family in greatly reduced circumstance, almost as a slave-labourer, on his elder brother's farm. On hearing his name, my master was at once reminded of the letters on the fragment of flagstone in the Sheas' ruined house: ORM. He realised that it was part of the name *Gorman* and had nothing in the world to do with the Ormond family, and so this Gorman became his main suspect from that time on. He had also surmised that Peter Maher and his henchmen were deeply involved, and were likely the actual machinery of the murders. Part of his reasoning was that Peter Maher was a great frequenter of Mary Kelly's shebeen, but apparently William Gorman was not. He had gently quizzed the drunken Mr Kelly on that on our return from the second visit to Fr Rourke. He asked Kelly about a distant cousin of his own father's named William Gorman who might live about the area of Slievenamaun, and he was told that there was bad blood between the Kellys and Gorman. It was all over the latter having taken a great umbrage at being ejected from their shebeen for obstreperous behaviour several years earlier. The Kellys had never liked him and there had been a bloody fist fight. By all accounts Gorman had been properly 'seen off', for apparently Mr Kelly was not so far gone down into the bottle at that time and was still handy with those great fists of his, and I could just picture them swinging at the end of those long, thick arms.

Therefore, my master reasoned, if Gorman was the instigator of the killings, from a misguided revenge at having been dispossessed for the benefit of the Sheas, and if Mary Kelly had advance information of any plans for a raid against the unfortunates, then she had to have it from someone other than William Gorman. Also, because of the bad blood that was already between them, she would not have been so reticent about informing on Gorman – she would not have feared him enough to stay silent. Peter Maher, however, was the most infamous of the local bully boys, and because of that and his behaviour at the mention of the crime, Mr O'Donovan figured him for the criminal who, with Gorman or on his behalf, caused the horrible murders to be done. All the circumstances pointed to Mary Kelly having had her information from Peter Maher himself, and he had also learned that Maher was reputed to have been the woman's paramour at one time. Now my employer added the proviso that those two points were, due to a lack of real evidence, merely reasoned supposition on his part, but as each of those suppositions supported the other then he believed them to be true.

He was to be proven to be correct on every point.

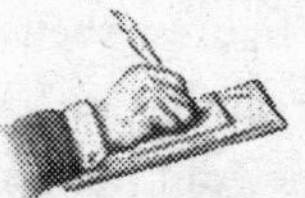

I went off to my own bed up in the shed loft and Mr O'Donovan said that he would rest a while as well, for it had been a long day. Though fatigued, I could not sleep for some reason, and I have been thankful ever since that I could not, for I was able to smell the smoke from the burning of my building before it killed me. I went down the ladder like a flash – thankfully I had not undressed – and I was out in the yard in seconds and could see that the whole roof of my former bedchamber was ablaze. I ran about shouting out 'Fire, fire!' and soon I had roused the whole population of the main house. People began to issue from the building and they rushed over to the burning out-office, but for what purpose I could not say, for they made no move to extinguish the flames nor had they even any means at their disposal to do so. One man did get a single wooden bucket from somewhere. He filled it at the horse trough and he threw a few buckets full up at the burning thatch but without any beneficial effect for his throw never reached anywhere near the orange blaze on the roof. The rest and myself stood helplessly by and watched the roof burn and begin to sag and collapse.

It was only then that it occurred to me – I must have been groggy – that this latest, mysterious fire was surely a ruse to get the able-bodied men of the house out into the yard, for I saw no way that the blaze on the roof could have started other than by being set alight on purpose. There was no fire in the building nor the means of setting one and it was too far from the main house and its chimney stacks to have been sparked from there.

Then I saw big Mr Kelly out there, near to me, swaying about, huffing and puffing, exhorting the assembled to save his shed, but I did not see his wife and I instinctively became alarmed for her safety. I looked back across the yard just then and by the light from the flickering fire I saw three figures, their shadows long on the white wall, enter the front door of the inn. They were grown men, fully dressed in dark clothes. They did not have the aspect of people who had hastily donned their coats over night clothes and so I knew that they were not of the regular household.

By this time some of Kelly's people had roused themselves at his urging and had entered the shed with the blazing roof and were throwing anything that might be saved from the lower floor out into the yard. I saw a single hames land at my feet and I picked it up for a weapon and it had all the aspect of a primitive war club in my hand. I dashed as fast as my old legs would carry me across the yard and into the house after the three interlopers. I went directly through the dimness of the taproom and the kitchen and on into the family's quarters, and I could hear a commotion already taking place within. The door to the room from which the noise was emanating was wide open and I ran over to it and looked inside. By the dim light from the room's fireplace I could see the three dark interlopers standing with their backs to me and I could also see Mary Kelly, already out of bed, pressed into the far corner of the room. I could tell that the men were masked in the lower parts of their faces and all were armed, one with a pistol and the other two with knives and cudgels. I have no doubt but that Mary Kelly would been a dead woman already but for one thing: my master was standing between her and her would-be assailants. He was facing them, armed with his blackthorn stick and his small flintlock pocket pistol. The leader of the men seemed to be the one with the pistol and he was screaming at Mr O'Donovan to stand aside, as they had only come for the woman and wanted no trouble with him. In spite of the masks and the dim light in the room, I could easily tell by his stature and his voice that their leader was Peter Maher.

Mary Kelly screamed when she heard those words from his lips and at that the three men moved toward her and Mr O'Donovan. It was then that I came fully into the room behind them swinging my hames at the head of the man nearest to me and screaming as loud as I could. I caught him a resounding blow across the side of the skull and I still recall that the brass knob on the butt end of the hames made a wonderful noise on the villain's close-cropped head.

He uttered not a sound but fell down directly and I turned my attention to the next man who had swung around already to face me and parried my next blow with his own cudgel in a most expert fashion. I realised at once that I was up against an experienced stick fighter and I retreated well out of range of his club. At the same time I saw Maher raise his pistol to the firing position and my master brought up his own little pistol and fired at once, without seeming to even take aim. Maher's big gun went off almost immediately after. The noise in that enclosed space was deafening, and the room was immediately filled with sulphurous white smoke. But Maher had been hit by my master's pistol ball somewhere in the upper body and his arm was useless and falling again when he discharged his weapon, and his shot did no damage to anything but the planks of the floor. Although solidly hit he was not silent, and he cursed loudly. He turned, even shot through as he was, and ran from the room. My opponent wisely broke off our tentative engagement and followed after him, taking one last wide swipe at me with his club as he went. His final blow at the full length of his arm unfortunately hit me hard across the right forearm and I yowled loudly and dropped my hames. I feared that he had broken my wrist. I went down on one knee and howled again with pain for after the initial numbing shock it was quite an agonising wound. Mr O'Donovan was at my side in a flash and asked me if I had been stabbed. In the firelight I could see that his face was most earnest and showed his concern for me, but when I explained that I had only received a belt from a club on my arm his concern for me ended abruptly.

Soon after some others of the household came in, for they had heard the shots and big Kelly was first among them and was asking what in blazes had happened under his roof and why we were in his wife's bedchamber. Mr O'Donovan bade all leave but ourselves and the Kellys, and as he trussed the remaining and still unconscious assassin up like a hen being prepared for a flit, he explained the scene briefly to the big man. He told him about his wife's testimony, which was to be given against Maher and the others, and said that somehow Maher had learned of it or guessed at it. It was very likely he was having her watched, for her behaviour must have been odd for many months, and he had finally come here to do away with her while everyone else was at the fire. My employer guessed that the last visit to the priest's house and Mary Kelly coming away with us must have been the final circumstance that impelled him to action.

Mr O'Donovan had been wide awake and sitting in the dark of his chamber with a loaded gun in his lap when I called out my alarum about the blaze, and he had rushed immediately to Mary Kelly's room rather than to the outside with the rest, for he felt sure that it was a ruse to get at her with no one about. He was expecting as much after my tale of the watcher I saw at the Sheas' cabin and the bullet fired at us in the night. He had arrived in her chamber just before the three ruffians and it was a good thing for the poor woman that he had been so suspicious of the fire. He later admitted to me that he had made a bad miscalculation. He had reckoned that Maher would make any attempt to put paid to Mary Kelly on his own. When he had arrived with his two vicious thugs behind him, my master had greatly feared for the outcome. He was extremely relieved to see me arriving 'like an avenging angel', swinging my club and roaring. He said that I had undoubtedly saved his life that night by my alertness and game readiness to enter the fray. I admit that I relished his words of praise far more than I should have, for that leads certainly to pridefulness, and that is one of the seven deadly sins.

Her husband damned Maher for a duplicitous rogue and was at a loss to explain how the man could come night after night to their hospitality and then try to kill a defenceless woman in cold blood. He vowed to choke the life out of his very body if he ever came within his reach again.

'I think that he is closer to the reach of the Almighty and his just judgement than to your long arms at this time, Mr Kelly,' said my master. 'It is dark in here, but I believe that I put my shot into a vital place and the wound will soon carry him off.'

In that statement he was likely right, for Black Peter Maher was never seen or heard from again and either he somehow healed and escaped from the country to America or elsewhere or he crawled off into some private mossy hideout and died alone, to rot where he lay. In either event it was definitely a case of 'good riddance to bad rubbish'.

The next morning a party descended on the manor house of Captain Despard, the magistrate. There was myself and Mr O'Donovan, of course, and both Mr and Mrs Kelly as well as the priest, Fr Rourke, all packed into the trap. Mr O'Donovan purposely sent no word to Grimes as to the true denouement of the case, for he had decided the man should be allowed as much time as possible to dig his own grave with his rabid fixation on the guilt of Lord Ormond. He was of the opinion that it was a just enough punishment for his hounding to death of the younger lord.

The magistrate had just breakfasted when we arrived, and on hearing the seriousness of our purpose, he bade us all enter his study. Mary Kelly told all in her own words and I was given the task, because of my ability to write very quickly, in spite of my much bruised and bandaged but otherwise whole wrist, of putting it down on paper. I have a copy of it before me as I write, but I will tell the story to you in my own words, for the poor woman was nervous and rambled and repeated herself and still left important things out.

William Gorman was an undertenant of Lord Ormond's estate. That was the lowest place in the numerous gradations of tenure into which almost every field in the land is divided and subdivided and subdivided again, almost *ad infinitum*, into patches too ludicrously small to be termed fields at all. The farther the undertenant is from the overall landlord, the heavier the weight with which the oppression falls on the occupier of the soil. The owner presses his lease, the lessee comes down on the tenant, who comes down on the undertenant and he on his own undertenant, and so, in this long concatenation of vassalage, the lowest man is made to suffer the most. He is, to use an expression from the great Lord Clare, 'ground to fine powder' by this complicated system of exaction.

William Gorman was dealt with most severely and abruptly by his lord in order to give his lease to the Sheas. He was distrained, sued in the superior courts, processed by civil bill – in short the whole machinery of the law was put against him. Driven from his home and his few fields, he made an appeal to Peter Maher, whose gang were wont to masquerade as some sort of league of peasants, although they were not Whiteboys or Thrashers at all but only common brigands. Gorman claimed that by accepting his stolen lease the Sheas had infringed against the 'statutes of the league' and that an exemplary and appalling vengeance should be taken of them. They must have been mad, all of them, to even consider the scope of what they did.

It was determined that their plot should be carried to completion on the night of Monday the twentieth of November. On the preceding Saturday Peter Maher went to the Kellys and secreted himself in a kitchen corner, where he busied himself in melting lead and casting pistol balls at the fire. Mary Kelly had heard all the public-house talk and rumours that some people about the area were determined to inflict summary justice on the Sheas and, being well aware that Maher was more than likely to be involved, for he had a vicious and cruel repute, and seeing him making bullets, she faced him with her suspicions and begged him not to take away life so needlessly. He laughed and answered her most equivocally, a true skill of the Irish peasant rogue.

During the course of that day, young Catherine Mullally, extremely heavy with child but a most happy lass, came to visit her cousin Mary. Peter Maher knew the young woman, indeed he had known her since she was a mere infant. He had the rude gallantry which is common among many of the men of the Irish peasantry and he engaged her in conversation. He knew that she was then residing with her husband at the home of the Sheas and he quizzed her gently about them. He had information already that there was a fair number of able-bodied persons living there with a view to defending the place, for Patrick Shea knew well he was in grave danger, and so Maher wanted to find out what serviceable firearms were in the house. How well armed the house was would determine the gang's course of action, you see. It is most probable and a great piece of irony that if there had been no arms to speak of in the place then the ruffians would merely have broken into the house in the dead of night, dragged Patrick Shea out into his yard and shot him dead, sparing all the others in the cabin.

Maher cajoled Catherine Mullally and joked and jibed with her for a while. The young woman was pleased with his attention and in her innocence, having no suspicion of him, gradually disclosed that there was a quantity of firearms in the house, loaded, primed and constantly ready for use. As she was leaving, she being big and encumbered, Maher actually put on her cloak for her, kissed her cheek and bade her farewell in the warmest tones of friendship. Mary Kelly had guessed at the reasons for his asking so many questions of poor gullible Catherine. After the girl had left, for she dared not speak in her presence, Mary begged and implored Maher, no matter what he intended to do – for she cared not a farthing for Patrick Shea – not to harm Catherine Mullally or her husband in any way. She finally extracted a solemn promise from him to that effect, and he left her with his new ammunition and his new information.

By the next day, however, and after due reflection, her alarm for the safety of her relative, to whom she was much attached, revived itself and that day her suspicions were increased by the signs of preparation which she observed between Maher and his confederates when they came to drink at her home. She dared not speak out, however, for in her own phrase, a wrong word or even a look would have been as much as her life was worth.

She was deathly afraid for her cousin's welfare by this time and knew no peace that day nor on the Monday. Late on Monday night when her husband, who knew nothing about the whole thing, was asleep in drink, she rose, put a coat over her night shift and left her abode. It was about midnight and she had advanced cautiously along the hedges of the fields until she approached Maher's own cabin. She hoped to find him home and alone, for she intended to use what sway she still might have had with him to ensure the safety of her young relative. But she stopped in the shadows near by, for she could hear the voices of many men gathered in Maher's hut. They seemed to be in some heated discussion, but at length the door opened and a large group came out. She hid in some brambles, squatting down so as to avoid being seen, and she marked the murderers in the light of the cabin door as they emerged. They all came out bearing arms and walked off into the night in a single file. Eight of them she knew and recognised from their voices and looks. One of them carried a piece of turf speared on a broken-shafted pitch fork, lighted at both ends and kept alive by his blowing breath.

They passed her without observation and proceeded on their dreadful journey to the cabin of the Sheas. She followed their retreating backs, trembling and terror-struck. She trailed after them from hedge to hedge and, seeing that they were in fact heading for the Sheas and nowhere else, she stopped at a spot from which their house was clearly visible. She waited there in great fear for the fracas to begin. She expected to witness the death of Patrick Shea, dragged from his home and butchered. She was shocked when she suddenly heard the sound of heavy hammering and then saw that a fire had started on the roof of the Sheas' long cabin. The wind was very brisk that night and the small patch of fire was rapidly fanned into a high flame and soon the whole roof was ablaze. It lit up the surrounding glen and enabled her to see all that occurred about the house as if it were daylight. The sounds of screams, shrieks and pleas for mercy began to emanate from the burning building, as the murderers had hammered and fixed the door shut with spikes so that it could not be moved. Far from them being moved to pity by the pleading voices from within, they answered the invocations of their victims with yells of insults and with ferocious laughter and war-whoops of exultation. When they heard the sound of the loaded weapons in the house being set off by the flames, they fired their own muskets and blunderbusses into the air in triumph.

Then they fell silent and in the stillness of the night Mary could still hear the low, muffled shouts, then the screams and agonised groans of the dying. The killers laughed again and started to shout imprecations at those perishing within once more and fired off their guns again, which was a foolish thing, as it brought unwanted attention to them. On the opposite side of the hill which adjoined the house, there resided a man by the name of Phillip Dillon who was friendly enough to the Sheas. Hearing the sound of musketry and coming outside his own abode to see the sky lit up from a great fire, he summoned all the men he could from his cabin; and, arming themselves, they set off across the brow of the hill to assist their neighbours. They advanced towards the house but arrived too late to be of any use, as they lacked the courage to attack the murderers, who had drawn up between themselves and the burning house with their arms at the ready. Phillip Dillon stood off and defied them to come on and fight in the open glen, but they declined the challenge and awaited his onslaught. Dillon's faction were inferior in both numbers and weaponry, however, and did not dare attack the assassins, as to do so they would have to cross the fire-lit yard. They stood impotently facing the others as the house burned and the groans of the dying eventually ceased altogether. Mary said the whole thing took at least a half an hour from first spark to the last moan.

Although the arrival of Dillon and his cohorts did not serve to save any of the Sheas, it still provided the means of convicting William Gorman. Among their number was young John Butler, the half-brother of Mullally. The youngster was in the employ of Dillon at the time and was sleeping at his house. The poor boy knew well that his brother and his young wife must be in the Sheas' house that night and even though he could not help them he worked his way as close to Maher and his band as he could by a flanking movement and was able to identify both Maher and William Gorman with absolute certainty. He later testified in open court, at Mr O'Donovan's urging, and provided the necessary corroboration of the evidence given by Mary Kelly. He identified Gorman, who, with no Peter Maher about, was not a danger to him, by boldly facing him and placing the black rod on his shoulder.

Mary told us that that night, after the roof had collapsed on the silenced victims, Maher, Gorman and their associates left the scene of the atrocity and went back to Maher's hut by the route they had come. They travelled as if they were kings abroad in the land, fearing no one, and took no trouble to hide themselves. They reckoned that by their strength of numbers and Gorman and Maher's repute for violence and viciousness, none would speak their names to the authorities. Once again they passed close by where Mary Kelly was in hiding and so she had another opportunity of identifying them all. She said that as they walked along the conversation of the murderers turned to the doings of the night and she heard William Gorman amusing the party by mimicking the groans and pleas of the dying, and mocking the agonies which he had inflicted.

As dawn broke Mary returned to her own abode, shaken to the core by what she had seen. Well aware of the consequences of any disclosure, she said not a word of it to her husband. She was in fact questioned by the local captain of police before a magistrate because of the ill fame of herself and her household and the nearness of her home to the scene of the outrage, but she declared herself to be totally ignorant of the crime and innocent in the matter.

I should note here that John Butler, who also did not speak out against the murderers of his brother and his family, had been enjoined by his mother not to do so, lest he and she should suffer the same fate as his brother and the Sheas.

The killers were right in their confidence of immunity, for in the intervening year and a half no information at all was communicated to the government. Mary Kelly was keeping silent and did not even dare to reproach Maher about the death of her cousin whose life he had promised to spare. She knew that he was aware of her knowledge about the matter and she feared that he would finally take the notion to make himself safer from prosecution and the hemp by eliminating her altogether. She kept well in with him, she waited on him at table and forced herself to smile at him as if nothing at all had happened, and she tried to live as normally as she had before, but a vivid recollection of the frightful events never left her. She was leading two lives. She said that she actually came to fear her own bed, for any sleep she got was haunted by the spectre of her dead kinswoman. She told us that she felt as if Catherine was lying beside her in her bed holding her child as 'black as a coal' in her charred arms.

She went to her local priest and even to the priest in Fethard to seek absolution and they both comforted her but pressed her to come forward and to see the culprits punished. She had resisted this through her great fear, until she was shamed into it by circumstances and by my master's manipulation of her mind and her innermost feelings.

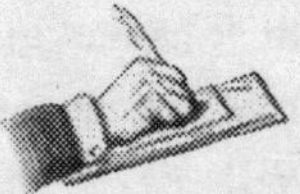

To do the local people some small justice I must say that after their own compliant silence of near two years they felt a universal horror at the definite guilt of Gorman and his associates and held no resentment against Mary Kelly and John Butler for their testimonies on behalf of the Crown. Those two shared the government reward, and young Butler was able to ransom his mother's leasehold and to add to it substantially. He later became a successful large farmer and a representative of the Catholic Committee in the area. Mr O'Donovan and I have corresponded with him and met with him in that regard many times over the intervening years and I can only say that he turned out to be a very sound man.

Mary Kelly used her portion of the reward in a much different fashion. She abruptly ran off from Kelly in the company of a handsome young agricultural lad, to set up house – and what kind of house you may well imagine – in the north end of the city of Dublin. Needless to say, she prospered, the vile woman, although my employer seemed to have gained a certain respect for her, and I never recall him saying a bad word about her.

William Gorman was arrested by an abashed and quite nervous Grimes, under a special warrant signed by Captain Despard. Even that was touch and go – I mean whether Grimes would comply, for Robert Peel had set up the Irish police not as a civil force but almost as a military organisation and they were very independent of the local magistrates and answered only to their Dublin headquarters. My master advised Grimes not to make matters worse for himself and to carry out the magistrate's warrant or face serious consequences from the Chancellor's office. When Grimes read my report of Mary Kelly's testimony he was forced to admit defeat, even to himself. His face a sickly grey now and with a shine of perspiration about his thin upper lip, the man knew his back was to the wall.

My master and I prevailed upon his new weakness to let us be in at the kill. We arrived in force at the shanty of Gorman's brother, where we found the culprit in a sound and drunken sleep. We had been quick about our business and he had no warning of our activities of the night before. I think that Mr O'Donovan was correct and Peter Maher was permanently out of commission and so unable or unwilling to warn his co-conspirator of the danger he was in. The wretch was dragged cursing and screaming from the hovel by four of Grimes's largest constables, bound fast in a cart, and brought to a cell in Fethard. The other assassins that Mary Kelly and John Butler could both identify were sought by the police and some four were taken in their homes, but, by late on the next morning, word of the new developments in the case was spread far abroad and the others were able to run off into the hills and, no doubt, make their way out of the country.

My master made a point of attending the trial of William Gorman and the other killers that the police could lay their hands on at the next assizes in Clonmel and he insisted that I accompany him as he put it, 'to see the risen loaf come out of the Bastable'.

I should note that by the time of the trial Sergeant Edmund Grimes had been dismissed from the constabulary in disgrace. He had caused a great embarrassment to the authorities in Dublin and London and to old Lord Ormond, whom he had nearly caused to be arrested on a false charge after hounding the man's only son to death. My master did all in his power to see that the arrogant prig was universally blamed for the suicide of the young lord and he became a pariah wherever he went. I eventually lost track of him, but I believe that he went out to India in some minor position with the East India Company. May the Good

Lord have mercy on our Indian brethren, if he wasn't soon carried off by some deadly and horrible disease of the tropics.

The case against Gorman was ably prosecuted by Sergeant Blackburne, a famous king's counsel in his day, and, based on the testimony of Mary Kelly and John Butler, the villainous William Gorman was found guilty of murder and was duly hanged along with his cronies, and if you ask me there never was a man who deserved topping more than that foul beast. Although it was normally very much against my nature, I made sure that I was present at his hanging, but let me say that I went, not from any sense of blood-thirst, but only to see for myself a great evil being excised from the world. None missed him that I know about and I suspect that even his own wife and children saw his end as a blessed relief.

THE MURDER OF DANIEL MARA

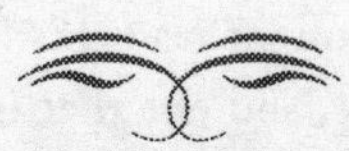

'Guilty, yer honner, I mane, my lord, we find the defendant, Patrick Grace, guilty of the wilful murder of Mr James Chadwick.'

The nervous foreman of the jury read these words to a hushed and tension-filled courtroom. Then, as the import of the words struck home, the chamber erupted into a cacophony of sounds, human and inhuman, shouts of dismay and various expressions of deeply felt grief and howling rage. My master looked over to where I sat in the public gallery and shrugged his shoulders slightly; by his eyes I could tell that he was very dejected and disheartened at the defeat, more saddened than I had ever seen him before at a reversal of his courtroom fortunes.

I apologise to any who might read this for my beginning this entry with such a dramatic scene, and one that is a fair way out of its place in the normal scheme of the story I intend to tell, but it is a new style which I am considering the use of. I must confess that I have recently forsaken my beloved Greeks, Thucydides, Herodotus and Xenophon and their noble kindred, for the writings of some of the 'sensational fictions' of our more modern scribes. At first my natural bent as a reader of the classics struggled mightily against these works but now I must further confess that I have come to enjoy them. Most of these books take the form of adventures and narratives of high crime and some are translations from French writers, which at times can only be described as salacious in the extreme. I defend my use of them, to myself, by claiming that I am perusing them for the sake of their style of language and their method of keeping a reader's attentions and in putting their stories out in a more entertaining, more thought-provoking if a somewhat more disorderly fashion. Telling a thing as it happens, in a linear form, seems anathema to them.

That is why I have set off this story as above but I fear that by outlining my new stratagem I have now squandered the effect of it, similarly as the jest of a witty man tends to lose all its humour when it has to be explained by him to some attendant dullard. You will see from the above that the maxim 'you cannot teach an old dog new tricks' is one that can certainly be applied to me.

In the spring of 1827 we were working in Dublin, although to be truthful we were doing less and less *bona fide* legal work and more and more toil on behalf of the Catholic Association, the successor to the old Catholic Board. As the struggle for Catholic Emancipation seemed poised to come to a successful conclusion, my master and I had been working, in concert with many others in the movement, to prepare the land and the people for it. We both looked forward to the day when Catholics in the kingdom could take their place as full members of society, unhampered or restricted by the last of the country's heinous Penal Laws.

I well recall the day on which we first met with young Alice Grace. A fine-boned and pretty young lady approached us one Wednesday at about ten in the morning, just as we arrived. Evidently she had been waiting for some time and had attracted a fair amount of attention, for many were staring at her as she stood demurely waiting by a large pillar. Now it was not an unusual thing to see those of the gentler sex in our precinct, but never alone, and a decent one would never be seen there unchaperoned, so a young, well-dressed, respectable-looking female alone in the rotunda of the Four Courts was a most startling thing.

The first words that she said to my master – she seemed somehow to know him at once – were, 'For the sake of God, Mr O'Donovan, you must come to Clonmel and save my poor foolish brother, for if you don't I fear that they will soon be hanging an innocent boy.'

As she finished this remarkable introduction of herself to our ken she seemed to weaken and I feared that she was about to keel over. I dropped my writing satchel and supported her arm. She smiled her thanks at me wanly and turned her pretty doe eyes up to my master once again in a pleading fashion, and a large tear, as lovely as a pearl, rolled down her right cheek.

My master is ever a man of great generosity of feeling and he assisted me in bringing the young lady to a private room in the building where we could find out more about her and her extraordinary claim. I remarked to myself that he was not mumbling his usual 'waste of time' and 'I can't be bothered with this' and 'more important things to do' as we went down the hallway in search of sanctuary. When she was seated and had collected herself a little, the young lady apologised for her behaviour and told us her name.

'I am Miss Alice Grace, sir, and I am the sister of a young man falsely accused of murder in Tipperary. I have come here to seek your help in averting a grievous wrong.'

From her clothing and the tones of her speech I would have put her at somewhere much above the run-of-the-mill peasantry and yet lower than the lowest rungs of the social ladder occupied by the various degrees of our self-styled country gentry. She was educated, from her clear use of the language, and I would have guessed that her parents had managed to send her for some years to a convent school of sorts. That would indicate that they had some money or at the least an uncle who was a Romish priest. She was dressed in a good and modest outfit that appeared nearly new. It was a rich dark green hue with a bit of white lace about its high collar which set off her slender, pale neck and fair straight hair, which she had partially covered in a black lace mantilla in the Spanish style. She had a very pretty face and I reckoned, as she was unmarried, that she would have had no end of suitors in her barony; from my knowledge of the practice among the Papists of marrying very early, and from the fact that she was at least twenty years old, I knew that she had, so far, been sensibly choosy in regard to them.

'I am Ambrose O'Donovan, but you already know that and this is my able clerk, Mr Noble Alexander, Miss ... er ... Grace. My, but you came to us in a tempest, didn't you just, and you have put the cart squarely before the horse, for we know nothing at all about your brother's situation and we can promise no help until we hear more from you.'

I could tell that my master was more than a little intrigued by her approach, as we usually learned of such cases from some hoary old solicitor who was attempting to interest my master in the matter on behalf of one of his unfortunate clients. I could also tell that he was quite taken with the young lady herself, for he was looking at her fine face in a most frank and admiring way. Now, please do not mistake me and think that my master was in the least a rake or a letch for he was far from it. His dear wife, Ellen, was still among the living at that time, although grown worse with her wasting malady and bedridden for much of the day, but he was always devoted to her in every way. He was human, however, and looked favourably upon beauty and that, combined with his sympathetic nature, gained this young woman his attention where many had been spurned lately because he was too preoccupied with other more important things.

'I am pleased to meet you, Mr Alexander, sir,' she said, giving me her gloved hand and smiling at me again. She made me regret my habitual bachelorhood if only for a short time.

'I apologise to you for the manner of my approach, but I have travelled far and quickly to see you. I arrived on the night mail coach from Clonmel and I have come directly here without refreshing myself and so I beg your forgiveness for any disarray in my appearance,' she said.

I looked at her golden hair combed back tightly under its lacy covering and contrived into an ingenious bun at the back and at her cool-looking, immaculate alabaster skin and wished that every female was in such a state of disarray, but of course I said nothing.

'Think nothing of it, my dear girl,' Mr O'Donovan said. 'You appear to have a great deal more trouble in your young life than myself and my decrepit old friend here, at the moment anyway.'

The girl was obviously made less nervous by his gentle manner towards her and began her sad tale for us.

'The whole unfortunate thing began at the very start of this past April. A man was murdered in broad daylight at Rath Cannon, near to my home. He was a Mr James Chadwick, the land agent for his own family's interests in my area. The Chadwicks are substantial landowners, but they all live across in England save him – or he did live in Ireland, until he was shot and killed. My poor brother Patrick was arrested by Mr Doherty, the magistrate, and he now faces a capital charge. There is said to be much evidence against him, but we do not know what it is nor what it can be for he is innocent of the killing. We have been told that because of the danger to them the witnesses against him must be held in protection until the trial. When we complained of that, Mr Doherty threatened to have the local military commander invoke martial law and have my brother hanged after a drumhead court martial. We could not allow that to happen to Patrick. He has always been a good boy, a blessing to my parents and my other brothers and sisters and he is only twenty years old. Ah, Mr O'Donovan, I see that you have already guessed my own age and yes he is my twin. He has always had a noble heart, if much too ready for what he imagines to be patriotic deeds. He lives much of his life in books describing the olden days before the coming of the Sassenach and has been far more active than he should have been with the local league of tenants. The truth be said, we have little in common with those people, for we are comfortable on our own farm, which is larger than most, and we are not even tenants, for my father holds our land in fee simple.'

I interrupt her tale here to point out that I had already assessed the girl as intelligent and this was confirmed by the fact that she anticipated our unasked question as to her age and that of her brother and that she knew at least something of the law of real property and the various methods of holding it. There was not a belle in a ball in Dublin who would have known as much, I would bank on it.

'My brother may be a hot-head, Mr O'Donovan, I'm the first to admit it, and he may think himself a great patriot, but he did not kill Mr Chadwick.'

'And how can you be so certain of that, my dear?' Mr O'Donovan asked her gently.

'Why, because he told me so,' she answered innocently, as if shocked at his query.

'But, Miss Grace, it has been my experience, and please do not take this in the least amiss, but my friend Noble here will back me on this, that persons in deadly situations do not always speak the truth, even to family members. I have seen men hanged who were as guilty as sin and yet whose families to this day aver their total innocence, in the face of any amount of evidence, simply because the condemned claimed it.'

My master had been indelicate in talking of hanged men, I realised it as he spoke, and the young lady displayed deep emotion to us, losing her composure for the first time.

'Oh, Mr O'Donovan, he must not be allowed to hang, not poor Paddy, it would kill my parents. But I believe he is innocent not for any purely familial reasons or from a misplaced loyalty to him, but because we are so close, we are twins and it is as if we are the same person in two separate bodies. I do not know if you can understand this but we think with the same mind and we feel with the same heart. I would know in an instant if he was being untruthful to me. It has always been so, for I cannot ever deceive him and he cannot deceive me either. We even feel each other's pain, and now I feel as if I am locked in cell under Clonmel courthouse, suffocating there with him.'

'Well, when is his trial set to start?' my master asked after a moment of thought.

'It has already started, sir, nearly a week ago,' she answered, apologetically.

That knocked my master back on his heels for once and I'll admit that I took some brief pleasure in seeing it for it was a rare thing.

'Then he already has a brief acting for him, surely,' he said, when he had recovered.

'He did have, a Mr Braithwaite, one of your Dublin Englishmen set up to practise in Clonmel. He opened the case for my brother, he was willing to take it on for money, where most of the rest wouldn't touch it, Catholic nor Protestant. As you can imagine, the killing of a land agent who is also a grand landlord's son is a great thing and the local gentry would not look kindly on any man who acted for the defence of someone charged in such a case.'

'I can well believe that,' my master said.

'This man Braithwaite has now suddenly excused himself from the defence. He claimed a serious illness, recently contracted, would make it impossible to continue and the judge adjourned the trial for one week until we could find another to make representations on behalf of Paddy. There is none to be had by us in Clonmel, I can tell you. I was desperate and I went to our priest for guidance or at least for his prayers. He gave me both and told me that I must seek you out. He has met you through your work for the Catholic Association. He is Fr Edmund Connell. He praises you greatly, both you and Mr Alexander, and says that you are the man for the job. He says that you don't care a fig for the good opinion of the gentry and their lackeys, whether in Clonmel or anywhere else for that matter, and so I have come to see you. Incidentally, that rogue Braithwaite was seen riding to hounds as late as yesterday and so his illness cannot have been so severe nor of too long a duration.'

She was silent for a moment then added, 'Please, for mercy's sake, tell me that you will assist us in our hour of need, Mr O'Donovan.'

As my master thought about what she said, the young lady was silent again, but then she added, 'Now, this might seem to be a piece of pure silliness to you, Mr O'Donovan, but I am afraid that if they hang my poor twin then I shall be choked to death at the very same instant ... wherever I may be.'

I think that her last little speech brought my master solidly to her cause for I know that even old Noble Alexander could picture her sufferings at the loss of her twin and I would have done anything in my power to prevent it, even at the cost of my own life. I thank God that I did not meet such a one as Alice Grace when I was a young man and that she didn't smile upon me for I might well have spent my days as her slave. My word, she might even have brought me to the folly of the Papists at the cost of my very soul.

My master agreed to accompany Miss Grace to Clonmel. For a few worrisome hours I feared that I would not be accompanying him at all, for his initial thought was to leave me in Dublin to continue the work of the Association, but eventually he relented and said that of course he could not do without my services and that I must accompany him to Tipperary. I was relieved to hear that, now I wonder if he was teasing me all along about the idea of my staying in

Dublin. I wouldn't put it past him for he seemed to take great delight in galling me at times.

We packed for the road that very afternoon and got seats on the night mail coach to the big market town of Clonmel. We were late in buying our tickets, however, and I had to take a seat on the outside, while my master and Miss Grace sat together within, and as a result I was not privy to any conversation that they may have had on our long journey.

We booked into rooms in the Grand Commercial Hotel and then went straight to the gaol-house to meet our client and to begin building our defence. The man's sister accompanied us and even though she had enjoyed no proper rest or toilet for over two whole days she seemed as clear and cool as could be.

We were soon in the man's cell and I had my first look at Patrick Grace. Even though I already knew the man and his sister to be twins, I started at the sight of him. While they could only have been fraternal twins, he was an exact male replica of his sister, which was unfortunate for him; where her looks made her a fetchingly attractive girl it did nothing to evidence any manliness in him. He had the same slender build as her, the same delicate hands and the same golden hair over what was almost a pretty face. He took my master's hand and then mine on being introduced by his sister and his hand was soft and not possessed of any great tensile strength. He had a very pleasant, almost gentle, manner about him and was evidently glad to see us. He talked with us for a while and then my master asked to be left alone with him and spent a full half hour so enchambered. When he emerged he told Miss Grace that he would represent Patrick and said that we must go to our rooms and prepare his case.

Once there I asked him if he believed the man to be innocent. He replied that the young man had just admitted that he was indeed a member of the Sons of the Hibernian Soil, a local land league of sorts, and that they hated all landlords and, in particular, James Chadwick – apparently Chadwick had been, at the time of his murder, in the process of bringing the police in among them – and fervently wished him dead. He had in fact volunteered to carry out the execution.

'And so we can take it that he is guilty after all in spite of his sister's spiritual feelings on the matter?' I remarked.

'The boy has a very misplaced sense of patriotism and believes himself to be another Wolfe Tone or Robert Emmet. He said that he was equipped with a loaded pistol and that the date and time for the killing had been set. Apparently that there was a deadly plot against Chadwick's life was well known to the local peasantry but they hated the man and his kin so much that there was no fear that anyone would tell him beforehand.'

'Then he is for the rope,' I said. 'What hope can there be?'

'No, he is innocent,' my master replied, to my astonishment. 'I believe he didn't do it.'

'But …', I began.

Mr O'Donovan waved me silent. 'He was certainly prepared to do it, perhaps mere hours from it, and he is very glad that Chadwick is dead and dearly wishes that he had put the ball into his head, but he did not do it, Noble. The opportunity to do it was taken from him … by preemption.'

'How do you know?' I asked.

'Because he told me so,' was his reply.

'But you said yourself only yesterday that people, when put to it, will lie to save their skins,' I reminded him.

'True for you, but he is not hiding behind a shield of total innocence, now is he? He has freely admitted to me, and to anyone else who will listen, that he was fully prepared to do the deed. In fact

I think that the misguided young fool would still be absolutely delighted to take credit for the murder to make his name in the pantheon of great Irish patriots and martyrs.'

'Well, what is to be his defence? If he did not kill Chadwick then where was he at the time?' I asked, trying to think like my employer. 'Surely there must be some alibi for him.'

'Apparently not. The deed was to be carried out the next day and he was secreted away on his own in the hills to await the appointed time and to avoid any possibility of early detection by the authorities. He has no alibi, he has not even attempted to obtain one by the usual method of perjury, and feels that he needs none.'

'How has he come to such an astonishing conclusion?'

'This is a different clime, Noble, a different clime than even our native Kilrush. Tipperary is a lawless place in many ways. Hatred and deep mistrust of the authorities are endemic and frankly with good reason. The land leagues of the peasants are all-powerful here in the minds of the people. They are greatly feared, and rightly so, for their ferocity; and Grace is convinced that none will dare to bear witness against him. It would be death to do so, and so the Crown's case will not be proven. He is calm over the whole thing and has said that he cannot give me any other assistance in the case.'

'And are you still willing to act for him in light of that stupid attitude?' I asked.

'I feel that I must. He has to have competent counsel after all, and if what he says is true, then there may not be any real case brought forward for us to answer. Now, so far in the court proceedings, in spite of the rumours of a mysterious Crown witness, all the evidence heard has been from the local coroner, as to the time and the method of the killing. I do wish that I could have examined that gentleman, though. There was some inconclusive stuff from the police. They are playing their cards close to the chest on this one, as to the scene of the crime and who was about the murder site at the time. It took place by a new police barracks that Chadwick was building, at his own expense and on his own lands, mind you, on the promise of a strong contingent of police from Clonmel being installed there. He knew that the local peasants were in a rebellious state and thought that the presence of well-armed police at his own beck and call would calm or at least cow them. You have to wonder that he never thought that it would drive them to murderous fury instead.'

'He appears to have been foolhardy then,' I said.

'Just so and the man was already detested in the area, but not because he was overly vicious in collecting and pressing the rents of his tenants. By all accounts, he was less odious in that side of things than many a factor who was not of the owning family, but he was hated nonetheless. It came more from his contemptuous and sneering manner than anything else. He was disdainful of the peasantry as if he were a true lord and that rankled the people and those in the land league, for he scoffed at them and called them verminous vagabonds and the like when he met them on the road. The average peasant will be happy enough to tug his forelock at a passing gent and will abide by his lease, but there is a line which he will not allow to be crossed. A line that separates duty and official oppression from abuse to his personal pride. It seems that in that area the late James Chadwick almost went out of his way to annoy them.

He was usually accompanied on his rounds by his under-factor, by all accounts a decent enough man named Cullinane, a man from an old Catholic family who had an ancestor who thought it expedient to turn himself to the Protestant faith. He did the actual work of the management of the estate while Mr Chadwick took his ease and grew fat.'

'I must say, sir, that so far nothing you have said makes me believe in the innocence of young master Grace or his henchmen in the "Sons of the Hibernian Soil",' I observed.

My employer looked at me but decided to make no comment on my feelings about the matter.

'The murder took place in the open daylight in the middle of the afternoon and yet none of the many travellers on that busy road had seen anything. Now I will go to the court and advise the powers that be that I shall be standing in for the "gravely ill" Braithwaite and endeavour to read the official record of what has been heard to date.'

And he did just that and the trial resumed the day after with old Judge Kilgour presiding.

Mr O'Donovan astonished me when he told me that the empanelled jury was all made up of strong Protestant farmers. I asked him how this could be in such a Catholic district and he told me that it was Braithwaite's doing. He had put all aside but those gentlemen and asked for no advice from his client on the matter of jury selection, nor for his part had Patrick Grace complained to him about it. It was obviously a piece of foulness and from it we could tell that Mr Braithwaite had certainly not taken the position of counsel to mount a defence for the young man but perhaps only, cynically, to ensure that the hemp was well around his neck, before excusing himself. And still our young client was not perturbed but bowed his head in acknowledgement of his cronies in the public gallery and sat as straight and composed in the dock as a Spanish grandee.

His trust in the fear of any in the populace to testify against him was sadly misplaced as it turned out, and the Crown's main witness was a total devastation for us. He was brought up to the witness table and sworn in, to the hoots and howls of the gallery. It was evidently a great shock to our client to see any witness there at all and especially to see that it was Philip Mara taking the stand against him.

The man testified in a clear but nervous voice that he had been working alongside Mr Chadwick on the new barracks on the afternoon in question. The other workers and the sub-agent, Cullinane, were absent on that day, for Cullinane had business on the home farm. There was no actual building going on at the time; Mara was merely working at clearing up debris from the site under the gaze of Mr Chadwick, when a man came up the road and calmly put a pistol to the back of poor Mr Chadwick's head and shot him dead. The murderer warned Mara against opening his mouth about it and then went away again as calmly and unhurriedly as he had arrived.

Mara said that he was deadly afraid of the local land league, and the killer was a well-known member of such a gang, and so he did not want to come forward, but he could not erase the scene from his conscience and had decided to speak out under the guidance of Mr Doherty, the magistrate. He said again that he was now in fear of his own life, but that he must do the right thing, and I could see that the jury were very impressed by him.

The Crown prosecutor then asked him if he knew the killer and he said that he most certainly did. When asked who had done the deed he stood and, when given the black rod into his hands, he pointed it at our client in the dock, tapped him on the shoulder and said, ''Twas Patrick Grace himself there that done it, for as I said he even spoke to me afterwards and told me to keep my mouth shut if I knew what was good for me.'

That hit the room like a bombshell and there were howls of rage and screams of anguish. I looked at the jury and they were all nodding sagely and looking at the prisoner in the dock with anything but pity.

The prisoner was momentarily stunned but managed to shout out, 'Liar! Mara, you are a foul liar! I was nowhere near the barracks that day. You are a traitor and you will pay for this.'

Mr O'Donovan leaned back to where I sat behind him and said that the man was certainly lying through his teeth, but he did not know why, as he had put himself in great mortal danger by doing it; he could never live in peace in safety anywhere in Ireland again.

He then proceeded to cross-examine the witness, but although he was able to shake him on some small details, he could not discredit him in the eyes of the jury . Looking back, I think that even if he had been able to show the man for a sure perjurer, that jury would have rendered a guilty verdict anyway. So strong a witness did he make, and unrelated as he was to the deceased and unconnected in any way to the defendant, that his word was taken by the court as sufficient to convict where usually a second witness would be required.

My master did, officially, lose that case, but I am still hesitant to put it down to the loss column of the ledger of his career, for the thing was impossibly stacked up against him from the start. His client did not help us much, for before the jury left the room he claimed that he was innocent, but also that he was glad that Chadwick was dead and wished that he had been early and had done it himself. The jury was plainly horrified when he shouted out that emotion. In fact that last speech got him the rope. The jury barely left the room before returning a verdict of guilty. The wrinkled, cadaverous old Justice Kilgour quickly put the black cap atop his horsehair wig and intoned a sentence of death by hanging, to be carried out one week later. The execution was to be held in public near to the very site of the murder and Grace's body was to be buried in quicklime immediately afterwards.

Our man seemed almost elated at this news and threw his hat in the air and shouted, 'Long live Ireland, death to the English!' A good many in the public gallery of the court hurrahed strongly at this and shouted their own curses at mother England. His family members were, however, inconsolably distraught; they were sensible, though, and did not apportion any blame for the loss to my master, but they were grieved and weeping and his twin sister, for once, was less than perfect in her appearance. Her hair was in disarray, her eyes were red and her cheeks flushed and darkly stained with tears.

We stayed in the area for the next week while my heavy-hearted master sent a post-rider to the Chancellor in Dublin to ask for clemency and to have the man's sentence commuted to deportation for life, but the answer came back by return in the form of a blunt refusal. If the previous Chancellor, Jimmy Griffin, the little Welsh rascal, had been in power, then we would have been successful in our plea, for he was in my master's debt; but the new man owed him nothing.

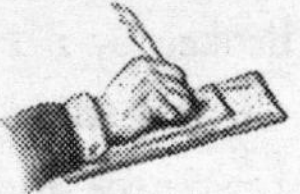

We were present for the execution, or the 'Funeral of Patrick Grace' as it came to be known, and it was certainly a grand affair. The publicising of it, meant by Justice Kilgour as a warning to the rest of the populace, was a great mistake, for fully fifteen thousand people assembled for it, almost to a man in support of Patrick Grace, and it caused the peasantry to be roused to red anger rather than to be cowed.

It took place in the grounds of the old Abbey of Holycross, one of the finest and most venerable sites among the Papists of the county aside from the Rock of Cashel. It was a beautiful morning of full sun, and an incongruously picturesque setting for the macabre act of a man's public hanging. The young man's deportment, courage and personal beauty that day attracted the sympathy of the masses to him more than ever. He was brought to the scaffold in the midst of a profound silence – you could not hear even the eternal clicking of the prayer beads. When given leave to speak his last words he asked God to receive his soul as another martyr for Ireland. He did not go so lightly into the void, for he asked for revenge on the false man who had caused his death; the traitor must die, he said, and demanded that it be carried out before he was a year in his grave. Having called for retribution, he finished by calmly proclaiming his innocence once more.

Even the priest beside him could not prevail upon him to confess his guilt and to ask forgiveness, and this moved the crowd to further fury, for the Papists put a great store in the veracity of one of their own kind standing on the brink of death.

Grace carefully took off and handed his fine white kidskin gloves to a man near the scaffold and then calmly faced his executioner asking him how it felt to be killing an innocent man. The man remained silent under his mask and Grace suffered the hangman to put him to death. There was silence even at that, until his dangling was stilled, and then it was broken by a universal wail from his female relatives about the foot of the platform. The sound fairly made the hair stand up on the back of my neck and my master, standing beside me, actually gasped at the primal nature of it.

Then someone, guarded by the anonymity of being deep in the crowd, shouted, 'Paddy Grace will be avenged!' and the same shout was taken up by others and soon the whole crowd was chanting it almost in a religious unison. The police and soldiers visibly readied themselves for action, standing tightly in line, shoulder to shoulder.

My master had stood beside me watching the whole spectacle, without betraying any emotion save for that one gasp. But as we drove off towards Dublin in the stage coach that afternoon he sighed deeply and said, 'I failed, Noble, I have failed. There must be something that I could have done, but we have seen an innocent boy put to death today, a foolish and misguided boy to be sure, but nonetheless innocent of the charges against him. Why, why did that man Philip Mara lie on the witness table, lie for the Crown and against his own kind? If I could only divine the answer to that ...'

I could have said a great deal to him. I could have reminded him of the paucity of time available to him to investigate the case; the inability and the unwillingness of his client to give him any assistance whatsoever; the make-up of the jury and the obvious duplicity of Grace's previous lawyer, but I did not do so. I feared that he would have found such assurances from me to be patronising in the extreme.

Philip Mara was, of course, no longer able to live in the country and so he was removed by the government for his protection, likely to England, where he would have to avoid all contact with people from his own county for the rest of his life.

We went back to Dublin and eventually when the season was over, to Kilrush, and all the time my master's heart remained heavy. He told me he could not let the case rest even now and he had, even far removed from the place, developed a theory about the murder, and he set about obtaining information to bear it out. I could not for the life of me imagine what quarter he expected to receive such information from, nor indeed why, for the poor lad was dead and mouldering in lime.

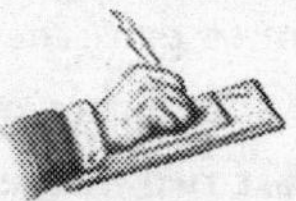

We had been home for only a month when we heard from the priest who had been giving guidance to young Grace in the prison at Clonmel and who had attended him at the time of his death. The clergyman had been in a turmoil of conscience since the execution. He had been convinced that young Grace would own up to his sin at the last as he stood on the gallows, for he knew him to be a devout Catholic and could not believe that he would dare to face his Maker without making a clean breast of things. After his neck was snapped by the rope the priest was convinced that the man's claim of innocence was totally genuine.

Now he pointed out in a letter to Mr O'Donovan, which my master showed me, that if Patrick Grace was innocent, that must mean that Philip Mara had lied under oath and had wilfully condemned him. Mara was safely away from Ireland, but he had left his wife and family and three brothers behind him and some men in the country had recently taken the life of one of them, a fellow named Daniel, in revenge for the death of Patrick Grace, and the two surviving Maras had now fled the country. The authorities, even though they strongly suspected who it was that had done this last murder, could get no one to give information as to the crime, for the population at large felt that the Maras were only getting what they deserved. Some few peasants had initially been arrested for the deed, but there being no real evidence against them outside of judicious suspicion, they had been released.

In February of the year 1828 there came another letter from the same priest, whose name was Connell, as I now recall. That letter was shown to me on a Sunday. I normally went on Sunday to services in another town from Kilrush, where the nearest Presbyterian church was situated. Since my master knew that I could never manage to travel the twelve miles there and back on my own, he had long been in the habit of sending his man to drive me to my worship in a fast gig. He would wait for me and then bring me back to Kilrush after our services were over. On at least two of the Sundays of every month he had his man bring me back to the O'Donovan family home late in the afternoon for an early dinner with himself and the whole family. He knew that I ate like a bird if left to my own devices and often I forgot to eat at all and spent my whole night with my neb buried in some old tome of the writings of the ancient Greeks. By feeding me a few times a month he assured himself that I was getting at least some nourishment and he knew that I enjoyed the warmth of family life, not all the time of course, but now and again.

On the Sunday in question I was made very welcome and I was delighted to see that my employer's dear spouse, Ellen, was up, if not exactly about. She was seated in an easy chair in the drawing room with a warm blanket over her legs. She was a dear sweet lady and always seemed genuinely delighted to see me for she made me most welcome.

'Why, Mr Alexander, how wonderful to see you again, you must sit with me here a while and tell me all the news you have,' she would always say upon my entering the room.

I would sit with her and even though I never had much by way of interesting news she still seemed to enjoy my company. I watched her fade from us through the decade of her wasting illness and I was saddened each time that I saw her, for she would be farther depleted than the last time I was in her company. I was heartsore over it and I can only imagine what grievous heartache my poor master and his little daughters endured.

I must admit that his daughters were the main reason that I treasured my visits to his home so much. The elder, Florence, smiled at me sweetly, but her place on my knee had by this time been usurped by her sister. 'Ruthie' was just six years old that year and was as precocious and precious as anything in the world. I adored her bronze-red curls and her cheeky face, and she had her daddy's great heart combined with her mother's placid and good nature. She was the only person in my life that I gave my heart to, freely and completely, and she repaid me well for it, for she called me 'Papa Noble' and used to hug me without being bid.

After I had been with Ellen and the girls for some minutes, my master entered the room and shook my hand in welcome.

'I beg your pardon for not being here to welcome you properly, Noble, but I was reading another rather interesting missive from that Fr Connell in Tipp. It was delivered to me by a messenger a short while ago ...'

'Ambrose,' Eileen Dubh, Mr O'Donovan's mother, intervened, 'let us not pester Mr Alexander with business details on a Sunday, and before we have fed the good man. Leave off now, we will be going in to dine in a few minutes.'

My master bowed to his mother and winked to me at the same time, and then began playing with his girls, teasing them and tumbling on the floor, throwing Ruth up in the air and catching the screaming imp as she toppled back to him. I was once again amazed by how gentle and subdued my master could be with his dear ones, for away from them he was normally not so placid or indulgent and easy-going.

After a decent interval had passed since our dinner, Mr O'Donovan whisked me off to his study. When we were both comfortably seated, amid the smells of furniture wax and fine leather and among the wonderful collection of books amassed by Mr O'Donovan and his ancestors before him, my employer handed the priest's latest epistle to me without comment.

This letter was more urgent than the last had been, for men's very lives depended on it. The authorities had made great progress in the investigation of the murder of Daniel Mara. It appears that the former magistrate, the energetic Mr Oliver Doherty, was now Solicitor General, and he had been sent back from his hard-earned post in Dublin to carry on the investigation into Mara's killing.

Even though the government had put up a reward of the enormous sum of two thousand pounds, the man was as unsuccessful as the previous investigators had been, but he then had an astonishing piece of good fortune fall into his lap. A young man, drunken to the point of inability, had been taken attempting a bizarre act of highway robbery and was soon sobered and facing a capital charge for what he claimed to have been the one criminal indiscretion of his life. Unfortunate to be sure, but to my mind it was but another grievous example of the evils inherent in any man taking strong drink. If only the native Irish were as temperate as myself the rate of crime in the country would plummet, I am certain of that, and the Irish might well gather themselves and take over the world. In any event the villain had sought to escape his own fate by providing information to the police on the murder of Daniel Mara.

The priest reminded us in his letter of young Grace's having given someone his kidskin gloves just prior to his death on the scaffold. That man had been one John Russell, a strong farmer of the district. Russell had drawn the gauntlets on with some ceremony and had sworn an oath that they would remain on his hands until such time as 'Paddy Grace was fully avenged'.

The would-be highwayman, Thomas Fitzgerald, told Doherty that he had been a confederate of the men who had killed Daniel Mara and would name them and testify against them if he was given a full pardon for all the bad deeds he had done so far in his days. Immediately upon Fitzgerald naming names, more persons were taken up and, anxious to save their lives, some of the more minor of these gave information on others. What it all boiled down to was that two men, Patrick Lacy and John Walsh, were arrested and charged with the murder of Daniel Mara. The priest said that the men were, to his knowledge, innocent of the crime. Like young Grace, they were delighted that Mara was dead and would have gladly killed him, but they swore that they had not done the deed. The clergyman asked my master to come to Tipperary again and to represent those men, for not one local barrister could be induced to advocate for them for charity or for money.

And so we were once again drawn into the thing, although in truth it was as if my master had never set it down in the first place, for he had recently received some correspondence from London which he said could have some great bearing on the crime and he had been very excited to get it.

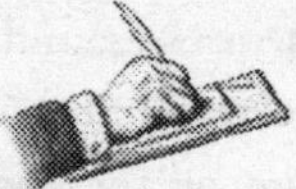

As the date of the trial, March 31st, 1828, fast approached we found ourselves headed from Kilrush to Clonmel, in our own gig this time with myself at the reins. I had discovered a penchant for driving and had come to enjoy it, not least because it meant that when our regular coachman, Shamey Didders, was unavailable – usually through drink – my master would not have to drive us. This was a relief, for his method of careering along was woefully detrimental to my nerves and a danger to all concerned.

I knew nothing of what he had received from London but I was not surprised that my master had taken up the case so readily, for he still suffered greatly from having had to watch the death of an innocent young man, and as time went on he seemed to actually blame himself more and more for his own shortcomings in the matter. Moreover, he was dreadfully bored in Kilrush – the legal work and even the work for the Catholic Association was stultifyingly tedious and repetitive – and he was nearly at his wits' end for lack of diversion. I don't know which spur was the sharper, but I sincerely hope that it was the one more tinged with charity than mere self-indulgence.

We settled into the Grand Commercial once more and very

comfortable it was, clean with well-made beds and a good kitchen. Then we visited with our clients in the company of the priest and the aforementioned John Russell, the man who had sworn to avenge the death of Paddy Grace. The facts of the Crown's case were few but very solid. They had their witness hidden away somewhere. The man had told them that he and several other men had gone to hunt out and to slay the three Mara men while they worked to complete the barracks where Mr Chadwick had been murdered. The place was to be completed on the orders of the new general agent for the estates of the Chadwick family, the former under-agent Mr Barry Cullinane. They had assembled and readied their weapons and had a few drinks of their dreadful poteen to steady themselves, and so had been late setting out on their mission. The three remaining Maras, Daniel, Timothy and Francis, had left off working by then and were headed homewards. They turned a corner on their route and nearly ran right into the party that had come to kill them. Some of the less addled assassins recognised them and attempted to fire upon them, but their few old weapons were in bad repair and poorly loaded with suspect powder and so some did not fire at all and those that did go off did so to no real effect. The Maras, spared through the slipshodedness of their would-be killers, dropped their tools and fled at once. Francis and Timothy wisely ran off in the opposite direction, but Daniel must have been made irrational by panic and he ran through the gang and tried to hide in the nearby cabin of an old woman. She was absent at the time, for it was market day, and the killers had followed Mara into her little cabin and had shot him in the head, killing him in the same manner as Mr Chadwick had been dispatched all those months ago.

The evidence against the two who had been arrested was plain and, because it came from an accomplice, it was heeded, for otherwise, as I have said before, the testimony of a single man would not normally have been accepted by a jury as conclusive evidence of guilt. Tipperary appeared to be setting some precedent in that area. My master interviewed the two accused in my presence and he elicited from them almost a complete confession for the murder. I sat astounded as he examined them on the evidence of Fitzgerald and they corroborated all that he had said in almost every detail. They had conspired to kill the Maras; they had armed themselves, with drink and bad firearms; they had sought out and met the Maras and they had pursued the fleeing Daniel to the old widow's home – but at this point the story changed. Daniel Mara had successfully barricaded the door against them and had so gained enough time to squeeze through her back window and escape across the fields. The last they saw of him was a clean pair of heels going over the hedge behind the house. They had apparently been too fuddled by drink, or just naturally too stupid of mind, to even think of sending a man around to the rear of the cottage to prevent just such an escape. Fitzgerald had been among the men who made an equally ineffective chase after the other two brothers and so had not seen what had really happened at the cottage. Most of the assassins had regrouped after that and left the scene, and it was an astounding shock to Lacy and Walsh that the man Daniel Mara had later been found lying dead in the cottage by the old woman, a Mrs Celia Cullinane, on her return from the town that day. They couldn't account for it at all, for they had not done it, but there he was 'as large as life, sur, only dead', as Lacy said to us with a serious face on him.

I thought that a jury, even one that was deeply and bitterly motivated to be against the government, would think the last part of their tale totally incredible and would find them guilty at once. They had chased the man into a lonely cottage but didn't kill him and yet he was found there shot to death later that day. Even the simplest gossoon would not have credited that tale.

We went back to our rooms and my master examined what documents had been provided to him, the coroner's report and the report of the lieutenant of police who had investigated the scene of the killing.

Mr O'Donovan said that the policeman who had prepared the report had learned his trade well and his description of the scene was full and detailed; as well, he had shown considerable artistic ability in his rendering of several sketches of the scene, including the body, and he had indicated where blood was found about the room. He even included measurements of the cottage's interior.

After reading through these documents several times, my master was in a much better mood and treated me to a fine dinner of boiled mutton, potatoes, turnips and parsnips in the dining parlour of our inn. He rather spoiled the meal for me, however, for his topic of conversation was the coroner's and police reports on the body of Mara and him with his head half blown off. I should tell you that I am a very squeamish man where blood is concerned. I had to beg him to stop, for I was in grave danger of giving back any food that I had managed to consume. He did impress one last point on me before talking of other less unsettling things. The coroner stated that Mara died from a shot to the head, but could find no other recent marks of injury on the body, no bruises or lacerations whatsoever. My master thought it odd that enraged murderers, with drink taken, would not have first given the man a healthy drubbing with their fists and boots and perhaps gun barrels rather than merely shooting him in the head in an almost clinical fashion.

We went off for a drive in the gig afterwards and my master asked me to stop by a little stream and stone bridge which looked very pretty in the gloaming.

'Do ye know, Noble, there is a great connection between the death of Mr Chadwick and Daniel Mara. If only I could put my finger on the real pulse of it, I would know all. I have my suspicions, I must say, but without official help I can do nothing, and the authorities are too hell bent on hanging our clients. I doubt if they would even listen to me.'

'Well yes, the connection is that Mara was killed by those louts in revenge for his brother having testified, falsely or otherwise, against the killer, young Patrick Grace.'

'Just think of what you have said, my dear Noble. Cogitate on it, for it makes a great deal less sense if you do. I am convinced that Grace was not guilty and that Philip Mara perjured himself, at great personal cost, and I also believe that the men in the cell in Clonmel are innocent – at any rate of killing Daniel Mara – and so the connection between the cases may not be the one which you have just now espoused.'

'What do you mean?' I asked. I admit that I was confused.

'Well, the motivation for James Chadwick's death is still a mystery.'

'That is easily told. He was building a police barracks and he was hated by the locals and there is a dangerous element among them,' I said, a bit too smugly.

'But, as I say, he was not killed by Grace, who had been designated as the assassin by his own organisation; and, since he did not do it, then the land leaguers could not have done it at all,' he replied.

'Supposing you are right about that, then who did do it?' I asked.

'That has plagued my mind for months, Noble. I previously missed something, something which is very basic. Let us list the personal motives available to us. First, there is the political or seditious impulse but I have now discounted that. Then, there is revenge for a slight or injury of a purely personal nature. Had Chadwick been in the act of robbing some honest man of his wife's affections, do you think? And then there is the oldest motive: we must ask ourselves *cui bono*? Who indeed has or could have benefited directly from Mr Chadwick's early demise? Not his family, that is for sure, for they will miss his services and anyway they are all in London; and so who is there who could have had a hand in Chadwick's killing and in the current matter as well? For I believe that, if Grace and the other two are innocent, then the same mysterious hand is likely behind both deaths and the motive will become clearer as we progress. We must just hope that we can prove it. We must begin our investigation into the current case, not with Daniel Mara but, with the late James Chadwick.'

I was as mystified as ever but said nothing in an attempt to mask my ignorance and lack of perspicacity from my master. It is always far better to remain silent and appear to be obtuse than to open one's mouth and prove it beyond dispute. If only I could always remember that!

We went back to the taproom that was attached to our hotel for that, in my master's opinion, was the seat of all useless and also some useful gossip in any town. It was a cosy and quite respectable place. I do not usually frequent drinking establishments, but it appeared to be above the norm and with a fairly decently dressed and reputable clientele. Once ensconced therein, Mr O'Donovan proceeded to ingratiate himself with a variety of customers by buying them a drink or two and chatting about various things, including the now seemingly harmless subject of the late James Chadwick.

He eventually found a man who knew Chadwick passably well, a solicitor, a red-faced Scotsman who had done work for Chadwick and who had sometimes dined and caroused with the man. This was unusual, for the would-be gentry would normally have little to do with a mere solicitor on a social basis – he would have been asked to enter the big house through the back door in fact. My employer had great skill in what one might call 'courting' a man, and he had soon won over the fellow by his good nature. He talked freely and we obtained a good thumbnail sketch of the deceased from him.

Apparently, for all his arrogance to the common people, James Chadwick was an affable enough companion to his own sort, and he enjoyed the free and easy social atmosphere of Ireland. He was unmarried and in his forties, but still had an eye for the women, and was not too particular what class they were from as long as they suited his particular purposes. The solicitor smirked knowingly at that and my master smirked back at him, while I sat there with a face like a biblical patriarch on me. The solicitor, however, on being prodded, said that he knew of no jealous husband or jilted lover who would have wished to harm the man. No wait, he said, Chadwick had been interested in a certain Mrs Bloom. She was the wife of a nonconformist preacher, a travelling minister who was away in the saddle ten months of every year. The wife of this dour missionary was a winsome enough girl from a nonconformist family that had forced her into the marriage. Chadwick had sought to alleviate her loneliness with his company and the liaison had, to the solicitor's mind, the seeds of a scandal about it, but he could not believe that the clergyman, Silas Bloom, would have taken any vengeful action in the matter or that he even suspected anything untoward.

Chadwick gambled a little but was not in debt to anyone that he wagered with and he enjoyed nothing more than a good bacchanal with his closest friends. Although on the surface he appeared to be a bit of a bumbler, and was tending towards corpulent laziness, we learned that he was in fact a meticulous businessman, who kept his records up to date and took pride in his work. He could meet any of his tenants on the road and, without referring to his books, he would know to the penny how far the man was in arrears in his rent and when he had last paid a penny towards it. This was a trait that did not endear him to the people, I needn't add, for he would call out his reckoning to the unfortunate tenant no matter where he was or what company he was in. He ran a huge amount of land on behalf of his family and, besides hundreds of small tenants, he also kept a good many sheep on his mountain slopes and several great herds of prime cattle grazed in the family's lush lowland meadows. He ran the estate, but apart from the meticulous accounting, he did no real farm work or even supervision of farm work himself and left all the 'unsavoury toil' to that assistant of his, Barry Cullinane. Mr Chadwick, we were told, had always been averse to getting cow dung on his boots.

After his death he had not been replaced by another family member, because none could be induced to come to Ireland, and so his former assistant and trainee had taken over the overall management of the Chadwick interests. Chadwick had always given the family in London a very good account of Cullinane and so he naturally assumed the mantle of estate manager.

My master prodded the man gently on the subject of the Maras and discovered that they had been very much Mr Chadwick's men and, as well as being his tenants, they had worked steadily about the estate and the home farms, as much as tending their own smallholdings. According to the man himself, they had been the only peasants that Chadwick would trust, and he had a high opinion of them in spite of their lower station in life. Also, they were the main source of his labour in building up the new barracks at the time of his death, for few others about the land would dare to take on the work, regardless of the recompense.

When we went to our rooms that night, after a light supper, my master was in a good mood. I heard him humming to himself as he brushed his teeth before retiring and I could not for the life of me see any palpable reason for his levity.

The next day he took me on a strange errand, at any rate I thought it very strange but you can judge it for yourself. We went, on information obtained from his Scots friend of the night before, to a man who was a pig slaughterer. I had never met such a man before for in the smaller towns each man kills his own swine, but the butcher shops in a large centre such as Clonmel sold a great deal of pork and bacon and so had a professional to do their slaughterering for them.

As we drove up, the proprietor came out to see who was arriving and he presented a sight to our eyes, I can tell you, which was worthy of a guardian of hell. His arms were gore to the elbows and the long leather apron reaching from his chest to his toes was stained with many layers and hues of blood in its varying degrees of freshness and corruption. My master spent a few minutes negotiating with the man and dropped a coin or two into his reeking palm before beckoning me to follow, bringing his small valise. We entered a little outbuilding that was white-limed inside but otherwise was a dirty, ill-kept and foul-smelling place. There he and the slaughterer arranged several old jute sacks about the floor and when all was ready the man brought in a large squealing pig by the use of a cruel twitch on its snout. Without preamble my master doffed his coat, threw it to me to hold, opened his valise, took a large flintlock horse pistol from it, cocked it, pointed it down to the middle of the top of the poor pig's head and pulled the trigger. When the noise died down and the smoke cleared, the pig's squealing days were over. The top of its head was quite disappeared and was now a red ragged mess.

'Come here and see, Noble,' my master said, though I could barely hear him for the ringing in my ears. 'Just look at the splattering of blood, bone and brains left behind by that unfortunate animal. See, even that wall a full ten feet away has blood splattered on it and on my very shoes and even on that door over there. And those sacks where he fell are covered with gore. Now, as you know, I have read the coroner's report on Daniel Mara, and he indicates that the man's head was half blown off by the blast of a gun of a large bore, but according to the police report no bullet was recovered from the body or from the widow's cottage. The police lieutenant made a good search for it but could not find it, although it must surely have passed right through the victim's head.'

'What does that signify?' I asked, for want of anything better to say, and being most anxious to get out into the fresh open air. As I have already admitted, I am not good in the presence of blood.

'It confirms my suspicion that the man was not shot in the cottage at all but somewhere else and his body was moved back to the cottage some time afterwards. I see your eyebrows arched at me, Noble, but it's true nonetheless. Just look at the mess the pig's head made of this room, and yet, according to the police lieutenant's reports, there was little or no blood splattered about the widow's cottage. I think that the omission of any description of a large quantity of splattered gore, bone and brain is a telling thing. So I am sure that the man was killed elsewhere after he escaped from that murderous mob, among which were our present clients, and his corpse was brought back later, obviously to incriminate them and therefore cover the real murderer's tracks.

Therefore, Mara must have told his real killer of the hunt for him and of his escape from the cottage. One can only imagine the panic that he felt. The murderer obviously wanted to be rid of him and at the same time to put the blame elsewhere, and it was a godsend to him to have the land leaguers be so co-operative in that regard. To be co-operative once more, in fact.'

I had to admit that the whole thing made some sense to me now and opined that once he had determined who the criminal was, then he would have the case solved. He laughed at that, and said that it would only be the beginning, for given the current climate, a great deal of proof would be needed to convince anyone at all of his suspicions. The authorities would much rather have a speedy trial and then hang our clients than actually have to look more deeply into the matter.

We went next, again on directions and information obtained in the taproom, to the small crossroads at a place named Ardhanna, but which should have been named Bally Mara, for the four Mara brothers had occupied land at each of its four corners and so their houses and out-offices were only a few chains apart from each other. The home of Daniel Mara had been burned to its blackened foundations by an angry mob shortly after his death, and that of his perjurious brother Philip had been treated in a like manner some time before that. The other two Mara men, Tim and Francie, had fled the country, leaving their wives and children in their houses; the families of Philip and Daniel had moved in with them.

Mr O'Donovan went to the door of the first Mara home and, remarkably, considering he was representing the murderers of a Mara, he was admitted. He was a fine-looking big man, immaculately if sombrely dressed, and he had a kind and open manner, when it suited him, which I recall women of all walks found to be very attractive. I tied up the gig and followed him in, unbidden. The room was quite large and surprisingly well furnished and much above what one would expect to see in the hovel of a man who held only a few acres of land and who laboured for the landlord's agent at a low wage on most of the days of his week. There was some fine furniture of an English manufacture, not a *súgán* chair in sight, and a great dark dresser full of good delftware, pewter and even a few articles of silver plate. There was a rich-looking Turkey rug on the floor, instead of the usual rushes, and the place was freshly painted. My master was seated at the hearth and there were three woman seated around him by the time I arrived. I had evidently just missed something, as all three women were tittering and laughing into their aprons. Some children played in a corner ignoring their fine visitor, but two others stood near by, staring at Mr O'Donovan's every move.

'I must sympathise with you on the loss of your husbands, ladies,' he was saying. 'It is a sore thing for women to try to keep a leasehold and to endeavour to raise children with no man about the place. Things will not go well for you, I'm afraid. Is there no chance that Tim and Francie will come back? I know Philip dare not, but the other two, after this whole thing dies down – well who knows?'

The women seemed to agree that their futures were not as rosy as they had been, but averred that the three surviving Maras would never return, for it would be certain death for them to do so. They all claimed that they were in no immediate danger of eviction, though, for Mr Cullinane was mindful of their situation and still deeply indebted to Philip for testifying against Grace and bringing the culprit to the rope for the slaughter of his dear master. They were talkative, and innocent of any of my master's real purposes, and I would say starved for the company and attentions of a fine-looking man, for they relayed a good deal of information that cuter women would have kept to themselves. My master was mining away at them when a fourth woman came in through the door with a child on her hip. It turned out that she was the widow of Daniel, and she was a different sort entirely from her sisters-in-law. She also knew right away who my master was and at once created a scene, uttering vile imprecations against him, and she soon succeeded in driving us from the house, and she even followed us out, brandishing a long broom at us, and cursing and screaming like an enraged banshee.

I was as white as a ghost myself, I am sure of it, for I hate such untoward scenes and have always avoided them, but when I turned to look at the effect on my master, I saw that he lay back in the gig chuckling to himself, with the pleased look of the cat that just stole the cream showing clearly on his face.

We returned to Clonmel, for my master said that he needed to think in the quiet of his rooms for a while, as the trial of our clients would start in only two days. The rest of that day I did not lay eyes on him until supper time and after that he retired to his inner room again until early morning. I took a notion and I went to the taproom on my own for a while to see if I could find out anything useful, but I do not drink or hold with drinking and I have not the same jovial manner as my master, and so I got nothing for my efforts.

The next day we went off in search of a labourer. It was all a mystery to me but I took direction from my master until we reached an out-of-the-way homestead near the Rath Cannon estates.

'This is the home of young Phelim O'Hegarty. You do not know of him, Noble, so do not rack your brain. I wonder if he is in, loafing about, or off working?'

His mother was in, but the young man was not. My master told her that we might have work for the lad and she indicated that he was not far off from us, just two fields over, thinning rows of turnips for a better-off neighbour. His mother said it was difficult for Feely to get a day's work at all since they finished with him at the new barracks.

With her very specific directions, for she obviously did not want to risk our missing him, we soon found the young lout sitting on his rear end by the road wall of the field and it only nine o'clock in the morning. By the looks of things he had only done a row or two out of the whole acreage by then. When he heard the clop of our approach it had no effect on his restfulness and it was only when we suddenly stopped that he leapt up and began snedding with his hoe in a feverish and industrious-looking manner.

'Hold on, Feely O'Hegarty,' my master called out. 'Don't give yourself a turn, we're not here to check on your progress at sneddin' turnips. Stop and talk to us a while.'

The boy relaxed and came to us over the roadside wall, still cautious and very suspicious of our appearance and at our knowing his name, but he was trained in his short lifetime to listen to and to obey his betters.

'How do yous know me name? I doesn't know yous at all,' he said in a reedy voice.

'We've just come from your mother and she sends us to you with her best wishes. We have a few harmless questions for you – and a golden guinea if you answer them smartly,' Mr O'Donovan said.

That got the lad's attention as nothing else would have and wiping his hand on his pantaloons he held it out palm up to us.

'No, after,' my master said curtly, but he pinched a coin out of his waistcoat pocket and showed it to the lad.

'What do yous want t'know or who is it yous want knocked over the head with a slane?' he asked, now eager for us to begin and so come to the finish and his reward all the sooner.

'You worked at the building of the new barracks with the Maras around the time that poor Mr Chadwick was killed, Feely, did you not?'

'I did, sur, I was the one that did nearly all the buildin' of it, so I was.'

'Quite so, and were you there the day of the murder?'

'I wus, sur, helpin Philip Mara and poor Mr Chadwick, God rest his soul.'

'Where were the other Maras that day, do you know?'

'They wus off herdin' the cattle on the big farm that day, sur, as far as I can remember.'

'Well, if you were there, did you see Patrick Grace shoot the man?'

'No, I did not, for I was gone for the day by the time he come and done it, sur.'

'But why, laddie, it was a Monday and only in the early part of the afternoon. Surely they work a strong man like you harder than that about here, to the Angelus bell at the least?'

'I wus jus tol' to clear off home for there was no more work for me that day – and 'tis God's truth I could have used the full day's wages, I can tell you, and a lot more besides.' The boy actually grimaced as he recalled his loss of that day.

'Was that so? Was there no work at all that you could do?' my master asked.

'No, sur, there wus plenty of work for me and plenty the next day and the day after that and on for weeks, 'twas the steadiest I ever wus in me whole life.'

I reflected that he must have been at the most about sixteen years old.

'I have one more question and then you can have your guinea, but I want the truth from you, you understand. Was there anyone there that day at the site besides you and Philip Mara and Chadwick, and was it that person who told you to go home?'

When we had the answer to that, we drove back to Clonmel and to a conference with the priest, Fr Connell, and Mr John Russell, who was paying my employer's fee in the matter. My master managed to tell them very little over the space of an hour and begged leave to go and prepare for the opening of the Crown's case the next morning.

The trial was to be heard before Mr Justice Moore, who entered in his red robes lined with black and had a face on him that indicated that he was prepared to discharge a dreadful duty. Surprisingly to us all, the Earl of Kingston was seated beside him, for he had come all the way from his home in Cork to observe the proceedings. It seems that, as he resided in a fractious county as well, he wanted information as to how best to deal with it. His menacing presence was also calculated to impress upon the judge the need to take strong action against rebel murderers. He was without a doubt using his right as a nobleman to be there to intimidate the justice and to make sure that he evinced no trace of fair play, never mind clemency, towards the men in the dock.

The whole of the first morning was spent laboriously selecting a jury. My master excelled at that task and did not merely look at a man's religion or political affiliation when saying aye or nay to a potential member – he told me on more than one occasion that honest men, capable of putting all bias aside, were to be found in every section of society – but asked the man a few pertinent questions and judged him well on his answers. He could spot a dissembler at once. After the noon break, the prosecutor, Oliver Doherty, now the Solicitor General, assisted by a Mr Redvers Harker KC, began to present his case against our men.

Our prisoners were ready and stood fearlessly in the dock. The younger one, Lacy, was a tall, good-looking young man with an honest countenance, dressed neatly and carefully in a green serge suit which accentuated his healthful colour and bright eyes. Walsh, his brother in crime, was a stout, short, square-built man with a sturdy look and with more of an aspect of fierceness about him than Lacy. Yet it was Lacy, for all his baby face, who, we learned, was far more a malefactor than Walsh, for he was reputed to have done many other desperate deeds in the land while Walsh had an excellent reputation and had obtained the highest testimony to his character from his landlord, a Mr Creagh.

The Solicitor General rose to state his case. He seemed to me to be impressed with the grave responsibility which was his and with a solemn and emphatic manner he narrated the facts of the case he was to prove to the jury. He had been in court a thousand times before and kept a close watch on the time he took, so as not to risk boring the jury – always a fatal thing for a brief to do, on either side of a case. He looked at the jury constantly, except when rendering a piece of evidence that would shock the prisoners, when he would look at them quickly to judge their reactions, and by doing so he quite naturally brought the eyes of the jury onto them as well. He made both the men start several times I can tell you, and was well pleased at the alarm they evinced at the extent of the knowledge of the government regarding their activities.

They preserved their composure when Doherty was detailing the evidence to be heard from Fitzgerald and another informer named Ryan. They were not unduly alarmed, for they knew, as my master had explained to them, that the jury could be made to ask for more evidence than the coincidence of swearing between two accomplices would give. It was enough in law to be sure, but in practice juries were in the habit of demanding a better foundation for their findings and before condemning a man to death they would prefer to exact a confirmation from some more pure and unreproachable source.

The first witness called by the Crown was Fitzgerald, who was brought in from his hiding place between two large policemen and taken to the witness table. He sprang up there with a light enough step and was duly sworn in. He took the witness chair, faced the prosecutor and gave his testimony, and all he related was the gospel truth – up to the point where Daniel Mara ran panicked into the widow Cullinane's cottage, that is. He had pursued the other two Maras and had left Daniel to the mercies of the two accused. He had not come back with the others, but had fled off to his home parish, which was some miles away, after the sober Maras had outrun them. He was not a local man you see but was brought in as a 'special', a hard case called from a distance to do the gory task. He testified that there were several other 'specials' in the band. He heard that the others had killed Daniel Mara later that day and he said that he was right glad at the time that the day had not been a true loss to them. He named the accused as the pursuers of Daniel Mara and described their weaponry as 'two great horse pishtils, yer honner'. He testified that they had been summoned by the relatives of Patrick Grace and his staunch friends to assemble for the killing of the Maras. They assembled in the house of one Jack Keogh, who lived near to the new barracks that the Maras were to be found working on most days. On the morning of October 1st they went *en masse* to an elevation covered in trees called 'the Grove', where a quantity of arms, lead balls and powder had been cached. The hill actually overlooked the barracks where the Maras were at work and they could hear the clink of hammers on stone and the shouts of the men to each other.

Another party joined them at that point and they went down the circular road from the hill to enter the main road which would bring them to the barracks. The rest was as previously told and resulted in the death of Daniel Mara at the hands of Lacy and Walsh. That concluded his testimony.

My master cross-examined him and asked him only two questions: he asked him if the Crown had excused him his previous criminal conduct for his testimony and whether he had honestly, personally, seen either of the accused shoot and kill Daniel Mara. He answered yes to the first and after looking at Mr Doherty as if in sorrow he answered no to the second question.

Next the Crown brought out another of the gang who had turned Crown's witness, a man of very ill repute named Ryan, and he told a similar tale to Fitzgerald and was asked the same two questions by my master and answered both in the same manner as had Fitzgerald.

The jury murmured at that and many in the public gallery made appreciative noises.

Then the Crown brought up a surprise for us, one who was not connected with the murder but was an independent witness. Mr Doherty turned towards the dock and, lifting up a shaking hand, pronounced the name of Kate Costello. It smote the prisoners with dismay and her name was like an explosion of a petard in the courtroom. We learned later that at the time he called for her, Doherty was very uncertain that she would actually appear to testify, for it would affect the lives of 'her people' to make her disclosures. She was the servant of our patron John Russell and was constantly about his house.

She was called once and did not appear and then she was called again but did not come. The Solicitor General sent repeated requisitions but without any positive effect. At length everyone began to conjecture that she would not appear at all. The prisoners were becoming relaxed at her non-appearance and Doherty had grown exceedingly nervous and red about the cheeks.

Suddenly the chamber door was flung open and one of the most extraordinary figures that I ever saw in an Irish Court of justice was introduced. She was a withered, diminutive woman who seemed unable to support herself and whose feet seemed about to give way at every step into which she was impelled by the court attendants who held her elbows as she tottered towards the witness table. Her face was almost covered with a shawl and it was impossible for some time after she had been hoisted onto the table for us to see her features. We could all see her hands, though, and they were as white and clammy as a corpse's and seemed already to have undergone the first stages of decomposition. They shook and shuddered as did the whole of her miserable and worn-out frame. After a few moments on the seat she shrugged her shawl from about her head and one of the most ghastly visages that I have ever been forced to look at was revealed to us. Her eyes seemed closed tight as if shrunken in by death and her lips were the colour of ashes and remained ever open but soundless. Her breathing was scarcely perceptible and as her head habitually lay to one side on her bony shoulder her grey mass of stringy hair fell in disorder down that side of her.

Now that she was produced, she seemed little calculated to be of any use to the Crown. Doherty repeatedly asked questions of her, but received no answer at all. She truly seemed unconscious even to the sound of his voice. At length, when she was given a drink of water and some more was flicked into her face by a bailiff, she responded very lowly, in such a bare whisper that it was exceedingly difficult to hear her. Doherty leaned close to her and repeated her own answers to her in a loud voice and asked her to nod if his rendition was an accurate one.

She stated that she had seen the two accused among a larger group of men on two occasions the day when Daniel Mara died. Once in the early afternoon she had seen them, armed with guns, walking in grim array, along the lane towards the new barracks; they had observed her and she had hurried off (though I do not see how that verb could ever be used to describe any of her movements) to her normal duties at the home of Mr Russell. She testified that she heard some shots soon thereafter, but did not go back to investigate the cause of them for she well knew it. She reached her employer's home and went about her duties, which seemed to consist mainly of sitting by the fireside and keeping her old bones warm. She said that her employer was in a state of great agitation and was pacing the parlour floor.

About an hour later the men that she had seen armed on the road came in – well, some of them at any rate, about five or six, including the two accused. They were as she put it 'near legless wit' drink' and made a great din as they entered. John Russell seemed to have been waiting for them and was soon busy shaking their hands and slapping their backs and they fairly lapped it up. John Russell's youngest daughter, a sweet thing of eighteen, remarkable in her good looks, ran up and asked the men if they had done a good thing that day and the leader, Walsh, had said there wasn't a buck Mara alive in the barony that night, for they had slew them all, stone dead. The girl was delighted to hear that and clapped her hands together and squealed with pleasure. She was apparently the sweetheart of the dead Patrick Grace.

Lastly old Kate was asked to identify the prisoners. The black rod with which culprits are identified was placed into her hand and immediately fell out onto the table with a clatter, for she had not the strength to hold it aloft. She was required to stand up and to face the dock and when at last she was able to do so and had the rod in both her hands before her, Walsh seemed to panic and shouted, 'O God! You are going to murder me! I'll not stand to be murdered, for I'm downright murdered, God in heaven help me!'

The judge asked my master what his client's complaint was and Mr O'Donovan stated that there were only the two men in the dock to be identified and so they were marked out with certainty to Kate Costello. The judge, to give him credit, in spite of the spittly remarks of Kingston in his ear, agreed and ordered that a few other prisoners be brought down from the jail to stand with the accused and that they be shown to the old woman in the midst of a crowd. As you can well imagine, a good deal of time was taken up with this task. My master leaned back and conjectured to me that the old woman might not be able to pick out our men from a crowd and so their lives would be safe. He doubted if she could have named what she had eaten for her breakfast the day before.

At last, the other prisoners came in and were put into the dock and their clanking chains and the soldier's muskets being grounded made for an ominous nocturne, as it was now fully eleven o'clock at night. The old woman's laborious testimony had taken nearly four hours to that point. The courtroom was grown sleepy and the second set of candles was beginning to gutter in their sockets and a dim and uncertain light was now diffused throughout the chamber. The frightful interest of the scene kept my own mind from weariness, I can tell you.

The new prisoners were all looking as if they had been stunned by the knacker's hammer as they had been roused from their cells and brought roughly to the court without being told the least detail as to why they were being herded there.

When all was in readiness, the old witness was called upon again to rise, to turn and to place the rod on the heads of the guilty. She began to do so and as her old hands were about to bring the rod to bear a lone female voice shouted out from the gallery, 'Oh, Kate'.

That seemed to stall her and she let the rod drop and Doherty's chin seemed to fall with it. Then she gathered herself and approached the dock again. This time her eyes rested on the quivering Walsh. She seemed not to recognise him, but after a few moments more she rested the rod on his shoulder and then picked young Lacy out of the little mob in the same way.

The court was hushed during this part of the trial, but when it ended there was a universal moan from the gallery and when I looked up at John Russell, he looked very nervous indeed, as well he should have looked, for he was arrested within the hour. Walsh collapsed and took no further interest in the trial, but Lacy appeared to remain alert to the end.

Then my master rose and smiled sweetly at old Kate Costello when she was seated again. He only asked her, gently, if she had seen anyone kill any man that day and she answered in her decrepit whisper, 'No, yer honner, I did not, I saw not a man kilt at all.' My master repeated her statement and asked if it was accurate. She nodded, vigorously for her, and I half expected to see her old neck snap like a dry twig and send her head skittering across the table.

The Crown ended its case at that and Doherty and Harker both looked pleased and not a little relieved. We were set to commence with the defence the next day as it was now very late in the night.

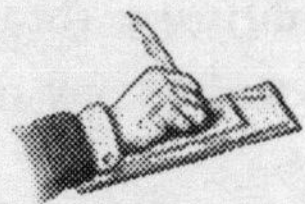

For the rest of that night I was in much more of a funk than Mr O'Donovan. He ate a good if belated supper and after reading for a while he retired and we said no more about the case until the next day.

He first called the police lieutenant who had examined the murder scene and the young man, an Englishman named Tulliver, seemed to answer his questions honestly. He asked him to describe the body, its position and the amount of blood and other matter that were found about the cottage. The man admitted that there was not much blood, bone or brains about, although the head was badly damaged by the shot. Suddenly he looked as if the significance of that had not occurred to him before and he reddened slightly.

'In view of the lack of blood and other matter, Lieutenant Tulliver, would you not agree that it is more than just possible that the man Mara was shot elsewhere and brought to Mrs Cullinane's cottage when he was already a dead man?'

There was a murmur in the court at that and one man roared 'Rubbish!' I happened to be looking at the public gallery at the time and I marked who was the shouter.

'Well, yes, that is a distinct possibility, I don't know why I didn't think of it before, but there seemed to be no point in such a theory, for we knew what must have happened,' the policeman answered, becoming more defensive.

'You thought that you knew what had happened, you mean? You were a long time in arresting anyone with enough evidence to support a charge, isn't that so? Why then did you not consider the possibility that the crime was done elsewhere?' O'Donovan asked.

The lieutenant seemed discomposed and answered that he could not really say why.

'So you will grant me, Lieutenant, that on further reflection, the murder could have been done elsewhere.'

'Well, I suppose so, there was not much mess there, so it could have been done elsewhere, but for the life of me I do not know how, or why,' the man replied.

'And if the murder was done elsewhere, then why would those two men in the dock move the corpse back to the widow's cottage? What could possibly be their reason for taking such a risk and at the same time incriminating themselves?'

'Well, er ... They would have had no motivation to do that, I suppose. They would have left the man where they killed him. It would have been simpler,' the lieutenant said.

'Exactly, sir. If the body was moved back to the widow's cottage it was done for one reason and one reason only – to incriminate my clients – and they would be very foolish men to do that themselves, now isn't that so? No, don't answer that, that there is no need. Thank you, Lieutenant, that is all I have to ask of you.'

The Crown questioned the young officer then, trying to put my employer's theory about the real murder site into disrepute, but in spite of any possible cost to himself he answered them boldly and honestly and if anything they only succeeded in strengthening my master's ideas in the mind of the jury.

Next, Mr O'Donovan called his second and last witness, the widow Mrs Celia Cullinane, and after she stepped daintily up onto the witness table and was sworn in, he asked her about the state of the body when she had found it and the mess in her home and if she could smell gunpowder smoke there when she returned.

The woman obviously had no idea in the world why she was being called as a witness, she was nervous at being dragged into the affair and she was visibly relieved at the simplicity of the questions put to her. She said that the body was lying on the floor near to the door and that there was very little mess about it and that she could not smell any burnt powder in the room. My master never left anything to chance, and he asked her if she knew what burnt powder from a discharged gun smelled like, and she said she certainly did for her late husband, God rest him, was the worst poacher in the barony when he was at himself.

That raised a good laugh in the chamber and I could even see the corners of the black earl's mouth twitch at the thought.

Then my master summed up for the defence. He had told the prisoners what he was intending to do and they agreed, for it was their only chance based on the weight of the evidence against them.

He proceeded to admit that all that the jury had heard from the prosecution's witnesses was truly correct, no matter how motivated. He told them that Fitzgerald and Ryan were telling the truth about the conspiracy to kill the three Mara men in revenge for the hanging of Patrick Grace. They had all set out that day armed to do the deed at the barracks of Rath Cannon. Kate Costello had seen them on the road, and she had indeed heard shots. They were ineffective shots, however, and neither killed nor wounded anyone at all. Furthermore, Fitzgerald and his friend Ryan had seen no one kill anyone and in fact they heard testimony from the police officer that the man could have been killed elsewhere and only moved back to the cottage later. The men seen by Kate Costello at the home of John Russell had been drunk and boastful, ashamed at their ludicrous failure perhaps, and had made up as if they were gallant killers when they came to Russell's home. They were conspirators to murder, that was beyond doubt and could be freely admitted, but they were on trial not for conspiracy, but for the actual murder of Daniel Mara. He also told them that the Crown had used dire threats to get old Kate Costello to testify. She had been identified to them by their 'stags' Fitzgerald and Ryan as a woman who saw them both on the road that day and also in the home of John Russell afterwards, and they had arrested her. They had threatened the frail old woman with putting her on trial as an accomplice and perhaps hanging her. My master had spoken to her that morning, without me being present, and had it all from her. He put it that if the Crown could allow itself to so abuse a helpless old woman then there was little of conscience to stop it from coaching her on whomever they wanted her to identify in the dock. The jury must therefore disregard her testimony and her identification of Lacy and Walsh, as it was forced from her on pain of death and that was against all the laws of the land. There were cries of 'Shame!' at this and hoots from the gallery, and Oliver Doherty grew beet red in spite of his best efforts to compose himself and ignore the cacophony. The jury, my master said, in spite of the Crown's extraordinary efforts, had heard no direct evidence for the killing itself, no one had seen it, and therefore they must find the defendants not guilty.

Now his speech was a good deal longer and warmer than that, but I have given you the gist of it, and it seemed enough to sway the jury, for they deliberated for four whole days before bringing in their verdict.

Immediately the jury was excused and sequestered, my master and I left the courthouse. As we were going down the steps a man approached us very brusquely with a scowling face on him.

'See here, sir, what do you mean by denying that those two scoundrels killed poor Daniel Mara?' he spat out at my employer. 'If you believe what you said in there you are a madman and if you do not believe it then you are nothing more than a scoundrel.'

Mr O'Donovan ignored him, and when the wretch grabbed his shoulder he shrugged it off and hurried away with me in tow. I was shocked at the manner of the man, for he was well dressed and had the aspect of a country squire about him and he spoke well. I was also surprised at my employer for standing for such rough treatment from anyone, for I had seen him often enough cuff men severely for much less. He hurried me along by pinching my elbow, until we had turned the first corner, then he wheeled around and took my shoulder.

'Noble,' he said, 'go back and follow that rude scoundrel, but do not let yourself be noticed. Let me know who he meets and what they talk about, if you can. Meet me back in our rooms in, say, two hours from now.'

I was puzzled, for I did not even know the man's name, but I dutifully went back to the street where the courthouse was and saw him talking animatedly with two rougher-looking customers at the base of the court steps. He seemed to finish his harangue of the two, took his watch from his waistcoat pocket and looked at it. He threw his cloak about him and hurried off immediately. I followed at a distance, and, if he feared being followed, he did not show it, for never once did he glance back. He made his way to a good hostelry with a large carved bull hanging above its door. He entered straight away, but I waited a minute before following him in. It was dim and smoke-filled inside and the mixed stink of tobacco, bodies, drink and cow manure nearly knocked me over. I stood with a knot of what appeared to be well-to-do farmers and cattle dealers near the bar and surreptitiously scanned the clientele seated at the various tables until I spied my quarry through the open door of one of the snug rooms.

I moved about so that I could see more of the little room. He was seated with two men of prosperous appearance, probably more cattle-dealers here for the market days. I stood near the door of the snug and tried to blend in with the crush, but as I was the only man there without a drink in my hand and speaking loudly about cattle, I don't think that I melded in very well, but everyone was so engrossed in their own business that I think no one noticed. I almost strained my ears to uselessness trying to hear what was said in that snug, but I couldn't make out a single word for they were speaking *sotto voce*. They were the only persons in the whole place doing so, which was suspicious in itself.

I waited there for nearly an hour before my quarry rose and left the inn as abruptly as he had entered. The two men he was with finished their beakers of drink and rose in a more unhurried fashion and sauntered towards the door. I went over to the bar and the innkeeper looked at me as if expecting me to order some of his foul poison. He was disappointed, though, for I merely asked him the names and business of the two men about to leave his establishment. They were at the door as I asked, and he told me straight off, almost like an automaton, without thought. He said that they were cattle buyers from north Cork and that they had a reputation for seeking out only the best beasts and would pay accordingly. If he had been given more time, he would probably have refused outright any information at all without seeking to know why I had asked, but the men were about to leave and I suppose he naturally blurted out their names before they went out of his sight. I remember thinking that I must tell Mr O'Donovan that little theory when I met with him.

When I left the pub, the two cattle-dealers were sauntering off towards a nearby dining parlour, but I could see nothing of my quarry for he had been given too great a head start by me and so I made my way back to our rooms and reported all that I had discovered to my master.

He was delighted: 'Capital, Noble, capital! You have worked wonders, you really have, and what you have told me just now puts a great head of steam behind our quest for the truth.'

I was delighted by his flattery and it almost made my going into that odoriferous den of iniquity worth while.

We were off in the gig within the hour of my return to the hotel. Outside he was clamoured by the people belonging to the defendants and the family of John Russell and the priest, but he would not answer any questions, except just to say that it was all up to the jury now, as I whipped up the horse. Once out of town, he had me relax the beast and we waited at the first crossroads for some visitor that he obviously expected. Within the quarter hour the young police lieutenant, Tulliver, rode up to us on a grey mare. He rode cautiously and he was well armed, for he knew that he moved in a very dangerous country when he rode out alone.

'Thank you for meeting with us, Lieutenant Tulliver. I trust that coming here has not discommoded you,' my master said by way of greeting.

'A little, Mr O Donovan, I must confess, but not enough to mention. I must say that I was surprised and a little perplexed by your note. Frankly, I have no idea why I am here, but I felt that in view of your reputation I owed you the courtesy. You did give me pause for reflection in court today, I don't mind telling you.'

'Well, sir, this might just be the first step on the route to making a great name for yourself. Tell me, how would you feel about that?'

I was watching the young man's face framed between his kepi and chin strap and I could tell by his eyes alone that my employer had aroused his interest, for he had recognised the officer as a very ambitious young man.

'He is a man of the commons, Noble, one can only guess what struggles were required to obtain him a commission in the constabulary,' he had whispered to me after the man's testimony that day, as he slipped me a note to be delivered to him, as secretly as possible.

'Well,' the young man said, not answering the question, 'if you have advice or information for me I would certainly take it under advisement.'

'If you would be so kind as to sit with me for a while in my gig I think that you will profit by it,' my employer told him. 'At any rate you can judge it for yourself.'

The young man dismounted and, handing his reins to me, stepped up into the trap.

We were there about another half an hour before he left us and we did not return to Clonmel as I expected we would, but my master told me to drive on towards the west.

Our destination turned out to be the manor house of the Chadwick family, situated on their large home farm. Even moving at a goodly clip the journey took almost another hour and I noted that the land improved greatly as we neared Chadwick Manor. The very best grazing land for beef and milch cows was close about the house, and the poorer outlying land only was let out to the small tenants.

'This is the place where the Mara brothers were once employed as farm labourers, primarily to tend the great cattle herds, according to their women anyway, Noble. Over a hundred years ago the Chadwicks were ambitious farmers and began to clear off the best of their lands to create a great space for their cattle to graze and they were once, and still are I suppose, the prime breeders in the whole of the midlands, perhaps in all of Ireland. Their cattle are famous, justly so, and are vastly superior to most others. They have imported selected animals from England and even from France; their breeding stock has always been carefully husbanded and they only sell on the fixed bullocks and cows too far advanced in age for dropping calves. My legal friend told me of it the other night in the taproom but I already knew a great deal about the reputation of their cattle.'

We did not go directly to the house but he had me drive around the perimeter roads of the estate and then drive many of the lanes of the property itself, where we saw the various herds that made up the family's cattle stock, and I must say that even as a devoted townsman I was impressed by what I saw. We were unmolested in our travels about the land and the few tenants we met merely doffed their caps on seeing two well-dressed gentlemen in a gig and kept their eyes down as we passed.

We came up the drive to the manor at last and I was very unimpressed with the building. Oh, it was much larger than any of the other buildings on the land but it was far from baronial. It was ramshackle to say the least. It was not nearly imposing enough to occupy the setting that it did amidst the thousands of fertile acres of the central estate.

'Time for a visit to the Cullinanes I think, Noble. Now, I understand that Cullinane himself is to be away at the westernmost properties this afternoon and so we may interview his people without any fear of interruption from him.'

I asked him how he knew that and he tapped the side of his nose and smiled at me.

He waited in the trap while I summoned the maid to the door with a good hard tug on the bell rope and handed his card to the woman for delivery to her mistress. It was a piece of flattery, as if we were calling on a grand family and not on a jumped-up farm manager and his wife, and it worked well on the woman, for after only a few minutes, during which I am sure there was a great deal of frenzied and hurried preparation, we were admitted to the 'good' parlour.

The lady of the house was seated and waiting to receive us and I could tell that she was delighted and surprised to receive gentle visitors. She rose to welcome us, ordering tea from the sordid-looking maid, who shuffled off grumbling to herself about people putting on airs.

'Charmed to meet you, Mrs Cullinane, I am to be sure,' said my master, bending over her hand, 'but I was hoping to meet with your good husband. I have an introduction to him from the Chadwick family in London. You see I am interested in improving my own herd of cattle over in Clare and have come to see him with the purpose of buying a good bull or two from the family's stock.'

'Please be seated, sir. I'm afraid that my husband is away for the day. He went to Clonmel to see those dreadful men tried and then he was to journey on to our west lands to see to the tenants there. I'm terribly sorry that you have wasted your time.'

'Meeting such a charming person as yourself could never be classed as a waste of time, my lady,' Mr O'Donovan said, in a most unctuous and treacly fashion, 'but I am devastated at missing him, I don't mind telling you, for I have little time and I must see him.'

'Well, I am sorry to tell you this, sir, but it would do no good even if you did see him for he will sell no breeding beasts. I do not really understand it myself, but he is under the strictest of orders to sell no breeding beasts, orders from the Chadwicks themselves. Believe me, we are inundated with requests such as your own, my husband tells me of them all the time, but we can do nothing to satisfy them at all, even to a fine gentleman such as yourself. It would be as much as his position is worth for us to do so.'

'Alas, I'm sure that you are correct. The Chadwicks, even though old friends, advised me as much. I knew that I had little chance of success, but I had to come anyway. Perhaps I could see the beasts at least, a tour of the farm, so that my journey is not totally wasted? The Chadwicks mentioned that you employ people named Mara to look after the cattle.'

The woman obviously had not left the manor for some time and had not kept herself up to date with all that was happening in Clonmel. She certainly didn't know my master from Adam.

'We did, to be sure, but no more. There is not a Mara left to us – all killed or driven away by the most despicable peasant agitators. They were my husband's best herdsmen and were a sore loss. He was very vexed over it and he has had to replace then with the Hallorans. They are working at the cattle now, but I could not tell you where.'

'Your employees were driven away from you – how so?' my master asked disingenuously.

'I can scarce believe that you have not heard of it. They were driven away by foul murderers, and this country is full of those, let me tell you. Do you know, I won't go as far as the gate unless I have to. One Mara was exiled for being a decent man and for testifying against the rebels, and another was murdered in revenge, and the last two have had to flee away. And, do you know, they would have died too if my husband had not hidden them safely away, and he gave them money out of his own pocket, mind, to get them away from here. My husband is always loyal to his men.'

'You don't say! Your husband seems a very commendable sort of employer, and that sort of thing must by turn breed a great respect and loyalty in his men,' Mr O'Donovan said in very a flattering tone.

The silly woman lapped it up. 'Oh, it does, the Maras were purely devoted to him. He was hardly ever out of their company, and they thought the world of him.'

Our tea arrived, and our hostess simpered and tittered at my master's flattery and *bons mots*. I was glad when we were on the road again and headed back to Clonmel, for I felt the need of a good wash.

In our rooms, my employer was in a very light mood – he had almost skipped up the stairs. He said that he expected that he had created doubt enough in the minds of the jurymen to get an acquittal for Lacy and Walsh and his other theories of the crime were solidifying and conforming to what he had surmised even before we had left Kilrush.

'How so?' I asked, for it was all still a mystery to me. 'Forgive me, but I mean the facts of the cases are very clear and the story that those men intended to kill the Maras, and went to kill them but did *not* kill Daniel Mara still seems pure fantasy to me.'

'That is your suspicious old mind at work, my friend, your pragmatism and common sense telling you to accept what you see as real fact.'

'Well, perhaps you can explain to me what it is that I am really seeing,' I said with rising asperity, for I could not abide my master when he appeared as smug as he did then.

'With pleasure,' he answered, taking a much-folded piece of paper from his inside breast pocket and opening it up. He stood near the evening light coming from the window and prepared to read.

'First let me say that I have as many questions as I have answers for you – more even – but do not despair, for I believe that finding the questions to ask is the first step towards finding the answers to them. I mean a lawyer makes his living by his questions and knowing what questions are to be asked, of himself or of others, forms the main part in any case, inside or outside the courtroom.'

He shook out additional, imaginary creases in the paper and read:

> Why did Philip Mara perjure himself at the trial of Patrick Grace? Why did he give up everything to do so? What induced him to risk his own life and the lives of his family for a lesser existence elsewhere?
>
> Who benefited from the death of Chadwick?
>
> Why was the young labourer sent home early on the day of Chadwick's murder?
>
> Why do the police reports contain no reference that Barry Cullinane was at the building site at all that day?
>
> Why on a busy road did no one else seem to see the murder take place or even an armed Patrick Grace on the road?
>
> Why did Mr Cullinane hide the surviving two Maras and fund their escape from his own pockets?

Why did Cullinane hire the Maras and only the Maras to herd the cattle on the estate?

Where was Daniel Mara actually killed? If we succeed in finding the location of his murder there is bound to be evidence of the crime even after the lapse of so much time.

Why was Daniel Mara moved to the cottage after his death? There must have been some considerable risk involved with that.

Why were there no other marks of violence on the body of Daniel Mara?

He finished and handed me the paper and said, 'When we have the answers to those questions, or rather the proof of the answers to them, for I think I already know the answers, then we shall have solved this case. What do you think, Noble?'

'Well, this Cullinane fellow benefited by the death of Mr Chadwick, for he was promoted to full agent after his death,' I said.

'Quite so, but I doubt that he receives much more remuneration for the promotion and he has had to hire another to do his former duties as sub-agent and so has lost the chance to squeeze any additional profit for himself from the poor tenants over and above their rents. I'll grant that he does now live in that big rat hole of a manor house, but that is hardly incentive to murder, for you can see why the Chadwicks never visit there. And his vacant lump of a wife can play the lady now in her dilapidated parlour, but that too is not enough profit for murder and the risk of the rope if anything went wrong. And the timing of the murder, in the late spring, made me, as a gentleman farmer myself, suspicious from the start, and now more so as I have learned of the meticulousness with which James Chadwick kept his estate records.'

'I suppose it is all put together not a great enough reward for such a dire act,' I said. 'But then, what was the motivation for the murder?'

'I would prefer to keep that to myself for now, not because I do not trust the seal of your lips, my old friend, but it is simply that I may be wrong and I am risking a good deal of embarrassment in pursuing my ideas at all.'

After that he would say no more on the subject but I was able to peruse his question list all the evening and I admit that I was no further ahead at the heel of that activity than I had been at the start.

The next day we spent in relative idleness, to my mind anyway, and the day after was shaping up to be much the same when we were summoned to the courthouse by the sudden news that the jury was finally prepared to give a verdict in the case of Lacy and Walsh. My master said that the lengthy deliberation was a very good sign for our clients. The courtroom was not so full as it had been for the trial proper, for the populace at large had been given little or no warning of the jury's readiness and so had no opportunity to assemble in numbers.

The foreman, grim-faced as Charon himself, stood and faced Justice Moore and declared that the jury had unanimously found a verdict of guilty against the two men. The families of the men, being those with the most interest in the case, had stayed near the courthouse for all the time of the jury's deliberation, and so the verdict was received with a low moan and then screeches of terror and grief from the gallery. The prisoners both slumped forward and put their heads into their manacled hands. The justice, Moore, still flanked by the ominous mass of Lord Kingston, quickly donned the black cap and pronounced a sentence of death on the two, to be carried out one week to the day, in public, at the place of the gibbet on the north road leading out of the town. In the old days, mind you, the sentence would have been carried out at once, especially in time of rebellion, but we were then in more civilised if not civil times and so we were allowed the space of a week, which was usually used to appeal for clemency, or a commutation of a capital sentence to exile for life. This appeal was made directly to the Lord Chancellor in Dublin.

I myself was aghast at the verdict for, like my master, I fully expected that he had muddied the waters to a sufficient extent to gain an acquittal, but I noticed that my master was not in the least perturbed by the reversal, certainly not as distraught as he had been when we listened to a similar verdict and sentence on the head of young Patrick Grace. We met with the heads of the families and we offered our condolences and arranged for a post-rider to go to Dublin with our plea for clemency. But in truth we could expect no mercy, for the murder of Daniel Mara had created a far greater stir and fright among the authorities there than even the killing of Chadwick himself and they would not let the culprits escape the noose for any reason, certainly not for compassion at any rate. They could very well stand to lose a landlord or an agent or two from their numbers – they were never in any shortage – but they could not stand by and see the Crown's witnesses shot or their families killed for that would put a great fear in anyone who might have been induced to come forward in future cases. It all makes perfect sense, if you think on it, brutal sense but sense nonetheless.

At last we managed to extract ourselves from the emotional turmoil of that family meeting and I was relieved when we got back to the sanity of our rooms. It was a Thursday evening and the next day was the time of the big monthly market. I had learned in the drovers' inn that it would be the greatest cattle fair of the first half of the year and there would be many in the town with their cows, bullocks and calves for sale, and near as many there to buy them. Dealers would be in attendance from all over the south and west of the country. I reckoned to my master that we should pack up and leave the place and journey back to Kilrush before the crush of the next day, but he said that we would wait a while in Clonmel, for we were not done here yet. I ventured that the appeal had been sent to Dublin and so it was out of our hands and we could go away without detriment to our poor clients, but he shushed me and suggested that we get a short spell of sleep under our belts, for we were to have a busy night.

After that enigmatic statement I lay on my own bed, but I could not sleep for wondering what was to happen. He roused me, from what was at best a drowsiness a few hours later, and I was surprised that he was dressed in rough travelling clothes, his riding clothes in fact, dark as usual, and black riding boots. His coat was buttoned up to the top and I could see nothing of his normal white neck stock at all. He told me to dress roughly, but to let no white show about me and then to get the gig ready and I did so, wondering all the while just what was afoot. He came down to the stable yard in a few minutes carrying a big pistol in either hand. He handed them to me, swung himself up onto the seat bedside me and took the reins from me without a word. I quailed inwardly, for obviously it was his intention that he should drive the horse, at night on a road with which he was unfamiliar, and if you have ever seen my master drive a fast horse and light cart you would know the reason for my great fear. Quite frankly I did not think that I would be alive to see the morn, but I was to be pleasantly surprised, for he drove as sedately as a royal coachman in a coronal procession and we arrived at our destination safely and in very good form. Our stopping point was to be the crossroads where we had previously met the young police lieutenant, and I was surprised to make out a group of men and horses already there in the darkness. We were greeted by the young officer himself and I saw that the group of five men behind him all wore the uniform of the constabulary.

'You're on the hour, Mr O'Donovan,' Tulliver said by way of greeting. 'Are you set to ride hard for a while? We have saddled horses here for you and your man.'

'We're up for a good hard ride, sir,' my master replied. 'My old fellow here sits astride his horse like a Tartar. If he hadn't taken up the law he would have made a great lancer, I'm sure.'

Now that was a lie if ever I heard one for I detest all horseflesh and I have a 'bad seat' as it is called, bounding about in the saddle like a sack of potatoes.

'We'll give him the wilder of the two horses then, in view of his expertise,' Tulliver said.

I was alarmed at once and about to protest until I realised that they were making a jest between them at my expense. My master had started it off, unrehearsed, and the young Englishman, seeing my figure, had picked up on it immediately and had carried it on. To my immense relief I was soon seated on a placid old mare with a seat as wide as a byre door and we set off. The ride was no less odious to me for all that mare's placid nature, as even I could tell that she had a foul gait. I jolted along a good fifty paces after the hindmost trooper, and I still did not know where we were going to end up nor of course why we were travelling at night at all.

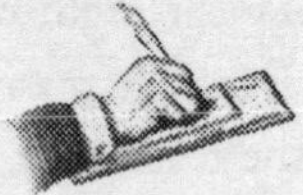

After an hour's ride we seemed to have arrived at our object or at least near to it. Our journey was not to end with that stop, however. We halted and dismounted and the officer had his men take up their short saddle carbines and follow himself and my master off into the darkness, leaving the reins to all our mounts in the hands of one of the policemen.

We tripped and trekked and shambled in the dark along several lanes and then across a field or two until Lieutenant Tulliver and my master were satisfied with our position and the men were set up, hidden along the hedge. I am no military man, but I could see that it was some sort of ambuscade that was being arranged. We three squatted in the darkness of the ditch and waited without a sound. When I tried to whisper a question to my master, I was rudely shushed and so I remained sullenly silent for the rest of our vigil. We waited for what I imagined to be two or three hours in the damp cold and I wondered what in hades we were doing there at all, for my every bone was beginning to ache and my every joint to throb with rheum.

'Well, Mr O'Donovan,' the officer whispered, 'it appears that your theory may well be quite wrong after all, they would almost need to be here before now if the market square is to be reached by dawn. This is, I fear, a wild goose chase.'

My master was, I imagine, about to answer this when we heard the lowing of cattle and the trample of their feet and the short, sharp, meaningless sounds made by droving men. The sounds grew louder as they were obviously approaching us in the dark. At once my master and the lieutenant were at action stations and after another wait of only ten minutes or so, the lane between the lying policemen and ourselves was thronged with beasts we could not see in the near dark, but which we could certainly smell. The lieutenant gave a shrill peep out of a silver whistle and suddenly the ambush was sprung. Two of the police were to the fore and two to the rear and the herd and herdsmen were trapped between them and us.

'This is the police!' the officer shouted and brandished a pistol. 'Halt at once, in the king's name!'

My master also had a pistol in his hand and I held his second pistol awkwardly in my own. He was near me, and in what light there was I saw him grab at a shadowy figure near him and try to clap his gun to its head. The other herders were not so easily apprehended and I heard a shot and saw everything that the blast of a gun illuminated for a split second. I recognised the sound of the shot as the report of a blunderbuss, and I heard and felt a shower of shot go past me and into the bushes beyond. There was a howl of pain near me and I guessed that one of the policemen had been hit. Then there was another flash of gunfire. I reckoned it to be from Tulliver this time and there was a yell in the darkness and a voice called out, 'Jasus, I'm hit, I'm kilt!' but whether it was herder or constable I could not then tell, for the ordinary policemen and the peasantry both have the same accents. There was another shot or two and then we heard someone yell out, 'Don't shoot no more. We surrendur!'

As it turned out it had been a crucial part of our plan that none of the drovers should manage to escape from us and for a frantic few moments the constabulary searched the road until they were certain that all the herdsmen were in our net.

My master called out to me in the darkness, 'Noble, are you all right, are you hurt?' His voice was filled with anxiety and I quickly answered that I was shaken but not otherwise hurt.

The prisoners were assembled and a candle stub was lit, and for the first time I knew with whom we had been fighting. As the most ineffective of the combatants I was then dispatched by road to fetch our horses and the fifth policeman, and after a few mis-turns I found the man at the crossroads near to the bigger road that led to Clonmel.

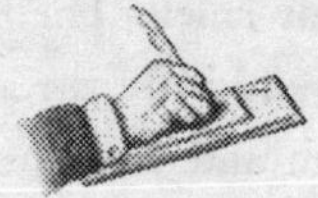

By the time we returned, two of the four captured herdsmen were stripped of their coats and pantaloons and bound well with rope. A third was wounded in the upper arm by a pistol ball and he sat dejectedly moaning to himself, rocking back and forth and holding his hand over the leaking wound. We left them, all but the fourth man, whom Tulliver and my master had determined to be their leader, seated at the side of the road and guarded by an armed policeman – the one who was hit, but only lightly hurt, by the charge from the blunderbuss; there must have been little powder behind the shot for the pellets had hardly even broken the skin on him but he was in a foul mood over it and I thought that his rude wards had better behave themselves. We rode on in the darkness driving the cattle before us and eventually we were out onto the main road to Clonmel and its Friday marketplace. I was at the rear of the odorous herd doing my piece with the driving, but my master rode ahead with Lieutenant

Tulliver and the fourth herdsman bound and seated on a horse between them. I heard them speaking to the man and I heard him answer them, but I was too far off and they spoke too lowly for me to be able to make any sense out of their words.

We rode along for several hours and I reckoned that we must be nearing Clonmel town. I must admit that I was drowsing in the saddle and no doubt I was on the way to taking a very painful fall from my high mount when a sudden halt was called. The first light of the dawn was showing well over the dark hedges on the horizon and the illumination of it allowed my master and the police to make their planned preparations. My master and Lieutenant Tulliver quickly donned the coats, loose trousers and black felt hats taken from two of our captives and they instantly had the look of rough peasants about them. The other policemen rode off rapidly down the road which we had just traversed, with all the horses, and they were soon out of sight from us. The herd was allowed to mill about on the road and those of us who remained squatted down by the roadside with the prisoner. I noticed that the lieutenant held his cocked pistol to the man's back the whole time. My master suddenly seemed to notice my black gangly figure among them and he told me to hide myself deep in the hedge by the roadside. I complied, grumpily, and so I began another cold and damp vigil. Thankfully it was not so long as the first wait of that night, for after less than an hour had passed, in the now full dawn light, a man came galloping up towards us from the direction of Clonmel town. He tore up at a great rate and I saw the three 'peasant' men seated at the roadside rise at his approach, with the prisoner snugly in the middle of the group. I saw that the rider was the same man who had yelled out in the public gallery and who had accosted my master outside the courthouse and who I had then followed to the tavern.

'Halloran, you foul bastard, why the hell are you sitting there on your dirty arse when you should have had these beasts in Clonmel and penned long since? What's the matter with your head, man?' the new arrival immediately screamed at the miscreant who faced him, shaking his leather riding crop at him. 'Didn't I tell you a hundred times that we must not be seen bringing them there in open daylight and you bloody well know it, you thick-headed lout! Move along there now, damn you and your miserable kin, or I'll take this crop to your backside.'

My master and the lieutenant both threw off their peasant's broad-brimmed floppy hats at that and the man nearly fell out of his saddle with the shock he got. Instantly he pulled savagely on his horse's bridle to turn him about, but the policeman grabbed his reins to hold him fast. The man cut at young Tulliver savagely about the head and hands with his crop, but Tulliver held on until my master came to his aid and shouted, 'Stop that at once, Cullinane, or by the Lord Harry I'll empty your saddle,' all the while pointing his big pistol at the man.

Cullinane quit trying to flee and began to bluster instead: 'What the devil do you mean by holding up a gentleman on the king's highway? If you don't desist I shall fetch the constabulary for you and see you swing for this. Leave us be to take our beasts to the market like honest men.'

'Lieutenant Tulliver of the constabulary at your service, Cullinane, and those are not your cattle, and you are far from being an honest man. You are under arrest for theft from your masters and you will accompany me with your man Halloran here to Clonmel to cool your heels in jail with him – and the rest of your cronies when they arrive,' the policeman shouted in return, still holding fast to the reins.

I could see a large red ugly welt coming up across his cheek and I imagined that by that point he would have shot Cullinane as quick as look at him.

'Why have you stopped me in bringing these beasts to market on my master's behalf?'

'These are your master's cattle, we don't doubt that for an instant, but you are not marketing them on his behalf, but for your own good,' my master shouted. 'See here, we have counted seventeen uncut bull yearlings among them and as many breeding cows and heifers, nearly all with their calves, and we know that the Chadwicks would never consent to the sale of even one such beast, never mind over half a hundred of them. The proceeds of their sale would no doubt be used to line your own pockets.'

The man blustered a while longer, but when his hands were bound before him in the saddle and with an armed man to each side of him he quieted himself, thinking no doubt that silence was the best policy open to him.

And so we made our way to the main police barracks in Clonmel. Men were sent to return the suspect cattle to the Chadwick farm and to fetch the other three Halloran brothers, and in the meantime we set about questioning the two prisoners that we had with us. If the lieutenant thought that the presence of my master and myself during his interviews was unorthodox in any way he did not show it. He was, to my mind, the very best sort of Englishman, with no side to him at all. As well he was both pragmatic and completely free of the usual self-important officiousness and he obviously felt some significant gratitude to Mr O'Donovan as well.

We could not get a single word from Cullinane now. His blustering was long gone and he refused to speak other than initially denying any wrongdoing whatsoever and saying that we would find his farm records all in order if we chose to inspect them.

We had more success with Dennis Halloran, the eldest brother of the four, who, having been caught in what he knew to be an illegal act, was more willing to co-operate with the authorities. He initially claimed that he was merely taking his master's cattle to the spring fair, at the agent's express bidding, and knew nothing about them being stolen beasts. He was reminded that they had been apprehended in the dead of night and driving the cattle without a light or lantern between them. He answered that Cullinane had told them to drive the cattle at night, to let no one see them and to get the beasts to the market stalls in Clonmel well before first light. His master feared cattle-thieves.

My master laughed at that, but Tulliver merely shrugged his shoulders and sighed at the man's obduracy, and reminded Halloran that they had fought a gun battle with the police. A capital offence in itself.

Halloran answered that they thought we were common cattle-thieves of the sort warned against by Mr Cullinane. Tulliver countered that they were plainly told that they faced the police and to halt in the king's name and that they had resisted arrest and that they had even put a few pellets into the hand of one of his men, and they could expect no mercy from the courts for the shooting of a policeman. Further he told the man that his master's instructions for a clandestine driving of the beasts to market should have alerted any sensible man to the illegality of the thing and that a jury would scoff at his protestations of ignorance in the matter. If not hanged outright he would certainly be deported for life with his three brothers, and his family would starve by the roadside or his children would be raised in the poorhouse. That shook him as nothing else would have for the peasants are usually fiercely devoted to their families and he said that he was prepared to talk to us, if it would be taken into consideration at his sentencing, and that his brothers were far more innocent in the thing than he was.

When he was assured of the lieutenant's plea for leniency for them all, he composed himself and began his story. He told us of the preparations made by Cullinane in the previous weeks, culling a few beasts, choosing which to take with a judicious eye, uncut calves and breeders only, to amass a secret herd at a pasture in the far reaches of the estate. It was his intention to sell off the precious and restricted breeding stock to some men that he knew, cattle-dealers, at a great price and under the guise of the open market. He had done it before at the last autumn market and had got away with it in broad daylight in the hustle and confusion of the throng. Previous to that he had sold the beasts off in ones and twos right from the grounds of the estate itself. Denis Halloran only and not his brothers had done such work for him before, most of it was left to the Maras in their time and the other Hallorans had only been recruited by Cullinane when the remaining Maras had fled the country. He knew that what Cullinane was doing was wrong, but they were only his workers, receiving just a small bonus for their night's work and he even tried to use the excuse that they were subject to their master's will.

The man was locked up once again, and I found that the next item for the morning was another visit to Chadwick Manor and the lovely Mrs Cullinane. A fair-sized squadron of mounted officers came with us on this occasion, once again led by Lieutenant Tulliver. A search of the house was conducted and my master took the estate records and especially those regarding the cattle herd into his possession. They also discovered a large amount of hard currency in Cullinane's private dressing room, cached in a niche rudely cut into the wall behind a chest of drawers. It amounted to over fifteen hundred pounds.

The rest of the men were dispatched to search every building on the property and that took almost all of the rest of the day. I had little idea as to what they hoped to find, and my master and Lieutenant Tulliver seemed as if they were ready to give up and to end the search, when one of the troopers rode up and summoned them to a lonely hillside byre deep in the estate grounds. It was a place evidently used to keep sickened beasts or to house calving cows in inclement weather conditions, which explained its remoteness from the main buildings. The place not much to look at, a low building washed with faded white lime, with no doors or windows hung in its vacant frames and a mouldering thatched roof, suspiciously low at one end. An observant policeman had seen past the accumulated muck of the years to notice a corner which had a great deal of rusty brown stains on the walls about it. We examined it in turn and my master, who for a lawyer was very experienced in the subject, confirmed that it was dried blood and that he thought the bothy could well be the actual site of Daniel Mara's murder. Tulliver was sceptical and said that it could be blood from the slaughter of some sick beast or from the detritus of calf birth and my master agreed with him that it was a possibility but he stooped down and scooped away the loose hay covering the floor. He knelt down and put his face close to the beaten earth surface in the dim light from the doorway, running his hand over it at the same time. After a few minutes he indicated a hole in the floor, filled up with small yellow chaff. Tulliver produced a folding knife from his tunic pocket, knelt and dug at the hole and soon he held up a dark object between the thumb and forefinger of his right hand. My master held out his own hand and the officer dropped it into his palm.

'My word,' my master said. 'A large pistol ball, a little flattened, to be sure, but a pistol ball nonetheless. Well, I suppose our friend Cullinane will say that it could have been fired to kill an ailing beast and that would make sense and probably a good brief could addle a jury with it, but I think that it will give us enough to let us winkle further information from the far less stalwart Dennis Halloran. What do you think, Lieutenant Tulliver, shall we give it a try?'

We went back to the gaol and immediately pulled Halloran out of his cell and into the room where we had questioned him before.

'Well, Halloran, we have some bad news for you,' said Tulliver in a surprisingly easy manner.

'You have, sur, what is it?' the man asked, unsure as to what 'bad' could entail, given his already dire circumstance.

'We have found the place where you and Cullinane took and

murdered poor Daniel Mara, where you shot him to death before you helped your master bring the body to the widow's cottage. She would not have known the difference, or if she did I believe that she would have been amenable enough, for she is a distant cousin of Cullinane's and would have been glad to turn a blind eye for the sake of future benefits.'

'Good Christ in his heaven, I killed no one, not ever in me loife, sur, I swear to it, on me mother's grave, so I do,' the man replied in obvious alarm, but I was watching his eyes and they betrayed some guilt as well as fear.

'Well, in this instant and because we have no evidence to the contrary, we must believe that you are the murderer or at the least his willing accomplice. In either event you will soon know the feel of the rope about your neck,' Tulliver replied, in a very breezy manner given the import of his words.

'We know that Cullinane did not transport the body on his own and so you will be charged, you and your three brothers, with being his accessories before and after the fact. I wouldn't want to be defending you ...' my master chimed in, to great effect as it turned out.

'I wasn't even in the byre when he was shot. 'Twas Cullinane did it all be himself. He called me in only after the man was dead. I was working for him in the meadow near by, that was where he kept the culled beasts, and so Dan Mara knew he would be about the place. I even seen Mara wit' me own two eyes, goin' in there like the bats of hell wus after him. Fairly winded, he wus, sweatin' and weepin' like a girl he wus. I didn't dare go in, for I knew Cullinane was in there and he has an awful temper on him when he takes a pick at a man. Then I went back to me work and a few minutes later I heared a shot and then Cullinane comes out and whistles and beckons me in. If I live to see a hundred I will never forget the sight of Mara lying there with only half the head on him and the smell of the pistol smoke still about in the air. I tell you it was like the back room of hell in there and I'm not right of it ever since.'

'Well, go on, man, we're listening to you,' Tulliver said, when the fellow paused in his misery and no doubt the horror of the memory of what he had seen.

'Cullinane would say nothin' about it to me, and only ordered me to get on wit' helpin him wit' the body. Or I would get the same treatment meself, and that if I told any about what had happened he would see to getting' me swung along wit' him. I was stood there, like a pig pissin' in a maze, like one of the statues in the big garden, and he had to give me a cuff on the ear to set me started. Then we wrapped up the man's head in an old sack and I got the wee cart from the main house and we took the side roads and boreens wit' him dead in the back until we got to the widow Cullinane's cabin. There was nobody about and 'twas only the work of a minnit or two to get him carried in and onto the floor.'

Tulliver looked at my master and he nodded at him and Halloran was soon taken back to his cell.

'Well, that solves the murder of Daniel Mara for sure,' Tulliver observed. 'But why did he do it? Why would Cullinane kill him?'

'To get him out of the way, I believe,' my master replied. 'He was a hangover, a remnant, with his brothers, of the original crime. He likely needed money to get away, perhaps he became greedy.'

'What original crime?' Tulliver asked.

'Why the murder of James Chadwick,' my master said casually and waited a few seconds for that piece of information to sink in. 'Cullinane did that crime as well. It started the ball rolling on everything since. I have been certain sure of it for some time, since before the murder of Daniel Mara even.'

'You're not serious man. Patrick Grace was hanged for that!' Tulliver exclaimed.

'Hanged in error, Lieutenant, although I will allow that he fully intended to kill Chadwick, but he was beaten to it by Cullinane. Poor

Cullinane, if he had only known that his problem was soon to be removed for him by young Grace, he could have solved his own dilemma by waiting a day or two and he would not have needed to lose the services of the Maras and to kill Daniel and now swing for it himself. He knew that the populace had evil intentions for Chadwick, but he could not know the hour of the man's death, and he knew that he was running out of time. But if you will wait for a day or so, we will be able to force Cullinane to speak with us, for we will have all the information that we need, with your indulgence and the use of your manpower – if you are willing to use it in a good cause.'

I think that the possibility that an innocent man had been hanged and that two other men were facing the rope for a crime which they had not committed had a great effect on the young officer, and he was quite amenable to anything that my employer might suggest.

The next day the town was abuzz with the news of the arrest of Cullinane and the Hallorans, although none but the police and my master and myself knew the where and the why of it. A major expedition was made to the Chadwick estates, and the police and some men pressed into service for the day laboriously counted all the cattle on the estate, every calf, bull, bullock and cow. The totals were brought in to the main house and compared with the estate's official records, and it was found that the numbers found tallied exactly with Cullinane's book-keeping. Tulliver was dismayed at that finding, but my master soon cast away his apprehension, for he had a surprise for us all.

He produced a copy of the records submitted to the Chadwick family in London by Cullinane only three months before as part of his year-end duties and over five hundred beasts were missing when the actual numbers were compared with those papers. Lieutenant

Tulliver was astounded and asked my master where he had obtained such a private document.

'I have suspected Cullinane for some time of killing his master. The whole thing was simple to me. I knew, I firmly believed rather, that neither Patrick Grace nor none of the other would-be raparees about the area had killed the man, and therefore I knew someone else had to have done the deed. I then had to consider who benefited by the death, and by the timing of the death, and the only name that I came up with was that of Barry Cullinane. At first I thought that he merely wanted to take over the running of the estate in an uninhibited fashion; I was sure that he was doing some wrong. But, I reflected, he had been in the position for ten years and so I wondered why he chose that exact time to rid himself of his master. From asking about, even in the remoteness of Clare, I learned of the jealousy with which the Chadwicks guard their breed. Indeed, it is the only thing that sets their estate apart from any other in the land, and I surmised that it might have had something to do with the murder. When I heard of the second murder I at first supposed it to be only a misguided form of revenge on the Maras, but I could never quite get Patrick Grace out of my mind. I knew that I would never be able to let his wrongful execution be. I wrote to an influential friend in London, and he was able to convince the Chadwick family to release a copy of their annual reckoning to him and he forwarded it to me, and as we saw, Cullinane has craftily changed the estate's records to tally them with his own misdeeds. With the Chadwicks' chronic absenteeism, his swindling of them could have gone on for many years to come.

I later found out, by the way, that it was James Griffin, once Lord Chancellor of Ireland, who had been my master's 'influential friend' in London, a debt repaid.

We returned to Clonmel and waited till early the next day before facing Cullinane with the evidence of his theft and the murder of Daniel Mara. My master thought it best to let him stew in his own juices for another night, and Tulliver now had respect enough for his opinions to fully agree.

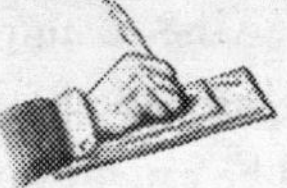

The villain was at first as stoical and silent as he had been on the day before, and Tulliver bluntly told him that a dumb man could be hanged as well as any other. First of all he was presented with the evidence of his theft of at least half a thousand beasts from the Chadwicks, borne out by his actions, by the genuine records from London, and by the evidence of Dennis Halloran. He was stunned by the strength of the case against him as he had imagined that his false records would be enough to cover his tracks. He now said that he had only been previously selling off the beasts on the orders of the late James Chadwick himself and the latest theft had been the only one that he had done for his own benefit.

My master scoffed: 'What rubbish, man! You were always the thief, and you killed Chadwick because he was about to find you out about your crimes. Young Feely O'Hegarty has confirmed that you were there at the new barracks and that he was sent home by you early on that day. It was obviously done so that you could shoot Chadwick and then slip away, knowing that the authorities would see only the local land league as the culprits. Later, you put the only witness, your silent accomplice, Philip Mara, up to laying the blame for it on Patrick Grace. That was after the police got wind that he had actually planned to kill the man. Mara didn't come forward until that time, weeks later, and that in itself was suspicious. Poor innocent Feely was not too pleased to lose a half a day's work at the time and he told me that previously James Chadwick had promised him a few days of good steady work in the next week, for he planned to make a full inventory of the beasts on the estate to balance his own records. Feely has also told us that to the best of his knowledge that count was never made after Chadwick's demise. He got no work at it in any case. You knew that Chadwick intended to make an inventory – he would have had no compunction about telling you of his plans; the poor man trusted you. He was only doing the count to satisfy his own vain meticulousness and not because he suspected you in any way. You killed him before you could be caught out by him.'

'That's nonsense, man, you have no evidence that anyone but Patrick Grace killed Chadwick,' Cullinane said trying but failing to scoff. 'Didn't the scoundrel hang for it?' I have found that a man with a dry mouth cannot make a very good scoffing sound and a dry mouth has always been a sign of guilt in a man.

'Perhaps you have covered that too well, but it is not that particular murder which interests us at the moment, for young Grace is dead and cannot be raised again by any agency of men. I want to have you charged with the murder of Daniel Mara which we *can* lay squarely at your door,' my master said sternly.

'You are a madman! Lacy and Walsh have only just been found guilty of that in a court of law and are to be stretched themselves in a few days,' Cullinane retorted with a poor attempt at his former bluster.

'Yes, once again found guilty in error, but this time they are still alive and we have a witness against you. Your man Dennis Halloran has told us all that happened, to perhaps escape the rope himself, and that is enough to get you stretched as – you put it,' my master countered.

'Halloran is a fool. I should never have hired him and his verminous brothers. I could at least trust the Maras, but the Hallorans are thieves and liars, the whole clan of them,' Cullinane said bitterly.

'Yes, the Maras are a most commendable lot to be sure, but we need no confession from you – the evidence is all there and we will try you as a common murderer,' my master said, and Tulliver nodded his assent.

Cullinane then claimed that the word of an accomplice alone

would not get him convicted. My master advised him that with the testimony of Feely as to his presence at the murder site and with the proof of his ongoing theft as motive, then no sane jury would find him anything but guilty. The interview went on in such a vein for some considerable time, with Cullinane trying to defend himself or at least to find a bolt hole. It was like a stage play but most tedious and repetitious and so I will not even attempt to record the most of it. But, suffice it to say, that between my master and Tulliver all hope of escape was closed off to him and at last he broke.

Cullinane said that he was not a common murderer and wanted to tell his side of the story. He said that he was ready to explain everything, and Tulliver summoned Mr Doherty, the Solicitor General, to hear it all, and once again in my career I found myself being pressed into service as the official scribe of the party. I still have my rough copy here with me and a gory read it is to this day.

> *Statement of Thomas Cullinane, taken at Clonmel Barracks by Lieutenant Edgar Tulliver, this fifth day of April in the year of our Lord eighteen hundred and twenty eight.*
>
> Present, Mr Oliver Doherty, Solicitor General, Mr Ambrose O'Donovan, barrister at law and Mr Noble Alexander, clerk and recorder.
>
> I was first employed by James Chadwick over ten years ago to be his assistant. He was the over-agent for his family's lands in the county and I was taken on as his under-agent. Mr Chadwick had the responsibility for the overall running of the estate and I was given the task of the day-to-day management of the tenants' affairs and all the actual supervisory work at the home farm. Several years ago, needing additional funds, I began to sell off

some of the farm's breeding stock to interested buyers who wished, anonymously, to improve their own herds. The Chadwicks have developed and own some of the best cattle in the midlands and have always jealously guarded the ownership of their breeders. They have always steadfastly refused to part with a single bull or able cow in spite of requests from even some who would be considered their close friends as well as valued customers. This created a ready market for me and, as Mr Chadwick never spent a great deal of time in the various pastures of the estate, I was tempted to secretly market and sell off some of the beasts. At first it was only one or two in any one season but it grew from that. While he was alive and I was sub-agent, I carried out my business at night selling a bull now and a few cows another time, but it all added up. It was a most lucrative business and the Maras were my accomplices and carried out the actual herding for me. I acted in the meantime as if nothing was amiss and the operation of the estate carried on. Mr Chadwick for his part was more worried about the fractious peasantry than any theft of his beasts, and so had recently incurred the even greater wrath of the locals by building a barracks near by to house a contingent of police amongst them.

For some reason, and I do not honestly know why he chose then to contemplate it, he announced to me that he was intending to do a strict count of the cattle on the estate. He said he intended to have every beast driven past him and his tally board and I knew that his records were fastidious and that any count would be short by several hundred beasts over what should be on the land. I believe that he may well have suspected the peasantry of perhaps taking a few, but that is all. The scale of the theft would be discovered and I could foresee that it would have been ludicrous of me to try and claim that I knew nothing about the missing animals for it was my responsibility to check on the health and numbers of the various herds on a regular basis and I had always certified to him that all was in order.

I was in a panic and I determined that I would either have to flee the land or remove the threat to me posed by Mr Chadwick. Not wanting to face my wife with the need for our flight, I chose the latter, and I arranged for him to be about the new barracks that day. I sent the boy off home early and I had Philip Mara on the roof of the building watching both ways, down and up the road, to make sure that there was no one coming near us. Then at his signal I shot Mr Chadwick. I did it from behind and he knew nothing about it and did not suffer at all, but simply fell dead. I left the site at once and made for the home farm to give myself the benefit of the alibi of being seen far from the murder scene and I had Mara go and fetch the police but to say that he had found Mr Chadwick dead on the ground and nothing more. The authorities immediately suspected the murderer to have been among the land leaguers of the peasantry and later when they lifted Patrick Grace, on a suspicion only, I had Philip Mara come forward. He did it for money, a large enough sum to make it worth his while. At my behest he confessed that he had seen the murder take place but had been too frightened to tell of it, but that his conscience had been too troubled by it to let him keep his silence forever.

He identified the man who shot Mr Chadwick as Patrick Grace. The young fool had been bruiting it about that he meant to do the deed and so it was easily laid upon his shoulders. I paid Philip Mara handsomely for his assistance and he was sent away to England, by the government, for his own protection. I thought that the whole thing was ended when Grace was hanged and I was made up to Land Agent.

I continued to take cattle from the estate and, as there was none to gainsay it, I grew ambitious to sell them off in larger numbers and in broad daylight at the Clonmel market. Then one day, up on the high meadow where we kept the culled beasts, Daniel Mara came running up to me and he was in a state of extreme agitation and swore that he was being hunted to death by the peasantry for Patrick Grace, both him and his two brothers. They had almost caught him and had chased him into the widow Cullinane's cottage but he squeezed out through a window and came to me. He was in a frenzy and feared that the buckos had already killed his brothers and he needed to protect himself. I told him that I would get him away to England and would give him some money. He swore that he would not sweat in the muddy fields of some English lord for a pittance away from all he loved like his brother Philip and that he knew all about Philip's perjury and was tempted to tell the authorities about it all and of my killing Chadwick. He was addled, and I think imagined it as a way perhaps to put himself right with those who were hunting him. He thought that it might even make him a hero to the people; he must have been mad. He imagined that as a consequence he would be able to remain with his family in peace in the area. He was demented by fear, of course, for those brutes would have killed him out of hand no matter what action he took and I tried to explain that to him, but he would not hear reason at all. I lost my temper with him and knocked him to the ground and as he made to rise I shot him dead. I don't think I even planned it, I just lost all patience with him.

Dennis Halloran was one of my new men, replacing Philip Mara in fact, and it was an easy matter to get him to help me bring the body back to the widow's cottage and so put the deed squarely before the doors of the conspirators. As you know, his brothers had survived and came crawling to me that night terrified at the death of their brother and they knew that those incompetent fools Lacy and Walsh were guilty of the deed for they had seen them chasing Daniel to the cottage door. I paid them some money, enough to get them away and they fled for their lives, to England I suppose, that very night, and if they have any wit at all about them they will stay there. Poor England, the riff-raff we send her.

And that is the main thrust of his statement and do you know the man actually expected us to feel pity for him in his situation and expected us to see that he had no choice in the matter. He acted as a man who had done no real harm, astounding as that may seem to any sane man. He treated two murders as a matter of course, as if they were mere nothings. I have known his like before as has my master and, fortunately for humanity, they are a rare breed. They are men, and women, for whom the only existence and welfare in the world is their own, to the total exclusion of a true tender thought for any other. They are simply born without any vestige of a conscience whatsoever. I could see that he was actually shocked at the revulsion that his confession had caused, plainly displayed on all our faces.

Oliver Doherty, the 'astute' investigator, was choleric red when Cullinane had finished, but from real anger or real embarrassment, I could not tell. He had already, to his discredit, put one innocent man to death and he had two others measured for their coffins and as a result he was in a stuttering confusion by the end of that interview.

He went off to see Justice Moore, who fortunately was still in Clonmel. By court order, Moore set aside the jury's verdict and put the sentence of death in abeyance, pending confirmation from the Lord Chancellor in Dublin, and within a few days the two erstwhile assassins were free men once again. Doherty was not to be pacified, nor nearly satisfied by that, though. He had a reputation that was badly in need of restoration and that made him a very dangerous man. My master warned his clients to take themselves off from the vicinity of Tipperary at once; they did not perceive the danger, though, and stayed to celebrate their victory. They tarried too long and were arrested on new charges, of conspiracy to commit murder and attempted murder and of belonging to a seditious society and they went on trial at the next assizes alongside their mentor John Russell and his eldest son and three or four others of the gang. They had already admitted to those crimes in court in an attempt to escape from the charge of murder, and so they were soon found guilty. Justice Moore was somewhat chastened by the recent episode, however, and, lacking the bullying presence of Lord Kingston at his elbow, sentenced them all to deportation to a penal colony for a term of ten years each rather than hanging them, as the law would have fully allowed him to do. My master, although requested by the defendants, politely declined to represent them. He explained to me, needlessly, that in his opinion men who take up arms cold-bloodedly for whatever reason to kill their fellowmen deserved whatever was meted out to them.

There ends this tale, two murders and two guilty verdicts, a sorry enough average to be sure, but my employer was able to at least avert a second execution of the innocent and to see the guilty man swing for his transgressions.

The whole credit for straightening out the convoluted mess went to Lieutenant Tulliver, with my master's sincere approval, and to Oliver Doherty, with my master's great disapproval, for it restored him to his position in the good graces of the powers that be. His treatment of old Kate Costello was an odious thing and my master could not forgive him for it. All in all, he was a reprehensible man.

Ireland was well rid of him when later he was 'unfortunately' shot and wounded by an assailant in a park in Dublin. He had been riding on his mare on the bridle path for some morning exercise when a young man approached him and shouting 'Revenge for Patrick Grace' had shot him in the stomach with a pistol of a very small bore, before running off. The assailant was never captured; and, although he survived a good while after the shooting, Doherty was unable to help the authorities in their quest for the assassin. In fact he did the opposite.

Doherty should most probably have recovered from the small wound but he took a poison in his blood and died in agony some weeks later. He was near delirious from after the first day and no real sense could be obtained from him by the police. They tried to question him as to a name or even some description of the attacker, but all he would say was that it was Patrick Grace who had come back from the grave to shoot him. He said that he would have known that fair hair and baby's face anywhere and he swore over and over that it was a dead man who had shot him.

I learned of this all from a former clerk of the late Oliver Doherty when next my employer and I ventured to the spring sessions in Dublin. The authorities had kept a strict silence about his ranting and raving, fearing no doubt the ridicule that would bring to the memory of such an esteemed man as the Solicitor General. Showing how the great man had spent his last days quailing in terror, like a child, at the thoughts of ghosts and goblins roaming about the city's parks armed with pistols.

In turn I told Mr O'Donovan all that I had learned about the death of Doherty and he scoffed, not at me, but at the powers-that-be, and the depth of their stupidity.

'It may well have been a near relative of the man, Grace, that did it,' I ventured, hesitantly. 'The authorities do not seem to have considered that at all. It would go a long way to explain the resemblance to the man if the killer was, for instance, a younger Grace brother. Doherty may have been partly right after all.'

He smiled at me. 'You are almost most certainly correct in your deduction, Noble; there is hope for you yet, so there is. But I think that you and I will not bother to assist the authorities by voicing our opinions to them, or to anyone else, in the matter, for perhaps the Grace family was owed a life. It almost certainly was a near – a very near – relative of young Patrick Grace who claimed revenge on his behalf from Oliver Doherty. But to my way of thinking it was a close relative on the distaff side.'